The PIRATE KING

By Annie Pearson

Rain City Series:
The Grrrl of Limberlost
Artemis in the Desert
Nine Volt Heart
The Pirate King

The Accidental Heretics Adventure Series:
(writing as E.A. Stewart)
The Blue Door
Bone-mend and Salt
Trebuchets in the Garden
Crux Lunata
Song of Valerós

www.anniepearson.com

The PIRATE KING

ANNIE PEARSON

Jugum Press

First print edition June 2016
ISBN: 978-1-939423-41-2

Published by Jugum Press
Find ebook editions at:
www.jugumpress.net

For Susan, who knows these people.

And for all the would-be startup kings
in Victrola on 15th Avenue East talking about their angel investors
and their derivative ideas.

...Sam's cheatsheet at the end is for those who
want the derivative ideas made plain.

For Susan, who knows these people.

Contents

The PIRATE KING

1

Morning Comes So Early in the Day

SOARING, LIKE RIDING A LONGBOARD over the top of a skate ramp. Gentle breeze tossing my hair.

Then splat. Pavement. Bleeding.

Wasn't that the story the last time I bolted a job? My previous escape from the world of national security contractors led to a year of cybergangsters on my trail, the FBI reading my daily email.

And yet I bolted again.

I'm Samsara Ada Byron—yes, that freak who caused havoc on Limberlost Island last year.[1] Being true to my inner sk8ter self, I once more performed a massive backflip—which is a good move that requires capable execution. Two weeks ago, when an adware corporation acquired the Seattle security startup where I worked, I rejected the new owners' job offer.

Instead, with my friend Natalia Dragon, the network security wizard, I took a flying leap, and we became Byron&Dragon, the world's best security forensics analysts—with no capital and no clients. We do have a basic idea about how to run a business. It's this formula, solved for ***x*** and ***n***, right?

[Cyber_Skilz @ $***x***/hour] * ***n***(Client_Hours) = ***enough$$***

[1] See *The Grrrl of Limberlost.*

We aren't looking to be Seattle bazillionaires, only to do good forensics work without facing a moral dilemma every day. However, the *enough$$* side of that equation must be resolved quickly, because insurance still hasn't paid my claims for last year's multiple debacles, which leaves unfilled financial holes. And our Client#1 is the kind of referral you get when you launch with no plan: an old friend called, asking my help.

"My stepmother's laptop has a virus," Zak said. We'd been security superstars together when I worked in Virginia. "I can't fly to Seattle to help her. So, how much will it cost me for the world's best forensics analyst to do a dumb job that's totally beneath her?"

"Five thousand dollars," I said, joking. Ten times what it costs at the help counter of a local Buy-CheapWare store. Zak arranged for a courier to bring me the laptop, and then thanked me profusely when I finished moments later.

"Yes, a trivial task." I reported back by phone. "That virus signature was the most common of its kind. The invoice will seem outrageous. I'll hand-deliver the laptop to ensure value for your money."

"I'd have paid ten thousand if you asked," he said.

"Why?" Me, an infant in the entrepreneurial woods, stunned.

"Trust. That virus scared her. Trust is worth more than gold."

Therefore, since Zak's stepmother lived near my office, I set out on foot far too early on a cold, too-bright October morning, crossing the residential north end of Capitol Hill, ready to meet our first client, looking as good as any hip Seattle professional: tailored vest, white dress shirt, and a black leather suit jacket scrounged at a Madison Valley rich ladies' resale shop. Along the way, my phone buzzed in my jacket pocket. I paused to flick on the screen with chilly fingers, expecting my lover Matt, who's away in Virginia training for a job.

> ✆1(323)#######:
> C'est moi. So happy to find u, cheeky monkey...

The rude buzz of a second message.

> 🖋1(323)#######:
> r u writing code now? Or only forenzix? I need u, my sweet, my dear heart.

Nope, I'm not found.

And I know a burnerbot when I see one: a fake forwarding telephone number.

Blocked that number. Shoved the phone into my pocket.

Any adolescent hack-bunny can text misspelled phukkery.

Block. Move on.

Because I'm the master of my universe. I'm done being alarmed by last year's cyberstalkers, done looking over my shoulder for fear of cybergangsters. Instead, I was out on the street at eight-of-the-freaking-clock in the morning to earn the easiest five thousand dollars ever.

And okay, yeah, I'm a big fat liar. Last year's adventures scared me to the core. It's taken a year to get my moxie back. And I'm enraged again each time some random jerk-faced hacker sticks a "LOL HACKD U!" message in my face. Gives me a crick in the neck, looking over my shoulder all the time while adrenalin runs through my veins and my brain tries to sort responses: Alarmed? Time to run? Mad? Time to fight back? Seems like each day, I'm teaching myself the same lesson:

Block. Move on.

Here where I live and work now, on the north end of Capitol Hill, the graceful boulevard trees wreak havoc on the sidewalks. In October, the fallen maple and chestnut leaves hide upheaved concrete. But see? Otherwise peaceful. No one's chasing me here. At East Aloha Street, where the sidewalk crosses into the wealthier parts of the neighborhood, I glanced at the email message that reconfirmed my client's address.

13-something Twentieth East, in the subdivision built for Klondike Gold Rush nouveau riche. Faux-Georgian mansions, faux-alabaster columns, faux turrets, expanses of leaded glass.

My client had included her door's security code in email: *"I'm often on the second floor and can't make it down as quickly as I used to."* At the massive wood-and-leaded-glass door, I punched in the security code, pushed open the door, and called out hello, quietly excited: me, I'm a businesswoman with a real client.

"Mrs. Monroe? It's Sam Byron. Zak's friend."

A long-haired snow-white cat meowed and brushed against my dress-up black trousers.

Two lovebirds whistled and chatted with each other, the sound echoing down the hallway from the kitchen.

A wild-haired tall person lurked behind the front door.

I yipped, startled.

Then felt my face burn, embarrassed for being spooked: an antique mirror hung above the high walnut wainscoting. It was just me.

Called hello again.

The cat mewed, more pathetic than the first time.

Deeper into the foyer, I discovered a library to the left. An attractive, formal-looking woman in a charcoal pants suit sat in a club chair. A woman of a certain age and definite class of wealth, immaculately coifed champagne hair, pale silk blouse with a floppy bow. I spoke her name once again.

It's more than a year since I'd seen that color.

My phone in hand, I tapped 9–1–1.

▪

Waiting for the EMTs on the front porch, I meditated on Zak's poor stepmother, waiting for a visitor that she'd never greet. Sitting perhaps as properly as she'd done in life, facing the doorway, eyes tastefully made up, but staring without seeing.

"We're here for you, Mrs. Monroe." That's what I'd said on the phone, talking about that virus. Though I didn't know her beyond one phone call and an email message, she sounded nice, twinsets-and-pearls nice. Exactly the kind of woman I saw from the walnut-paneled foyer: she lounged in a lush cream-and-ivory interior, rocked in the bosom of Abraham, clutching her day-planner, waiting for our appointment. That nice woman's misfortunes and happy times were now over.

Thumb hovering over my cell phone, I prepared to call Zak. But was it my place to call? What could he do at this moment? My finger twitched. Better to let the authorities call first, the way they're trained to do. I'd call after—

After someone else roused and responded to his raw emotion? I'm such a coward.

Across the street, a big-leaf maple had dropped enough leaves to reveal a bird's nest in the top branches. The webbing of my computer bag's strap rubbed at my neck. Farther down the block, a garden crew roared fallen leaves into the street, the smell of the gas-powered blower drifting my way. The workers, decked in ear protection, hats, and sunglasses, seemed oblivious to the world, but stepped aside when a pedestrian approached. Along with the gas smell, the air carried the faint decay of autumn from the veggies and annuals growing in the parking strips and the ungleaned Italian plums that littered the sidewalks.

Everyday life. Everywhere but in that nice woman's library.

To stay in my own Real Life while waiting, I sent my daily email to Matt's daughter Pippi. I begged for details about her new piano teacher and shared a math puzzle that'd make her laugh. The rest of the world melts away when Pippi and I share private jokes and stories. It's only a couple of weeks since she and Matt left for Virginia, but I already miss that girl like crazy.

My cell showed three minutes since I'd called for the EMTs. Felt to be three hours. Under my hovering thumb, my cell buzzed again, and I still hoped for Matt, my absent boyfriend, in the midst of my disconcerting morning.

> 1(206)#######:
> UR so cute in yr lether coate. Glad u didn't cut yr hair. Bye - Nicky

My cold hands trembled. Last year's shards of fear. Block that chill twitching up my spine. I smothered an instinct to call Matt for comfort, amazed at my childish response.

It was only Nicky. Who else in the world but Nicky would be nuts enough to take risks just to tell me I'm pretty, when I'm not?

> Sam:
> Nicky? Seriously? You must know the FBI is still looking for you. And they read all my messages.

Last year, Nicky, a former coworker, decided he was in love with me and through a series of unfortunate events got the White Knights of the New Russian Revolution chasing after me, those mobsters from upstream of the Sea of Azov and downwind of Chernobyl. The FBI still wants to catch those rats. So I dutifully forward stalker messages for an anonymous security contractor to analyze. Nicky, however, isn't a threat, just a pest. Block. Move on.

Flashing lights rushed up the street, putting an end to my existential impulse to call Matt. I straightened my secondhand jacket and prepared to be the First Responder I've been trained to be. A young uniformed officer came with the EMT crew. After exchanging identification, I answered his questions, which always proves to be calming. Just the facts.

"Her name is Doreen Monroe. I didn't touch her to offer aid. As you see, it's clear she's dead."

"Did it frighten you?"

"Um, no." Seeing that woman made me sad, not incompetent. I'm a totally adequate First Responder. "Why would I be frightened?"

"Your hair looks…"

He made an uncertain motion with his hand that made me check my reflection in the glass door. I must have run my fingers through my hair while twitching on the front porch.

"Yeah, it gets out of hand. I looked better when I first showed up for our meeting."

"You had an appointment?" The officer was blond, wore a wedding ring, and kept his hair soldier-short.

"For eight o'clock. Her day-planner or journal was under her hand, as if she'd just looked inside."

"You know Mrs. Monroe well?" His SPD shoulder badge—Seattle Police Department—rose and fell as he wrote notes.

"Not really. She's a widow. Her stepson Zak, her next of kin, hired me for the project that I came to discuss with her. This was our first live meeting." Sad word choice.

He looked at his notes, made one more jot, and then his blond brows beetled up. "Wonder why she sent you a code but left her back door wide open." It was a remark, not a question.

We were done after I gave the officer Zak's phone number. Soon my friend would be getting That Call. *There's been an unfortunate event.*

The call I was too cowardly to make.

▪

Early-morning sun broke through the tree tops when I headed back up Capitol Hill, longing deep in my soul for espresso, watching that I didn't stumble on chunks of sidewalk. Behind me, Mrs. Monroe's front door stood ajar, the emergency-response people not yet done.

Just as I stepped into the crosswalk at East Aloha, a new-model black SUV sped up. I scrambled back from the curb.

The SUV's tailwind spooked me, reminding me of last year's armed ambush by the White Knights of the New Russian Revolution, who weren't knights, weren't political or ethnic Russians, and weren't looking for revolution. Mere looters, taking advantage of the cybernetic chaos of the modern Internet.

A deep breath. Let's be real: no one is chasing me. Anything I knew when I was an NSA contractor? Out of date by two years, minimum. I no longer possess knowledge of value to even the most clueless cyberthug. Let's call that past event the White Knight Affair, so it no longer sounds scary. Block and move on.

Espresso on Fifteenth Avenue was in sight. I could smell the burnt-bitter tang of just-ground beans. Did I imagine hearing the *ssst* of steam over the traffic noise?

My phone vibrated with a message from Karl, my attorney.

Karl:
That offer on your aunt's house? It did not go through.

My Aunt Lucky requires long-term memory care, and to finance it, I need to sell her house on Limberlost Island. I hold my infirm aunt's power of attorney, but it seemed that all I had the power to do was write checks to an actual attorney, who does the baseline work that will ensure her care. When he isn't arguing with my insurance company.

Sam:
Rats. Need the money from that sale now.

🖑Karl:
Worse

"Samantha!"

Brad Jones pulled up beside me in a Maserati, the top down, calling my name wrong on purpose. Florida frickin' Georgia Line played too loudly on his satellite radio. You can be as frat-boy cute as a Clean-and-Wholesome romance hero and yet have bad taste in music.

"It's Samsara, as you know."

"Why aren't you at work?" His voice reverberated like a cello. But did that tenor tone remind me of Colonel Brandon or Hans Gruber in *Die Hard*?

"I am at work, Brad. New business. Visiting my clients."

"But we bought Quinn's startup. You have a job with us."

"Actually, I'm self-employed." And here's why: Brad Jones's Big-Data ad-rendering corporation represented spiritual death to both Natalia and me.

"But we hold Quinn's non-compete agreements." Brad seemed more puzzled than assertive.

Ah, the bane of Silicon World work-life: that non-compete clause in employment agreements, where you promise not to go to work with the corporation's competitors for two years, by which time all proprietary information learned at the old job has rotted.

"Quinn only paid me as a contractor on a few software projects. I wasn't his employee."

"But we have your code." Brad wore the upscale, exec version of the tech-manager uniform: pressed Dockers and a business-blue, silk-like Tencel shirt with a button-down collar. "We now own your research into secure-code solutions."

"In Quinn's documents, I'm a named contributor. So I earn a portion of whatever your company earns by using my code. Shall I explain the math?"

Brad grinned, acknowledging our shared history. "I have minions who do my math."

In ancient times, when I was a young grad student at Princeton, Brad was an older back-for-an-MBA student, certifying his ability to supervise geeks. He was on the vice-president path, his managers having recognized his innate abilities, which some call sociopathic. On all our group projects, I did the math. But in the much-touted meritocracy of the software world, the VP role always pays better than does genius-programmer.

"Seriously, Sam." Using his privilege, Brad set the handbrake, left his car double-parked, and pursued me down the street, the driver's door open and security bell dinging.

Me, I wanted espresso. And to ask Karl what *worse* meant.

Brad almost touched my elbow, but sensitivity training got the better of him. "We have problems only someone like you can solve."

"Someone like me?"

"You. Specifically you, Sam. In grad school, you wanted to save the world. I am offering that opportunity."

"My hourly rate is five K, with a twenty-hour minimum."

"We need you in our Clean Room. On our payroll."

"Regretfully, I have my own business to run."

"What business?"

With Mrs. Monroe's laptop tucked under my arm, I invented an answer. "Concierge security for the wealthy. For people like you, who need their families to be secure but don't have time to play personal Home Help Desk."

"You do research, Sam. There must be two hundred guys in Seattle selling security services."

"Other firms can't deliver what we do. Who else can you trust with what's most precious to you?"

"C'mon, Sam. You're joking." He laughed, but then noticed I didn't join in. "You can't be serious. How can you do the genius work you're known for without a support infrastructure?"

"I'm touched that you care."

"You need the tools and backing of a major entity. You're settling for less."

"I certainly hope so."

He softened. His VP personality kindled into full flame, personal warmth glowing, the flare that separates top executives from us worker-bees. "Truly, Sam. You are special. We can offer work only you can do. Opportunities you will never otherwise stumble upon in this lifetime."

Brad touched me then—verboten in geek culture. He put a hand on my shoulder, like my brother Pete does, and looked deep into my eyes, as if he cared. I fingered the business card in my pocket, only slightly frayed from twitching it while I waited for the EMTs. I handed it to him.

"Take my card. Tell your mother and her friends where they can find true security. Don't you worry about the malware that arrives in her email every day?"

Yes, indeed: I offered a facetious response when he claimed to care about my wasted talents.

Brad's perfect brows dipped in classic, executive sadness.

"Sir? Sir?"

Lovely Rita pulled up in her weatherized cart, pointing to his double-parked car. Brad nodded to her, but had to call after me so that he got the last word.

"Call me when you're ready to do the best work you ever dreamed of. Work only you can do, Sam."

Even last year I'd have been intrigued by that kind of an invitation:

> "Only you, Sam Byron, can find the trail through this code."

Save the cyberworld. For God and country.

Like when I saved the local power grid from international terror in the White Knight Affair. But then mobsters sent their armed cousins after me. That made me I'm cautious where I used to be a rebel. So now, at the ancient age of thirty, I check both ways twice before I cross the street. I hope that deep inside, the Real Me wants to step to the brink for the view over the edge. But for sure, the Real Me cannot go back into the corporate world merely for a paycheck.

"Only you, Sam Byron."

Yeah. No.

2

409 in Your Coffee Maker

⁝

"WHAT CAN I GET FOR YOU?"

The kohl-eyed barista, a baby's footprint tattooed on her forearm, asked that question each of the ten days since I moved to the neighborhood. She never remembers my usual order.

"Shot-in-the-dark." Other possible answers to that question:

Safety. Cash. A creative challenge.

I buy my caffeine at an espresso store on Fifteenth Avenue East, the one with the scratched painted sign on the glass door. Espresso and Shoeshine is kitty-corner from the marijuana shop. The sign formerly read "Barber" instead of "Espresso." The building has been there since the early twentieth century, about the time Seattle's Gold Rush robber barons installed their families on the top of this logged-off hill.

The barista didn't look up while she made change and handed over my paper cup. "Cream is on the left counter."

Every cell in my body screamed for caffeine, but I stood at the bar to drink, looking (I hoped) as cool as every other hipster sipping espresso. The sun broke through the window. And I felt bad once again about Mrs. Monroe. And Zak.

Since I'd skipped breakfast, I decided that a handcrafted artisanal donut would not be amiss. When I returned to the espresso line, an older woman stepped in front of me, seemingly dazed and amazed to find herself suddenly In Real Life.

"Want a refill?" The barista prompted while the woman tried to remember what she wanted to say.

Two men entered Espresso and Shoeshine, squeaking into line behind me. One had a horsey face and wore the working man's version of Brad Jones's Pacific Northwest Silicon Forest uniform: off-brand khaki trousers and a blue perma-press shirt, top button undone, white t-shirt peeking out. I glanced down to confirm my prejudice: indeed, he's wearing low-rise Timberland hiking shoes. The too-tall guy behind him appeared exceedingly Capitol Hill hip in a washed-out black hoodie, jeans, and Doc Martens, and so thin that in a mare's nest dreamland he'd pass for Slender Man. More so because it wasn't possible to see his face with the hoodie pulled up. Then I revised my judgment: not a no-logo hipster; rather, a cubicle-dwelling software geek in a hard-to-obtain American Giant zippered sweatshirt.

"I need help," the woman in front of me said. I started to answer, but she spoke to the barista. "I bought a newspaper earlier, but when I put the coffee away at home—remember, I always get it ground for gold cone drip—it wasn't there."

"Really?" The barista pursued her lips. "Receipt?"

"You didn't give me one." A five-dollar *New York Times* in hand and dressed in an upscale purple velvet tracksuit, the woman likely emerged from high school when my mother did. Her lipstick was slightly off color for her skin tone; perhaps her hand shook while she applied it. Even this early in the morning, the color bled into the thin lines around her lips. Her eyeliner wasn't quite symmetrical, in the same way that her helmet-hair wig was skewed. "So I came back for my paper."

"That happened last Tuesday *and* Saturday," the barista said.

"Truly?" The woman's eyes opened wide, astonished. "My son is right. I'm too forgetful. Do you think that rubber band idea works, where you snap it to remind yourself why you put the band on your wrist?"

"I don't think—"

A kid rushed up, dressed in the dusty rags of junior high skaters, inadvertently nudging Memory Lady in the back with his skateboard and knocking into my five-thousand-dollar laptop bag. I clutched the bag closer. He waved for the barista's attention.

"Hey, someone's shooting up in the john. Don't give out the door code for a minute."

"No one's in there," our barista said. "No one asked for the code to get in."

"It's 1776, same as yesterday. How do you think I saw the dude? Huh? How?"

The barista uttered an expletive that wasn't in her training.

"Don't bunch your thong. Just keep people out till he's gone." The kid moved again, knocking my bag.

"Don't be rude." Khaki Guy had his cell in hand. "I'm calling 9–1–1."

"Hey, assbite!" Skater scowled. "There's no reason for the cops. And they won't come anyhow. Not in this neighborhood. Just leave the dude alone. He'll be gone soon enough."

"It's just rude," Memory Lady said. "Heavens. There's a changing table in that bathroom. Is there no shame?"

"There's no baby right now." Skater shrugged. "That table's just convenient. Capitol Hill doesn't have a safe injection site."

"It's illegal," Khaki Guy insisted, shifting his stance, color creeping up his neck. The crimson shade of guys genetically programmed to go off in a rage as the first emotional response in any situation. Bet he yells a lot. "If you let one go—"

"One broken window and Capitol Hill becomes West Baltimore?" Skater sneered. "Righteous people like you just want users to die in the street, right?"

The barista's hand hung over her cellphone on the back counter. Unsure.

"No one's hurt." Skater persisted. "No one's in danger. No property theft. Don't call."

"Can I get a double espresso?" Slender Man called from behind us. Barista returned to her steampunk espresso machine, biting her lip, trying to decide about what's the right thing.

"I'm calling 9–1–1," Khaki Guy insisted, cell still in hand as his weapon of choice. Meanwhile, Slender Man got his espresso before any of us.

Curious, ready to warn the occupant, I tapped the restroom security code. Like the sign over the lock said: Vacant.

Memory Lady evaporated.

Junior-high Rag Boy was out the door. Though from the politics of his disputation, I'm now betting he's in high school.

"Excellent grift," Khaki Guy said, speaking to me as if we were in on the secret. "Superbly executed. But so much effort for only a newspaper."

Startled that he spoke to me (it's not our way with strangers in Seattle), I whipped around.

"I'm Victor." He moved to shake my hand, one of which was in my jacket pocket, the other holding my now-cold shot-in-the-dark coffee.

"That's nice." I used the most pleasant voice I can manage after finding a dead woman and chatting with police and the espresso not yet kicking in.

The barista wiped down the foamer nozzle. "I'm sorry. Corey's supposed to be here. He's late." She recognized me. "You drank that fast."

"Another doppio and a latte, please. And two donuts, the maple frosted ones." It occurred to me to act like a leader and bring coffee to the office staff. Which consists only of Natalia.

"You want that to-go or for here?"

"In a paper carryout box, please."

Khaki Guy still awaited his extra-hot no-foam three-pumps vanilla venti latte when I left, following Slender Man who turned left when I turned right.

At that point, I felt that I'd been quite nice to people for it being a tightly wound, screws-stripped kind of morning. And once again I felt glad to be back in Seattle, living in a serio-comic postpunk thriller, inhabiting the part of the city where you have to show your sleeve tattoo just to rent a room.

Time to be at work in the new office I can't afford.

Outside, a glorious October had settled over Seattle. Temperature in the fifties, no humidity, brilliant sun that hadn't yet dipped into the lower Seasonal Depression latitudes. One of the 1910s prefab mansions down the street had its Halloween flag flying, waving valiantly over the stone lions that guarded its xeriscape front yard.

A block from my office, I crossed what was formerly the banks' redline along the middle of Capitol Hill: you white people over to the north, we'll give you a mortgage; you people with melanin, stay on the south side and rent. One of the uprooted sidewalk chunks forced me to stumble.

I'd walked as far as Galahad House, that old brick apartment with its name cast in plaster over the entry way, its nearby architectural brethren christened Arthur, Merlin, and Guinevere. Galahad contained the one-room studio where I skated into my first heartbreak. A dorm-sized refrigerator and toaster oven in the closet formed a kitchen. Books piled everywhere, mattress in the corner. A jade plant in a glass of water, rooted from a cutting, needing to be potted in soil. Tony's clothes stashed in a duffel, as if he might leave at any moment.

Which he did.

But that's what college is for, right? Like practicing jumps on a ramp, you practice human relations with those who leave and yet haunt you. I'd forgotten when I moved back to Capitol Hill that I'd run into lost memories along with tree-heaved sidewalk chunks.

At the end of the alley that runs parallel with Fifteenth and Sixteenth Avenue, that grifting beige blond from Espresso and Shoeshine was letting herself in the side door of the Galahad building. That skateboarder rolled past, fast as the north wind, like Mercury carrying a message from the gods.

The woman's light fall jacket wafted in his tailwind.

Or did I imagine that?

▪

"We have no new clients!" Natalia called from a dark corner of the office. "Not one response to any of fifty email queries. Good thing you scored at least one client."

Here's a pair of Capitol Hill small-business owners, leasing an office in a brand-new building—one of the boxy monstrosities encroaching on the antique village that lines Fifteenth Avenue East. It's also where I live alone now, in a top-floor unit slightly larger than my first dorm room.

In our new office, Natalia had buried herself in research. We're both in black trousers that day, but where I still exude whiffs of too-tall skate-punk who hasn't decided if it's okay to have breasts, Natalia is pure European sophisticate, ultra-feminine, and perfect. Perfect nails, hair, makeup. Her shirts are starched and pressed. She floats when she walks in high-heeled boots, an incarnation of grace and fashion sense. Me, I'm still a fourteen-hole Docs kinda grrrl.

Setting down my offering of coffee and maple donuts, I described our new business model, as I'd explained it to Brad Jones: concierge security for rich people. Network security and laptop restoration.

"So, no in-depth forensics?" Natalia wrinkled her perfect nose.

"No. We just ask basic Help Desk questions."

"Like, 'What were you doing when this happened?'"

"Exactly. And we add a surcharge for repeat customers. Those who never learn. No moral dilemmas for us."

"Freyja preserve us!" Natalia laughed until she got the hiccups, calling on one of her pagan gods for protection.

But I didn't get around to telling her we'd already lost Client #1. Whenever I began to say anything, I felt overwhelmed at the thought of Doreen Monroe dying all alone. There's no reason in the world to bring other people down.

And anyway, a male voice rang from the office doorway. A beguiling baritone, a cosmopolitan Brit accent.

"It's well hard to find you, dear heart, though I'm indeed chuffed to succeed."

Of all the security-forensics joints in all the world, Tony King walked into mine.

"I need your help, my love." He smirked when he saw he had our attention.

"No," I explained.

"Oh, dear heart, I promise I'm not the wanker you think I am."

Anthony Hong Moon King—in dark-blue bespoke silk suit, more London than New York and certainly not Seattle for daywear; reeking of rich man's charisma—filled the doorway to our office, fresh from the deep fraud-and-theft Internet mud he's inhabited since we said goodbye. I must have conjured him, lost in memory as I passed the Galahad Apartments.

Tony, the Pirate King.

"You!" Natalia poked up from under the table where she'd been connecting network cables.

"Natalia Dragon? How *do* you do!" Tony drew back as if surprised. His asymmetrical face and mannered body language are difficult to read. You get lost while figuring where he's from: too umber to be golden, too Asian to be African, too tall to fit human spaces, too friendly. "Aren't you a perfect pair? Sam for code, Natalia on the network."

Natalia for detecting other people's horse pucky. Me for accepting people at face value, right up until they say goodbye. Oh wait. Tony never said goodbye; he just vanished into the darknet.

"What in Freyja's name are you doing here?" Natalia called again on one of her gods, hands on her hips.

"Instead of in jail. Or SuperMax." Which I'd muttered when he surfaced at a blackhat event in Naples two years ago.

"Have you two dear hearts quit Special Forces *and* the French Foreign Legion? Now leading a quiet life in the forensics suburbs?" His smile, if that's what it was, showed teeth, a manicured expression Tony purchased with his tailored shirts. If you didn't have to always be figuring what he was, he'd be any metrosexual guy, tall, dark, but not handsome; his face is too disconcerting and his size intimidating. You think you've interpreted his expression, and it drifts away, like an emotional chameleon. "Oh my darlings, I wager you're even married."

"May the gods save me from ever satisfying your curiosity," Natalia said, at the same moment that I said, "Seattle is a city."

"Ah, yes, Seattle, a cosmopolitan hamlet under grey skies."

He's exactly the wanker I think he is. Has always been.

"What's with the fake Brit talk?" I met him at university—University of Washington, not Oxbridge. Back when he claimed to be all-American mongrel. "Are you running a new man-of-mystery con?"

Tony King, the Emperor, the Caesar, the Khan, the King of Pirates. In my first job, I cut my wisdom teeth chasing his DVD bootlegging enterprise across Asia. And then pursued his web of illicit cons while he burrowed into the ever-expanding darknet.

"Rubbed off, from where I abide." He offered a card from his silky inner pocket. I didn't accept it. "You are my only hope, Obi Sam Kenobi."

"Help *you*?"

"To protect my mother."

"Seriously? I don't do elder care." Actually, I do, if we're related, like my Aunt Lucky. However, Tony isn't in that circle—and he's too good a hacker to need help from me.

He made eyes at me, old-fashioned made-for-each-other eyes. "You appear to be the Sam I have long known. Your life among the petit bourgeoisie is merely a masquerade, is it not?"

He tugged at my shirt collar, an intimacy that only Matt has ever been allowed.

"Yet here I am, Samsara Ada Byron, shop owner." I resisted knocking his hand away. "The Hero with a Thousand Faces."

"Well and good. I need a hero. Though I'm knocked sidewise to find a CEO instead of a hacker at the end of my search."

"You, Tony, remain the same con artist as ever. Shinier suit. More expensive shoes. Haven't seen you around."

Then again, I haven't *been* around. Staying out of sight has been part of my master plan after last year's overexposure.

"Took a break," he said. "Then I needed to be seen again to make progress. However, now, I need to disappear."

"Sorry. Can't help."

"Don't require your assistance for that. I need you to protect my mother."

Tony glanced around, which caused me to wonder why there remained this much move-in chaos in the new office, since both Natalia and I tend to be hyper-organized.

"Do you have a private office where we can speak on this matter?" Tony asked.

Natalia said, "We don't accept work that isn't one hundred percent legal."

"And if we take your case, we will all be involved." I swept a wave to encompass the mostly empty office. "Natalia supervises network issues. It takes a team."

Tony touched the hand I'd waved, slid a finger up my sleeve, pressed his thumbnail lightly into the Celtic tattoo at the web between my thumb and forefinger.

"Not everything is about business," he murmured, hinting at an intimacy that excluded Natalia.

But it's not as if I'm still seventeen and one touch from Tony sends me to my knees. And my phone was vibrating in my breast pocket, most likely Matt. I tapped to ignore it.

Tony followed me into our Clean Room, where we do forensic work that can't be tainted by networks or other machines. The building owners expected to lease this space as a restaurant, but had no takers, so we got this space at a bargain. What was intended to be a walk-in cooler proved perfect for work we needed to do with no outside contamination.

Yet I let Tony inside the Clean Room.

He sat on the edge of a tall stool.

"Natalia likes me." Tony folded his arms. A familiar gesture: asserting that he'd won a dispute at the same moment he started it.

"She sees you for the snake you are."

"And you, dear heart, mean to insult snakes by that. I shall learn to live with your judgment. Meanwhile, my mother needs your help."

"Give her my number. Have her call me."

"Alas, just like you, she won't take advice from me." He had hold of my hand again. "You are the only one I can trust."

Me =/= Trust =/= Tony

"Back when you told Tony-as-a-young-boy stories, you claimed your mother abandoned you." How we bonded in college: proving to each other what sad orphans we were. "Back when you didn't have a British accent."

"She and I reached rapprochement. And I want her safe. Her computer system's been hacked. Some spook is spying on her. You need to find the spook—and protect her."

"What can I do that you can't? After all, you claimed the hack in the Hang Seng Affair."

A couple of years ago, Tony hacked the Hang Seng stock exchange, causing a shut-down by posting a cautionary on the darknet about how easy it was to do; the freeze also halted a computer-generated run on the market. He'd texted me with glee. I refrained from saying that my team solved the Lights Out In Estonia hack and restored the power grid. I don't need to flash my Tuff Cybernetic Skilz to prove I'm the queen of the cyber forensics universe.

He said, "My mother has messages from two chums who received email threats. I believe she's also a target."

"You hack your mother?"

"Only to read her email. But also to make sure my enemies aren't trying to get to me through my mother."

"Please stop touching me like that. You need to respect people's boundaries." And stop breathing pheromones on me.

Tony didn't retract his hand. "Yesterday I was in Hong Kong, so I contacted one of her chums to offer help."

"Can we stop a minute? You don't peer over my shoulder like that, do you? Hack my email?"

"You wound me to the very core, Sam," hand to heart, "for you to think I'd ever—"

"I do think so."

He folded. "Only on social sites. And only to protect you, my dear one, if you need it."

"Never penetrated my machines or servers?"

He offered that infuriating guilty-boy grin. "Only once, for about fifteen minutes last winter. All I checked was your location data. To find where you went after Virginia."

"If I do one single favor for you, I'm bound to learn something I don't want to know."

"Just find who's spooking my mother's email. I believe the threats her friends received are intended to draw me out."

"And you can't fix it yourself, because why?"

"I'm in the midst of crucial work. And you're a better hacker than I am." He held out a palm-size caddy for a solid-state disk drive. "This contains the threat her chum in Hong Kong received. It's a starting place for your research."

Smothering my curiosity, I didn't reach for the caddy. "Have your mother call the FBI. Best choice for death threats."

Tony leaned forward, listening intently, like the guy you see in the coffee bar, wanting the girl to like him. "Unlike most West Coast women, you don't have that voice uplift quirk. Your body language, as much as it's gendered, is at times more male than female. Which makes people uneasy. You do that on purpose—am I correct?"

Not to be distracted so easily, I repeated, "Contact the authorities. I'm not playing ten-dimensional chess with pirates and hackers."

"My mother would kill me if the FBI called her." The Brit accent disappeared. His voice became utterly Pacific Northwest again. "With her own hand. And a dull knife."

"You've sent the authorities after your enemies before." Not that I'd pat him on the back for it, but Tony contributed intelligence that brought down one of the greatest bitcoin grifters of all time.

"Oh sweet thing, I'm the good guy, seeking the truly bad guys. Here's her address." He forced that business card on me, ink scrawled across the back. And from another pocket, he retrieved a pay-as-you-go phone. "Call me after you meet her. You're the only one I can trust."

In the Clean Room, Natalia had hung a battery-run clock, its face as plain as any clock you endured in high school, watching time fail to pass. Except the second hand didn't sweep, it jerked and twitched. In the silence, you could hear the tick just before each spasm.

That clock would have to go.

"Why me, Tony?"

"Because deep inside, you're still one of them." His devilish grin again. He meant the NSA and their contractors. "And you will do the right thing, instinctively."

"I am not one of them." I'd left the national security apparatus just before Snowden did.

"But your old friends still watch out for you, Sam. Be a hero. Help my mother without drawing attention to me."

"Is this illegal? Dangerous?" With great effort, I resisted wrapping my arms around my core, not wanting to give Tony any sign that I needed protection from him. Or from *them*.

"For you, dear heart, there's no danger. And what's illegal about finding the spook who hacked my mother?"

"Put it there." I pointed to the workbench, where he could leave the hard-disk caddy. "All I want to do is the best possible job with the most social good. If this work doesn't meet my criteria—"

"Oh, it does. In spades."

"Yeah? We shall see. I'll send you a project link." I asked for his email address and created a Krypptikk project. "Check your email now."

Krypptikk is a web program Byron&Dragon uses for shared task lists and secure communications. We can access it from any device to save and share encrypted information, create job tickets for projects, and send encrypted email.

"It's safe?" He stared at his phone, a damned pirate asking if I'd sent him a safe message.

"Two-factor authentication. Not just server-side crypto."

"Make this private. Just you and me, dear heart." He crossed his arms, as if he needed to protect his core as much as I did. "Add your crew later, when you've identified the spook."

KRYPPTIKK JOB: CLIENT#0_SPOOKS_PRIVATE
Invited members: sbyron; PK323
SByron:
Ticket #1: Analyze referred client network.
Ticket #2: Analyze customer-provided disk.
Baseline charge = $10,000 USD plus $500 per hour research and consultation; due upon project completion.
SByron:
Project criteria: Legal. Sane. Safe.
SByron:
Query 1: Laptop or desktop?
Query 2: Personal or business computer?
Query 3: Recommended probe?

"PK?" Tony, head bent over the screen, read the Krypptikk message on his phone and tapped a reply with his thumbs.

"Pirate King. The number is the area code from that creepy blind text you sent this morning."

[PK323 accepted and entered project]
PK323:
Query1 & Query2 - no information.
Query 3 - onsite research required.

"This is ripping good fun. Though the messaging isn't as fast as texting."

"Are two authentication PINs too much to ask of a pirate?"

He grinned. "It's rather like playing Fatal Fury at the same time as playing Doctor, except with crypto. I shall happily show you mine."

Wanting Tony out of my space, I pointed to the door. I take full responsibility for each decision about who I go to bed with; however, Tony was a decision made before I reached the age of reason.

Which, for me, was approximately last year.

In the main office, Tony called a farewell to Natalia as if she were his own dear sister.

3

Girl Can't Help It

WITH NO REAL CLIENTS—the Pirate King's mother? really?—and therefore no work to help me stop fuming about Tony entering my professional space, I did just what normal people do in the office: took care of my personal business, checking items off the list as I went.

First: returning texts to Karl, my attorney.

Sam:
What's worse than no house sale?

Karl:
Her new neighbor is suing. Claims your aunt has infringed on his beach access for years, that she has no waterfront.

Sam:
I need to sell a water view AND waterfront. Not a rickety farmhouse ready for demolition.

Karl:
Relax. It's what you pay me to solve.

Sam:
How long will this take?

Karl:
The whole time. Starting research now. Also, your incorporation papers are ready to sign.

Sam:
We sign electronically, right? Do you need security specialists to review your network and processes? Latest research shows 75% of law firms don't know if they're breached.

Karl:
1. Yes. 2. No, we just paid someone for that. But I have a client who could use your help. Talk later?

Okay: Still broke. Or maybe, more broke than before. But hopeful, at least.

Next up: Office finances. Even though we're sitting in the same room working, Natalia launched a Krypptikk project to discuss the deficiencies of the cocktail-napkin business plan we'd made last week. Her first message:

KRYPPTIKK JOB: #SALES_PRIVATE

Invited members: byron&dragon

NDragon:

Received first bid.

We need $97K for datacenter hardware.

SByron:

All my cash is tied up in the lease and expenses.

NDragon:

Are we in business or not?

If it takes days instead of hours to execute a research query, how many clients do we get?

SByron:

We need clients if we want Dogs of War.

NDragon:

Then we need another investor.

Dogs of War is our pet name for the datacenter-scale hardware we use for forensics research—paid for by our corporate bosses in our former jobs.

Natalia looked up from her monitor and spoke aloud. "We don't either of us want to do less than our best work."

"Never." It wasn't pleasant, hearing her echo what Brad said earlier.

"Then we need to spend a hundred K at the hardware store. Not the five K you just made off that boring malware."

An invoice that I couldn't ask Zak to pay under the new depressing circumstances. I deployed a delaying tactic.

"Let's do some serious malware bounty hunting."

We'd made twenty thousand over Labor Day weekend, collecting a bounty on a significant-but-hard-to-detect security flaw in software that is likely running on your computer right now. The bounty was part of why we believed it possible to make a living on our own.

Natalia sniffed at the idea. "Bounty hunting with our weak-ass laptops and Muppet-sized servers?"

"Let me finish my coffee before we talk about this."

Yes, I failed to share details about my first client. Or about Brad's offer. Or, for that matter, about the morning's stalker text messages. Why keep silent? Because I found a dead person, and I wasn't prepared yet to talk about it.

Next, time to text Matt—though it's not as if I treat my personal affairs of the heart like an item on my day's task list. But it was the first moment when I could send a message without the impulse arising from fear or a need for comfort.

> Sam:
> Missed you last night.

Matt, my—what? Partner? Significant other? More than lover!—had joined the FBI, and now must spend time training in Virginia. Though I'd argued for other jobs suited to his new law degree, Matt argued that this was his life's dream. I cannot counter such a claim. Nor can I live in Virginia again. So I'm alone in Seattle.

> MattOwens:
> Up late working last night?

> Sam:
> You know me

Frankly, late last night I'd been out playing guitar in a garage on Twelfth Avenue, with people he's never met, the first time in a year that I played music without Matt.

Not at all like sleeping with someone else.

MattOwens:
How's work? Did you meet your new client?

Sam:
Meeting got delayed.

We share an ocean of trust, more than I've ever known in this life. Yet I didn't have a good reason to ruin his day with a sad story…that I didn't want to talk about yet.

MattOwens:
Did you think about my proposal?

Scrolling up through his texts, I didn't find an unanswered question. Not a *proposal*, I hope. Matt knows that I don't do Happy Ever After, only happy for now. And that morning, I wasn't happy. I prevaricated with a French word, not a Spanish one.

Sam:
Si.

MattOwens:
What if this is too much? Time to talk now?

The gap between us—the entire North American continent—was my fault, because of my need to avoid the tentacles of the national security state, which strives to pull me back into its maw. Begging me to serve my country. With mathematics. Because I couldn't get over that dread, I was here instead of in Virginia with Matt.

Sam:
Hands full. Later

Which is why we love text messages. No intonation. A gallery of emojis for self-expression. Perfect for fibbing like a child who thinks she can escape the consequences. And for avoiding a discussion with the love of my life about unhappy truths and unknown proposals.

And yet, through that text, I felt his presence, a gentle reminder that left me missing Matt and Pippi like a pair of phantom limbs. We're friends, family, who need each other.

As penance for that cowardice, I found my courage and bucked up to speed-dial Zak Monroe.

Pressing the phone closer to my ear, so Zak's grief wouldn't leak out to where Natalia was busy at work, I listened closely while he seized his first chance to talk to a friend.

"When Dad married Doreen, I was fifteen and cruel. Then when he died, Doreen let me cry and offered me solace. Now I sit here feeling that I never truly knew her."

"If you need me to do anything here, just ask," I said.

"I wish—" Zak sniffed. "Last night on the phone, she opened up to me, maybe for the first time, talking about the fear that virus caused her. I could offer so little reassurance over the phone."

"It should have occurred to me to go pick up her laptop. I could have reassured her. I'm sorry."

"No, she wanted to talk about the past. For some reason, that virus called up old memories. And I made silly attempts to placate her fears." Zak cracked his phone against something hard. Silence.

Hoping we were still connected, I said, "Some rat made her last day miserable."

"Let's chase that rat down. Then send the cavalry to pound his ass into SuperMax. We could work on this together, fighting evil again. Though I don't want to take you away from your other work."

"I'll research the virus further today. Let's put all the details we find in a Krypptikk project file, so we can both see—"

Muffled voices begged Zak's attention. He interrupted his mourning. "Gotta go. We have a major crisis. I'll be buried."

"Call if you need to talk," I said. "I'm truly sorry for—"

Dead air. Zak was gone. Reminding me how it is in Virginia: No time for your own tragedies because you owe twelve, fifteen, or twenty hours to fending off the next cybernetic Armageddon.

KRYPPTIKK JOB: CLIENT#1_MONROE
Invited members: byron&dragon; Zak Monroe
SByron:
Ticket #1: Research ransomware source.
Original client files archived on byron&dragon server w/ this folder name.
[ZakM accepted and entered project]
ZakM:
Excited to be #1 client 4 U!
Let's find this bastard.
[NDragon accepted and entered project]
NDragon:
What is bill rate?

But I didn't start any research then. Instead, I wrote checks, which was next on the day's task list.

> October school fees for Pippi, because it turned out that private school was the only reasonable option where Matt lived in Virginia. And I wanted to be involved.

> The next month's advance and last month's extra charges at the home where Aunt Lucky lives now. (I say "home" because it's more like that than like an institution labeled "memory care facility." That's why it cost so much.)

> Attorney's fees—I didn't used to wince when I wrote checks that size.

However, I, Samara Ada Byron, free spirit, chose each of these ties to other people. I am not complaining.

Those tasks about exhausted the details of my personal life—attorney (no money; new hassle), love (misunderstanding; longing), and grief (malware forensics as an act of mourning). Therefore, I was about to do what I'd promised Natalia last week: contact people I knew at the FBI in search of contract forensics work.

But Harley Owens appeared in our office doorway.

▪

"Good morning, ladies."

My father-in-law. Yeah, no, that's not the right term, since I'm not married to Matt. But still. Harley Owens, the former sheriff of Limberlost County, the man who made it his personal project to scare me straight when I was in high school.

"Surprised to see you in the city, Harley."

I accepted a light-touch Pacific Northwest hug from him. The Owenses are huggy people. I'm not. But when you're next-door neighbors and sleeping with their son, you learn to adapt.

"Yeah, I'm wondering, can you rent me office space?" He shifted a battered leather computer satchel from one shoulder to the other. "I got invited to work regional cold cases."

Harley pretended to be casual, but I detected pride. Harley's goal since he retired: state or federal cold cases, as a contractor.

"Congrats! Does 'they' mean FBI?"

"Can't say." He flashed that conspiring grin of his. "Now I need a fast, secure network to practice research. And maybe a tutorial or two."

Emerging from the dark side of the room, Natalia came to shake Harley's hand, congratulating him. "You want to learn to search deeply on the net? I'll teach you."

Natalia cleared a chair and a door-and-sawhorses desk, and then set Harley up on the network with one of our computers. Tiny Natalia in high-heeled boots sat beside Harley, who has the build and beard and glinting eyes of a Viking berserker. Dressed as he does these days, you'd think "biker" if you didn't notice he wears the same riding boots as cops do. He also wore the kind of plaid cotton shirt and corduroy jacket that makes you think "air marshal."

While they discussed real-world opportunities where Harley might practice, I swallowed the idea of working beside my father-in-law. And had an idea.

"Harley, want to practice being a sock puppet? You could watch my social media accounts. Pretend to be me." I'd abandoned most social media last year after the White Knight Affair. The online harassment got boring. But if I was returning to the professional security world as more than a private researcher, I needed to reawaken those accounts.

"Like a female impersonator?" Harley's voice rumbled. Natalia and I exchanged looks. He caught us. "Not PC, huh? Am I pushing my privilege in *female* spaces?"

Jerking my chain.

He'd heard sufficient rants from me about being labeled "female" in the Internet Warz. Natalia, too, recognized the tease. She said, "We don't have a dress code. Or an estrogen detector."

In ten minutes, I had Harley set up with all my login details, plus a basic idea of how to save anything needed for deeper consideration. And also: how to ignore the twice-a-day promises from antagonists who assure me that they can hack in ways I'd never be skilled enough to discover.

"Here's the tool we use to save data and notes. I'm adding your name to the project."

He pursed his lips, looking wry. "If you say 'Harley Owens' loudly enough, will the NSA watch me, too?"

"It's the FBI that follows me," I said. "My personal watch-dogs. The NSA doesn't need me anymore. They've already recruited a thousand new mathematicians."

We introduced Harley to Krypptikk and the magic of encrypted communication everywhere.

> ***KRYPTIC JOB: #DEBRIS_BYRON***
> Invited members: byron&dragon; Harley Owens
> *[HOwens accepted and entered project]*
> *[NDragon accepted and entered project]*
> *NDragon:*
> Who to bill for this?
> *SByron:*
> Me, I guess, since it's my personal problem.

"On this account," I pointed to a place on his monitor, "you can see who's following me."

"Following?" Harley echoed. He retrieved his reading glasses from his worn leather satchel. "That's what people do on the Twitter? Or is this the Facebook?"

"Not Facebook," Natalia said. "Not cool enough of a hangout for Sam's hacker boyz."

One day last year, for fun, Natalia and I had a contest: in ninety minutes, who could generate the most robot followers on a social media account? I won, but only by a couple thousand robots. Which meant my profile, on a social account I hardly used, came to look like I was a major voice on the site. And I posted a message for the robots:

"I am the Red Queen. I can haz all yr robotz. Off with yr headz."

As a response, and as part of a malevolent indecency on the world-wide web, some hacker wannabe posted a picture of me holding a skateboard and tagged my name, and the words "code" and "security" and "bitch" appeared in the same sentence in a web story. Then my face appeared all over darknet forums, identifying me as an NSA informer. Harassed and doxxed on blackhat forums.

Doxxed? You know, when a basement-dwelling twerp decides to win an argument by posting details on the Internet, like your address and pictures of your closest relatives, friends, and their school-age children. Here's Sam with Matt and his daughter Pippi at the Fremont Sunday Market. Here's the house where they live together on Limberlost Island. To cap off the White Knight Affair, I had to redo my identity and credit last year.

And I joined my cyber-sisters in the morass where loads of promises of sexualized violence are shoveled into our social accounts daily. Rather than me sharing that verbal vomit, including words and pictures that children shouldn't see, I recommend you perform your own web search, to see what everyday life looks like for professional "females" whose careers receive excess exposure on the Internetz.

It's of no use to call the cops, unless the same messages are actually nailed to the door of your house or sent through the U.S. mail. It will take us all the entire next decade of organizing to get anywhere. I'm not convinced that legislation can do much about broken people who publish garbage online.

But I'm special, right? I advise others on privacy protection, but surrendered mine in exchange for personal protection. I don't have to explain that at length, do I? The FBI wanted to see my email messages to find the people who were chasing me. So I forward personal threats to my FBI minders. I have all my anti-doxxing and anti-hacker moats and barriers in place. And I live in a building where every inhabitant has a personal security code (my neighbors can't grant entry to anyone looking for me).

"Have we no coffee here?" Natalia, buried in code, tugged at her hair. "We need cabana boys or Georgian footmen."

Harley was in the john, else he'd likely volunteer. I slipped out to Espresso and Shoeshine.

The store's front door banged into me, scuffing over the top of my boot. Dark-hoodie Slender Man exited, didn't look my way, steaming down the street. Inside, the early-morning barista had finished her shift, replaced by a feather-weight guy with a half-sleeve tattoo. Steampunk dragon and mechanical roses. He was on the phone, back to the door.

"Dude was such an asshole, like I interrupted his day by asking what he wanted while he was texting. Didn't even look me in the eye while ragging." A pause. "Oh, I totally decaffed him. Not one iota of guilt about it."

The barista noticed me, clicked off his phone, and clicked on his best helpful manner, happy to make a foam-heart in my macchiato.

"What does it mean to decaf someone?"

He blushed. "I'm sorry. That was rude of me to say."

"But what does it mean?"

"To have any control when we're hassled..."

"You give total jerks decaf instead of regular." I tried to think if I'd ever called down barista decaf wrath upon my head.

He said, "Only in the most extreme situations. With all these tech guys moving into the neighborhood, it's a tad more tense than it used to be."

After dropping the tip I always do, I carried coffee for three back to the office. As I set hot paper cups before Natalia and Harley, I didn't see behind me when they both looked up.

▪

"Excuse me? You're Sam, right? Can you help me?"

Jason Taylor, in all-black jeans and no-label hoodie, leaned on the doorframe at the office entry, his lanky frame far more elegant than our secondhand Ikea furniture.

"Karl and your brother Pete said that you'd help me."

Not the best self-intro, using my punk-ass, perpetually problem-producing brother Pete as a calling card. But I know who Jason Taylor is, the avatar of second-chances-come-true in indie music. Perhaps better known in Europe than Seattle, but a good guy. And I like boys in eyeliner—I mean, just to look. I have my own boyfriend, who doesn't do eyeliner.

"Networking problems? Malware? A new studio that needs cyber-security?" I'm the freshly minted entrepreneur, internalizing the always-be-selling message. Wait, it's always be closing. Jason was perfect if we wanted to pursue that day's hilarious idea of a business model: security concierge for rich clients.

"I need a partner for a PSA event," he said, perking everyone's attention in the office at the mention of Public Service Announcements. "Someone who knows what she's talking about. I made a mistake."

Ah, that's where our new business intends to hit its sweet spot: *I made a mistake*. So easy to do if you try to handle your own cybersecurity.

"Fine." I waved to circle Natalia in. We'd agreed that she'd be doing anything public, since I prefer to stay out of the limelight. Not that I'm still spooked by the after-effects of the White Knight Affair. "We'd love to help. When is your event?"

Jason glanced at his watch, a wholly analog device. "Thirty minutes? My car is right here. I'll drive."

"Blessed Freyja, I cannot help." Natalia flicked off her monitor, as if she were leaving. "I have to pick up my kids at daycare. The late fees are more than I can afford."

I'm loath to say no to a would-be client (unless it's Tony). But I had to. "Sorry, Jason. Public speaking isn't my thing."

He incarnated disappointment. Then shrugged it off. "Panic attacks, huh? I understand."

"No, troll attacks. I become their target when I speak at cons." In fact, I hadn't been to any convention or meetup since the White Knights came after me.

"Can I convince you for a special case?" Jason twitched with eager excitement, as if someone flipped his On switch. "This is just some kids, bright ones at a Central District high school. I'm a witness for how hacking screws up real people. We'll talk for just five minutes. Then I promised to jam with any kids who are musicians. You can jam with us."

Okay, this appealed. I'd make Jason my pretend-boyfriend if he let me jam with him in real life. The other client who requested work this afternoon wanted me to babysit his mother. At least our business model was evolving with the times.

4

Mark Me Absent

ON THE WAY TO THE high school, while Jason chatted about how his website kept getting hacked and could I help secure the site so his band could host their house recordings, I politely said yes to everything while fielding texts from Matt.

MattOwens:
I offered that proposal because you won't join us

Sam:
Not fighting about that again

MattOwens:
Yes. That's why I want you to feel free. Just in case

I'm always free to do whatever I want, so that message confused me. My brain was scrambled from the stalker text, and I'm not good at this permanent boyfriend business, having never practiced before Matt. I'm not good at hidden meanings. *Just in case*—what?

MattOwens:
Are you there?

MattOwens:
We never made promises. You're free to do whatever you want, right?

Oh screw me. This is exactly what a guy says when he's about to start up with another lover. You'd think Matt was too busy, especially with his mother living there with him to help Pippi get settled. Oh well.

Sam:
Do what you want. Whatever.

MattOwens:
Whatever?! That's what you said when I told you Quantico was my dream job.

Same dumbass answer now as I gave him the last time we argued. What fulfilled my dreams? *"Living a continent away from Virginia's covert cybersecurity scene"* didn't sound inspiring. So I'd ended our last argument with *Whatever.* Brilliant.

Sam:
Gotta go – meeting with a client

Time to silence Matt's texts. I'd played with other musicians the night before. And now I'd let myself be beguiled by an invitation to jam with Jason Taylor. So, to my way of thinking, I didn't have much runway for arguing whether Matt was free to sleep with other people, even if sensibly:

Playing Music with Strangers =/= Sleeping Around

"So you agree?" Jason's question roused me from my pathetic love life. And I lost context for his question.

"I'm thinking about it. Talk details later."

"This little event is going to be easy."

Jason parked at the far end of the visitors' lot at Garfield High, the way people in BMWs do. Except he drove what seemed to be a battered secondhand Prius. I guess that's a thing with superstars at home now. He lifted a guitar from the back seat and lugged it in with him.

School was out, but the lot seemed full of teachers' cars, those stuck in their after-school toils. As we crossed the blacktop lot, my phone buzzed with a Krypptikk message from Natalia.

KRYPPTIKK JOB: #SALES_PRIVATE

NDragon:

What's the project and billing rate for Jason Taylor?

SByron:

#PR. Pro bono

NDragon:

For a rich dude? I think not.

When we entered the main building, Jason's teacher-friend met us. We shook hands, all jolly. "Appreciate you coming out," the teacher said. "School's only a half-day on Wednesdays, for planning. But I find it's the best day for kids like this to find something interesting to do."

"What exactly do you want me to say?" I asked them.

"Pete Byron said—" Jason cited my brother, again "—that Sam knows scary stories about how hackers get caught and what happens to them. How they aren't as hard to find as they think they are."

"Like scared-straight stories?" I held up my hand in defense. "Not my thing. And it doesn't work on kids."

"Maybe try, 'Here are better things to do with your skills'?" The teacher, your prototypical high-school math guy, with a receding hairline and an ironic necktie, had that encouraging, kind tone that I'm not good at replicating.

By the time the teacher pushed open the door to the auditorium, I still hadn't agreed.

But we instantly faced not five, not ten, but a hundred freaking people, with cameramen from both the local CBS and local PBS stations. That guy Victor from the coffee shop was with the media, a pocket recorder peeking from his pocket, a notepad in his hand.

The trick is not to let them see or smell your fear.

While the teacher introduced Jason, I lurked out of camera range, practicing First Responder calming techniques on myself.

Just breathe for a minute. Another breath.
Help will be here in just a moment.
Let me check your pulse.
Let's stay calm and make rational decisions.

When I woke from assessing the degree of danger to my physical well-being, Jason was speaking. That skater dude from Espresso and Shoeshine sat front and center on the bleachers, busily eyeing me while Jason spoke.

"I get it. It's a game," he said, "where people like me—any name you've heard of—become the target, as if you're just playing a first-person shooter game."

With only his mouth close to the mic, Jason imitated the soundtrack of a shooter game. Kids in the bleachers stirred. He turned the sounds into a beat, then into a song, then into "Smells Like Teen Spirit." People began to clap and then sang the chorus. He wound the crowd up, then brought the sound down, and signaled the ending, as if everyone in the room had become part of his personal band.

"An oldie but a goodie," Jason said when the room quieted enough to hear him speak again. "My point is this. From the monitor of a mean-spirited hacker, it looks like a game. Like egging a house on Halloween. But on my side—for anyone who becomes a hacker's target—it's more like a mo-fo cherry bomb in a shit-filled toilet."

The kids um'd and hummed, since that wasn't a word heard often in this auditorium. Even though each of them punctuated every other noun with that word.

"My friend Sam Byron has an interesting story to tell."

Okay, sure, yeah. With no preparation. However, though I'm nigh-on thirty, I can still pull it off. Stuck my hands in the pockets of the second-hand rich lady's leather jacket, and slouched, my hair uncombed since before the sad experience with Client#1. I can still look like any punk with a bad reputation singing "Gloria."

Three years ago at a blackhat conference, I did a white-girl rap that—well, it had sad consequence, but that's a world away from a gym one-quarter full of high-school geeks. The first two lines go like this:

"Scan for weakness
Exploit weakness
Hack for sleekness."

Then I rapped a litany of semi-notorious kiddie-script hacks that basement-dwellers use and re-use to vandalize websites.

A call-out response came from the crowd when one kid recognized a script. More shouts as I continued—like the little freaks thought this was a call-and-response testimony.

Winding down to a whisper near the end, I seek to be like how any singer gives you the chills in "Gloria." *She come round my*… Everyone listens closely when you whisper. I got to a peak point and stopped.

Then:

"But tell yourself the truth. It's re-using a trashed stencil to tag a San-I-Can. Creativity? Mastery? It's three-year-olds coloring inside the lines, just like Barney says."

Lots of stirring. No stomping. Skater in the front row leans forward, chin on his hand. I raised my voice to match how you scream *"Gloria"* at the peak.

"Break free, brothers and sisters. Learn the math. Learn the logic. Write code that changes the world. Don't be the finger-puppet at the San-I-Can, dancing while a fake Guy Fawkes pulls the strings. Be truly great in the world."

It's silent for a heartbeat. Then some douche in the bleachers squeaks.

"But girls can't code."

Though I responded in an honest and plain way, some might claim that what happened was my fault. Though I only spoke the truth and said exactly what you'd say in that circumstance.

"Are you fucking kidding me? What jerkoff bullshit."

▪

Our teacher-host moved to close the session, likely because I said the F word out loud in school. Most of the kids—and several teachers—crowded around Jason, wanting his autograph.

"My mom will cream herself when I bring this home."

"Hey," Jason said, "I'm more your age than hers."

"But your music isn't."

"Try me," Jason said.

"When?"

Et cetera until Jason prepared to bring everyone on stage who wanted to play music. The teachers all stood by the door, pretending I wasn't there. Which I wished, also.

When I headed for the door, Jason called, "Thanks, Sam. Maybe we can jam together soon."

Yeah, thanks. Since I can predict the future, I predicted right then that all of Jason's trolls would switch to me by dinner time. Instead of waiting for a ride with Jason, I went out to catch the Number 48 bus, only to find a police car in the drive-up lane, with two plainclothes guys leaning against the car.

"Sam. Good to see you."

It was Detective Jeremiah Francis, whom I'd met more than a year before, when we discussed our mutual granola-fed childhoods and, more pertinent to that occasion, a dead person.

Behind me, an adolescent male voice called out.

"See, it's like they said. She's a fed, a collaborator."

In the officers' car, Jeremiah sat in the back with me. We chatted briefly about family, a polite catch-up since we'd last met over the blue-guy dead in the coffeehouse freezer last year, the first victim of the White Knight mobsters. I wiggled in my Chelsea boots, impatient to hear what he really wanted to ask.

"We need to check some details about Mrs. Monroe's death," he said. "Let's just chat until I can take your formal statement."

At the East Precinct station, Jeremiah was joined by his partner, Carlos Gabriel. My friend Jeremiah is tall and always appears in Pacific Northwest formal wear: khakis and Gore-Tex. Carlos, better groomed, wore a dark suit. The bony ridge that formed his brow gave him a grim demeanor. He was, as I learned in the conversation, a serious guy.

The two detectives gave me coffee and prompted a review of the same details as I'd given to the responding officer, though this time they recorded it, and they meandered back and forth through the questions.

"And where were you last night between ten o'clock and one a.m.?" Carlos asked a serious and slightly alarming question. I confessed that I'd played rhythm guitar in an automotive body shop on Twelfth Avenue.

"Here's the manager's card." I passed over the band's crumpled business card. "He's a friend from college, which is how he knew to invite me."

Jeremiah, my personal and friendly detective, said, "Tell us more about your work for Mrs. Monroe. Her stepson says you removed a computer virus that frightened her. What was that?"

"Ransomware. Do you know what that is?"

"It freezes the computer's files," Carlos said. "Holds them hostage and demands money to free them."

"Correct. The version on Mrs. Monroe's was the most common and easy-to-remove variety." Cold in the interview room, I'd folded my arms, waiting to hear why they'd sought me out, why the ransomware mattered.

"Except?" Jeremiah asked. "We don't know each other well, but you just closed up in the middle of our friendly conversation. What was different about this virus?"

"A ransomware banner always includes a scary warning, like, 'Pay or your life will be ruined.' Or, 'Pay or you'll wish you were dead.'"

Both detectives sat forward, listening even more closely. Carlos asked, "And this one?"

"The splash banner read, 'Pay as a promise you and your friends will never speak. Pay by Friday or die.'"

"You didn't mention this to the officer at the house."

"It didn't seem relevant. And it's Tuesday, not Friday."

"Anything else you noticed at the scene? Anything that didn't seem relevant then?"

Closing my eyes to concentrate (and now unnerved), I ticked off each item again, from cat and lovebirds to people I noticed on the street. How Mrs. Monroe sat formally in her library.

Carlos stood. "We'll just be a minute typing up your statement. As soon as you sign it, you can leave."

After he departed, I asked Jeremiah why they came looking for me. "You could have just called."

"Mrs. Monroe wasn't holding a day-planner like you described. Nothing similar was found in her house."

"Perhaps I misremembered." My voice sounded weak. Because if I saw what I saw, then someone was in the house while I stood on the porch writing email jokes for Pippi.

"Perhaps," Jeremiah said. "But also, your email with the security code for her door? Talking with her stepson…" He glanced down at his notes.

"Zak," I said, being helpful.

"Mr. Monroe said he last spoke with her, she was on her cell phone, which we didn't find on the premise. When he checked Mrs. Monroe's phone records, it seemed to have been hacked. That means that…"

"Someone was inside her house." As if the interview room wasn't already cold, a chill settled in my bones.

"So we wanted to talk to you again. And we asked the medical examiner to take a close look." Jeremiah leveled a gaze—that's what it's called, right? When an officer of the law glances your way, asserting a deeper meaning.

Tiniest cough before I managed to open my throat enough to ask a question. "Have you talked to Zak about this? He's likely to call me later."

"We're in touch. Please don't speak about this with anyone else." Jeremiah rose when his partner reappeared with a typed statement for me to sign. "We'll likely request her computer. You have that?"

"Yes, both the original disk image with the malware and the repaired computer." The Byron&Dragon protocol: save every image, unless the client requests it be deleted. You never know when more research is required.

In another minute, I was back on the street, my spine tingling. I declined Jeremiah's offer of a ride back to my office. It was, in spite of the doors of hell opening, still a beautiful autumn day. I sought diversions from the inner voice that kept pinging me:

Mrs. Monroe wasn't alone while you stood on the porch.

▪

One deep breath and I started down Twelfth Avenue, then up the hill to Fifteenth.

The core of Seattle is scattered among seven hills, one of which they took down and dumped into a swamp. Because of the hills, the city is a collection of geographically–bound villages. A few diagonal boulevards were overlaid on the street grid, connecting outlying villages directly to downtown, originally via streetcars. Those tracks are long gone, and the diagonals are now arterials that lead to freeways. On Capitol Hill, just a mile by bus and three hundred feet of elevation up from the skyscrapers, the village hasn't decided yet what it will be in the twenty-first century. There's the plain old American Fifties architecture of a home-town bank, now owned by a Delaware corporation, across from a two-story wooden house that had once been a doctor's home and surgery, until a disciple of the Ascended Masters moved in, lowered the blinds, and retired into the previous century.

Up the street, the core of the old village stands: single-story storefronts from the Twenties, together with two-story brick-faced stores from the Thirties. The old organic grocery now sells high-end vitamins and holistic remedies. A marijuana store on one corner, a chain drugstore on another. A no-brand dollar-store staffed by friendly Muslim cashiers had replaced the old radical bookstore and now is one of the few places in the village where you can get what you need.

Forcing my mind back onto the Real World, I considered what best to do. I needed to dig into that malware, beyond just the opportunity to work with Zak again. Intending to text him, I glanced at my phone.

While I'd shivered in the SPD interview room, the Internet suffered a new Invasion of the Trolls. And, damn it, Harley! Instead of just looking at my social media, he must have turned notifications back on for all my dormant social accounts.

Bonfires burned in all my social media accounts, and my effigy was the strawman tossed on the pyre.

Someone had posted a U-toob video of the fiasco in the gymnasium, with both audio and bad video. (I should have combed my hair.) More than one geek had logged onto 4Chan to report his encounter with the infamous and insidious hacker-hunter and NSA pawn, Samsara Byron.

Most of the harassment, so far, was adolescents peeing vitriol on their keyboards, slamming in naughty words they can't say in front of their mothers. I scrolled rapidly through the repeated plans to slice gendered parts of my body.

What does this prove? Most significantly, it proves that the whole FBI setup I agreed to is worthless. *We'll protect you.* I remained paranoid:

glancing over my shoulder, spooked by shadows; forwarding to the FBI every text message that wasn't from Matt. *We'll protect you.* One time last spring, I red-flagged my data-mining cyber-minders and forwarded what turned out to be a credit card payment notice. After that, I managed to get a grip. And what did all that FBI involvement get me? A new shit-storm, and no FBI raincoat to protect me from slime.

Busy with "turn off notification and dismiss all" tasks, I discarded notification of ten bazillion adolescent postings from each social media account. However, that task was interrupted by a text message.

> 1(206)########:
> I'm glad I found you again. I see you walking down the street right now. Makes me soo happy.

What I most dreaded: a stalker who could hack past my block.

And who was quite close by.

Hoped it was Nicky, because he means me no harm. He just drags hellhounds behind him, wherever he goes.

▪

Around the corner from the toy store on Fifteenth Avenue, a man struggled to jam a dozen helium-filled birthday balloons into the backseat of his double-parked Mercedes. As he tucked in three, two escaped. One popped, the sound echoing between buildings like a pistol shot. More wrestling.

Another pistol shot.

I twitched inside my jacket, even though I expected the ricocheting sound. That kid will not get a dozen balloons.

When you suddenly feel vulnerable just walking down a city street, and when it's only four o'clock and you've already endured the fourth or fifth worst day of your life, the buzz of a text message and the sight of a friendly name is like a rainbow after the Flood.

Mercifully (or so I felt upon seeing his name), the next text message was from Matt. Except:

> MattOwens:
> I truly want you to be free

Oh, perfect for a craptacious day like the one I was having! In my experience, this message should always be decoded as:

"I Want You to Be Free" = ("So I Can Do What I Want")

What did I expect when Matt packed up to chase his dreams and I didn't—*I just can't*—go along? But, then, this always happens when it's solar-system–sized long distance relationship. Though if anyone asked, I'd say Matt is as constitutionally incapable of disloyalty as I am.

And besides, isn't this what you want for your partner: to feel freer than they'd be if they were alone? It's what I want.

> Sam:
> When wasn't I free? Or you?

What I wanted to ask: when did he stop feeling free, so that he had to ask me for permission?

> MattOwens:
> I only want it to be clear. With me here and you in Seattle.

While he's doing whatever he wants, I can be happy, once more doing all the adult things alone. I've been adulting on my own since I was sixteen.

> Sam:
> OK. Sleep with whoever you want to. I have to meet with a client right now.

> MattOwens:
> wut? No!

Truthfully, I did need to speak with a client—I needed to perform that welfare check on Tony's mother. And I needed to pay attention to work and not relationship phukkery. When did I ever let the cruel junk of love interfere with work?

Fetching the business card from my jacket, I double-checked the address. Unfortunately: same address where Tony used to live. Just down the alley where earlier that day I'd drifted into memories that conjured Tony back into my life.

At the front door of the old-fashioned Galahad Apartments, I studied the names on the bell panel, seeking any resembling what Tony had scrawled on a business card. Choosing one, I pushed the white button next to it, on a panel so old the buttons must be Bakelite. A buzzer sounded and the speaker crackled, but no one spoke to answer. I pushed it again.

Behind me, the heavy glass-and-oak door pushed open. I tried to squeeze past whoever was departing, since I intended to knock on Door #3, the number on the panel that matched Tony's note. But my way was blocked by that skater-geek from Espresso and Shoeshine and the high school assembly, skateboard once more in hand and now wielded like a shield.

"Are you following me?" I scowled.

Not that a new stream of online trolls and a possible stalker made me paranoid.

"Shouldn't I ask that?" he said. "You're on the outside, and I'm inside. How d'ya think I stalked you from in here?"

Tried to wiggle past him.

The little ones can be squirrelly, and I made no progress. Without his hoodie, he proved to be only as tall as my chin, thin to the point of emaciation, and of indeterminate ethnicity. Caucasus or Kunlun Mountains? Tibesti or Virunga Mountains? Or Polynesian shores? And how long since any forbearers migrated to Seattle? Probably generations.

"She doesn't like visitors," the kid said, his voice deeper than a dude his age should possess. "If she wanted to see you, she'd answer when you ring."

My eyebrows asked a question that he rushed to answer.

"We were together when you rang." He shifted his board, preventing me from getting past him without touching either him or his board.

"I have a message from her son."

"Let me give it to her."

"It's personal."

"Want to put it in an envelope so I don't see it?"

An unnatural, unwomanly feeling rose from deep inside me, a primal response to this challenging male, an urge I hadn't felt for a long time, the kind of sentiment that runs counter to both personal philosophy and ethics.

My key desire: freedom to pound the arrogant twerp.

But before either of us could carry our challenges further, a woman appeared behind skater-dude.

"Who is it, Tim?"

First—not that it matters, but you'd notice it, too—she was white. As pale and lucent as bone china.

Second, she was the grifter in a velvet track suit who stole the *New York Times* from Espresso and Shoeshine.

Tim said, "She claims she has a message from your son."

The woman batted her lids and smiled at me, the same pleasant way she'd handled the barista who questioned her grifting forgetfulness. Not a glimpse of any DNA that matched Tony. "I'm sorry, dear. You must be mistaken. I don't have a son. What's your name?"

"Sam."

"Do I know you? Are you the girl who raises funds for Planned Parenthood on Broadway? Or is it Greenpeace?"

Tim spoke again. "Samsara Ada Byron."

"Oh?" Her raised brows didn't stir her beige-blond wig. "Like the famous mathematician? It must have been hard to have that man for a father."

Indeed, having Huck Byron as my father was hard, but she meant Ada Lovelace and Lord Byron.

"The countess's 'poetical science' helped her escape the bounds of her origins," I said. A wave of recognition passed over Tim, indicating he wasn't stupid. "Tony says you are in danger from his enemies. There's a spook in your system. He wants me to help—"

"Who's Tony?" She seemed curious, but my Spidey sense told me a grift was in play. "Is he that ragged man who preaches at the Olive Street bus stop? He always says I'm in danger. But doesn't he say that to every woman who passes him?"

My phone rang.

"We'll let you answer that," she said. "Bye now."

"I'll give Tony your message." I called after the Grifter Twins, but they disappeared from the archway before the heavy glass door swung shut behind them. I backed off the steps, glancing to see who rang: Matt. He'd hung up and didn't leave a message. I texted an answer.

> ↳Sam:
> Missed you. Phone if you can.

Must have been a butt-dial, because Matt didn't call back.

At least my Client#0_Private home visit went somewhat better than my visit with Client#1.

▪

Inside our half-unpacked office, Harley stared at his computer screen, not even looking up to say hello. And Natalia was there.

"Thought you had to fetch your kids."

Like Harley, she didn't glance up to greet me. "That was just an excuse. You're better with older kids than I am."

No use arguing over it. And I was starved. "Is there food? Girl cannot live on artisanal donuts alone."

But before I solved that problem, I had a phone call. No, it wasn't Matt bugging me to be free.

"Hi, Sam. Listen, if you won't join me, make me your client. My mother's computer has a security problem, and I don't have time to fix it."

Brad Jones called, likely from his executive suite, settled into his plush Italian leather chair. No, I hadn't seen that particular executive suite, but I know the brand. I put him on speakerphone, so Natalia listened too.

"Great news. Byron&Dragon has extensive experience." I blocked any thought of Client#1 and moved straight into creating a Krypptikk project for Brad, using the email address on his business card. "Check your email, Brad. I'm sending you an invitation right now to a project dedicated to resolving your problem. You can contribute details and review our work via encrypted communications."

"What?"

"We'll schedule the best time for meetings and—"

"That's what I want, Sam. A meeting. You and your partner. My company needs your help. And not to fix laptops. Come see what we have. As a personal favor."

"Pretty sure I know what offices look like. I'm sitting in one right now, at my own business address." Drinking coffee dregs. Opening my snail-mail: new business credit cards from the bank. Another envelope that appeared to be a bank draft, the return address an acronym I didn't recognize. "Do you see the Krypptikk invitation in your email, Brad? Works just like messaging, but over the web without installing an application. Oh, look, my partner is already busy on your project."

"Yes, I see."

He didn't see that the project title lied about our client count.

KRYPPTIKK JOB: CLIENT#202_JONES
Invited Members: byron&dragon; Brad Jones
SByron:
Ticket #1: Determine tasks to clear malware.
Query 1: Laptop or desktop?
Query 2: Personal or business computer?
Query 3: House call or office delivery?
[NDragon accepted and entered project]
[BJones accepted and entered project]
NDragon:
Baseline charge: $10,000 USD, due upon project completion.
Confirmation message will launch contract work.

"Can't we do this over email, Sam?"

"Don't you prefer security? Besides, you know me, Brad. I like to compartmentalize tasks. With Krypptikk, it's like naming the rooms in your mental castle and then putting things where they go, where each room has a unique lock. Your task is stored in the closet with winter coats and snow boots and—"

"Honestly, Sam. I get it, I do." Brad was pleading, not reading the new Krypptikk project messages. "Different intelligences between us, different aspirations. But you don't truly think I'm an immoral corporatist. You haven't even heard what we're offering as a focus for your talents."

See how years of corporate VP training works in the world? Persuasion through kindness and insight. Anyone else would simply ask me to stop being such a bitch. Brad, however, had reached the lofty heights of chief executive officer. He persisted, because that's what he's paid to do.

"Coming to work with me isn't like trolling for the NSA. Or code-breaking for the Russian mafia." Brad made a joke. "Come visit, if only for a hardware tour, Sam. Meet our dev leads."

"Hardware tends to all look the same. And I know several aDVers lead developers. You bought most of Quinn's."

"We're pretty far beyond Quinn's setup. It'll be the turn of the next decade before mom-and-pop startups like yours, or Quinn's, have access to hardware like ours."

This caused Natalia's head to turn from her computer screen. Like the little girl in *The Exorcist.*

"Can you visit for just a day?" Brad was well practiced. Ask for only a little. "At the last security strategy meeting, our CTO beat on my ass to get you through the door." CTO: Chief Technology Officer, the guy who purchases and staffs the hardware-plus-software solutions, sets security strategy. Hearing the old corporate acronyms gave me hives. Brad's voice deepened into the charming CEO speech to be used in persuasive, non-adversarial encounters. "He's impressed with how you saved the power utilities last year. He wants to meet you. Please, I'll owe you a favor. Come visit."

"Who's your CTO?" I didn't pay enough attention to the startup scene in Seattle.

"Daniel Llewelyn."

Natalia's head spun around twice.

Though Brad hadn't added the other part of Llewelyn's name: IV. From major wealth in the Pacific Northwest (starting with trees where all wealth began in an earlier era), he was first in his generation to couple wealth with enormous intellect in the computing sector. After retiring from a local software giant, he'd become a major force in two realms: high-profile philanthropy and low-profile angel investment. That he served as CTO for Brad's corporation signaled deep interest in that business and its mission.

Which is Big Data research. And that must make aDVers an industrial espionage target. Which had to be why a significant tech figure like Dan Llewelyn served as CTO.

Natalia left her chair to hover over me, breathing heavily.

Not because Llewellyn is one of the five richest men on the West Coast. She and I have both been at the table with the super-rich, so wealth isn't an attractant—they pull their pants on one leg, et cetera—but Llewelyn was interesting because of the path he'd followed, because in the early days he'd taken his Stanford math degree, added moxie, and built an important tech company from a not-that-significant trust fund.

"Still there, Sam?" Brad prodded from the speaker phone.

Natalia returned to her keyboard, glared at me while typing. My phone buzzed with a message.

KRYPPTIKK JOB: #SALES_PRIVATE

NDragon:

If u say no, you'll destroy Christmas.

"When is this field trip to your farm?" I asked Brad.

You could hear his sigh of relief.

"Let me set up a meeting. I'll get back with you."

By the time I hung up, Natalia was literally in my face. I tore open that piece of mail that promised to be a bank draft. Money in the mail!

"In no world do you meet Daniel Llewelyn without me, Samsara Byron. We're partners."

"It's just rich guys showing off their toys." The envelope didn't contain a check that I could deposit in the bank; it was a notice from the U.S. Office of Personnel Management.

Natalia still breathed down my neck. "I love toys. You don't love toys. Take me along. You won't even know what you're seeing."

Waving the letter, I asked, "Did you get one of these? An OPM letter? Zak told me his came weeks ago."

A while back (no one admits to precisely when), the U.S. Office of Personnel Management—OPM—got hacked. Who knows how long it took the data owners to discover that all the security-clearance research for government employees had been stolen.

"Mine came weeks ago." Natalia paused, thinking. "Your name is earlier in the alphabet than mine. Wonder how they choose who to warn first."

Hard not to laugh at that form letter. Yet I went online to type in my PIN, allegedly to protect myself. As if the Social Security numbers in the list were what cybercreeps valued most. That list was likely on the darknet, attracting bids on information far more valuable than SSNs. Anyway, I already had a new SSN, thanks to last year's doxxing.

▪

Rifling through our office mini-kitchen, I found a jar of peanut butter and two grocery-store bagels. I started to chuck the peanut butter, worried about Pippi's allergies, but of course she's in Virginia and wouldn't sniff my allergen-ridden breath. Still, I shoved it to the back of the cupboard out of loyalty. A sudden gust of regret filled a cavity in my chest. It's been only fifteen days, and it felt as if an organ had been cut out of my insides.

Pondering that hole, the one named Pippi and Matt, I settled for the remaining half of Natalia's discarded sandwich.

Natalia glanced up from her monitor. "Sam? It's obvious from your posture that something bad happened today. Was it Tony King? I swear on Freyja's falcon cloak, you can trust me. Tell."

Harley also glanced my way, peering over the top of his reading glasses, waiting for my answer.

"Okay." I swallowed, finding it hard to get an unexpected constriction in my throat. I kept it simple. "I had a dispiriting morning. Then Tony appeared out of nowhere. And that school thing with Jason Taylor turned into a debacle. Don't want to burden with details."

"Let me choose whether to be dispirited." Natalia waggled her index finger. "Unless children are involved. In that case, don't tell me."

"No children."

"Spit it out. I'll raise my hand if I can't handle it. It's Tony, right? Every blackhat drags a black hole behind him."

"No. He only referred me to another possible client." Not exactly a lie. "When I went to deliver that malware fix to our first client, the owner turned out to be dead."

"Trip for nothing? So we won't get paid?" She lifted her well-tended brows in query.

"I found her body."

I underplayed the drama, but Natalia sat still as a stone. Harley took off his reading glasses and turned his cop eyes on me. "Had to converse with the EMTs and the cops. Then I've chatted with Zak in quick bursts. He's under stress at work, and I'm the only one he can talk to about losing his stepmom."

"Oh no! I'm so sorry." Natalia's voice warmed. She came over and sat on the countertop where I busily disassembled her stale sandwich to find the good parts. "Grief over a common computer virus. The sad stories we could tell."

Pretending that cold chicken and wilted lettuce kept me from speaking, I took that moment to decide how much more sharing I should do. "We need to look at that code more closely. It's ransomware. I added a research ticket to the project."

"Unusual delivery?" Natalia straightened at the opportunity for research. "New ways it eluded the anti-virus checks on the computer?"

"Don't know. But the malware banner wasn't the usual pay-or-we'll-delete-your-files threat. It said, 'Pay as a promise you and your friends will never speak. Pay by Friday or die.'"

"And now she's dead?" Alarmed, Natalia shoved against the counter, scattering pieces of her lunch over my hands. "Do the police need our help?"

"They don't connect her death with the virus." I didn't really lie. "But we should find her friends. In case they're in danger."

And my detective friend Jeremiah asked me not to talk about details, so I omitted parts, like Mrs. Monroe disposing of her day-planner while I stood on her porch. And I did a silent kick-flip over Tony's request and flew right past discussing his grifter-mother. I needed more information about all of that. Instead, I redirected attention to the trouble Jason Taylor stirred up.

"Worse, Jason Taylor opened Pandora's box and shook it over my head. He does *not* get to be my boyfriend."

"You have a boyfriend. Jason has a wife." Natalia returned to whatever had her attention before I interrupted with my story.

"It's a metaphor." I wrapped up the remains of the damaged sandwich and stuck the wad in the Seattle-mandated compost pail. "Next time a cute guy pleads for my help, I'm moving this office to the far end of a dirt road on Limberlost. Wait till you see what's happening in my social stream. "

"Harley already noticed." She tapped her upper lip while thinking. "Can we monetize your reputation as a danger to evil hackers."

Hearing his name, Harley once more looked away from where the computer engrossed him. "I'd heard about what you girls have to put up with on the Internet, but—" Harley halted when Natalia glared at him. "*Women.* Sorry. It's a generational thing."

"We're grown-ass people," Natalia said.

Harley accepted that. "You're harassed by foul-mouthed boys, if you don't mind my judgment."

"Jason Taylor prodded the giant awake. It's everything I've worked to avoid." Rifling through our office mini-kitchen, I found a can of sardines in mustard sauce, apparently left by a malevolent elf. "We need the kitchen stocked. And an espresso machine."

"I'll add a ticket in Krypptikk to send Jason a bill," Natalia said. "You solved his problem. Trolls aren't screwing with him now. They're all out soiling themselves in your mentions. Time for a block-chain on every account where it's possible."

Natalia leaned in to work beside Harley.

Finding two pieces of cold pizza buried in the fridge (left over from move-in day), I indulged in yet another thirty seconds of missing Pippi and Matt, with an extra helping of self-pity. Why not indulge? I had spare time while the microwave ran. However, watching Natalia and Harley work together, I also felt a sense of gratitude: for Harley's help, by clicking Block every ten seconds on each social media account I follow, which kept me from getting tendonitis; for Natalia, who'd spot any security hole I might miss.

"Holy smokes!" Harley whistled through his teeth. Then he began to read messages out loud.

5

Box of Rain

■
■
■

"I'VE READ ABOUT THIS," Harley said. "But I thought you had to be famous to be plagued with such garbage."

> "Bitch is at it again."
> "Thought we put an arrow through her tits last time."
> "You should die for the things you tell kids."

"In some circles…" I began.

Natalia shook her head. Harley watched us both.

"Since you girls are in the secrets business, I won't ask." He scooted back his chair, rose, and slipped into his mail-order leather jacket. "I'll stock the kitchen tomorrow. High protein, low-carb, right?"

Then Natalia left, this time truly on her way to pick up her kids. Her goodbye included a prod to check her #Sales notes, so before I headed to the Clean Room to study Tony's hard disk, I made a cup of tea and read.

KRYPPTIKK JOB: #SALES_PRIVATE

NDragon:

> Check these web links so we're informed at the aDVers meeting tomorrow.

She'd collected links to two dozen articles that mentioned either aDVers or Daniel Llewelyn. I hadn't yet made it to my Clean Room work by six o'clock, when that throwaway phone from Tony buzzed inside my jacket pocket.

> ✆1(323)#######:
> She didn't listen, did she? Dinner?

Tony's burnerbot number. Not a great message, but not so bad as cyberstalkers or faux-Russian mobsters.

Outside in the waning October light, Tony held open the door of a for-hire cab, a far less elegant ride than one might expect for a Pirate King in a bespoke suit. His suit cost more than the cab did brand new.

"Come along, dear heart," he urged. "I'm knackered. Must eat before catching my flight."

We sat in the back of the cab, with a broad expanse between us, while Tony probed for details about my encounter with his wacko mother.

"You didn't say she lived *there.*" It didn't seem whiny till I heard myself say it.

"Owns the building. Or so she led me to believe. Are her doors and windows alarmed?"

"They seemed quite serene," I said. "Just like she was."

"I meant—"

"Yes. There's a keypad inside her door and a sign outside the apartment entryway. And two deadbolts on her door."

He sat back, hands under his armpits, rocking as if distressed, watching out the window as we caromed down Lakeview Avenue. The last of the day's light bounced on the south portion of Lake Union while Queen Anne Hill rose up to block direct beams on the north end. The cab passed where the dirt-bike trails take off under the I-5 freeway.

"There's where I first defeated you." I pointed to the acres of freeway pillars, the trails now masked from view by Himalaya blackberry vines. "Fair and square. I think the City of Seattle put up a commemorative sign."

Tony glanced past me to the forest of concrete pillars. "Of course you remember it that way."

"You bit off too big a bite. Because you love a challenge."

"Yes, I admit to that."

I mimicked his braggadocio from back then. "'A skinny girl loses to greater muscle mass every time.' So you let me choose the course."

"It was a gentlemanly act to allow the woman an advantage."

"You *condescended* to allow me to choose the course."

"And you showed up with that antique dirt bike. You cheated, dear heart."

"No. Just better tools for the job." I settled back into the cab's vinyl seat.

"And foreknowledge of the terrain."

"And Tuff Skilz."

"You still have skinny legs."

The car dipped down to Eastlake Avenue and across the University Bridge. This early in October, we're still promised a long twilight. The cab made the unmarked three-hundred-and-sixty-degree exit after the bridge, turned west on Northlake Way, and then disgorged us at the Salmon House.

"This is where you want to eat?"

Tony opened the heavy door and stood aside for me, offering no excuses for his choice. The hostess performed the familiar and subtle double-take I remembered from years past when out in the world with Tony: large dark man. Famous ball player? Dangerous? Tony flashed a smile and, in his fake Brit accent, begged her to accommodate us.

"He's not often in Seattle," I murmured while the hostess checked where to seat us. "But when he is, he chooses Ivar's."

"A gem in your fair city, Sam. Have you forgotten what we poor students thought was grand?"

Seated near a window, I hesitated to answer the waitperson's request for drink orders, not able to focus on the menu. Tony ordered fernet branca and troll-caught salmon for both of us.

"You don't mind, I trust?" he said. "You ate fish when I knew you. Or was I being too efficient and failed to consider personal boundaries?"

"You're paying the check."

Tony stared out at the dramatic view, looking south down Lake Union to the city center, where one building blazed orange in the last of the autumn sun. Meanwhile, I studied him, seeking what I once saw, versus today's pirate. Maybe that's where I developed an allergy to charismatic, cosmopolitan men.

We commented on the view, the authenticity of First Nations and Northwest original art, not saying anything substantial. Our food appeared when I was in the middle of calculating the last actual meal in three days that wasn't old pizza, old sandwich, designer donut. I stopped counting backwards and ate my salmon.

"She's really your mother?" I asked between bites.

"That's what she told me. I didn't question her." Tony caught me watching him. "Like you, I never do full self-disclosure."

"So I once came to understand."

"But, Sam, it is true that my mother left when I was fourteen. Sent me to boarding school and disappeared. We talk, but she will never take kindly to interference from me."

"Are you taking me off the Mother-in-Jeopardy Affair?"

"No. I'm certain she's in danger because of me." He pushed his plate aside, having eaten only the salmon. "Tomorrow, beg her to let you find the spook in her system."

"She says she's never heard of you."

"She's protecting me. Show her this."

Tony pressed a lump of plastic in my hand. A cheap U.S.S.R. pin, a figure of Lenin in red and yellow.

"Nostalgia from the Fremont Sunday Market?"

"She gave it to me when she left." His hand lingered near mine. "Do you remember how we connected when we met? That neither of us knew our mothers?"

"But now yours turns out to be alive. Playing the Mother card doesn't grab me."

"Truly, I worry for her," Tony said, blowing right past what I asserted. "You've made it clear that you aren't sentimental."

"I do have sentiments," I said. "Besides resentment."

"For instance?" He offered me the same beguiling smile that convinced the hostess to seat us by a window. "I wager you cannot name one thing that makes you tear up. And no fair saying 'hidden bugs' or 'wankers who leave' or—"

"Okay. What are you wagering? What are the rules?"

While he considered, his hand inched closer to mine, slinking up like the Little Prince and the Fox, while he's wearing a musk cologne known to make girls' panties fall off in timed trials.

"One hundred thousand dollars." He slipped a thin wallet from inside his jacket pocket and laid a cashier's check before me. Not Monopoly money. "U.S. dollars, not bitcoin."

"You've hacked into my business communications?"

"No, but I know what kind of server hardware you need to do what you want."

"It's outside what this gambler can cover." I folded my arms. "I don't have that sum stuffed in my mattress."

"Wager me a day of security services in return. That's worth a goodly number of American dollars."

"Did you steal this money through a web scam?"

"No, it was a gift from my grandfather. That I choose to apply to the task of protecting my mother. So let's play. When do you get misty and have to nab a hankie?"

Challenged, I plunged in. "One. The opening lines of the original Sesame Street theme song."

"Oh, sod off, dear heart. Surely—"

"When my Aunt Lucky rescued my brother Pete and me from our father's chaotic commune, we ate Cap'n Crunch and watched PBS kids' shows nonstop for a month. To make up for years of tofu and granola. I'm sentimental that Aunt Lucky made us safe and comfortable."

"You never before said—"

"Two." The first one indeed made me sentimental, so I recklessly ripped off the covers. "The first chords of 'Box of Rain' from *American Beauty*. D. A minor. E minor. C. Opens the tear-dam every time." Not because the Grateful Dead howled continuously on the commune's ratty CD player. "Because that song represents who my acid-head father longs to be. He just hasn't arrived yet."

With one finger, Tony scooted his cashier's check in my direction, but stared out the window.

"Three." Going for it now. "The chorus riffs in 'Psycho Killer.' Because it was the first riff I learned to play. *Fa-fa-fa-far* better than any freaking folk song on nylon strings."

"That's aesthetics, not sentiment."

"Except I was desperate to make the boy next door fall in love with me. I'd shred anything for that. Made the same freaking mistake not three miles from here." I got the waiter's attention and asked for coffee. "So don't say I'm not sentimental, that I don't have feelings like normal people, whatever that means."

He had his hand on mine again, stroking it with his long forefinger. "It's a wonky moment, seeing you now, thinking how you scared me when we first met."

"Nice to know." More than one person has described me as scary. But Tony? I've long wished he feared me.

"You, Sam, were the first genuine person I knew. When you're wrenched out of childhood the way I was, the question isn't 'Who will I be when I grow up?' Instead, it's 'Who will I pretend to be?'"

"So I've never met the real you?"

A man like Tony doesn't shrug. He doubled down, tenderly stroking my hand. "You must admit that I'm talented. I'm the Zen master. I can be fifty people in the course of a year, each unrecognizable from the last incarnation."

"Except I've recognized you now and then."

"That's why I need you now. When I perform the true, the real Anthony Hong Moon King, then—" Tony leaned forward, so close his breath brushed my cheek. "There's a crisis I must attend to. Immediately. And I can trust only you."

"You keep saying that. Why?"

"Honestly? Because, dear heart, I refuse to entertain any notion that I should think otherwise than to trust you. Have done, always."

"Wow. That must be nice. I can't imagine."

He stayed close, not affected by my spiteful response. "I trust without asking return, dear heart. Know full well I haven't earned it."

"Didn't then. Couldn't now."

"And yet, I have to ask—"

"You've been asking repeatedly, and not telling, Tony."

"Sam, when you were doxxed last year, it gave me pause."

"That was a bit of a drag."

"I'm sure." He didn't pay attention to the coffee the waiter set in front of him. Me, I was inhaling that elixir when Tony spoke again. "The pictures. The girl with you, in so many pics?"

"Pippi."

"Pretty."

"She'll be thrilled to hear—" My hand was still in his, and he now rubbed across my knuckles so intently that it irritated enough to wake me to what he really asked. "No, Tony. She's my friend Matt's daughter. Adopted when his partner was killed at work. And two years too young, at least." A distinct tension lessened around his jaw. "You said you trusted me. Wouldn't I tell you?"

Quick dip of his head, acknowledging that. 'When you have no tribe, there can be moments when it's hard to—"

My phone vibrated, disrupting the tension between us. Tony released my hand. I glanced at the display.

MattOwens:
In bed - don't make me start without you.

I tapped an autoreply: *Later.*

MattOwens:
It's never going to be anyone but you.

"Business?" Tony pried.

"Boyfriend." Putting it mildly. Seeing Matt's name twanged that sentimental string I'd tightened earlier. "I finally made the boy next door fall in love with me."

"That blue-collar undercover cop with whom you sleep?"

"How do you know who I sleep with?"

He didn't answer that question, asked another. "It's serious? Are you making your own wee little law-enforcement babies together? Sam, if—"

"Is this a job interview? The kind where they illegally ask if you're married with a family?" I do have a family now. Matt and Pippi. We just don't live on the same side of the country. "No, I'm merely loyal. And don't snoop in my business."

"Wish I were so lucky." A tone in his voice caused me to shiver, like an autumn wind stealing the last of the leaves. Then he came back, the ever-persuading Tony. "Let's work together. A good team makes it safe to take risks. It's not the math, it's the people that solve problems."

"Or that create them."

Tony signaled for the check, paid in cash, and had us on the way before I finished my coffee. The for-hire car still waited, the way a limo does.

In the twilight, a yellow band of sunlight lingered on the western horizon. The downtown towers were alight as if on fire, the radio towers on Queen Anne glowed red. In the cab, Tony looked out the window, his face and form hidden in night-time shadows, streetlamps flickering across his profile at thirty-miles-per-hour. One thing I learned from Tony: that my sense of being a misfit was merely the small-town junk of high school. This man fit nowhere in the world: abandoned by his mother, claimed by no family, no cultural tribe. His extraordinary physical being declared him outside every category, every community. Yet he performed his movements through everyday life so gracefully. A perfect pirate, hiding in plain sight. Because no one ever claimed him.

"What risks? What danger are you in?" The question for which I most needed answers if I was going to commit to Tony's problem. "They say that bitcoin guy sent hired killers after you."

"Except, as it turned out, the twit hired undercover FBI."

"Still. And that fire in your DVD manufacturing unit in Thailand—"

"I'd left that business behind four months before."

"Shall I describe more? Your life in the darknet—"

"Are you declining to help my mother because I'm personally often in danger? Dear heart, no."

He asked the driver to stop in front of my building and then ran around the car to open the door for me. We stood on the street, the cab's taillight blinking red on Tony's silk suit.

"Don't know yet, Tony. Keep your check until I decide."

"No. In fact, cash it tonight. You must need the money. And I'll double it if you find who hacked into my mother's system."

"I'm not broke," I said, not lying exactly. I fumbled the security code for the front door of my building.

"Listen, Sam. I've uncovered immense secrets. Secrets your NSA friends are struggling to keep in a box. Secrets that attract ruthless people, who'd do anything they could to find me before I find them."

"Tell me more. Like why you won't call the FBI."

He folded his arms, as if it were cold. Shuffled his stance. Then rested his hand on my shoulder. I didn't mean to, but I stepped closer, because he whispered. "I'm once again pursuing a rogue agent, just like that bitcoin affair years ago. Remember what a good guy I proved to be then?"

"Like in a Bond movie?" I stepped back, thinking he was joking. But he stepped closer, still whispering.

"No, Sam. In the manner of real life. The past few weeks, everything I do, he knows—whoever he is, he knows immediately where I am, what I'm doing, and…" Tony hesitated. "From what happened to a friend last week, any word from me to the FBI gets a special agent killed. Right now, I don't dare go near my mother."

"But you want me to…geezus, Tony."

"Believe me, I'd never endanger you. You're just a freelance forensics analyst." He touched the side of my jacket where I'd pocketed his check. "No one can see any connection to me."

"This is giving me a fatal case of dry mouth."

"Just block the spook in my mother's system. Even if you can't identify who it is. Please."

"I—yes. Okay."

Tony laid his hand on my shoulder. Gently, with only his forefinger, he lifted my face toward his, tracing my jaw.

"We were good together," he whispered. "I wish I'd turned out to be someone else. My dear, dear heart."

▪

Upstairs in my smells-like-new living unit—too small to call an apartment—I put Tony's cashier's check in my scary-clown cookie jar, a Depression-era relic that hasn't held cookies since Grandma Flo sold it to me at a garage sale.

And checked my email: Pippi had solved the math problem and sent me a joke she'd made up that relied on a misspelled pun. She added that her grandmother Roz had captured part of the second piano lesson with her new teacher, the video coming my way in other email. About the new piano teacher, Pippi writes:

> "She's a witch. She makes you think she's kind and nice. And then pow! The metronome!"

In the video, a pretty young woman gently guided, deciding over the course of the lesson to focus on correcting bad habits. But, thankfully, she wasn't one of those sadistic teachers out to groom each student for high-stress competitive piano. I folded my arms, rocking while watching the video, intent on finding Pippi in safe hands.

Done with my moment of world melting, I then did what any professional does when not one row got hoed all day: I went down to the office and focused on priority tasks.

With a few sips of lapsang souchong tea and the right Icelandic trance music, I prepared for a night of it: first to check that code from Tony, and then to work on the revenge-for-grief research project that Zak and I planned. Here I was, doing socially relevant work without the oppression of corporate masters or moral dilemma of national security overseers.

The new workspace in the Clean Room provided all the amenities I require: decent lighting, a comfortable chair, a table that doesn't wobble. The heating was built into the floor and worked well enough that my fingers wouldn't get so cold they stuck to the keyboard, like it does in the ancient farmhouse where I lived with Matt on Limberlost Island. I didn't have to interrupt my thinking to chat with another late-night dweller or the people who empty the trash cans. With Matt in Virginia—and it was long past his bedtime—I didn't have to stop for any human interaction. Just before I prepared to hunker down and work in the Clean Room, my phone buzzed.

> ✆1(206)#######:
> U should't work so late

> ✎Sam:
> Nicky, take a flying leap. Quit stalking me.

Switched off my phone. Huffy.

However, only ten days into the new digs, I kept interrupting my work whenever an unexpected sound whispered in the room. The condenser in the refrigerator turning on. A bump when a car drove into the secure underground parking. The buzz and ding of the elevator. Those creaks when a new building settles, like a woman getting comfy in a chair, polite popping of whatever the equivalent is of synovial fluid in new construction.

Ten lines into my first pass through the Client#0 laptop code from Tony, I got up to verify that I'd locked the office door, and then called my security system upstairs to make sure I'd locked that, too. Of course, I had. Outside the window, I noticed the Tom-Waits-at-the-diner lighting of the streetscape, which fit well with the music I'd chosen.

To be honest, this hyper-checking came from the day's creep factors. Yet it's what any woman does when she's alone in a new place. How to be safe is what you learn first from new friends when you start college. Then it's like riding a bicycle. I hadn't forgotten how after a year living with Matt. That reflexive safety muscle always works.

About one a.m., I went upstairs and made a frittata on the hotplate that passed for a kitchen in my new digs, my brain still immersed in Client#0 code as I sipped club soda while my food cooked, the bubbles tickling my thoughts. Then I pulled three plates from the wire rack over the sink, only then rousing sufficiently to realize that I'd cooked for three people while on autopilot. I put Matt's and Pippi's portions in a washed-out yogurt container, jammed it in the mini-refrigerator, and sat down to eat my portion. That tiny place inside kept complaining about being lonely without those two eating beside me.

Then I jammed the plate in the mini-sink since there's no mini dishwasher in these digs, just mini basics, as if I'd eaten one of Alice's down-the-rabbit-hole pills and my arms and legs might pop out the mini-windows any minute now.

Downstairs in the Clean Room, I eased back into work after performing safety checks again, making sure every ingress and egress was known. Not scared. Just careful.

Two hundred lines of logs and code from the hard disk Tony gave me, my eyelid started twitching. While I pressed with a forefinger to make it stop, I scrolled down to the next line in the log. And then the next.

Trained to be skeptical, I'm hard-pressed to believe in coincidence. Yet this was the same intrusive code as on Doreen Monroe's laptop. The same ransomware that Zak asked me to remove. The identical garden-variety malware, demanding a ransom by wire-transfer to a bank where the workers are sunburned all to hell and at the end of the day sip drinks with tiny colorful umbrellas.

The same warning on the splash-screen billboard:

> "Pay as a promise you and your friends will never speak. Pay by Friday or die."

Creeped out, I did the most logical thing. I went out into the main office and searched the private online forums where people like me trade current information and heads-up cautions about fast-changing trends in malware. No one in any forum reported this message. I posted a cautiously worded query about any newly detected changes in this common hacked-and-adapted ransomware. Then: how to find the "friends" being frightened into silence. How did these two women know each other?

Since this friend of Tony's mother lived in Hong Kong, I searched the hard disk for her name and the GPS location where her computer was last powered on. Then I went out to the main office and put that name into an online search, including a search that translated the name and the location because, unlike Tony, I don't read Chinese.

Wendy Logan—a nice British sounding name, but a U.S. citizen—leased a penthouse in a Hong Kong high-security building where American executives and rich expats live. Her husband was CEO at an import-export business. They'd resided in Hong Kong for ten years.

Scanning U.S. records, guessing her age, I hunted for history. But with such a common name—and perhaps changed when married—all my results came up grossly ambiguous. Pennsylvania? Florida? Montana? A dozen Wendy Logans were researching their ancestors, none of whom had ever met each other.

The expat news sites, which I could read in English, contained about what you'd expect. Cultural exchanges. Fundraisers for folks who needed special medical assistance. Chairing a committee to welcome newbies in the consul world. Hosting send-off parties for friends returning home. At some point, I hit the refresh button on one of the expat news sites, and there was the banner news of the day.

Mr. Logan came home to find Wendy dead yesterday. Natural causes. Services planned for…

Switched back to the Chinese official sites. No word yet.

It didn't have to mean anything. On Monday in Hong Kong, Wendy gave Tony her hard disk in that penthouse. In Seattle, a graceful older woman sent me her laptop by courier and inked our Tuesday appointment in her day-planner. My eyelid twitched again. The day-planner that wasn't there when the EMTs walked through the front door ten minutes later.

Time to send Tony an update via our Krypptikk project. Remembering his finger along my jaw caused me to shiver. I swear that's why I shivered, not that I'd creeped myself out with what I found in both Client#1 and Client#0 projects.

> ***KRYPPTIKK JOB: CLIENT#0_SPOOKS_PRIVATE***
> *SByron:*
>
> > Original hard disk source secured on byron&dragon server with this folder name. All work is on clones.
>
> *SByron:*
>
> > Ticket #1: Research malware source and package contents.
>
> *SByron:*
>
> > PK: This disk has same ransomware as another project. 2 instantiations, 2 threats realized. 2 dead women. Curious?

No response. I waited ten minutes while running more forensic tools on files from both Client#1 and Client#0 hard disks. Then created my own burnerbot phone number and poked Tony again, this time on that throwaway phone he gave me, choosing the top number on the list.

> ⇗2068888888:
> Early to bed?

Which made me look at the clock. Three a.m. How time flies when you're in a quagmire. The phone leaped on the desk, vibrating an answer. The cell number was Matt's.

MattOwens:
No, up at usual time. R U still working? New phone?

W-the-ever-loving-F. How did Tony have Matt's number, much less choose to program it on that throwaway phone? Determined to run forensics later on Tony's psyche, I focused again on what I'd found on two computers from opposite edges of the Pacific.

Each researcher has an ethical duty to report malware, but I didn't yet have research to report. Only a grungy sense in my belly because of two dead women with the same threatening malware. Yet, this ransomware might be on many more computers, perhaps so many that two dead recipients was a statistical likelihood. Come U.S. working hours, I'd likely find more instances discussed on the private forensics forums. Then I could report what I was learning from my own research.

It wasn't as if I faced deep, existential decisions:

> Am I the law-enforcement stooge those high-schoolers scream that I am?
>
> /* OR */
>
> Do I know the difference between statist invasion of personal privacy and dangerous criminal activity that requires attention from law enforcement?

Yes, I do know the difference. But I also heard Tony describe his alarming predicament: *One word gets a special agent killed.*

Treading carefully, not mentioning anything related to Tony, I sent a Krypptikk message to Zak, that I'd seen anomalies in my research and intended to share his mother's computer with law enforcement.

KRYPPTIKK JOB: CLIENT#1_MONROE
SByron:
... unless you want me to insist on a warrant.
I'm freaked by all this. Are you?

ZakM:

Oh yeah. Definitely freaked.
Go ahead. Let them have all details.
Though it's not as if locals can do better research than you and I can.

Then I sent email to Evan Mulasky, the FBI agent who'd misdirected his professional passion last year when I was trying to save the local power utility from a cyberattack. I'd agreed to let his crew monitor threats from my mobster enemies. Of course I share crimes I find in my research. It had been six months since I last found anything worth their notice. My message to Evan included the SPD case number for Mrs. Monroe's murder in relation to the code package I submitted to his lab. Then I packaged a copy of that code and loaded it onto a secure cloud repository Evan's crew created for me last year.

Next, fetching my favorite detective's card from deep in my jacket pocket, I wrote to Jeremiah:

> "My initial research indicates a need for deeper studies of Mrs. Monroe's computer virus. Our company standard is to share information about cybercrimes with the FBI. Please ask agent Evan Mulasky for forensics details."

Finally, I surveyed the pathetic array of hardware in our new Clean Room. I set another batch of automated tools to run on Client#1 code, but it'd take hours before I could run the same tools on Client#0 code. In all my previous employment, I had a full hardware armory, with research assistants. Instead, it was if I'd set out to run an organic farm with no electricity, no tractor, and no forged iron tools. I needed to turn Tony's $100K check over to Natalia and let her go shopping at the hardware store. And I needed an answer before Friday: who else had received that dire warning?

With nothing more to do at that moment, I rechecked all the locks and turned off the office lights. Then I switched my phone back on and rode the slow-mo elevator upstairs. I got ready for bed. Flossing. Brushing my hair a lot less than one hundred times. Putting clothes away, because there's no room in this so-called apartment for anything to be anywhere except where it belongs. Checked all the locks once more. Listened to the building sigh and settle in the night.

Staring into the dark, just the LED display on my phone advancing slowly toward four o'clock.

Zak's loss. The sadness in his voice.

Actions inside Doreen's home while I stood on the porch.

My mobster stalkers reappearing.

Tony and his bewigged grifter mother.

Would I be able to find other people who received that ransomware threat and—what? Save them, like the Lone Ranger?

My new narrow bed proved significantly uncomfortable. I was not enjoying moments of solo time, unlike the delight I felt my first night here. Then I began to think how different it'd be if Matt hadn't gone to Virginia. At a minimum, after a hard day like the one I'd just endured, I'd crawl into a warm bed, rest my thigh on his, feel his chest rise with deep, consoling sleep breaths. He'd rouse enough to pull me closer, drag my arm around him, squeeze my forearm in that way I find reassuring, until sleep embraced us both.

That many time zones away, Matt was awake.

Perhaps a moment for escapism through phone sex?

From my own phone, I called Matt, but he was already in the car with the guy he commutes with, so only I spoke. Not satisfying for either of us. The cell battery made my hand hotter than the conversation.

If any of my security-mining minders were listening to the call, they all got a soft-on.

Then another voice intruded on Matt's end of the call. Syrupy, Virginian, female. Near enough to be heard quite clearly.

"Matt, sweetheart, we're here. The guy at the gate wants to scan your badge."

6

Daniel Saw the Stone

■
■
■

WHEN I CAME DOWN TO the office—way early in the day, morning-mouth still overpowering Dr Tom's toothpaste and seeking a coffee coating—Harley was already at work, busy outside, scraping the glass front door to remove an upside-down-and-circled bright red anarchist's A.

He opened the door for me to join him on the sidewalk.

"Careful." He pointed to the slippery, soapy walkway. "Had to sluice it. Someone peed all over the doorway."

"Do the security videos show—"

"Hoodie-wearing faceless punks? Why, yes, they do!"

Back inside, Harley settled down at his desk, flipping on monitors and the small cabled television that usually showed the security footage from the front-door camera. He switched to a home-remodel channel on mute, since he had the same view of the street from his desk as the security camera captured.

By the time I returned with espresso—neither the barista nor geeky Slender Man said hello or recognized me; I'm anonymous on the Hill if not on the Internetz—Harley was already glued to his computer screen. Instead of hello, he said, "I report these death threats to the FBI, right?"

He asked did I want a debrief on what he'd found. Or did I want to look at the details saved in the #Debris_Byron project?

"No, I have a rough idea of how many adolescent males want me to go kill myself or wish for badness done to my body parts." I touched his shoulder. "Harley, there's nothing to report. No one has time to chase adolescents jacking off in their basement. Block and move on. If it's a site that tries to control harassment, report their accounts."

"When I was sheriff..." He stopped. No one looks more judgmental than an ex-cop, but Harley adds a certain Viking berserker flare. "I made my guys take threats seriously. Better than dealing with a domestic gone horribly wrong later."

Peering over his shoulder, I discovered that Harley had taught himself to capture screens and web addresses, and was continuously adding information to the #Debris_Byron project.

"The Internet is bigger than Limberlost Island." I was reassuring Harley, though he'd volunteered to review my web trash.

"A playground where there's no garbage collection, and the bullies are unsupervised." He seemed pretty dang glum.

"Let those rats screw themselves for a while, Harley. Please see what you can find about this person." I passed over the card Tony gave me, with the name and address of his mother inked on the back.

Harley opened a search window on his monitor. He did a minor double-take and then changed the cable station to local news. "This is no good," he commented mildly. He kept the TV on mute, so together we read the trailing news ribbon displayed under the on-the-scene reporter: another armed militia squabble, this time with the Forest Service at the Potholes Reservoir just across the Cascades. Here in the Pacific Northwest, we proudly brew an unlimited number of conspiracies and shelter angry sovereign citizens under every unturned rock. Harley seemed amused. "Muzzleloader deer season starts about now. Bet lots of hunters hope the feds clear up this new standoff before the loonies screw up duck season in the Potholes."

Unlike the paving gaps that Seattle drivers deal with on all our streets, the Potholes Reservoir is a twenty-thousand acre irrigation project managed by the state Fish and Wildlife people, though it's part of the federal Columbia Basin Irrigation Project. The reservoir fluctuates wildly from floodland to wetland with sand dune islands, and it's bordered by irrigated farmland, sage scrub land, a national wildlife refuge, and county parks. On an outline map, rather than looking like a dammed lake, it rather resembles my hair blowing in a full breeze.

"Why are they in conflict now? Someone's cow got on the wrong side of a fence no one maintains?"

"Something about freedom and federal encroachment," Harley said. "With irrigation and leopard frogs in the mix."

"With AK-47s?" I never came to be a fan of armed rebellion, in spite of hearing all the conspiracies from the crazies among my father's cousins and the never-pay-taxes tripwire vets who lived up the unpaved road from his commune.

Harley pointed to a detail on the screen. "That guy's holding an Armalite AR-10. Not an AK-47."

"Good to know. Is he defending the leopard frogs?"

While we watched, the TV news station christened the event the Potholes Deadlock.

"I'm thinking," Harley studied the video feed from the confrontation with great intensity, "that the frogs are being asked to look out for themselves."

Natalia joined us, rushing in from daycare dropoff, just as Brad's admin phoned. I put my cell on speakerphone. The admin said that the convenient time for Mr. Llewellyn and Mr. Jones proved to be nine-thirty. That very morning. "Is that satisfactory, Ms. Byron?"

Natalia nodded a strong affirmative, so I agreed. We had forty-five minutes to travel two miles.

"Did anyone pick up the drycleaning?" Natalia asked as soon as I hung up.

"Do we have anyone on staff to do that?"

She looked thoughtful—which means drawing together her perfectly groomed brows, her tattooed eyeliner crinkling at the edges of dark eyes. The picture of how the demi-urge Sophia must appear. "We need an executive admin."

"We need a cash flow," I answered.

"And we need to find who delivers laundry in this neighborhood." Harley switched screens.

Because both Natalia and I might end up giving testimony at any time of any weekday, we'd stashed appropriate clothes in the coat closet, this office having a larger closet than the one in my ascetic's cell upstairs.

Natalia checked her makeup while I'd only gotten as far as sniffing which shirt to wear.

"Skirts?" she asked.

"Ix-nay." I pulled my go-to-court suit jacket over my black t-shirt. Did not kick off my Chuck Taylors in favor of go-to-court shoes. "Last thing we need is Brad Jones believing we're trying to impress him."

"Let me do your eyes." Natalia came at me with a fresh, new eye-liner pencil. We compulsive types don't share pencils. "You look like you stayed up late in a dive bar. Playing music again?"

"Scrolling through code." Can't say much while an act of compassion is being performed on your eyelids. Besides, she was breathing directly into my face. I decided to tell her about the second instances of the ransomware, and second dead woman, after we visited aDVers.

"Let's hit the road." She slung a super-expensive Italian tote over her shoulder with an elegance I can never master. Though I'd worry about being mugged for that bag if I ever mastered that kind of grace. I grabbed my scuffed messenger bag.

Harley glanced our way, peering over his glasses. "Superman in the phone booth, eh? Pretty impressive. I'd trust you ladies to know what you're doing."

I held the door for Natalia, who frowned at the "ladies" tag.

"If kicking ass and taking names is what you're out to do," Harley said, turning back to close the computer window that held the stream of what the universe spewed at me over night. He studied the card I gave him and then two-finger typed Tony's mother's name on the search screen.

▪

At the aDVers front desk, the receptionist examined our ID, collected our cell phones, thanked us for helping with their security protocols, and then called for an escort.

When Natalia and I appeared at Brad's office door, he hurried out to meet us. Our kick-ass eyeliner seemed to be effective, because he blinked rapidly and opened his mouth twice without introducing us to his companion, who had the kind of manners that put everyone at ease.

"You're Samsara Byron. And Natalia Dragon. I'm so happy you could come today." The man held out his hand to shake mine, his palm cool and parchment-dry. "Please call me Dan."

Brad's twitching gave me extra seconds to recoup my own surprise. I'd seen Daniel Llewelyn's picture in the news, and I'd watched from the nosebleed seats once when he spoke at a white-hat security conference years ago. But now that we stood this close, shaking hands, I recognized him from another event.

In Virginia.

The high-domed forehead and rich man's groomed white ponytail. A neat Van Dyke replicating the triangle of his face, framing a sensitive mouth. The pale, you might say bloodless, complexion of an older man, once blond, now white with age. Watchful, crystalline topaz eyes.

After we restored power in the Lights Out In Estonia Affair, my Z-Crypto team presented to a dozen national security advisors, only three of whom were introduced to us by name. Dan Llewelyn was one of the anonymous, silent majority, not dressed as he was now in Carl Sagan-like turtleneck, but then in the anonymous white shirt, tie, and charcoal suit that populates that part of Virginia.

This time, we both recognized each other.

"It's a pleasure to have this conversation," Dan said. He spoke in a dry, whispery voice, spending two minutes making Natalia feel welcome.

If you won't go to Virginia, does Virginia just come to you?

Brad motioned for us to enter his conference room.

In any conference room when you sit with an exec like Brad or Dan, another person sits off to the side typing notes, often not even introduced. In this case, that person bent over his work, not looking up when we entered. When Dan pulled a notebook from his pocket, the amanuensis offered a pen, but Dan waved it away. Unlike other super-rich men I've met, Dan didn't have a pocket man. He had a phone tucked in the breast pocket of his suit jacket, where gentlemen formerly carried their handkerchiefs. He wrote with a fountain pen on a Moleskine notepad, jotting down what you said while he murmured, "Interesting," as if compelled to record your every precious thought.

We began the meeting.

Where Brad played wingman while Dan seduced us in ways only a grand master can.

Natalia and I refused the designer pastries and French-press coffee. "I don't eat while I'm working," I said, which was a lie, since I often don't realize I'm hungry until I sit down to work.

"A woman after my own heart." Dan smiled.

Not like how Brad smiles, in the habitual way of a glad-handing corporate vice president. Nope, every smile is personal, just for you, like a secret Dan chose to share with you.

"No slides today," Dan said when Brad reached to turn on his laptop. "These people can understand what we're doing without pictures."

"Before you start, I have to say, we don't do Big Data." Natalia presented our gambit. On the ride over, we'd discussed what we learned from online research. Brad's new company, aDVers, was recruiting Big Data mathematicians out of eastern schools and West Coast businesses. "We came only because you honored us with an invitation."

Brad glanced nervously my way, as if he expected me to harangue him the way I did on the street the day before. "What do you have against Big Data?"

Natalia made an expressive case: "Big piles of consumer data sliced and diced and served up for advertising? We work like cowboys busy checking that the barbed wire fence is in place?"

"Guarding a store of personal information in service to online advertising?" I truly was my most polite self. "We did look at your business before we agreed to this visit."

Dan pointed to Brad. "You're succeeding. Congratulations." He tapped the table beside me, an eyelash away from touching me. In that dry voice, every word like a personal confidence, he said, "I wager my grandmother's Christmas cookies that you'd consider working on 'Big Data for advertising' as a professional compromise."

"In my world, most all math is a moral dilemma." Yet I liked it when Dan smiled in appreciation of that I'm-not-kidding jest. "And Natalia is right, fence-building in service to online ads is not interesting."

"That sort of problem is trivial in comparison to what we need from you." Dan had his pen in hand, as if ready to take notes. "We want you to build protection inside our code, not just to tweak our processes. You'll finish the security solution you began on Quinn's research team."

"Advertising is boring." I resisted folding my arms to emphasize my innate stubbornness.

"How I wish you'd give me credit for knowing that." Brad pulled paper from a folder. "Before we go on, I hate to ask, but we do require an NDA."

In this life, I've signed so many NDAs—nondisclosure agreements—that I could paper my aunt's kitchen and dining room walls with them. Working life in Virginia required so many NDAs, you'd think waiters might ask you to sign one before taking your lunch order, forcing you to promise not to repeat proprietary secrets.

"Use mine." Dan handed me his fountain pen. Natalia was already signing with the gold Cross pen Brad offered. Her pageboy hair shielded any sight of what she wrote, but when she passed the paper back to Brad, I saw her gorgeous European-girls-school signature.

Pen poised, I could not make its point touch the paper.

"These agreements are one way." I locked on Dan as I spoke. "Where I promise not to tell your secrets. And yet you've dug into my secrets already. Let's just trade our words of honor that we won't cheat each other."

Brad's jaw actually dropped, since this just isn't done in pre-hire interviews. But before Brad could argue, the silent scribe passed him a note, which he looked at for half a second and then stood to leave.

"Please continue," Brad said. "Dan is best at describing what we're doing at aDVers. If you'll excuse me, I'll be back in a bit."

▪

Dan pointed to the door, a motion intended for the scribe, who then departed, notetaking laptop in hand. For a moment Dan stared out the conference room's glass wall, where Brad conversed with a bevy of guys in logo'd jackets. A security crew?

"I'm pleased to see Brad learning to delegate." Dan rasped that confidence like a benevolent father. "For a long time, I endeavored to handle all the tough work myself. It took me a while to learn that to survive in the executive suite, you have to delegate most things."

You'd have to be swift to notice the glances that Natalia and I exchanged. I spoke.

"Yet here you are recruiting two girls who declined to even drink your free coffee."

Natalia leaned forward, earnest. "But I will accept a free tour of your hardware."

"Word of honor." Pointing to the unsigned NDA, I repeated where we'd paused before Brad departed. Outside the glass wall, Brad stabbed the air with his finger to make a point.

"Word of honor." Dan seemed satisfied, though who knows how much interpretation I was applying to every nuance of expression. "I won't beg you to sign an NDA."

"Nor interview us, since you have HR research in hand."

"Yes, Ms. Byron. I've made several attempts…to bring both of you onto my team." Beside his whisper, Dan paused at odd points when he spoke. "My investment in Z-Crypto cost a bit, as did…our acquisition of your friend Quinn's research startup."

"I'm flattered." Z-Crypto is where I used to work. Where Zak is still employed. "But buying companies like that is 'a bit' creepy. Why did you think—"

"You made more…progress toward unlocking certain security code than…anyone ever before, Sam. Did they tell you that?"

No, they didn't. "I relied on my partner Zak. I don't specialize in breaking crypto."

Natalia stirred beside me. "Hi, I'm still in the room. Do you guys want to include me? Or do I ask Sam to explain later?"

"My apologies," Dan said. "That was rude. When Sam was employed at Z-Crypto…" He pointed my way, indicating that I should tell the story.

"Zak and I were invited to participate in a decode-to-penetrate contest, representing our company."

Natalia nodded, instantly understanding. "As part of a vendor selection process?"

"Indeed. The sponsors expected only partial analysis, just identification of the challenge. The candidate technology was better masked than Zorro." At my remark, Dan smiled broadly. I resumed the story for Natalia. "Zak and I conjectured, based on mythical data-protection technology we'd heard about. As mythical as a gift from Greek gods."

Another smile from Dan. He liked that metaphor, too.

"How'd you win?" Natalia asked.

"First question!" Dan raised his hand as if this were a classroom. "How'd you guess?"

"Zak and I read disappeared research. One paper described a digital camera that might embed a biometric ID in crypto. Another proposed a watermarking security solution for relational databases. Yet another—"

"Disappeared research?" Dan shifted, distinctly interested.

"On Tor, people share papers that disappeared between peer review and publication." How some geeks amuse themselves on the darknet. "Most of us assume the government snagged the disappeared research. So, matching up several ideas, Zak and I decided that the code we were looking at was a species of digital watermarking."

"That was the mythical gift from the gods? Major-league security geniuses detected DRM?" Natalia was not impressed. Dan was laughing.

Most people know DRM from their DVD collections: digital rights management. It's a form of digital watermarking, which is like watermarking paper. If you hold paper money or an expensive piece of paper up to the light, you can see the papermaker's watermark. But I can't show you a digital watermark, because if it were detectable, it wouldn't be doing its job.

"It wasn't commercial DRM. Zak and I guessed that the code came from a mythical project called Prometheus. We presented a protocol to unmask the beast."

"Did your solution work?" Natalia glanced between Dan and me. "I'm assuming yes."

"No idea. Z-Crypto won the contract, but we never saw a single line of that code again."

"Prometheus isn't a…myth." Dan seemed to be deeply enjoying that story, a flash from the past. "It's an extension of the digital watermarking my first team created for…" One of his irregular pauses went on for an uncomfortably long moment. He finally concluded, "For more than mere copy protection."

"And you're still involved?" I stated the obvious, since we'd last met in the company of heavy-duty NSA guys.

"I consult occasionally. Like…that invitation to review your efforts. And then the presentation after your success with the Estonia power crisis. I've wanted…you on my team ever since."

"For penetration testing? Not my favorite." How disappointing. "It's just a set of prescribed tasks."

Natalia heaved a melodramatic sigh. "Your personal preference, Sam. Me, I like planning and executing a good penetration test. It's as pleasant as chopping wood and lighting a fire on a cold winter morning."

Again, Dan's flicker of a smile. "That's exactly why I want both of you. We require the world's best protection."

Natalia's eyes passed my way for a nanosecond. "Sorry to repeat myself. But we don't do corporate Big Data. It's just not interesting. You have many other candidates to choose from."

Dan glanced past me to where Brad was gesturing to the logo-jacket guys. Then he focused his crystalline, penetrating eyes on us again. "We don't do commercial Big Data here. Though we'd like the world to think so." He leaned onto his elbows, hands folded as if in prayer. "We are building on the gains made in the last decade via machine learning and virus mutation."

"Like the folks using mathematical models to understand how HIV DNA mutates?" Natalia tapped that curve above her lip, pondering. She and I had discussed one interesting place outside national security and social media where mathematicians find jobs in the new economy: biomedical research, especially research related to DNA. For example: viruses mutate, so let's understand how and then learn to affect the pattern.

"Quite similar." Dan approved of Natalia's interruption. He didn't speak for an extra unexpected second. I was guessing that he had a physical problem, maybe one that went with his chalky complexion. "But we're…exploring degenerative neural disease rather than virus DNA. When I describe our work, it sounds like we leaped the Mississippi in a single bound. By advancing the pioneering work we did with digital watermarking, we've engineered a way to halt the advances of Parkinson's. It's executable cell biology, functioning like a vaccine. Or, better analogy, an antidote. We're next exploring ALS and Huntington's chorea. And a few other rare neural conditions."

Certain moments in life generate so much awe that no words come. A baby just born. The peaceful death of the grandmother you adore. Discovering that you have inside you the ability to love and fully trust another person.

Mathematicians finding solutions to pernicious, debilitating disease.

Gave me chills.

Dan broke the silence. With his odd whisper. "We hold a solution in hand, ready for human subjects in the United States."

While Dan explained his personal passion (a mother and sister lost to neural disease), I stared through the conference room's glass wall, picturing myself back out there in the corporate bustle, excited to be changing the world. Get up every day, go downtown, get coffee, hole up in my cubicle—no, Brad would give me my own office. All-glass outside walls, full-spectrum lighting, coffee robots from Starbucks. Stand in line with other developer-types at the food trucks to get tacos for lunch. More coffee. Plan with my team what to do. More coffee. Home at night, where I'd spend more than half my time solving problems for aDVers. Helping to change the quality of life for humankind.

"We've redirected press attention about our work. But we expect extreme publicity next year." Dan rousted me from daydreams.

"Not my favorite."

"No. Nor us. Since we aren't structured on the traditional principal-researcher model, we won't be parading superstars. Instead, we will be emphasizing our team approach to research."

Dan paused, smiling, as if waiting for Natalia or me to speak.

Brad opened the conference-room door, but then turned back to the men he'd been meeting with. "You are empowered to create and execute strategy. I don't want to make tactical choices. That's what I hired you for."

When he closed the door, Brad nodded to Dan. "Feels like I'm imitating you. 'Don't ask me to make the decisions. Do your job.' I was an intern when I first heard you say that."

Then he glanced between Dan and us visitors. "Dan explained our work? Then you know why we need you. We need to protect more than our data store and code. We must protect every individual on the team, from the outside world and from any possible errors they might make."

"From Brad on down to the receptionists." Dan leaned back, steepling his fingers again.

"And your first safe act?" Natalia asked. "Limit publicity?"

Brad nodded, that CEO tactic of agreeing with you before saying the opposite. "Once we announce our vaccine, the media will descend. But our plan is to only answer questions."

"Vaccine?" I repeated that, even though Dan explained their solution wasn't that, precisely. "Human trials take years."

"It would, if we began in the U.S.," Dan said. "But we've been at this for a while. We have sufficient data in twelve countries to accelerate approval in the U.S."

Brad shuffled his folder from one hand to another. "This might sound like hubris, but we expect a National Science award next year, if not a Nobel nomination."

Dan waived away that idea as trivial. "All that matters is the success of our efforts. Talk of...prizes distracts from the work we have yet to do. And we need the profound reassurance that we'd have with...you, Sam, and you, Natalia."

He spoke for a moment about the ravages of diseases they intended to halt. When Dan's pitch veered off into passion, I noticed two things. Brad listened raptly, his face lit with joy. He nodded at each key point. This was a sermon he loved, though he must have heard it often. You didn't need to tattoo "True Believer" on his forehead to convince me of Brad's devotion. His work at aDVers meant far more to him than just finally serving as CEO of a significant tech company.

The second thing? Dan's hand, near mine on the table, trembled with passion as he spoke. And my hand twitched in response, as if his urgency traveled by electric transference.

"You're the first and best choice for this work." This time Dan touched my hand, just grazing the edge of my little finger. "After you ensure we're running smoothly, let our profits pay for your other research efforts over time."

"What exactly do you want?"

"We want you to build protection inside our code," Brad said. "Extend the basics of digital watermarking so that no one can unlock our code and repurpose it."

Brad continued the pitch, speaking to Natalia, since he'd likely internalized that he couldn't convince me that gravity is real. "We're offering you the best hardware you might need to do all you can in the world."

Since I'm not good at seduction—doing or receiving—a fountain of doubt burbled inside me. For one, I say I'm the world's best forensics geek, but I know my limits. The hard sell put me off. "We've started our own business. Natalia and I can serve as consultants. Even promise you eighty percent of our time for the next ten months."

"It will take one hundred twenty percent of your time," Dan said. "Which of course you know."

"We need you as employees." Brad's mouth twitched when he realized he was arguing with me. "The company requires your Standard Form 86."

At this point, my spine froze. The ice flowing in my veins caused my fingertips to sting.

"Why would the federal government be involved?" Natalia asked, eyes wide.

Dan crossed his legs, shifting, his shoe near my jeans but not touching. "You guessed, didn't you, Sam? When I shared this with my national security friends, they perceived the same problems you do."

Natalia folded her arms and sat back in her chair. My heart jerked with the effort to pump frozen blood.

"The possibility of reverse engineering is," I managed to speak the word, "terrifying."

"Bioengineering by terrorists. Or bad state actors." Brad couldn't refrain from stating the obvious. "Our security friends insist we employ the best possible protections."

"At our last review, your name was mentioned again, Sam." Dan sat back, mirroring Natalia, hands in his lap, easy, trusting.

"Your name keeps being mentioned," Brad said. "Which was why we acquired Quinn's research team. Now—" He turned up the dial to peak executive sociopathy, the most warmth possible from a human being. "We wish to give you all the time in the world to make up your mind. But we need to have our security team named by Friday if we're going to start U.S. human trials in the next year. We have an alternative identified, who's eager to say yes. But we want you. Sam. Natalia."

"By Friday." Natalia's voice didn't uplift with a question.

"Tomorrow or Thursday would be better." Brad's smile was bright and human enough to warm the chilly conference room.

Privately, I couldn't stop wondering whether NSA interest was solely to guard against misuse. Was there no chance that someone in the NSA wasn't considering the actual implementation of malevolent uses? However, this wasn't the place to ask a question that's best asked on the open Internetz soon after aDVers announces its "vaccine."

Sensitive, Dan noticed my withdrawal, my nerve endings retreating from all that bonhomie we'd exchanged throughout this conversation.

"Let's talk more." If you didn't watch closely, you wouldn't catch Dan checking the time. "Before you say no, I beg you to meet our team, including board members and key developers. Brad, will you be so kind as to arrange that?"

"Of course." Brad turned up the sociability heat. "Perhaps you can join us for our team's happy hour this afternoon."

"I'd love to," Natalia said.

Though I loathe work-team functions, I accepted. Dan gave us his personal phone number as part of the invitation.

When Dan rose to leave, he tucked his pad into a leather pouch, which he carried over one shoulder like a student, though it was fine Coach leather, not battered canvas. He flipped the handy gold stylus between his fingers, like a magician pondering the next trick. Then he shook hands, promising that the morning's pleasure had been all his.

▪

Brad asked his assistant to schedule a hardware tour for Friday, and then he said goodbye, though he couldn't refrain from additional sales.

"It's exactly what I promised, isn't it, Sam? Best work you ever dreamed of? Work only you can do?"

"You cannot even imagine our best possible work," Natalia said. "We are the Kurosawa-Mifune team of excellence."

They drifted into a movie discussion while I wandered into a forest of ideas I couldn't sort. About Dan Llewelyn buying companies in order to hire me. About NSA folk pushing my name on aDVers to support new life-saving technology that had the potential to be misapplied to—

Brad said, "My first lessons in leadership came from watching Kurosawa movies with Dan, when he was explaining to the team how the king tempted fate in *Ran*. Afterwards, two of the younger developers on the team said they'd commit hari-kari rather than ever betray Dan. Can you imagine?"

"Sweet Freyja!" Natalia exploded. "You don't think crap like that do you, Brad? Cuckoo-cult talk?"

He laughed. "Of course not." He caught me staring at him and stopped laughing. "To tell the truth, I think people honor his leadership because they know he'd do the knife thing rather than betray the people on his team. Metaphorically, I mean. This isn't the middle ages."

After the receptionist returned our cell phones, Natalia and I checked messages as soon as we hit the street. (No replies from Evan Mulasky or my friend Jeremiah; Nicky-the-stalker made it through my block again with a new phone number; a text from Dan thanked us for our time and chuckled again at my "math is a moral dilemma" comment; Matt wanted a we-need-to-talk conversation come nightfall.) Then we caught a cab back to the office, both of us with research tasks that needed attention.

Natalia remained silent half way up Capitol Hill, while I pondered that sense of connectedness I felt with Dan. As if I'd found a (sane) brother. Or a (civilized) uncle.

Then she said, "In the old country, my grandmother looked behind the door for dust-bunnies every time she closed it. Brought the habit with her when we immigrated."

"So, we say no?"

"You can also look for dust-bunnies before opening the door."

Leaving me to guess what she might be thinking. I've known developers and leads who say "far out" or "you fukken-kidden me" when a response is required but no commitment is desired. Natalia typically spins a story. Or maybe tells lies?

> "In the old country, my grandmothers did what mothers here do, because our mothers were in the army. Or were sent to Turkmenistan to train nurses."
>
> "In the old country, we were forced to double our math training with Olympics-style physical training. If you couldn't keep up, it was the armed forces or factory work. Less demanding."
>
> "In the old country, we rode in ice-cold buses to the Polytechnic, where they fed us gruel and pig trotters. Where you stood in the freezing courtyard if you failed to solve logic problems."

The old country always sounds like some far northern Soviet Bloc nation, which cast particularly grim color on Natalia's stories. Yet to my knowledge, she's the daughter of a U.S. noncom G.I. and a German embassy liaison officer in Berlin. And subsequently she went to school in various International Baccalaureate programs wherever either her father or mother was stationed. She was visiting an aunt in Kosovo during an historic moment, but she claims those horrors didn't overwhelm her childhood. Or maybe she was never in Kosovo.

A few steps outside our brand-new office door, Natalia stopped unexpectedly, so I ran into her. She shook her head, rolled her shoulders.

"May Freyja wake me from this beguiling dream." She grabbed my arm. "It's like a bad old lover, begging you to come back and it'll be like the best of times. Right?"

"We're saying no?"

She took a breath, air hissing over her teeth. "We aren't saying yes. Yet. But this is a huge decision. I have to talk it over with my partner."

That was my moment of epiphany, when I realized what a sucky girlfriend I am. Matt had discussed his job decision at length with me, as if my opinion had equal weight with his. Me? It hadn't occurred to me to talk with Matt about Brad's job offer. Didn't even hear whispers of Matt's voice in my head. I tussled with only two thoughts:

> Was our new business so fragile that I'd toss it off after ten days?
>
> When a proposition seems too good to be true, is it always true that it's false?

"Meanwhile," Natalia said, "More research into Dan Llewellyn. Might as well munch on facts."

"And let's look for any clues we can find about the aDVers technical focus."

"And Brad Jones. And every other board member or employee they want us to meet."

Then I described to Natalia the last time I worked with Brad. I was seconded with Zak to a business that had just hired Brad as chief technology officer. He brought us in because of suspicions about data theft that he couldn't trace. Back then, Brad wore this hip GQ-douche look, always with two days' beard, loafers with no socks. He'd buttoned up since then, perfected the corp VP look and manners. And was no longer stuck (if the story about aDVers is true) with shepherding a pack of losers.

In the consulting gig, Zak and I zeroed in quickly. We were only there for a few weeks to find security holes and shore up the system Brad had inherited. The work was butthead simple, because the kinks in the system were designed by a butthead, but it allowed me to experience what it's like to sit at a desk every day in an airless room, your brain being burned by subtly twittering fluorescent lights, while you're breathing the same air as the most dysfunctional team in the history of the universe.

Sniping.

Calling in sick.

Taking credit for other people's work.

Brown nosing, by complaining repeatedly that others do it.

Freezing out one team member, who seemed to have been elected scapegoat via secret ballot.

Bullying lower status team members.

Bullying a guy who wept at his desk for three days because his mother's dog died.

Crying by the noisemakers drowns out the quiet and sane.

Insisting on their traditional tools and processes.

Seeking credit for "winning" based on bad metrics.

Blaming the last person who left the team.

Repeating scurrilous rumors about managers.

Complaining about the last manager, who allegedly poisoned the executives' view of the team.

It's all politics, no merit for rewards.

Fucking H-1B visa robots are stealing all the jobs.

Everyone pissed at direct managers and leads, the specific people most powerless to fix anything.

Okay, that list depresses ninety-eight percent of anyone working in the software and data world, because everyone's been on that bad team at one time, a time that seemed to go on forever. For me, it represented only three weeks as Brad's consultant, but it felt like that dream where you're sucked into a swamp and every struggle drags you deeper. I swore not to be sucked into any corporate maw, where such illness is more than humans should endure.

Brad? To my knowledge he fired, moved, and promoted people until that team transmogrified into a crew of satisfied and productive developers. But that's almost a decade ago—four or five generations of change if you measure it in software-development cycles, which ages you faster than dog years.

▪

At the office, Natalia and I found take-out sandwiches, courtesy of Harley. Above his desk, the muted TV showed a public news broadcaster interviewing a broad-chested militia man in camo, with "Updates from the Potholes Deadlock" scrolling across the bottom of the screen. The camera panned to show a phalanx of black Suburban and Expedition carryalls, which meant that a large number of federal agents had been called to participate. Therefore, that day I was glad Matt was in Virginia and not rolling out to work in a tactical vest.

Seated at the front desk, Harley leaned back in his chair, applying get-the-red-out eye drops.

"Is the #Debris project harder than you thought it'd be?" I asked. "Technically, I mean. Time for a tutorial?"

Harley screwed his lips in the disgusted way he looked at us in the sixth grade when he caught my brother Pete and me smashing pop bottles on the highway. "Besides craving a shower every thirty minutes?

And using quarts of eyewash? Can't see well with all the garbage I'm staring at."

"You'll get used to it." I touched Harley's shoulder, which passed for deep intimacy between us.

"Hope not," he said. "Sam, you don't have to argue that you're tough, that you can take tumbles no one else can. Or that you're smarter than all of us."

"Not smarter than me," Natalia said.

Harley waggled a finger to acknowledge her truth. "However, I been ass-deep in your online alligators for two days now. Sure, lots of basement boys paste bad words over your avatar. But here's a few that differ." He handed me a printout of the report he'd been building, which meant that he'd figured out the wireless printer on his own. "You need to call your law enforcement friends."

"They aren't my friends." I sounded unreasonably sulky.

"Maybe not. But the dogs in their kennel can do more than I can. That is only about one percent of all messages." He tapped the sheaf of pages. "I'm pretty sure eighty percent of these demand investigation. The other twenty percent fit the pattern. If you brought this list into my station, I'd have an armed guard at your house within the hour. These threats are very, very personal."

Natalia nabbed the pages from me and read aloud.

"From Nicky. Our boy Nicky?" she asked. I shrugged, not ready to get all het up over my personal stalker from last year. Nicky, the misguided tester, who'd dragged me into that huge hassle with the mobsters and then disappeared while I was busy explaining to the feds what happened.

> "You didn't allow a proper end to our affair."

"Sounds like Nicky."

She continued to read in her best effing Eastern European accent.

> "We found Nicky, so we found you."
> "No cop watching over you day and night now."
> "You fucked our business. We come fuck you."

> "You so smart, Miss Forensikz? The more your customers wake up dead, the closer we come to you."

"You can stop, Natalia. I get the idea."

"Oh, here's another from that twerp Nicky." She imitated his weird accent.

> "You are in danger but I will protect you. I'd risk my life for such joy. Not my fault."

"We're supposed to think the White Knights found him." I was convinced this was only huffing and puffing intended to scare me. But then, I had other thoughts buoying up my free-floating anxiety. "Go ahead and send these to Evan Mulasky at the FBI." Evan hadn't yet answered my previous night's email, though he'd sworn to continue investigating the hellfire that Nicky's love wrought previously. I pointed to the Potholes Deadlock images on the cable TV. "The FBI is all tied up right now. Only send messages if you've captured enough data that they can trace servers and find the sender's location."

Natalia offered the pages back, but I declined. I'd had sufficient cyberjunk shoved my way the previous year that I didn't need to preserve a paper record.

"And maybe I should travel with you for a while," Harley said. "When you're out on the street."

Natalia started to laugh, then couldn't stop herself. Had to sit in a chair. Pretending to be overcome. While she laughed, I shed my go-to-court suit jacket, pulled on my leather one, and grabbed my messenger bag.

"No?" Harley said.

"No. Especially since I'm off to visit our Client Number Two. I'm not dragging a sheriff into Brad Jones's mother's house because bogeymen are hiding in the Internetz."

7

Mother's Little Helper

WHAT I DIDN'T TELL MY faithful Byron&Dragon crew: before I headed downtown to help Brad's mother, I had a Krypptikk ticket to complete: tussle once more with Tony's mother.

Not yet understanding why the universe burdened my professional life with three men's mothers, I slipped into the QFC grocery on Fifteenth Avenue for a protein bar. QFC might be another local landmark from my misspent undergraduate days living on Capitol Hill, except Kroger bought the local chain, so there's not a trace of nostalgia or regret when I walk through its sliding doors.

A clutch of Tiger Milk bars in hand, I got in the ten-items-or-less line behind a lady who hoisted a shopping basket with nineteen items onto the checkout stand. And then the clerk had to call for prices on apples missing their stickers and a marked-down package of thin-sliced pork chops. I thumbed through screens at my phone, as one does to keep from turning into She-Hulk in the checkout lane. Natalia sent a Krypptikk message.

KRYPPTIKK JOB: CLIENT#1_MONROE

NDragon:

Finished search for phone-home details from malware.
PDF report in job folder.
Now I'm seeking the install path.

When I glanced up from my phone, I recognized the person holding up the checkout line. Not a beige wig this time. Curley maroon hair and dressed like a clerk at the Department of Motor Vehicles. I tapped her shoulder.

"You know this?"

I opened my fist to present the Lenin pin from Tony.

She brightened. "Why, yes! From the Seattle good-will exchanges with the Soviet Union. The first tourists brought back bucketsful."

"I mean this *particular* pin."

"The Fremont antique market?" She pursed her lips, as if thoughtful. "Amazing what they charge for brittle plastic."

"Tony gave it to me last night."

The clerk called for the price check again, tapping his foot, impatient about the line growing behind us.

She lifted the pin from my palm. "The Soviets couldn't even make cheap plastic. Makes you wonder what they hoped to bring home from Afghanistan. Or Cuba."

I snatched it back. "An oil pipeline and '57 Chevy engines."

"Hard not to be nostalgic for the Cold War, isn't it?" She was open and friendly, so grifting must be happening while we waited to learn the cost of pork chops. Only I couldn't see the grift.

"Before my time." I folded my arms, hoping to look tough. How do you bully a grifter? "You need to talk to me. Wendy Logan is dead. So is Doreen Monroe."

You could detect the tiniest change in her eyes, as if she controlled everything but her pupils. "How sad. Friends of yours?"

"Mrs. Monroe died yesterday, waiting for me to deliver her computer, freed of ransomware. The same ransomware Wendy Logan wrote to you about."

"You aren't selling Lenin pins door to door, dearie?"

"No, I'm not."

"You're his little agent." A coldness in those golden eyes.

"No. I'm a mathematician and don't believe in coincidence."

The clerk finally had the prices, pushed his buttons, and pointed to how she was supposed to swipe her card, which she performed as if she'd never seen a pin-pad in her life. Her receipt in hand, she gazed past me, not at me.

"Let's have tea."

She exited through the sliding In-Out door, never glancing back to see if I followed her after paying for my energy bars.

For the two blocks to her apartment, the sole answer she gave to any of my questions was, "Parabolic microphones, dearie."

In the alley, she unlocked a side door, which opened into a tiny, icy-cold foyer where three steps led up to the first floor and a dark, twisting stair led down below the building.

Inside her apartment, she switched on one table lamp, but otherwise left us in early October ambient light from the half-shaded windows.

It wasn't identical to the room where Tony crashed in this building as a student; no mattress on the floor or paperbacks stacked against the wall, no Marcuse or Camus or Wollstonecraft vindicating the rights of women, positioned for seduction. In fact, no books at all. But it was the same pre-WWII space, the romantic flats of Capitol Hill, with foot-high mopboards coated in another half-inch of multilayered paint, rounding all the edges. Wide, multilayered casings wrapped old windows that contained enough lead they appeared to be melting. Every surface a color that might be called white but an organic, living shade, unlike the bright, unreasonably white lobby outside my office. A kitchen the size of a closet, a sink too small to hold more than a bowl and a cup. (A tradition they've revived in new Capitol Hill apartments.)

Her scant furnishings seemed to have been culled from a BBC nostalgia catalog: rattan chairs from a Thirties movie set in rainy Singapore; reed-thin bamboo roller shades, letting in daylight like a tempestuous drama in the Yucatan. Reproduction paintings from Picasso's Blue period, either from a street vendor in Paris or picked out of alley trash behind Seventeenth Avenue East, right here on the Hill. The kitchen, with a Lubitsch-era round-edge refrigerator, gleamed, immaculate. In fact, everything was extraordinarily clean, spare, utilitarian, and not from a year before 1950.

No cats (not to admit I'd cast her as a type).

No knitting.

No craft magazines.

No antimacassars like the ones Grandma Flo spreads everywhere.

"I'm Samsara Byron. What shall I call you?"

"Clarissa."

She pointed to a straight-backed chair, its varnish scuffed and scarred from years of use.

Where I sat awkwardly through the moment when hostess should be offering coffee or tea. Instead, Clarissa stood over me, arms folded, a finger to her lips, studying me with a dispassionate—I'd have to guess, analytic—expression.

Me, a paramecium under a microscope.

Beyond that maroon wig—a disguise, not an accessory—everything about Clarissa had angles. Cheekbones. Shoulders. Eyebrows. A strong jaw, a mouth full of bright white teeth, which I'd first noticed when she laughed at me in the store, but now seeming ready to bite and chew an enemy.

She clapped her hands, as if surprised by a memory.

"Tea. I promised you tea."

She tripped the switch on an electric kettle, her back to me, and lifted two delicate china cups and their matching saucers from a diminutive cupboard.

"Why do you keep pushing your way into my world?" she said. A mild, inquisitive voice.

Accepting the china from her hands, I arranged them on the diminutive table, smoothing the embroidered tablecloth.

"We both know Tony." Time to get down to it, after all this foreplay. "You and I know what no one else does: that Doreen Monroe's and Wendy Logan's deaths are related. That you are the connecting point. And that you too are in danger."

The light in the room was strong enough to reveal that her pupils dilated again; she showed no other sign of recognition.

"Both dead." I persisted. "Both writing to you about their frightening malware."

"Is this a warning?" She blinked in her maddeningly blank way. "'If you break this chain letter, Satan shall take your soul'?"

"I found Doreen." Why didn't this impress her? "Tony says there's a spook in your system. Related to their deaths. If anyone knows about spooks, it's Tony. He's the Pirate King."

"You're sure it's not you that Tony led into danger?"

"You admit you know him?"

"Just repeating the name you use to harass me."

"This pin," I had it in my open hand again, "was to convince you to trust me. To help find the spook in your system."

"There are spooks, and then there are real spooks. My friend Tim says you're an NSA contractor. Do you greet one moral compromise after another each morning?"

"No, I don't work for the NSA. I'm a private business person." I set the pin on her tiny table.

"Who reports everything to the federal government."

"No, I don't. And Tony asked me not to contact law enforcement. He says that bad guys are trying to get to him through you. Which puts you in danger. Please let me find the hack in your computer system."

The tea kettle whistled. She ignored it. "If Tony's involved, law enforcement isn't far behind. I don't need that kind of help."

"Fine." I shoved the delicate china cup aside, letting it clatter in its saucer, and rose from the rickety rattan chair. "Since you won't take my help, I'm talking to the SPD and FBI. I need to find out whether other people are in danger. Besides you and Tony."

The sibilance in her voice hissed behind me as I jerked opened the door. "You call him the Pirate King? So silly."

▪

As usual in Seattle, bus lines didn't exist from my current location to where I wanted to be, so I walked downtown to meet Brad's mother.

Harley and Natalia had gotten under my skin enough that I walked only open, well-traveled streets, looking around for black SUVs filled with White Knight mobsters. At Boren, the extended time waiting for the cross-light had me rocking on my heels.

Boren provides the four-lane speedway that natives use to race from the eastside freeways into downtown. On Boren, "there is no there there." No parking. No attractions. Only sun-blocking apartment buildings. Nothing to slow speeding drivers except the stop lights, which downhill traffic tends to treat as optional for the first fifteen seconds after yellow changes to red. Pedestrians, bicyclists: grave danger can be found here as you traverse the chasm between Capitol Hill and downtown.

Just as I prepared to cross Boren and the I-5 overpass, that sk8ter-boy passed me, obvious from his goofy right-foot-forward stance, speeding down the car lane on Pine, faster than the taxi he was passing, youthful disregard for the outsized accident rate at Boren and Pine.

Like, just yesterday, I was that young. Now look at me: crossing the street only when the little LED man is white. Me, I have a regular stance, left foot first—and spent a year of my adolescence feeling bad because Matt described something about me as "regular."

At Ninth Avenue, the dude pulled up, kicked his board into the air, grabbed it, and then walked beside me.

"Hello," I said. "How do you do? My name is Samsara Byron. I believe we've met, but I didn't get your name."

"Temistocle Speedwell." His hands curled into fists, pressing his board to his chest. "And don't repeat that stupid joke about testicles. You can call me Tem."

"Tim, I—"

"Tem. T–E–M. Say it right. It proves that you listen."

"Pleased to meet you, Tem-with-an-E. I've seen you so many times since yesterday that it's an amazing set of coincidences. It's as if I met you in a previous life."

"We just work the same streets." He fished in his hoodie pocket and yanked out a crumpled piece of notepaper, pale green with a light brown grid, the kind engineers use. "You probably block everyone, but I think these two are real."

He held out the paper, shaking it until I took it from his hand.

"Are you stalking me, Tem? Do I need to have a word with your mother?"

"My mother's dead." He said it with no trace of emotion. "I follow several dark forums closely. Most of what people shovel at you is garbage. These two are different."

"All this harassment began after I saw you yesterday with that hacker crew."

He hugged his board closer to his chest. "None of those guys started anything major. They're just kiddie-script people. Someone else used that—" he searched for a word "—event to create problems for you. But those—" he pointed to the note in my hand "—aren't schoolboys freaking on you."

"So you hack?" When my voice is roughed up from too-little sleep, I make *hack* sound like an extrusion of body fluids.

"Mostly I just listen. You don't think I'm like those guys, do you? Fercrissakes. Lulz for nothing, just online hand jobs? The world is fucking falling apart. If you're doing actions, they should add up to something. Have a social purpose."

This whole while, we were wending our way down Pine Street, dodging shoppers and beggars and street musicians, pausing at lights amid the afternoon mob.

"Anonymous?" From the way I asked, anyone might think anything, but he and I knew what I meant: the leaderless league of hackers who attack and dox individuals and organizations they oppose, such as Westboro nutcases or ISIS. "The global brain? Perpetually replicating itself without mitosis?"

"I help when it's important." He sought to show no emotion, but he wore his hair too short, a #1 buzz. His giveaway: deepening creases near his ears, so his ears waggled ever so slightly. If he decided to play poker, he'd need to grow his hair longer.

"As if you're helping Robin Hood?"

"Most don't steal anything. Just take power away from evil."

"Wow." The way I said it, Tem knew that word was meant to express profound existential doubt.

He shrugged, the way kids do these days, slipping free of an unwanted burden. "I'm not a member of any group, not even one that doesn't believe in hierarchy."

"Well, put a good word in for me with your cybermob."

"What?"

"To leave me the fuck alone."

Tem leaned away, thinking, as if considering my advice. "You and I are both the good guys. It takes mucho kinds, the way the world is now. Check out those freaks." He tapped the paper in my hand. "They seem sincere. If not about killing you, they want to scare you silent."

He slapped his board down and skated south on Fifth Avenue, deftly dodging people on the sidewalk.

The green engineer's paper, unfolded, held torn printouts of four messages, taped in place. The first two were hacked versions of Anonymous screed.

> "We are Multitude. Your transgressions are never forgotten. Your trespasses are never forgiven. Anticipate our action."

> "Expect cyber destruction. We are Multitude and stronger than you. You cannot prevail against our anger."

The third was entirely familiar:

> "Friday is a good day to die."

All were signed by someone who called himself Biktop, with a tagline: White Knights of the New Russian Revolution. The fourth taped-on item was a more than decent discovery path, leading to the ISP (the Internet service provider) that hosted these messages.

I paused at a touristy coffee bar on Pine Street, sat down at one of their tables, and took pictures of the sheet. And then sent the pics to Harley to forward to his law-enforcement buddies. Done, I tucked Tem's homework into my messenger bag, stepped outside, took a breath, and looked both ways before I crossed the street.

If I'm scared, the terrorists win, right?

Let's settle for cautious.

I must remain free to do whatever I want.

▪

Even on a weekday in early October, even after the summer crowd had departed, the Pike Market downtown can feel like a buzzing hive with no queen, and visitors consume parking for blocks around. To avoid the crowds, I walked north on First Avenue toward Belltown to find the high-rise condo where Brad's mother lived.

The concierge knew to expect me and rode up the elevator with me to knock on Ms. Yates's door. (*"She kept her name when she married"*; Brad bragged about that, because he's truly a sensitive guy.)

I'm cool enough that I didn't gasp at the view of Puget Sound from a penthouse on the twenty-third floor, the water shimmering on a sunny autumn day, the sky now mottled by clouds drifting up from the south. But I felt my cool slip away in the presence of an elegant creature such Patricia Yates.

A tall, pencil-thin woman in casual silks, as casual as a four-color ad in *The New Yorker*, shook my hand the way a business woman does, firmly. Me, I'm in black jeans and plain Chuck Taylors, looking as professional as any has-been punk on the streets of Seattle. Don't ask me why a sophisticated woman trips my moxie when not a single one of Seattle's five billionaires fazes me. Before I could get myself too wrought up, however, she said, "Perhaps you don't remember, but you testified in a case two years ago when I was sitting as judge pro tem."

"Yes, it was unforgettable. You had astute questions about our forensic methods. We don't always know that the judge understands or can instruct the jury about what our findings mean for a case."

"Thanks for saying so." Patricia smiled, tilting the severe angles of her hair and accessories. "I miss that world a great deal. You knew I had to retire for health reasons?"

"I'm sorry. Brad didn't mention that."

"And you know Brad from…?"

"Grad school. We were on a winning hack-a-thon team."

"And if I know Brad, he did a great job of convincing people to work together." A wry look overcame her stern features. "While you did the heavy lifting."

"Well, I wouldn't say—"

"Of course not. But math isn't his strongest talent." She laughed. She knew the guy better than I did. "I'm grateful that Brad recommended someone he trusts. It's so embarrassing to have a virus like this. You are kind to come to me."

Now we'd returned to the awkward part, where I don't have enough social grace to keep the conversation going.

"Brad seems to be doing well." I fumbled it.

"Yes. He and Dan are eager for you join their new venture."

"They've been persistent. Perhaps flattering me too much."

"Have they sent you on a journey to be persuaded by their workers and friends?" A lift of her nicely penciled brows. When I nodded, she said, "It changes your life, getting to work with Dan. Not just because of all the good he's done in the world."

"I'm learning things I never knew."

"It's personal for me," she said. "I spent only a month working as his assistant. By then he'd talked me into law school. It's not wrong to say that I'm one of his many protégés. He mentored Brad as an undergrad. Introduced me to my second husband."

Since I didn't need any more pressure about aDVers than I'd already experience that day, I asked after her laptop. She led me to a corner table where she worked. Puget Sound and the Olympic Mountains filled the nearby window.

"It's silly to have this problem," she said. "However, I promise you I'm neither careless nor incompetent. And I've heard several law firms have been hacked this way, though not my firm. I led our team when we implemented the plan for secure computing."

Patricia described her security. If Brad set it up for her, he did a great job. No ordinary person could hack this puppy without a great deal of knowledge. Still talking, she powered on her laptop.

"Perhaps I should just pay them what they ask."

"No, never—oh, Geezus F. Christ!"

When I swore, she glanced at the now-familiar splash screen. The same ransomware. The same pay-or-die warning. I powered it off, closed the lid.

"Judge Yates—"

"Call me Patricia, please."

"Do you—" I set out to speak gently, to ask discreetly.

"Sam, that case where we met in court was gruesome. And you're pale as the jury members when the coroner's team testified." She pointed to the window seat. "Let's talk."

Perched on the corner of her expansive window seat, I asked my question. "Do you know Wendy Logan? Her husband is a businessman in Hong Kong."

"It's not a familiar name."

"Doreen Monroe? Lived on Capitol Hill?"

She angled her head, thinking while studying me. "Was she married to William Monroe? Our firm defended his company when a patent troll sued for infringement. I believe he died a couple of years ago. But I never met his wife. Do friends of yours have the same virus?"

"I worked with Doreen's stepson in Virginia. How about…" I blinked, trying to remember the name I'd seen on the call-button at her apartment building. "Clarissa Dalloway?"

Embarrassingly, I heard the fiction in the name as soon as I said it aloud. But instead of laughing, Patricia Yates turned a color to match her ivory-and-cream upholstery. She folded her thin arms across her chest, the first protective motion she'd made.

"No."

For a lawyer, she wasn't a good liar.

Which meant I could tell the truth, as far as I knew it.

"Doreen's stepson asked me to visit her yesterday. I found her dead. And Wendy Logan was found dead yesterday in her apartment." I watched Patricia, but she didn't seem to react—until I finished. "They received the same ransomware."

She didn't clutch her pearls. As tight as she'd wrapped herself up, one finger sprang loose, stroking her clavicle, the finger running back and forth across that boney ridge.

"Wendy and Doreen each knew Clarissa. Do you want to tell me what that connection is?"

"Ask Clarissa. I'm not at liberty to say anything." She folded her long, elegant hands in her lap, sat more still and erect than ever. "You know that as an attorney I'm limited—"

"I can't persuade Clarissa to talk. She knows about Doreen and Wendy, but she won't let me help. I don't know whether more people are in jeopardy. Now that I've met you—"

"Let me make inquiries." Patricia's inner lawyer seized control. "I'll call you. Perhaps later tonight."

"Will you trust me with your laptop for a few hours? I can bring it back later. I'll remove that malware. And I'd like to run some tools over the code."

"Certainly. I'll pay you the same amount those hackers demanded. Do you need my password?" She recited a string that was a good and sturdy password. I memorized it.

A call rang from the lobby. Her concierge offered to bring her mail, which seemed to be a daily practice. I gathered my jacket and her laptop and said goodbye, promising to be in touch.

"It's hard to live without my laptop," she said. "It's my lifeline, so the world doesn't pass me by."

"When I get back to my office, I'll clear the malware and then bring this back." Mentally, I calculated: meet with Brad for that after-work social thing, transport up to the hill. "Perhaps by ten o'clock, but that's not a promise."

A few more stiff pleasantries between us, and Patricia opened the door just as her concierge had his hand up to knock.

"Take the east elevator," the concierge said. "It's an express."

"Patricia." When I called her name, she glanced my way, the sunlight a bright flash behind her as clouds raced into view outside those panoramic windows, then shadowed when a cloud bank rolled over the sun. "Please call."

▪

At the espresso shop across First Avenue, I procured a doppio espresso and drank it black while standing at the bar and watching crowds hurry toward the market, skirting homeless guys who begged on the sidewalk, with and without cardboard signs.

First, I sent Pippi an email. If I delayed any longer, I'd miss that hour she gets on the Internet after homework is done. I sent her a link to a video of a cat skateboarding. And tried to affirm her piano teacher's approach without sounding like yet another adult making rules. Matt makes too many rules, as if he's scared Pippi won't grow up perfect without sufficient rules perpetually applied; but meanwhile, look at me: I grew up with no rules whatsoever, and it's not as if I'm an immoral, sociopathic beast.

> "Hey, Pippi. The metronome is a city-gnome who's the drummer in your band. You can ask for a slower beat, but you can't

fire the metro-gnome unless he throws up in the back seat of the car more than once."

Done with world-melting break (that hole aches in my belly, the empty place that's missing Matt and Pippi), I stirred my coffee, watching the foam swirl, while I swam in a morass of ideas that refused to solidify. I fetched the thin-point Sharpie marker from my pocket and attacked a bar napkin, attempting to draw the elements of the puzzle, since Tony might be right: *it's the people, not the math that create problems.*

The first circle: Zak in Virginia. He hadn't seen the ransomware code yet. I needed to get him access, to see if we might indeed find the rattphukker together. But that had to wait while a national security emergency consumed all his time and attention.

The next circle was Doreen Monroe, just down the street from where I live. Zak saw her only at Christmas, and they spoke infrequently. Mostly what they shared was a last name.

The circle for Wendy was way over in Hong Kong. But she wrote to Clarissa. Like Doreen did. So all three belong in the same bubble. And so did Patricia, as it turned out. Two of the four alive, those two not telling me anything.

A felt-tip pen line connected Zak to the bubble. Then two more spokes for two more sons: Brad, who didn't know the details of Patricia's malware, since he was busy with aDVers; and Tony who, God only knows why, I believed to be a good guy, at least in this morass. What did the spokes have in common with the inner hub of four women?

Technical craft—Zak and Tony for sure; Brad knows enough that he could remove a hack like this ransomware. If he had time. But Brad couldn't know how to create it.

Distant or estranged relationships with the women in the bubble—except for Brad.

A life, for better or worse, spent wandering the darknet—except for Brad.

Frequent engagements with national and international law enforcement—except for Brad, who needed to hire me for that.

Seattle background, but none of them have lived here for more than a decade—except for Brad.

None of the sons knew the other women. Or each other.

No connections beyond me sketching on a small square napkin where spilled espresso made the ink bleed. That throwaway phone from Tony tugged at the lining of my inner jacket pocket. I sent him a simple text.

> ↳2068888888:
> No progress no insight

Then I put the same message in our private Client#0 project. And got no answer from Tony either way. Snapped a picture of my drawing and added it to that project, although the drawing was incomplete.

Back on the street. The sun was now occluded and rain threatened. I wiggled past a trio of street people who seemed to be amusing themselves by hassling pedestrians. I balanced on the curb edge, impatient for the Walk sign. One of the trio called after me.

"You'd be pretty if you smiled."

My phone buzzed with a message from Dan Llewelyn. Hell, I'm the one who claims to know rich people casually, so yeah, I get personal invitations via text.

> ↲Dan:
> I'm downtown for after-work drinks. Join us?

> ↳Sam:
> Finishing a client meeting near the Market

> ↲Dan:
> Please come

He sent a nearby but unfamiliar address.

> ↳Sam:
> 1 drink maybe. I have a lot of work tonite.

The address was on the edge of Belltown, just north of the downtown core. That neighborhood now consists of eight- and ten-story apartments that look like they came out of Ikea boxes, having replaced most of the old union hiring halls. Wrought-iron gates across street-level archways, which open only if you know the digital code, serve to keep the homeless from sleeping anywhere but flat-out on the concrete sidewalk, which is usually wide enough that you can walk past without stepping into the street.

On First Avenue headed north toward Virginia Street, another guy catcalled, hoping to provoke a response from my stoic resting face—not bitch-face, just serious. I responded the same way as every woman that dude might catcall; that is, not at all. We all learn to ignore that by seventh grade, right?

Dan:
I'm nearby. Send my driver to pick you up?

Sam:
Will walk. Just blocks away

My cellphone rang. Patricia's ID. As I thumbed to answer, a hand reached from behind and jerked it from my grasp.

"Hey!"

When I turned, a palm mashed the phone into my face.

Pain wracked through my legs. I fell to the ground.

The next thing: fire in my head.

Maybe I lost consciousness for a moment. I tried to move, but seemed to be paralyzed, like in a dream. *Can you breathe?* My First Responder kicked in, checking whether I was conscious and breathing. When I finally opened my eyes, a frisee was licking me. No, that's fancy salad. A Bichon Frisé, a fancy dog, licked my face.

The owner, attached to a retractable leash, stood ten paces away, huddled within the safety of his dark-blue parka, hands jammed in his jeans, a Seattle mist clouding his glasses.

"Do you need help? Should I call 9–1–1?"

Do I look like I need help? "Can I get a hand up? Please?"

Though I reached out, it felt like I'd best lay still a moment longer, but it also felt like filthy, broken, oily pavement. My face was wet from mist and dog spittle.

The dog sat back on its haunches, head cocked, eyes brimming with compassion. The guy stood, shuffling one glowing white Adidas sneaker, hands still in his pockets.

"A guy shoved past me at the corner. A dirty, skinny bum. One of those guys who…"

He went into a diatribe about the rude homeless, their jaywalking habits, their aggressive panhandling when all he wants to do is keep dry while waiting in line at Cinerama for a Star Wars movie. How they pee in doorways and the police won't do squat about it.

Struggled to my feet. No phone. No messenger bag. No ransomware laptop.

Wallet and Tony's throwaway phone still in my jacket pocket.

Dog-walker said, "I'll call the cops for you. But I bet they won't do anything."

Trying not to jar my bruised bones, I managed a few shaky steps to the corner. When I passed the guy, he stood straight.

"Oh. You're not a guy." He swapped the leash to his other hand and reeled in his little dog. "You sure you're okay? Shall I call a cab? Can I help?"

"I'm meeting a friend just down the street." *And you, my ineffective Samaritan, are useless.*

Cute dog though.

8

Season of the Witch

IN BELLTOWN, MY HEAD STILL aching, looking over my shoulder so often that I stumbled three times on trash and sticky walkways, I followed the convoluted directions in Dan's text message. On Fifth Avenue, the monorail cast moody shadows where new South Lake Union construction had not yet extended its modernizing claws.

If I'm scared, the terrorists win.

If I'm a girl and I text while I'm walking, the muggers win.

Mind you, I'm not victim-blaming.

But remind me to change my middle name to Derp.

When I found the address, it was a metal-clad door with an excessively buff guy in all black standing out front. I told him my name. He swiped a badge to open the door and wished me a good evening. The rubberized, nonskid treads, worn down to the wood in the center, amplified the sound of my footsteps as I climbed what felt like two stories without an interim landing.

At the top, another security guy, also in black, again asked my name and then swiped a badge. Double-doors swung open, like an old-style passage into a restaurant kitchen. I asked the guy for the ladies room, and he pointed down the nearest hallway. I slipped in to repair the worst effects of my face being pressed against oily pavement, preparing to be social when what I most wanted was a shower and solitude.

The girls' john offered cotton hand towels. I smeared alley grime off my leather jacket, which now looked like it had never met a rich lady. Finger combed my hair. Thumbed what was left of my eyeliner so I appeared less insane. Wiped away alley grunge from my face, macadam crumbs leaving red scratches along one cheek.

Then I returned to the main room, one of those new faux-speakeasy night clubs. Under the dusky light, I made out an old saloon-style bar on the far side. A few young tester types leaned against it, holding schooners of beer aloft as if to check the color in the dim light. At one far corner of the room, a small, single-riser stage overlaid with Persian rugs held a trap set and several guitars propped on stands.

It also held Jason Taylor and that shaved-head guy from his band, who seemed to be leading a guitar clinic. From what I could hear, the topic was tuning and string choices. My crossing the room disturbed the shadows enough that Jason looked up and then recognized me. After a few words to his friends, he crossed to shake my hand.

"Hey. I didn't get a chance to thank you yesterday. You were as heroic as your brother Pete claims you are."

"No big deal." Dammit.

"Come to jam, Sam?"

"Dan invited me to meet some people."

"Okay. Come play with us before you leave."

"Love to, except I'm here for work."

"Everyone is." He laughed. "Ian and I are getting paid a ridiculous sum to drop in and have fun. Billionaire creating a playground for yuppie scum, eh?"

Jason went back to his clinic, leaving me to think, hey, I'm a mediocre guitarist. You could pay me a mediocre salary to hang in a fake seedy club and show people how to tune a guitar. I can also teach you to play "Gloria" really LOUD.

Dan sat alone in a booth diagonally across from the bar. In the dark corner near Dan, everyone at the other tables were all guys, save for one woman, whose hair and manner announced ex-mil. I glanced down.

Cop shoes. All of them.

Of course. No one with Dan's wealth walks the streets of Seattle unprotected. As I approached his table, Dan rose and greeted me, the friendliest smile I'd received since—

I don't know.

My guard goes up when people are friendly in this business. Someone always wants something from me, and Natalia has repeatedly made the point that I don't know how to value myself on the market. And I'd come here, agreeing to meet others in this marketplace. I scanned for Natalia.

As if reading my mind, Dan said, "Natalia has a sick child and can't make it." He held up his cell, showing her message.

> ♂NataliaDragon:
> Anything Sam says is true for me.

There we were, in what passes for gritty in the new Seattle: a fake grunge bar, booths with real Naugahyde upholstery (free of duct tape patches), a real musician pretending to be casually hanging. Guarded by high-end security muscle.

After a brief gesture from Dan, I had a drink in hand (faux Prohibition Era cocktail) and then was meeting people he motioned over to our table: the group of tester-type guys at the bar, and then a pair of women from a developer team. They each seemed too nervous to say more than how-do-you-do.

Brad Jones slipped into the booth beside Dan, first nodding hello, then seeing me under the grunge light.

"Sam, you're hurt!"

"Only mugged. And my cellphone grabbed." I didn't want to call attention, but couldn't dodge it.

"In this neighborhood? What did the police say?"

"I'll report it later. They aren't going to catch the guy."

"You need to report it now." Dan scolded me gently in his raspy, whisper voice.

"They can't do anything about it."

"You must add to the statistics." Dan paused. It's not that he's breathless when he speaks. It's just—odd. "The City Council needs data to make downtown safer."

Hovering at the edge of our table, a third person: that horse-faced reporter from the high school gym and the morning line at Espresso and Shoeshine. I'd been busy being nice, so I don't think I scowled when I greeted him.

"It's Victor, isn't it? You didn't write about yesterday's debacle, did you?"

"No, Ms. Byron. I'm working on a deeper story. Sorry I didn't recognize you yesterday morning."

How reassuring: a tech reporter in Seattle didn't recognize me. After all of last year's headlines. But Victor kept talking.

"And I thought you knew me."

The *tabula rasa* expression crossing my face seemed to prompt Brad to rescue the situation. "Victor's book made quite a splash last year. You remember *Trolling the Generals*?"

"Of course." Yes, that silly claim about cyber psy-ops in the Middle East, describing nothing more sophisticated than what that auditorium full of script kiddies might deploy. I can write a book: *Cyber Charlatans I Have Known.*

In a brief few moments, everyone came to know how Victor and I met. Victor, invited to sit with us, wanted to remark on the astounding coincidences. Dan, however, redirected everyone's attention to my street adventure. He motioned to Brad, who held out his cell, offering to help.

"Belltown has been a disaster for years," Dan said. While he talked, Brad displayed the website for my cell carrier, so I could lock my stolen phone. My jacket pocket still dragged against my breast, but I'd wasn't keen on using Tony's throwaway to call the cops. Dan continued his complaint. "The merchant association isn't strong, though it's a better lately. But independents need to work together to create the world they want."

Brad next had the SPD website on his phone, so I could report being bashed in the face and robbed. Dan continued. "Several great restaurants have fled the area. If you don't work here, there's no reason to come to Belltown for business. It's a difficult cycle to undo. Now it seems to be solely on the backs of the tech sector to mend things."

While nodding and saying uh-huh, as if I'd gotten a certificate in human sociability training, I tapped details on the phone screen, and the SPD form sent a confirmation to my email, with a promise that the police will be contacting me, plus a report number for the insurance.

"It's Patricia's laptop that's lost." I handed Brad back his phone, having to admit I'd lost his mother's computer.

"Believe me, her files are well backed up," Brad bragged. "Otherwise, what's the use of having me for a son?"

"Fantastic." Actually, the best news in the past hour. "Can you get me access to the backups?" I sounded far too eager. "I'm curious how that malware came to be embedded in such a secure system." I was also thinking that I'd call Patricia as soon as this social hour concluded, for another conversation about her connection with Clarissa Dalloway. Or whoever that damned grifter might be.

Brad thumbed through screens. Under the noir lighting of the fake speakeasy, Brad's face glowed white, reflecting the light of his phone, giving him the look of a monk bent over his manuscript. But then his phone buzzed and the screen-light dimmed when he swiped to switch to read messages. His eyes widened, and he rose in such haste that Victor's drink sloshed onto his tweedy sports coat.

"I'm sorry, Dan. Sam." He nodded my way. "My mother's bio-alert went off. The EMT guys are there now. I have to go."

▪

I'm a mathematician. I don't like coincidences.

But I said that already.

▪

Brad shoved past Victor. I wanted to go with him, to see Patricia. So badly that I stood at the same moment he did. But Brad sprinted through the club and out the swinging double doors.

"Brad is a good man." Dan watched the departure. He set down his cup, which was when I first noticed that he drank tea, not a cocktail like he'd ordered for each person who joined him. "The real thing. Perhaps the most sincere man I know."

"His poor mother." What the hell—I'd called Doreen and then Wendy *poor woman* in the wee hours. My pulse pounded, and I gripped that stupid cocktail glass far too hard.

"Are you all right? Sam?" Dan looked up where I still stood. Shaking inside.

"Maybe she hit her head," Victor offered.

Yes, I'd been unconscious, for however many seconds. Yes, a First Responder knows to consult a doctor if there's a loss of consciousness.

"Let me call my physician." Dan had his phone in hand.

"No, I'm fine." I sat down, feeling worthless. Hadn't protected anyone. Hadn't found a single clue. Yeah, zero steps forward on my way toward doing good in the world.

And everyone was staring at me.

I sank back onto the butt-warmed Naugahyde bench. "Just worried for Brad's mom."

Victor and Dan seemed to be negotiating some detail, which was when I gathered enough awareness that Victor had a writing project related to Dan.

"But not aDVers," Dan was saying. "Only historic projects."

"Yes." Victor flipped pages in a notepad. "I have the names for interviews and restrictions from your assistant."

"One of your interview targets is right there." Dan pointed across the room, where a clutch of men in jeans and flannels stood watching while Jason taught guitar techniques. One guy held up an empty pitcher, signaling the bartender for more. "Seize the opportunity."

Victor offered me a common-place farewell and joined the table of beer sippers.

Dan again said, "I'm happy we have a few moments alone." Which meant that the cop-shoe guys at the corner table didn't count as company. "Brad and I were too eager to tell our story this morning. I want to hear yours."

"Oh, yes." I shifted for a comfortable seat. My shoulder ached. Likely I hadn't been hit on the head. "The champion salesman's secret: let the target talk."

"Ah, you wound me to the core." He pretended to clutch his heart. "We earned that, your cynical view of us. All that talking, pushing you to say yes."

"Natalia and I remain committed to our new venture. You and I can enjoy this evening more if you accept that 'no' is my likely answer. We can move on to other topics."

"Fine, Sam. I'll stop harassing you. Though you know I hold a secret hope you'll change your mind. Now, satisfy my curiosity. Tell me how you ended up here."

"I walked down Pine and then over to Virginia, with that slight side adventure." I offered my brightest smile, assuming Dan might take a friendly joke as warning.

"You won't credit me with being genuinely interested?" His eyes twinkled, if that's possible under the faux-noir lighting.

"Best guess? My adventures this afternoon are the only detail missing in your recruiting staff's research." I disliked the Simple Syrup-laden drink, but pretended to sip it. "That, and what I had for lunch after we met this morning. You're free to ask, Dan, but your recruiters must report that I'm an extraordinarily private person."

"Perhaps, like me, you have to be." He considered it, and then nodded as if deciding. "Yes, you and I must be alike that way. Especially after the beating you took online last year. Slim reward for being a hero. Which you were."

"Thank you for saying so. In fact, being attacked in every single online forum turned out to be a time saver. A simplified life is a good life."

"Brad and I shared our secrets today. Couldn't you return that trust and share with me?"

"There's part of my sandwich left over, back at the office. I'd share that." I shrink at the idea of secrets. "Your recruiter's research people probably already know."

A wry, lopsided smile floated up the left side of his face, wrecking his symmetrical Zen-like calm. "Fine. Let's trade pretend secrets. Tell me one of your sock puppet names. I'd enjoy following what your secret identity does online. Do you ever troll yourself? "

"I decline to incriminate myself."

"And I cannot help indulging myself. Here's one of mine." He scratched on the drink coaster with the pen from his inner pocket. "Every time Daniel Alfred Llewelyn, the philanthropist appears in the news, I troll along with the disaffected, complaining that he hasn't done nearly enough for the local community. The *Seattle Times* comments are the most enjoyable."

"You're DougFromTukwila? 'If Daniel Llewelyn really cared about Seattle, he'd bring the Sonics back.' That's you?"

Dan tipped an approving finger my way. "'If he dug the spare change out of his sofa, we'd have an NHL team.'"

"And an arena to play in? Or does DougFromTukwila want King County and the City to pay for that?"

Dan sobered, as if a switch had been toggled off. "I don't enjoy those trolls' claims, that if only I'd do the right thing, there'd be no poverty in the Greater Seattle area."

"A communistic notion."

He raised his left shoulder, a small but characteristic move I'd begun to notice, like a young boy embarrassed by praise. "I can't plead my case to the caustic public, that I'm plowing every spare penny into the work at aDVers."

"Are you pitching me again?" I shoved my sticky-rimmed drink aside, having no conceivable reason to fake drinking. "Because I get it, the importance of what aDVers is doing. I'm profoundly moved."

"Thank you again, especially since we both agree you aren't interested in flattering me." Dan held up his tea cup, inquiring whether I wanted the same. In the blink of his topaz eyes, a fresh pot and two cups appeared before us. "Here's what I don't understand. How can your new business support both your sense of social responsibility and your extraordinary talents? Both yours and Natalia Dragon's."

When I started to answer, he held up his parchment-pale hand. "Please don't mistake me. I don't mean money or measures that—"

"The kind of measures that are valued by corporate masters?"

"Ah, but if you collaborate with me, I promise to never consider myself your master." He poured tea into the two cups. "You will always be free to do what you believe is right. Sugar?"

"Selling again, Dan?" I covered the cup, indicating no to either sugar or milk. In fact, we were enjoying ourselves. That sense of friendship that had grabbed me in the conference room settled in place, interrupted only every twenty heartbeats or so with thoughts of Patricia Yates in jeopardy.

"I'm worse than your online jackanapes." He grinned. "Can't stop begging for your attention, whatever you say."

Jason struck a chord just then. On stage, a woman had taken up the bass and one of the tester dudes sat at the traps. Even before Jason began to sing, Dan nodded with the beat.

"Perfect. A stalker song. You'll think I even paid Jason Taylor to persuade you."

Jason sang the first verse of "I Put a Spell on You" and then played it as an instrumental, since this was supposed to be a lesson for the bass player.

"'Pushin' Too Hard,'" I said.

"'I Will Possess Your Heart.'" Dan bit his lip, pretending to be shy of his own joke.

"'Changed the Locks.'"

"'Can't Stand Losing You.'" Little-boy shrug again.

"'Run For Your Life.'"

"The Beatles?" Dan pondered that. "You're too young to have that in the soundtrack of your life."

"My father was devoted. They came to America the year he turned fourteen. Had a profound emotional impact."

"We're the same age then. Tremendous impact on my adolescence. Then I found Dylan, The Cream, and later influences."

"They always ask musicians about their influences," I mused. "But no one asks coders. It's got to matter."

He sipped his tea. "I'd like to meet your father. To see how a child like you was molded—"

"Oh no, you don't." I laughed at him openly. "Surely your recruiters reported that. Family is off limits."

Jason was singing another verse, signaling to the players to raise the intensity, which raised the sound just when one of the jeans-and-plaid-flannel guys loomed over us.

"Hiya, Dan!" Our visitor had the booming kind of voice that can never be quiet, so had no problem speaking over the music. "This here the little girl you told me about? That you need so bad? Or did you pay Joan Jett to date you?"

Emotion wiped from Dan's face faster than Jason's arpeggio. The happy tone gone from his voice, Dan said, "This is Samsara Byron. Sam, please meet Luke Connor."

"Pleased to meetcha." Luke stuck out a huge paw and grasped mine before I was ready.

"He's an aDVers board member these days," Dan said, "but we've worked together since—"

"Since God made mud." Luke choked, laughing at his own hokey joke. A stocky guy, not as tall as me, so maybe five-eight, Luke was the one who led your high school wrestling team to State and then never let you forget. He had the lumpy face of a badly aging rock star who smoked and—in contrast with the signature Pacific Northwest plaid flannels—dyed his thinning hair a shade too dark. And he reeked: the barnyard odor of a pipe smoker. "Bet ol' Dan's been telling about the old days, huh?"

"No, we—"

"We be the best back then." Luke clearly liked conversation, but only when he was speaking. "Like winning Super Bowl five years in a row, eh, bro?"

Dan stared at the table, the way you do when someone is embarrassing you. Jason was still teaching his pupils to wail on "Put a Spell." I tried to speak again.

"We're discussing whether I'd like working at aDVers. That idea seems to be—"

"You Millennials. Wanting it only your way. Don't you see? You gotta serve your time to learn how it is." Luke nodded in agreement with himself.

At that moment, Victor appeared beside him. Luke draped an arm over Victor's shoulder, though I didn't see Victor wanting to cuddle up with him.

"Look, here." Luke continued with the conversation that no one else could join. "Dan says you and I gotta talk, so you can hear from the horse's mouth how good it is to work in ol' Daniel's business. And Dan says I need to sit still for Victor's interview. Why don't we wrap it all together, and you both come by my house tomorrow?"

Dan nodded once. "A fine idea. Can you and Natalia be free, Sam? Just a last favor before I…'Give You Up'? "

"I'll check with Natalia." Automatically reached for my phone, which was, of course, gone.

"Brad will come, too." Dan seemed free to commit for Brad.

"Works for me." Luke had a carnivorous grin. "If I gotta be bugged twice in a month, then you-ones gotta bring it on all at once."

The last chords of "Put a Spell" finished while Luke and Victor were saying goodbye or otherwise consulting over which set of insults to next shovel onto me. The sound system screeched, the way certain musicians know to do on purpose.

"Sam Byron?" Jason's voice purred into the microphone. "You promised to play with me tonight. Come show us amateurs how it's done."

▪

"You looked like maybe you needed rescue," Jason said. His partner Ian surrendered his guitar to me, claiming he wanted a break. "That guy and his friends began shouting Led Zeppelin song titles at us as soon as they got here. Didn't seem like he was charming you either."

"Thanks. What to play?" I strapped on.

"Your brother Pete says you do a mean 'Witch'."

"Hope he was talking about a song. And not Donovan's."

Jason struck an E chord. "Nope. The Sonics."

His student drummer did just fine when Jason indicated the count. *Well, you better watch out.* Because I hadn't needed to wail on those strings in quite that way for a long time.

You better be careful.

About the time we hit the Sonics' warning to be careful, I heard a gap in the bass line and turned to see.

Dan replaced the student. And quickly set the bass line again. I'd been so focused on the white hair, white complexion, the whispery voice, I'd begun to think of Dan as infirm.

Jason, the master of the long interlude, kept us at it, as if he understood how much I needed a long, hard bout at the guitar dojo, and after I'd screamed for a bit, he transitioned us to "Psycho" and had the three of us, heads together—Dan and I are the same height, Jason a hand taller—playing like the Garage Band of the Gods.

▪

"Sweat's good for you."

Dan and I accepted towels from Jason. We'd only played four songs, but you'd think it was a Pilates class instead of a faux nightclub. Jason shook our hands, promised we could jam any time, and then greeted the next students for his clinic. His partner Ian reclaimed his guitar. And I was ready to go home.

"Stay a moment longer, Sam?"

Dan motioned me back to his dark corner, now lit by votive candles. He glanced at his phone. "Oh, good news. Brad's mother is in cardiac intensive care, but doing well." He showed me the message, which I appreciated.

After an exchange with the bartender, asking for Armagnac, Dan coughed politely. "May I tell you a story? Will you indulge me? I feel compelled to prove I share the same concerns as you."

"Please. You've been patient while I keep saying no."

"Back in the early Nineties—"

"In the old Wild West?"

That flicker of a smile he shared when he appreciated my humor. "People had been inventing like crazy for a decade. Gangs of post-graduates and dropout geniuses hoping to be Bell Labs or Menlo Park."

"But in garages or office parks."

"Yes, Sam. Backed by modest corporate sponsors or no sponsors at all. Using their own cash to survive,"

"Someone," I said, "still needed to invent angel investors and IPOs and corporate acquisitions."

Dan grimaced, an acknowledgment. Our Armagnac arrived.

Not yet sipping, I said, "I feel bad, introducing the devil of capitalism into your story of the halcyon days."

His eyes twinkled again. Or maybe it was the candlelight. "Back when team leaders sold weed to meet living expenses? Yes. Back then. I worked on the most inventive, creative team I've ever had the joy and privilege to be part of. Perhaps everything I've done since is to recreate that energy and comradery."

The moody passion with which Dan described that team threw me back to the Clean Room in Virginia where Zak and the rest of us worked insane hours, thrilled by what we'd achieved while subsisting on coffee and box lunches delivered by the admin assistants, who performed their tasks like empathetic zookeepers. I nodded and uh-huh'd to urge more story from Dan.

"My team—mostly from Burlington and Princeton—was intent on driving the notion of digital watermarking to its logical extreme. We called our work Prometheus."

"Stealing fire from the gods?" I'm a mathematician, but I paid attention in my pass-fail World Lit class.

"Yes. We knew it was an extremely competitive race. You can see the depth of the competition in the papers submitted to journals back then."

"Or in disappeared research on the darknet." The light of the votive candle flickered in his eyes. He liked my barbs and asides, which only encourages me. "And at the end of the race?"

"We lost. Don't pretend you don't know." Dan tapped the table, his voice barely loud enough to be heard over the faux speakeasy noise. "Tirkel and Osborne got there a hair's breadth before us. Filed their patent and closed groundbreaking business deals with the major media corporations."

"That must have been—"

"Devastating. Only word for it." He leaned close, sharing a confidence. "You and I are discovering ways we're alike. Yet I don't know if we have that similar experience. Having the greatest creation in your life come to—nothing."

The palpable emotion he expressed gave me pause. Dan tipped his long, narrow face as if in prayer, pondering loss.

"Yes, I have experienced that. When Z-Crypto was sold into the national security system of contractors, so we could no longer pursue pure research. Only solve assigned problems."

Dan glanced up, startled. His hand lifted, as if beyond his control, trembling until he resumed his usual calm. My simple claim included an accusation: that he'd engineered the sale of Z-Crypto in pursuit of employing me. And neither of us benefited.

"I'm guilty," he said, "of gambling without knowing the consequences. And I just did it again, didn't I?"

"Most of the developers you bought last month claim they like working for you. Even though they weren't your intended acquisition target."

"But my hidden agenda negatively affected your life. I apologize. Sincerely. It's the kind of corporate…interference that I hated back in the old days."

"Me, I was born too late for the old days. Back when developers programmed to bare metal."

He grinned. "You've had other old codgers claim that, eh? Back when we coded uphill both ways through the snow."

"But do you see now how we're different?" I said. "For me, my work is not about the size of the battles I seek to win. I don't need my own Wikipedia article, whether it claims I won the patent battle or only came in second. I don't care."

Dan sat back, rubbing his chin, deep in thought.

"That's the gulf between us." I wasn't inclined to provide a topological map to describe a path through the gulf.

He accepted my claim. "Let's explore that idea more. Do you know how my team recovered from that loss?"

"You switched to Zeus, your secure BIOS work. Then got bought by one of the eight-hundred-pound gorillas in the computing industry, making you all rich as Midas."

"And our original watermarking solution, which contributed to the mythical Prometheus?" He prodded. "How good is your knowledge of early history?"

"Pretty limited. Did a patent troll buy the watermarking inventions and then sell to the government?" Patent trolls buy inventors' rights but then are more likely to sue other inventors for "infringing" than they are to invest time and money implementing the invention.

More of that twinkling, professorial smile, with crow's feet at the corners of his eyes. "We created our own trust, and worked as our own patent trolls. The trust has only one customer."

"The U.S. government." I struggled against physically pulling away from him. "We aren't alike at all."

"Oh, but yes, we are. I have the profound assurance in my life that you seek in yours. My best work, so far, is being used for good. It was like selling safety equipment that can't be weaponized. It's used to protect my nation's secrets."

"And that's why you turned up to observe our efforts in that 'mythical watermarking' trial." I'd long been used to anonymous suits wanting details about our security research methods. "Don't know how I'd have felt that day if I knew the inventor was in the room. Were you laughing at us? What did we miss by guessing?"

"The Prometheus solution included steganography."

"How humiliating that we didn't see it." No exaggeration: I felt my face flush at a research error from two years ago.

"The message was hidden." He pursed his lips, laughing at his own joke: Steganography is the ancient art of hiding a message in an image.

"What else is special about Prometheus?" I felt free to ask, because we were trading stories about work, and because talking with Dan offered the most interesting conversation I'd had in a while, aside from the last year's close work with Natalia. "Fibonacci sequence? Medieval Arabic numerology?"

He started to answer, then stopped, mouth still open when Jason Taylor counted out the start to another song.

"One. Seven. Eleven."

Dan pointed toward the band with a laugh: Jason led his student musicians in a Black Flag math rock song, dissonance with an excessively non-standard time signature.

"Can I brag about Prometheus?" Dan did that thing guys do, pretending to be modest while preparing to boast.

"Please. Especially after the embarrassing flattery you heaped on me today." The music volume forced us to sit close and shout our secrets.

Dan said, "We invented an extraordinarily sturdy mathematical solution for extracting the digital watermark from the media where it's embedded."

"Is it a backdoor into the whole solution? Were Zak and I on the right track?" A backdoor is a code secret added to a cryptographic security solutions. Anyone who gains possession of a system's backdoor secret can subvert that system's security.

"Someone less sophisticated than you might call the Prometheus extraction solution a backdoor. You'd call it—"

"A trapdoor." That means the complex encryption math is like the key to the padlock that locked the door to begin with, rather than a secret that can defeat overall security.

"So no actual backdoor?"

"Our customer did request a true backdoor." Dan's whisper-voice caused me to lean even closer. To hear the secret he shared. "But rather, there are dozens of false entrances into a maze. You, Sam, were on the outer edge, identifying individual trees in a large forest."

"They keep asking, the NSA and FBI. Demanding backdoors, as if by magic they alone will have access." I fumed over this technological and political sore point. "If your customer had half a brain—"

Dan smiled, nodding in agreement, but raised an admonishing finger. "Institutions do not have brains. And, yes, we agree. That customer resists understanding the broad negative potential of back-doors. They also want strong fences, to ensure no one else can find that backdoor. Therefore, we're still called to consult. My old team, I mean. The few of us left."

"Who are they?" I tried to call up that history, but my memory returned null. Couldn't picture a single face or name. The band played an especially dissonant bridge while I pondered.

"My generation isn't doing well for longevity. Of the six of us, all that's left are Luke, Charlie Thomas, and me. Charlie was a tester, not an inventor. But in those days, we were committed to sharing equally."

"Luke Connor? Who—"

"Insulted you earlier? He's not the most socially aware member of the developer community. Libertarian philosophy has a seductive attraction for Luke, in spite of how good capitalism has been to him."

"At least he's a genius," I said. Most Ayn Rand disciples I've met don't approach genius in their code. But if I say so on the Internetz, Harley will be shoveling my Sisyphean stables till Doomsday.

"Luke had his role on the old team and still performs for this new team. I hope that little fiasco earlier didn't put you off meeting with him tomorrow."

"No. But then, 'no' is what I've been telling you all day." Jason's make-do band built a skin-crawling crescendo to punctuate my "no," reminding me that this conversation about mathematical secrets was in an off-kilter nightclub.

Dan set down his empty glass. "Sam, here's an easy question. What's the biggest challenge for secure computing?"

"Quantum computing." What's more fun that geeking out about technology in a rich man's fake bar with live music in the background? "Hardware is ten times more powerful than what we had ten years ago. Leading to neural networks that can easily break most authentication algorithms."

"And what's the solution?"

"Migrating to quantum-resistant algorithms. Taking the Web beyond HTTPS."

"And what can you personally do in your new business to help meet the greatest challenge?"

"We'll find our way." My voice sounded like a confused undergraduate. Sleep, that's what I needed. After I returned to my own Clean Room to examine the ransomware problem.

"I hope so. Meanwhile, I'll not harass you."

"Thank you."

Dan made another covert signal, a motion of his hand that could be mistaken for a tremor; one of those cop-shoe guys started a discussion with the bartender.

"But my offer is always open to you. And Natalia."

"That's what you want to do?" I believe my smile was as friendly as I was feeling. "'To Wish Impossible Things'?"

"'Boys Don't Cry.'"

▪

Different from how you fall in love: the moment you recognize that a new acquaintance is a friend. An actual friend. For example, Natalia and I began at dagger-points with each other professionally, but then one day we walked over to the federal courthouse to testify in a computer fraud case. In the shadows under the monorail, two goths kissed, smearing their black lipstick. We each broke into exactly the same line from The Cure: *Kiss Me Kiss Me Kiss Me.* Natalia stopped in her tracks, grabbed my shoulder, whispered in my ear.

"Why can't I be you?"

From that moment, we've been trusted friends, watching out for each other, second-guessing needs or giving space as the moment requires. Yeah, it doesn't sound rational, but the result—deep empathy—never sounds rational.

I digress in order to explain why I let someone like Dan inside my wall. *Someone like Dan.* What does that even mean? Twenty-some people in the world who might approximate the basic elements of "Dan" likely couldn't match guitar licks with me. Probably fewer than twenty people in the world get my jokes, much less laugh at them.

Like the music we'd played, there's a rhythm to the birth of a friendship. With a lover, there's rhythm in bed and then later finding you can walk down the street together in sync. With a friend, there's the thrill of being understood in mutable and changing layers of meaning and experience. And the grace of silences. Is that when you know you're truly friends, not merely kindly acquaintances—when you're both comfortable with silence?

Of course, Dan offered me a ride home. When I declined, he offered me a guy from his security detail.

"Or a woman, if you prefer." He stood when I did. "If you come work at aDVers, you'll have your own personal security. But I can lend you help now, from my personal crew."

"Thanks. You're kind, but I don't need it."

"You were just assaulted." His forehead wrinkled in concern.

"Random acts in the city." And my own embarrassing gap in the business of paying attention. Also, a Seattle grrrl in black jeans doesn't have a security detail. I pointed across the room. "Look at Jason Taylor. Rich. Famous. No personal security."

Dan actually bit at his lip, as if to keep from saying something, then shook his head, disappointed at my refusal. "Well then, stay safe, my friend."

Since I was downtown, I stopped at the phone store, just before they closed. They confirmed that my old phone was blocked and sold me a new one. We looked for calls made after the phone was stolen: None.

No jail-break of the phone. No sign that my mugger conquered the phone's PIN to call his mother. Or order pizza. The GPS wasn't announcing a location, so the phone must be off.

After I retrieved my data from the cloud, I felt bruised and battered enough to justify a cab ride. Dan sent me another thank-you-for-coming text. I switched his name in my address book, which he noticed right away, and then he started another jokey song-title exchange.

DougFromTukwila:
Call on Me

Sam:
Call Me the Breeze

DougFromTukwila:
You Can Call Me Al

Sam:
Why'd You Only Call Me When You're High

DougFromTukwila:
Just Call Me Lonesome

Sam:
Call Me Irresponsible

Common sense stopped me part way through tapping "You Call Me a Bitch Like It's a Bad Thing." Okay, dumb. But I needed dumb and funny after that day's events. And I had to stop fooling around in order to answer another text.

MattOwens:
Come to VA this weekend. Miss you too much.

Yes! Take a cab directly to Sea-Tac, the next flight to Ronald Reagan Airport. A rental car—and then I could snuggle up with Matt and Pippi. Send out for pizza and ice cream. Watch a top-chef cooking show.

Sam:
Can't. Have a client. 2 clients.

In the office, Harley still huddled over his work, with two more monitors now surrounding him, as if he were expanding his real estate as fast as he was proving useful.

"Hey, Harley. Catching the last ferry home?" He, among all the Owenses, was the only one holding down the homefront on Limberlost Island, since his wife Roz was in Virginia with Matt and Pippi.

He glanced at the clock—either he or Natalia had moved it out of the Clean Room. "Lost track of time. What is this?" He pointed to an image on one of the monitors.

An image I'd seen before. "Some guy jizzed off on my Twitter picture. Follow general practice: block and ignore."

Harley expressed dismay, finally turning around to talk. He blinked a couple of times, likely adjusting his distance vision after too much screen time. He didn't like what he saw. "What happened to you?"

"Is it that bad? I thought I fixed most of the damage."

Then I repeated the story for yet one more outraged man to express dismay. And reassured him that I'd filed a police report.

"We can file for insurance tomorrow."

"It's not just about for the insurance." He was shaking his head. "I'm feeling badness in my bones. Makes me sniff the air like in the old days, trying to find which direction there's a fire burning, and whether the wind is fanning the flames."

"Stuff happens. I let my attention slip for a minute—"

"There's too damn many coincidences, Sam. These messages coming over most every cyberwall you showed me. Jackholes threatening rape and knives to your delicate parts—"

"Oh, Harley. I shouldn't have given you that job. Those aren't threats to me personally. It's just bad behavior on the playground."

He huffed, like we were back fifteen years, and it's a school night, and he's asking me how this car got fifteen miles from where it was last parked to being where my brother Pete and I are hanging at the city park, swinging and smoking unfiltered Camels (my smart-ass mouth tasting like five camels actually caravanned through it).

"There are coincidences one creates for oneself," I said, indignant about Harley's supposition that I can't take care of myself. "And others the universe creates."

"The universe didn't mug you. Did you include information about this harassment in the police report? Or explain what's on that stolen computer?"

"I sent a message to my detective friend. But what can SPD do with the data we have? They can't trace malware on a stolen PC. In fact, they can't trace the stolen PC if it isn't turned on."

"Stalking and harassment have precise legal definitions." Harley gave me a Viking king stare, intended to bring not-innocent juveniles to their knees, to accept his scolding. "You visit two women with the same malware, and they end up dead or in the hospital. And you're lying semi-conscious in an alley saying it's a coincidence."

"I'll let my detective friend know about this second instance of ransomware." I meant Patricia's. I didn't mention Victim#0 in Hong Kong, which I hadn't yet discussed with my office crew. "But what can law enforcement do when we can't provide any connections? Or even point to how to make connections?"

"What did Matt say?" Harley asked, not answering my key question. "Does he have ideas about what's best for us to do?"

People always say they can't read me. Except Harley seems to read emotional braille.

"You haven't told Matt about the mugging?"

Twitched an eyelash in confession.

"Or about the high-school hackers harassing you?"

One hair in my left nostril jittered.

"And you didn't tell him the White Knights found you again." Harley pointed to the bank of monitors where he'd spent the day living my online life.

"Do I get any privacy in this new business arrangement?" Yes, I was grousing.

"Let me guess." He had one hand on his elbow, one on his chin, looking philosophical. "If you say it out loud, if you tell Matt, then you'll have to admit there's real danger."

"You Owens boys tend to infringe on my privacy."

"You get yourself killed, my dear friend, and the morgue report won't be private."

"You are exaggerating, Harley."

"I'm talking to the locals tomorrow on behalf of the business. Guarding against loss of business assets and advocating for the safety of personnel."

"Okay. I agree. Make sure you include that ISP address from the photo I sent you. And I swear I'm being cautious." Way more cautious than not texting while walking. "Natalia and I have to meet another aDVers board member tomorrow. Will you be in the office come morning?"

"Yes. I appointed myself receptionist." Harley began stashing his things in pockets of his jacket: reading glasses, a pen, a packet of tissues. Not the typical armaments of a Viking king. "Here's a printout of Natalia's report on that malware."

A formal memo:

> From: NDragon, network security analyst
> To: SByron, code forensics specialist
> Re: Full Report on "Phone Home" Methods and
> Broadcast Destination for Client#1 Ransomware

Then a blank page. Very funny, Ms. Dragon.

"She says it doesn't call back anywhere. Just puts up a billboard message and—"

"Fine. Do you have more reports for me?"

"Left a folder on your desk with my report on the sole Clarissa Dalloway who doesn't seem to be fictional."

He went on his way, checking that the door was locked when he closed it, while I searched for the file with Harley's report, which turned out to contain the same overwrought memo as Natalia created. In the middle of the otherwise blank PDF was an obituary notice for a woman who died in the early Seventies and was buried in Lakeview Cemetery. Remembrances to St. Joseph's Church, please.

9

Mine Smell Like Honey

UP IN MY MONK'S CELL, the shower streamed as hot as I can ever stand it, though not as hard as I needed to wash away memories of hitting the filthy pavement in that alley. At the top of Capitol Hill, new construction or not, there's no water pressure.

By the time my fingertips wrinkled, I still didn't know what to say when I called my friend Jeremiah at SPD in the morning. What more could I report? Two women died after being threatened by malware, then a third woman nearly did?

My proof of a connected crime is what, exactly? Garden-variety ransomware? Simple logic? What's my recommendation to law enforcement for their investigation? Hire Byron&Dragon to spend a great deal more time in the Clean Room? We needed to identify who sent that malware. Then the FBI might be able to find the perpetrators and perhaps learn why this was happening.

Meanwhile, Brad sent a Krypptikk message.

KRYPPTIKK JOB: CLIENT#202_JONES

BJones:

Added access permissions to the cloud folders so you can research backup files from my mother's laptop.

SByron:

Thanks. Copying to byron&dragon servers with same

folder name as this project.
I'm sorry she's ill. Wish I could help.

BJones:

Nothing much to do where I'm sitting.
About to go home for the night.
See you in the morning.

SByron:

Hope she's better soon.

This gave me three sets of ransomware-infected data to research, though (reluctantly) I'd tell Natalia about only two of them, preserving Tony's plea for secrecy. I left notes for Client#1 and Client#202, so Natalia could start her tasks in the morning.

KRYPPTIKK JOB: CLIENT#202_JONES

SByron:

Ticket #2: Search Client#202 backups for malware.

SByron:

Goal: Find backup version that contains malware.
Then write new ticket for the research.

Although I'm good at math, the available data neither adds nor multiplies. There's no algorithm, that is, no rules of logic to follow. The only apparent process available:

n(repeated stabs in the dark)

A factor—or perhaps more than one—is missing in the problem definition. And I'm damned sure Clarissa holds that factor inside her skull. Maybe that sk8ter dude can help knock it free, if I can convince him that it's an opportunity for service to a free society.

And I start talking about math when my blood stream is roiling with emotion I prefer not to feel, when there are tears I want to weep but my brain cries *nonsense.* I didn't even know Doreen or Wendy. Until yesterday, their lives and their travails and joys weren't part of my universe. Yet my heart wanted to break amid the animal rage I felt.

Innocent women died. Justice must be paid.

And if turns out that they weren't innocent for any reason, well then, courts and jurisprudence are supposed to judge and punish. Not a death sentence from nowhere.

Tied, somehow, to a piece of too-common malware code.

The First Responder sense is strong in this one, when the human damage comes from code. I worked twenty-hour days when Zak and I were mired in the Lights Out Affair, not because the math and related problems were beguiling, but because I kept thinking of the old people and the babies who were freezing in the dark, frightened, helpless. I worked as if only our efforts might save them.

Thinking about Zak, I checked Krypptikk, and found a hasty message from what must be about one a.m. his time.

> ***KRYPPTIKK JOB: CLIENT#1_MONROE***
>
> *ZakM:*
>
> > Can't help now. Not sure when. A real crisis this time, instead of the soap opera stuff you and I used to see. Showdown at the OK corral with a crowd of territorial white hats gunning for each other.

Made me laugh, thinking of Zak absorbed in battling white-hat cowboys in a national security range war. Made me sentimental about that simple time.

> Manager:
> Customer wants you to test for XYZ intrusions.
>
> Sam & Zak:
> Okay. Done. Intrusion was caused by their own secret backdoor. Give us another task.
>
> Manager:
> Customer wants you to find and close an XYZprime backdoor.
>
> Sam & Zak:
> Okay, we did that. Give us another task.

In that old world, clients didn't die. A simpler time, closer to pure math than sorting through the spaghetti problems I currently had, with my only income being the $100K in my cookie jar, which Tony paid me to play Family Feud moderator with his grifter mother.

My hair, still damp from the shower, was beginning to spring wild and free, Medusa-like, so I forced a comb through and braided it while I studied my drawing on the bar napkin, hoping to see what was missing. I held it at arm's length, my thumb over the only blank space in the drawing.

"What makes the picture complete?"

A voice in my head asked that question, as if a Bowie song played as the soundtrack to my thoughts. Before I found an answer, or got ready to go downstairs to work, Tony rang my video doorbell. Viewed on the surveillance camera at street level, he twitched with anxious energy, repeatedly looking over his shoulder to scan the street. I texted him the elevator code and opened the door so he could let himself in. While Tony rode that puny elevator upstairs, I pulled on jeans, my least rumpled t-shirt, and raggedy Vans over bare feet.

▪

"Prepare to be gob smacked!" Tony burst in like an overexcited ten-year-old, eager with his news. "I have it at last, dear heart. A genuine and useful clue!"

But I had to say what was on my mind first.

"Near as I can tell, the trouble began, when a dear friend called on me to help his mother."

"Believe me, I appreciate what you—"

"No, I mean, a real friend. My old partner Zak." Pointing to where he could sit, I stood over Tony, arms folded. "While I'm walking through fallen leaves to meet his mother, that nice woman sits down and dies."

"I'm sorry for your loss—"

"The Pirate King, my long-time nemesis, begs me to help his mother. She serves me bitter tea and buffalo chips."

"But now I know—"

"A classmate from Princeton, a stranger to you, asks me to help *his* mother. She gives me a laptop locked by ransomware. The same as on the disk you gave me."

"Another one?" Tony sat up in the chair, eyes wide.

"The third one. Then someone hits me on the head and steals my phone and that laptop."

"God, Sam. Are you all right?"

"That nice woman sits down and—but for the grace of modern bio-electronics—almost dies."

"I never meant—"

"Now you, my long-time enemy—"

"Competitor."

"You appear again. Do you have plain truths this time?"

"I've sussed out who Clarissa's chums are."

"Who else do I need to rescue by Friday?"

"It's a set of names on the OPM list. Though I'm not sure yet exactly which names."

The OPM list? The stolen list of U.S. employees' security data. My spine tingled, guessing what this meant. "They say the list includes—"

"Undercover agents? It does, though it'd be difficult to identify them—even for you."

"It'd require additional data to triangulate." I still loomed over him, stern as possible, given how scared I ought to be.

"Want to sit down, dear heart?" Tony invited me to be comfortable in my own home. "The feds are playing whack-a-mole in the dark market to find who's buying the list." The dark land where Tony lives. Where he must have bought a copy of the stolen list.

"My OPM notice came in yesterday's mail." A beside-the-point thing to say, since people weren't targeting me with ransomware.

"It's taking the personnel office a while to get to contractors." He ran his hands through his hair like a man distressed. "Generations of spycraft, protecting agents, detecting double-agents. Then a hacker kipes a list that should have been bound with seven seals."

"Meanwhile, we have to take our shoes off at the airport to be safe." I bucked up and returned to what he implied about this list. "Your mother's friends are on that list."

He leaned back in my one chair, looking a tad bit satisfied with himself. "They worked as federal contractors in Seattle."

"Wendy Logan and Doreen Monroe are on the list?"

Tony slowly licked his lips, another gesture he'd carried from the past into present day; it indicated uncertainty. "You found their names on the hard disk I gave you."

"Wendy's disk had the same ransomware as my client's laptop. So I dug to find her name. Didn't you see my message last night?"

"Too busy. Your client is one of Clarissa's chums?"

"Was. She's dead. So is Wendy Logan. Did you know?"

He stared out the window into darkness, instantly drained of all that self-satisfied, boyish energy. I sat on the bed and dragged a checkered cotton blanket around my shoulders, the one Pippi gave me for Christmas.

"Tony, did you know about Wendy Logan when you sent me to visit your mother?"

Tiny shake of his head. "I found out a couple of hours ago. The Hong Kong police uncovered a blurry image of me on the surveillance video for Wendy's building an hour before she died. Two hours before I flew to Seattle."

"Are they looking for you here?"

"Ostensibly, no one knows I'm in the U.S."

"That makes me I feel safe."

"And yet whoever I'm chasing seems to be right on my tail. I need to disappear for a while."

"Listen, Tony, if working with you will get me blown up, then I decline to participate." For a split second I was bomb-deaf again, recalling the White Knight attack on Limberlost Island. "All my decisions this year ensure I'm not a candidate for guns and grenades again."

"I do not endeavor to—didn't believe I dragged you into my world. Sorry."

"Sorry?" The word was too small in this case.

"I'm unhappy that you are uncomfortable."

"How does your mother know these women? C'mon, Tony. You hacked her email. You must know."

Chirping crickets. Then he made a suggestive move like in the old days, pulled me close, and whispered in my ear. "I think my mother is a spy."

"Think?" I wiggled away. "Like Yoda said: Not think. Know or not know."

"Nine-nines certainty. Can't prove. Most likely she's retired." Nine-nines: the certainty required for reliable server performance. Ninety-nine-point-nine-nines percent uptime. Tony folded his arms, dipped his head, shrank in size. "My guess? She's part of an old apparatus from the Cold War, kept around by the Russians. And that's what's getting her friends killed. She gathered intelligence, and they worked for her."

"Okay, James Bond. You made a leap across the rooftops that I didn't follow. I told her that Doreen and Wendy were dead. She didn't show a spark of emotion."

"See? It's why I'm King. I was trained in the womb, bred to be the Superman of the darknet." He stopped in the middle of this bravado. "That's me, gagging for a drink. I'm dying here. "

"Not a great turn of phrase." I poured a shot of whisky from the bottle of Mischief that Matt gave me for my birthday, then stuck the bottle on what passed for a kitchen shelf in the closet that pretended to be an apartment. "Given what I lived through today."

He swirled the amber liquid and sipped, lost in thought, not commenting that I'd given him expensive liquor in a jelly jar instead of a glass. After a moment he shook himself, like a swimmer emerging from icy water.

I sat on the bed, tired of looming over him. "What did you get me into?"

"You aren't involved, dear heart. But I want you to pass a crucial message. And help me with an investigation for an hour or so."

"For one hundred thousand dollars? I suppose if that was my hourly rate, I wouldn't have to consider an aDVers employment offer."

"Damn, Sam! aDVers wants to hire you?" Tony sat up, Mischief sloshing in his glass. "Do it. For more than safety. They'll let you be more productive than anyone can."

"Safety? What makes you think about that?" I hadn't focused on that part of Dan's offer.

"Long ago I was helping to battle a protection racket that was affecting American businesses in—let's say, a warm country. One of the threatened subcontractors was a friend of Daniel Llewelyn's. A couple ex-Secret Service guys came to say that Mr. Llewellyn wanted to help, because he's very loyal to his friends."

"And?"

"A Llewelyn company bought the subcontractor's business and put strong enough security in place to cover that business and all its neighbors. So, dear heart, I'd say his kind of safety leads to productivity."

"It does seem that aDVers has tight security."

"Why?" Tony wrinkled his nose, puzzled. "Doesn't aDVers do machine learning on business data? What are they up to?"

That promise made instead of the NDA I didn't sign? Therefore: "Can't say. But I'm flattered they want me to help strengthen their cybersecurity."

"But you want to go it alone."

"Dan offers an unusual chance for doing social good in the world. Better than running messages to your mother."

"'Dan'? You're on a first-name basis?" He sipped whisky again. "But didn't you once complain about the One Percent having undue influence? That it's not good for society to have a rich man running his own social agenda? Didn't you claim to prefer democratic processes?"

"It's not—I hadn't thought about it that way. He's just a guy. It's not like he's playing the Great Man in the world."

"You are very like my mother, always justifying—"

"Please stop. No intelligent man ever asserts that I'm just like his mother."

"Okay, you aren't like anyone's mother. Ready to get busy and work with me?"

"No. Just tell me the other names on the list, so I can warn them. The FBI needs to know to look out for them—"

"Stop. The locals and the FBI can't handle this." He squeezed his empty glass, distressed. "I want you safe, dear heart. After our work is done tonight, beg to find the spook in my mother's system."

"And then?"

"If you find anything crucial, talk to your old NSA pals. The ones who stepped in after you saved the utilities last year. It'll be faster and safer than going to the FBI."

"You want me—your ex-girlfriend—to save your mom, who's a spy for SPECTRE for all I know." I scooted away from the sphere of his pheromone influence and wrapped my arms around myself, sheltered in Pippi's blanket. I'm my own best comforter. "Because neither you nor Clarissa wants the government—or your thugs—to help?"

"I don't have thugs." He frowned. "Clarissa doesn't want my help, because I *am* the government. She's so critical that I made that choice."

▪

Perhaps I'd feel better about my poor depth perception if this were the first guy I'd slept with who turned out to be someone else. Here's me, trying to solve math problems and not get involved with people's secrets. Turns out I am freaking Bambi frolicking in the forest, pretending everything is just fine and that the shot I heard didn't destroy my world.

▪

At this point, Anthony Hong Moon King, the Pirate King, riffed on how he was Superman, international cyberbait, luring bad guys into clever traps for a decade. Honeypots: the cyber equivalent of the honeycomb into which a criminal Pooh cannot resist sticking his fist.

"My boss calls me Honey Bear, since I've served as a walking, talking honeypot for so long. Now that goo stuck to me—the Hong Kong video—they want me back home. As if that problem is worse than what's been chasing me the last couple of months."

Similar to your life passing before you in a near-death experience, here's a survey of everything I thought over the next three seconds:

In my old Z-Crypto job in Virginia, I deceived myself in thinking that all the investigative hacking I did was one hundred and ten percent for the betterment of a free society. I hadn't put clear words to what disturbed me until just before Edward Snowden pulled back the curtains of deception.

Fleeing that world, I deceived myself in thinking I could investigate criminal hacking within the safety of Quinn's startup research business. My family and friends barely escaped a world of hurt from the Russian mobsters who wanted me because of the work I did in Virginia.

My new escape to independent business with Natalia was to ensure that I'd use my skills for social good, choosing my clients. But another international security threat walked in my door—that I used to sleep with—and drew me into personal jeopardy once again, where I can't determine what safe or moral action to take.

My arch-enemy claims he works for the good guys. Always has. And, it appears, I have no capacity for judging what's real in the world. It took those three seconds for my throat to allow words to escape.

"That's why you disappeared back then."

Years ago, three week after I knocked on the door of his empty apartment, Tony's two pals from the university's computer lab were arrested for hacking into government servers. Since then, whenever I saw Tony at a hacker event, I saw a rotten fish who always escaped the hook.

Not sugar in a honeypot.

"How does a freaking federal agent afford designer suits?" Perhaps not the number one question, but it's what first fell out of my mouth.

"Show up early at Asset Forfeiture auctions."

"Why didn't you tell me?"

"You want an invitation to the next asset auction?"

"I mean, why—" spluttering each individual word, "why didn't you tell me you're an agent?"

"Damn, Sam." He stood up, astonished. Sat down again. Stood and paced my tiny room. "What did you think?"

"You're the Pirate King, getting rich off the darknet. Your schemes, the piles of money—"

"Then what were you? Javert pursuing Jean Valjean?"

That crackly place inside, what you feel when people are laughing at you? When maybe you deserve to be laughed at? I bravely entered the breach. "I believed that you tossed your enemies my way just so I'd destroy them for you."

"What about the Bitcoin Affair?"

"You traded a bad guy to get the feds off your tail."

"Shit. I'm really, really good." He sat down again, laughing hard enough to shake the chair. He'd lost the faux-Brit accent. "Did you tell Clarissa how good I am? That I'm the Pirate King? I can't tell her myself."

"Or I could say you're a freaking liar."

"Okay, okay. I suppose I've omitted details. I did that when we first met, to protect you. These days…I thought you knew."

"You've lied to me since the day we met."

"And you, Sam? You claimed back then that you were nineteen, not seventeen, when—"

"Which proves…" I stumbled, recalling the omissions in the last few days' texts with Matt. Who's protecting and who's zooming whom? Weakly: "When does lying ever help?"

Tony still hadn't wiped that glee off his face. "They recruited me out of the boarding school where my mother dumped me. I always assumed they'd recruited you, too. You're one of us. Orphaned misfits who need a place in the world."

"I keep saying no." We'd circled back to my basic goal: avoiding the NSA contractor net.

"Oh dear heart. You said yes when Z-Crypto hired you out of college. Paid for your master's degree. Paid you to unravel secrets."

"That was all private industry, up until—"

"Until Dan Llewellyn bought Z-Crypto and turned it into an NSA contracting agency?" He was laughing at me again. "It was always NSA and CIA money. That's why I thought we were on the same team."

"The moral quandary." I was squeaking out words. "It's hard to make my way through."

"It's not hard to tell the good guys from bad. If you have the right team supporting you." He settled down, stopped laughing. "I'm walking proof, Sam."

"That it's possible to live your whole life as a lie?"

"That's a brutal way to put it." Yet he kept on with all that smiling. "I'm proof you can't go it alone in the world where you and I live. That there's no reason to do it alone."

"I don't live in your world. I just build walls to help keep people safe."

"That's Natalia's job. You take walls down, Sam. Elegantly." He freaking kissed the back of my hand at this point. "Which is what I need you to do. I need you to do what you always wanted."

"What's that?"

"Get a gold star in math, like when you were nineteen… Seventeen? Oh geez. I screwed up the intelligence on that one, didn't I? Anyway, I need your Tuff Skilz."

"What math?

"Data discovery and triangulation. Between my mother's friends and whatever put them in danger."

"You're Superman. You do it. Or are you flying back into the darknet with your support team?"

"Because of Wendy, they called me in. Whatever is happening, I'm likely out of play for a good long while. Unless I can prove that this affair isn't about me." He laughed, that rueful bark of the doomed. "They don't even know about your client yet."

"Who are the women?"

"Clerks in an archive. And Clarissa isn't on the list."

"Perhaps she has another name."

"Or she's a spy, except it isn't for the United States of America. As I feared."

"That's why the Lenin pin?"

"And also why in the next few days of debriefing, it might turn out I should have told them about my mother when they recruited me," he said. "Help me for an hour. Let's dig into some data, like in the old days."

"Sorry. Not doing more work. Not unless you show me everything." I took away his jelly-jar glass, trickled in a drop of dish soap, and rinsed it in my tiny sink. "You want me to run risks blind. I won't do it."

"I'd need to give you a Standard Form 86."

"Based on my OPM letter, my last form is still on file."

He sat silent, impassive, as if thinking it over.

"What other women," I prompted him, "are staring at a ransomware message that tells them to pay by Friday? Or who might be killed before Friday, like Wendy and Doreen?"

He glanced up, a deep frown scoring his forehead. "Are you sure it was a stranger who mugged you?"

"A bum. A guy with a dog saw him."

"A guy and a dog. The bum had no face?"

"A hoodie—"

"A hoodie is what I'd choose. A hoodie is good."

"It was dark."

"And so was the hoodie, I bet. What color was the dog?"

"What? White. Are you taking my bruises seriously, after scaring the crap out of me about your end-of-the-world problem?"

"As seriously as the bum who nabbed your laptop."

"Patricia Yates's laptop. My phone."

"But not your wallet," he said. "A bum with a plan."

"Are you creeping me out on purpose?" I sat on my hands, drawing in, checking my breathing in the same way as when I lay on the cold cobbles.

"No." His body changed, softened; his face warmed. "Sam, I'm sorry I dragged you into this." Hands through his hair again. "Though I didn't bring you the first client. Or Patricia Yates. We need to see if Ms. Yates is on the OPM list."

"Is it illegal for me to touch that list?"

"We don't have time to research that."

The digital clock on my radio flipped to midnight. I needed sleep to do what I'd signed up for in the morning. And whatever the right thing might turn out to be, an hour working with Tony seemed the most logical thing to do.

"What are we researching? Tell me everything, or leave."

"Clarissa got involved in something years ago. Now it's come back through the conspiracy that I'm tracking."

"We've got forty-seven flavors of conspiracy today, and half are organic. Which of them?"

"There's a security technology that people are searching and bidding for in the darknet. For years."

"Old crypto?" I was more than skeptical. "Last decade's crypto cannot be useful.

"Whatever. This technology is like Voldemort, though. To even mention it brings the full force of the U.S. government to your house and up your arse. Often times, it's been me knocking. Rumors rise, then get laughed off the net. Or whole accounts and servers disappear. That's usually me, unless it's someone I hope to close in on."

"Your mother stole this crypto technology for the Russians? And Doreen and Wendy? They're Russian spies, too?"

"Maybe just my mother's dupes. Maybe they're innocents in a maelstrom. Or, yeah, maybe they're all spies."

"They all ended up in rather lofty public places for retired spies. Not even hiding, just there in plain sight. Why now? And how are you involved?"

"Our team is chasing through darknet alleys, seeking bids and offers for that stolen crypto."

"Baiting honeypots?"

"Yes. The Pirate King has a significant bid out to purchase. But every lead turns up false—rumors or cyber bags of junk code. Your friends the White Knights are also making offers."

"Are they at the heart of this?"

"Maybe. Can't tell yet. Perhaps Clarissa is selling stolen crypto for them."

"Is your mother that smart?"

"Maybe. Though I haven't found any evidence she's selling anything. I want—"

"What? If she's a spy who stole critical code, I won't cover it up. What do you want?"

"To find out exactly how Clarissa's involved. I don't want surprises when they begin debriefing me tomorrow. And tonight is all the time I have before my four a.m. flight. You know, coming in from the cold."

"Okay, Tony. We need to get busy. I have other work tomorrow. And I want to find out who else needs to be found. And protected."

"Thank you, Sam. Let me pay my driver and grab my bag."

"You left your bag behind? The infamous Pirate King—"

"Just my running shoes."

He took the elevator down to the street.

Below my window, his shadow lengthened and shortened as he crossed under the cones of mercury-vapor streetlights, the tall man I knew and didn't know for more than a decade. The for-hire car idled near the corner. Tony pulled a gym bag from the back seat, and then reached into his pocket, probably to pay the driver.

Dangling the bag by its long strap, he looked up toward my window. Grinning. Pointing to, what? I couldn't see.

When the bag flashed.

A white streak in the night, like a bundle of bottle rockets gone all wrong.

My phone and blanket in hand, I grabbed my jacket and sprinted for the street, taking the stairs, jumping two or three at a time, punching 9–1–1 yet again.

The for-hire driver stood by his car, also punching 9–1–1. No. A flash. He was taking a picture. I wrapped the blanket around Tony and worked to apply pressure—where? What to do when it's the torso? Chanting my First Responder training. Talking to him, calling his name.

"Stay with me, Tony. C'mon. Breathe. You can do it, Tony. It's just a moment—"

Watched him slip into shock just as the EMTs rolled up, guys able to do far more than I could.

The for-hire car and its driver had disappeared.

10

A View of the Harbor

■
■
■

ONCE THE EMT GUYS PULLED me off First Responder tasks, then I had to jerk all possible calm from deep inside while telling the SPD officer that, no, this wasn't a gang thing. Yeah, he's dark; yeah, he had a wad of cash and no ID. But, I pleaded, Tony is an international businessman, a personal friend. Begging for—and losing—permission to ride in the aid car, I described once more what had happened, while repeatedly calling a dispatcher for a cab to take me to Harborview hospital.

Then, sitting in the visitors' room on the trauma care floor, I rubbed my hands raw waiting to hear news. And I lied once more, claiming Tony was my brother so they'd let me stay, promising to cover his bill until his insurer could be identified. No passport in Tony's pockets, no ID at all.

Feeling how lonely it is in the abyss, I texted Matt at what must be sunrise in Virginia. I imagined the meticulous way he brews coffee and how he makes sure we all eat a good breakfast.

> Sam:
> Have time to talk?

Then I changed my mind and sent a never-mind text.

> MattOwens:
> What? What's wrong?

Sam:
Lonely. Did I wake you?

He called. "What's wrong?"

"Overworked. Missing you." Lying. I'm scared the White Knights are back, but like Harley guessed: if I say it out loud, then maybe it will be real. Much better that Pippi and Matt are both on the other side of the country, physically safe, emotionally free. "Sorry about the confusing texts yesterday. My embedded extrasensory devices got crosswired and—"

A female voice near Matt asked a question, sounding distressed. "Go back to sleep," he said, not even muffling his phone.

I'd nearly punched End Call when I got rational enough to recognize Pippi's voice.

"What's wrong with Pippi?"

"Her nightmares returned. We can't figure it out. School seems to be fine. Maybe it's stress from moving." Worry clouded his voice.

When we three first came together, I instinctively knew how to soothe Pippi, gradually easing her out of the trauma of losing her birth family that brought on nightmares and woke us all with her screams.

But I'm not there with her now. It was weak of me to let my former entanglements with the NSA cloud what I owe Pippi. Her voice over the phone sounded far, far away, but she hadn't gone back to bed. "Let me talk to her."

She came swiftly when Matt called.

"Hey, girl! Miss you big time."

We talked, the phone's battery slinking down to nil for the long while we needed to spend together.

"Pippi," I whispered, "do you have any secrets to tell me?"

She negotiated with Matt to take the phone into the bathroom. After the door closed, she whispered too. "I found you on Facebook. And I saw what those men said."

"Oh, Pippi. They're just naughty boys doing bad things. Harley is going to make them stop."

"I'm afraid they'll hurt you."

"No. They can't even find me. Now, tell Matt and Roz why you're upset. They can help you not worry."

"But then Matt will find out that I have Facebook. I'll be in really bad trouble."

"Honey, you already got yourself in trouble. And I'm sorry you saw that. This is exactly why Matt says no Facebook until you're twelve."

"Please don't tell Matt I did a sneaky thing."

"Cross my heart, I won't. But you have to tell him. That's the deal, right? You tell the truth, and we take care of you."

"Okay. But if he kills me, you'll know why."

"Don't even pretend about getting killed. Give Matt the phone so I can say goodbye. My phone's dying."

"Bye. It's a three-day weekend. Can you come visit while there's no school?"

"Don't think so, sweetheart. But I'll call every day."

By the time Matt said goodbye, and I'd switched my phone off, you'd think I'd gotten over my own waking nightmares. Or decided to take the same advice about truthfulness that I gave Pippi, and therefore 'fess up to Matt about being scared. I checked with the nurses' station again, and slumped back into the visitors' room. But no. Not just that I didn't want to burden Matt, but what I had to deal with: it wasn't so immense that I couldn't handle it.

This is a problem I've never had to deal with before. Coming from a series of Friends-with-Benefits experiences, I have no knowledge to guide me. If you're in this thing called a Relationship, do you have to perform revelations of all weakness in front of your partner? I don't have any inclination to let other people see my weak points. Does True Love with the Boy Next Door cancel all that? I am striving to see the benefit of personal revelation. Here's Matt, who I want to think better of me than anyone else in the world. Why reveal that I've done stupid stuff? That I'm scared? That I don't know the right thing to do?

The best thing would be to go back to my tiny hovel and sleep. I'd had none over that last night, four hours the night before, and again the night before that. Tony was in the best possible place in Seattle for care.

Rummaging in my pocket, hoping to resurrect a protein bar, I found the bar napkin I'd scribbled on the previous afternoon. I once more studied that tattered, stained drawing, hoping to see what was missing.

"What makes the picture complete?"

That voice played in my head again, smoked by age, with a breathless inflection. The Socratic Method on multi-play repeat.

My art history professor, in an undergrad Humanities elective. The same academic quarter as when I was doing my homework in Tony's furniture-free studio apartment.

"What makes the picture complete? The viewer."

Lord, I'm as slow-witted as a three-toed sloth.

Bad things happened to these women.

Zak talked to his mother, and then called me.

Brad sent me to his mother.

What if it wasn't the OPM list that drew attention to those women?

What if it wasn't Clarissa at the root, but instead Doreen calling Zak, and Zak calling me? What if Doreen writing to Clarissa just widened the span of evil attention?

What if Clarissa wasn't in danger because of Tony, but because I'd knocked on her door?

What if Tony caught on fire because he came to my house?

My White Knight stalkers' repeated message:

> "You fucked our business. We come fuck you."
> "You so smart, Miss Forensikz? The more your customers wake up dead, the closer we come to you."

And then repeated warning:

> "Friday is a good day to die."

▪

"Your friend isn't dead. This isn't a homicide."

Along about three in the morning, Jeremiah sat beside me in the trauma-care waiting room, taking one of the colossally uncomfortable club chairs. Carlos Gabriel sat on the stiff sofa. Jeremiah looked suitably disheveled for that time of night, Carlos was still pressed and tidy.

"We don't believe in coincidence. It's like a religion for us," Jeremiah said after we traded hellos. "When the same woman calls 9–1–1 two days in a row and files other police reports about physical and property damage, we tend to put our heads together."

"It feels like the universe is out to get me. Missed me and got my friend this time." I made a joke, though nothing was funny.

"Want to walk us through what's happening?" Jeremiah offered a weak smile, also not finding any humor.

Always serious, Carlos was now just plain grim. "We have all the time in the world to listen. We can't work on the Monroe investigation, since you sent that code package to the FBI."

"And meanwhile, the Potholes Deadlock has the FBI's full attention," Jeremiah added.

"But let's work together on tonight's event." Carlos prepared to take notes.

For his benefit, I recounted what had happened the year before, when the White Knights first came after me. While the battery warning beeped, I showed them on my phone screen the deadly threats from the previous day.

"They must have hacked my contacts." I endeavored to weave the threads rapidly and tightly, explaining the stolen OPM list, what it contained, and how my enemies seemed to have used it. "They bought the list on the black market, and then managed to make connections back to people on my contact list. Then they found and damaged people who know me. Or their mothers."

Carlos rubbed a finger along the bony ridge that formed his eyebrow. Jeremiah shuffled his feet, but didn't stand. He said, "And the person who got himself blown up outside your apartment? Is he on that list? You knew him before today?"

"Don't know if he was on the list. We knew each other in college. And we're more or less in the same professional field." How to describe Tony in a way that mattered? "From the hacking community. Tony claimed he'd uncovered a conspiracy that involved the stolen OPM list. He wanted to work with me to discover who else might be in danger. He went to his car for…he said it was his gym bag."

"And you're sure this is him?" Carlos held out the notepaper scrap where I'd written Tony's name and mine at the emergency desk, when I asked the clerk to enter my name as next of kin.

"Yes. Anthony Hong Moon King. Only," time to own up, "I'm not his next of kin." What did Tony say? *My mother would kill me if I...* "He's an orphan. At admissions, I told them I was his sister so they'd let me stay."

"Did Mr. King leave anything behind at your house? His coat? A wallet? A phone? Anything that might help us find his real kin?"

"No." My uncomfortable butt, wiggling in the chair, was sitting on my jacket, which contained that business card with Clarissa's address. And that throwaway phone.

"Now, please don't be alarmed," Jeremiah said.

Oh, that put me totally at ease. *Don't be alarmed*—because things can't get freaking worse.

Carlos, the team's task master, said, "We can't find any record of a person named Anthony Hong Moon King. And the fingerprint checks we've done haven't found anything. We have to wait on DNA checks, but so far he seems to be a ghost."

Jeremiah cleared his throat. "We don't believe you are involved in any crime. However, we have a warrant to search your house for evidence about who he is. Do you want an attorney?"

"Um, no. But why would I?" Mentally, I was seeing that $100K check being slipped from my cookie jar into an evidence bag. Good fortune deferred once again. If only I'd already passed it to Natalia.

Controlling body language, not folding my arms protectively, I presented my detective friends with open-and-honest body kinetics. "He went to the UW. That's how we knew each other. Maybe you can find those records." I cited the year.

"We also want to trace messages from him on your cellphone, Ms. Byron. Do you mind passing that over? Or do we need a warrant?" Carlos dangled an evidence bag. My dying phone held Matt's texts but no clues about what the universe had dumped on me this time.

"He's never called me."

"How about text?"

I dropped my brand-new replacement phone into the bag.

Shortest life for a handset I'd ever known. I watched him write a receipt for my phone, not asking about encryption. Not that it contained one byte of data that'd help this case. The number Tony used to text me was from a masked burnerbot account. The email he used for Krypptikk? None of that data was on the phone anyway. "That's a brand-new phone. Mine was stolen yesterday."

"We have your mugging report." Carlos glanced at his notes. "Do you believe it's related?"

"Perhaps." The answer leaked out of me. "Can you consider one more possible crime?" When I asked, they didn't groan, but there was a lot of side-eye happening. "Before I was mugged, I visited Judge Yates in Belltown. She had the same ransomware as on Mrs. Monroe's computer. When I was mugged, the guy stole that computer and my phone. And moments later, Judge Yates nearly died. Can you ask her doctors to make sure no foul play was involved? Just in case?"

Jeremiah closed his eyes as if in pain. Though I'm the one who'd been up all night helping Tony not die in the street. "How is that man in there," he pointed toward Tony's room, "involved with Judge Yates?"

"He isn't. The judge's son asked me to help with her computer. That's one more reason why I believe the White Knights are attacking me through other people."

"You're sure?" Jeremiah said.

Yeah, I hedged: how to answer?

> Tony suggesting that bum who mugged me wasn't a bum.
>
> Tony not being who I believed he was.
>
> Tony being called in by his master because he wasn't safe.
>
> Yet Tony asking me not to go to the FBI. The rogue agent he pursued might be watching.

"I'm not confident," I said. "But Tony said he was a federal agent. He'd uncovered a conspiracy connected with the White Knights."

Jeremiah screwed up his face. "So who do we call to tell them to come get their spy?"

"If I have to guess, he's FBI. And collaborating with NSA cyber-terrorism people. Unless he's CIA."

"Do you happen to have their number handy?" Carlos made a note in his little book. "Or will we find it on your phone?"

"Evan Mulasky isn't answering my requests either. I don't have data that proves the NSA is involved. Just my gut feeling."

"So what's your gut say about how mysterious Russian mobsters managed to blow up a spy outside your door? How did they know the timing of your friend's tryst with you?"

"A tryst? That wasn't—"

"Who was the target? You or your mystery friend?"

Oh, yeah, I was totally not alarmed.

▪

Carlos and Jeremiah agreed to wait until Harley arrived at the office in the morning before coming to look for evidence about who Tony was. I didn't want to leave Tony yet.

Left alone, I tugged Tony's phone from my inside pocket, the one he'd dropped on the street. It was, as I'd guessed, a burner phone. The call and text history were erased. It had no PIN. I set one and installed an encryption application, then configured my own burnerbot account to send my calls and texts to this phone. And I once more sent email and texts to my trusted FBI contact, Evan Mulasky, who seemed to have been absorbed into the chaos of the Potholes Deadlock.

Yes, after deep consideration, I took a calculated risk about Tony's rogue agent finding him. But as it was, there was no one else but me to fend for him.

> ✆2068888888:
> PRIVATE DO NOT FORWARD. This is Samsara Byron. One of your agents is in Harborview trauma unit - Anthony Hong Moon King. Nicknamed Honey Bear. Please send protection. Also, let SPD know he's yours.

Too late at night—or early in the morning—to expect an answer. Without a personal contact, if I just called with the thin information I had accumulated, anyone at the FBI would put my name on the crazy-lady list. Or Tony's rogue agent would learn of it quickly. I closed my eyes, thinking of who else might act for Tony—and whose number I knew without my phone contact list. I'd memorized only one other FBI number besides Evan's.

Matt.

Who went to Quantico to fulfill a lifelong dream.

Who'd always believe me, without arguing.

I merely had to explain—

Nothing. I didn't have sufficient information for Matt or anyone to take action. Except for what I'd texted to Evan. Nothing to gain by sending that message through Matt. I'd just alarm him when there was nothing he could do.

Over the phone, I couldn't get from Matt what I most wanted: to curl up at his side, his arm around me, a blanket over us, smelling Matt-ness, feeling his warmth, hiding in the dark.

Instead, I washed my face in the women's room and practiced the tricks I'd taught Pippi about how to corral unreasonable fear.

After pacing the visitors' room, finding yogurt in a vending machine, drinking lukewarm tea, and sleeping a couple of restless hours on a scratchy trauma-care visitor's chair, I checked with the nurses. No change in status, no I couldn't visit, and yes, the SPD had placed a watch.

To ease the kinks and to make up for no sleep, I decided to walk the two miles back to Capitol Hill in the dawn light. I needed to move, and I still had enough time for a shower before Brad dragged Natalia and me out to meet Luke Connor, to listen to another pitch for why we wanted aDVers in our careers. Dan's offer of security and protection hovered at the back of my mind, nearly as beguiling as the opportunity offered to do security work for a cybernetic mission to save lives.

Outside, a November-style wet-wool blanket of clouds hung overhead, and a fat-drop downpour filled the gutters, so the old rain-forest streams flowed again, burbling in potholes and filling lost lakes along every curb. I ducked back inside the hospital to ask the info-desk clerk for my umbrella from the lost-and-found.

"It's black. The cheapest drugstore kind." I lied, helpfully. Then I hit the streets, choosing the lesser traveled roads (fewer cars to drench me as they plowed through waves flooding the streets), pondering what to do next while trudging along the deserted Pike-Pine corridor that runs up Capitol Hill.

Block by block, the crumbling commercial edifices of this corridor (formerly the place to go for mattress and down-vest factories or electric and plumbing supplies) are giving way to six-story apartments with street-level commerce: upscale noodle houses, farm-to-table cider houses, and unexceptional boutiques. Although the builder-landlords desire upscale, the core of Pike-Pine remains pho shops, skateboard outfitters, soggy pizza, and a rainbow collection of thrift shops. At night, there's a crowded onslaught of tavern-migrants seeking the proper drink-and-music dispensary for their specific tribe.

Me, walking back from First Hill at dawn, I'm hoping that whatever's on the sidewalk won't stick to my shoes. It's Thursday, the day before Friday, the day the ransomware warned those women to fear.

And neither Natalia nor I had traced the malware source, so what more to tell the police? Whom do we warn? Whom do we ask to help with the research, since Zak is fully occupied with his own cyber crisis?

Except, as Tony requested: Clarissa.

Even with that crummy umbrella for protection, by the time I was back on Capitol Hill, my leather jacket had lost all remaining attributes of its rich-lady pretense. The back of my neck was damp from the humidity. My sockless feet slipped inside my soaked-through, threadbare Vans, which made rude squishing sounds when I stopped to grab espresso and a seed-laden energy bar—my Tiger Milk bars disappeared with my messenger bag. When the downpour let up, puddles still filled every dip in the sidewalk, and the gutters remained fast-flowing creeks.

Two sips of espresso and thirty paces up Fifteenth Avenue East, I sensed I was being followed. Side-eyeing everyone who passed, catching reflections in storefront windows, I took an abrupt left turn, a right turn on Malden, and then circled back to Fifteenth East and down the alley above Sixteenth. Back out on Republican, I waited. Then shouted.

"Hey, creep!"

That skater from Clarissa's building.

When I yelled, he kicked up his board and held it as if to fend off blows. It was a janky, big-wheeled skateboat, hand-built for rain-sodden days. Low class, but a decent weapon.

"Tem. I told you my name is Tem."

"You're harassing me. I'm calling the police." I held out that throwaway phone like my own shield, feeling naked. "Did you send those death threats?"

"No. Didn't you believe me yesterday?" Skateboard under his armpit, the dude held out both palms, a universal symbol of nonaggression. "We're on the same side. At least, I think so from current data."

Tem, unlike I'd first judged, was scrupulously clean.

A ridiculous comment, except in my previous encounters with the man-who-would-be-called-Tem, I'd seen him as a dust rag, a high schooler pretending to be a street person. But in fact he'd adopted an urban camouflage made up of dust-colored jeans, a mottled tan sweater, dirt-colored Vans, where a big toe peeked out the wet front edge. Ragged, fingerless mitts might indeed be less clean. A much-washed brown hoodie.

Not tall enough to be my hoodie-wearing mugger.

"Want me to help stop your trolls? I'm good at creaming dumbasses." A mellifluous tenor-sax voice—or would be if it didn't break reedy and breathless at the higher reaches.

"You? Help *me* block hacker wannabees?" Like, I'm Samsara Byron, world's greatest, et cetera.

"The reality of today's geopolitical environment changes everything. Things move fast. You've been out of the scene."

Out of it? I must have blinked, betrayed a moment of unease.

He said, "Are you going to visit Clarissa again? Seriously, I can help." Like a Boy Scout offering to help this little old out-of-it lady across the street.

"She'll talk to me today."

"Mmm." He pretended to ponder the idea for a millisecond. "No. Yesterday she called you a security slut for the NSA. Doesn't want anything to do with you."

"Clarissa's in danger." I shrugged off the name calling. "Can you make her listen?"

"People should worry about being in danger from her." Like a kid on the playground: *my mom can kick your mom's skinny ass.* His board hit the pavement. Splashing through puddles, he skated beside me as I headed for Clarissa's apartment. The taste of espresso lingered on my tongue as a memory of the sole, sad pleasure I'd had since midnight.

"Okay," he said. "I'll help."

"I've got exactly forty-five minutes to get her to listen. Then I have to be elsewhere."

He skated around me in a circle. "You're wearing the same clothes as last night. Have you been home since then?"

"You are stalking me."

"Just happened by, lady."

"After curfew."

"I'm eighteen. No curfew. I told Clarissa what I saw. That's when she said that NSA slut stuff."

"And that was her son lying on the street." Didn't want to say a word, but Tem dogged me, rolling on my heels. "How cold is this White-Bone Demon that she—"

"Not cold. Just cautious."

"Called me a slut, I can call her a cold bitch. She—"

"No! She—she saved me." The name-calling burst a dam. "When my dad died, she made it all work. Fixed the legal stuff so I could live on my own. Kept Dad's affairs out of court, so I had money. For three years, she's the only one who—"

He ceased declaiming when we rolled up on the apartment entrance, the cream-colored concrete arch framing the door through which Tem could gain entrance for me. I glanced up and down the street: cars parked nose-to-nose and tail-to-tail on both sides of the street, crowding driveways, front tires up on the low curb edge: Seattle style parking. Subarus and Toyotas, no black SUVs. No one hovered in a car or lurked in other doorways.

"Hey, Tem. The authorities are bound to link Clarissa with these women at some point. Tony says there's a spook is lurking in her network. So someone already has—"

"Don't call the FBI. She can take care of this. With my help."

"Your help? What? You'll whap your skateboard on anyone who comes through the door?"

His nostrils flared. "It's me that's in her system. I'm her guardian in cyberspace."

Conflict with Tem would not get me through that door. I eased off. "Tem, get Clarissa to listen to me. Tony left me with a problem. I need her help—and yours—to solve it."

"Promise no FBI? It's like you have cooties on you."

"Can't promise. But I don't want to be involved with national security either."

"The oligarchs fear us," he said. He punched a security code to open the Galahad Apartment's front door. "The truthtellers support us. The valiant join us."

11

The Real Pirate King

THE WOMAN GAZING OUT THAT half-open door seemed to be a cousin of the grifting Clarissa-in-a-wig, the one who dithered and lied.

This Clarissa destroys steel beams with her cold-gold eyes. Makeup perfect, nearly undetectable. Her hair cut in a swept-back bob, a luscious autumnal brown, a white streak dashed back from a widow's peak.

Two sensations struck me as I endured those golden eyes probing my soul. First, this woman was so astoundingly beautiful that age hadn't lightened her grip on the power of beauty. Second, she'd have no qualms about cutting me open if what she needed might be buried inside me.

"Tony's in the Harborview trauma ward." Though tired, I shrugged off any notion of Clarissa as a superior being. "He spent the hour before he was attacked begging me to help protect you."

Those golden beams shimmered, gazing past me to where Tem hovered near my shoulder. She walked away from the open door.

"I suppose you must come in."

Tem and I followed. She didn't glance back. Bet she never looked back once in her lifetime. Music played softly, though not from the pseudo-antique "wireless" in the living room. The two women began the Flower Duet from *Lakme*. "*Viens, descendons ensemble.*"

Indeed, let us descend together. Into the dragon-mother's lair

Clarissa seated us at her tiny table, poured tea from a floral china pot. Again with mismatched paper-thin china cups. She held her own cup and saucer, standing against the pantry door.

"Your Tony will live?"

"*Your* Tony." Too tired to play her game. "The doctors are optimistic. If you want to see him, go now. His people are likely to come fetch him soon."

"It was that explosion," Tem said, speaking to Clarissa from the shadows, as if watching a game.

"Who did it?" She sipped, calm. "What's he gotten himself involved in now?"

"He believes something he's investigating became a problem for you. I assume whoever killed Wendy and Doreen—and tried to kill Patricia Yates yesterday—tried to kill Tony."

"My problem?" She shook her head, which she did more elegantly than you or me. Men in the Seventies likely killed themselves when tossed off with that shake of her beautiful head. "Tony can't know one true thing about my affairs. Consider his world. International thieves. Internet scoundrels. He's been tracked by the most ruthless of the ruthless for a decade."

"Ah, progress! You do know Tony." I snapped my rain-chilled fingers. But did I feel better that she knew only the illicit Tony? No, because it didn't help me believe or understand either of them.

"I can't help him."

"Or won't? Doesn't matter. I'm here because Tony believes these women worked for you. They were government contractors when you were working as a spy."

This seemed to stop Clarissa in her grifting tracks. I leaned back in my delicate rattan café chair satisfied that we were finally serious with each other.

Then she did the most extraordinary thing. As if we were living in a Charles Dickens story, she stepped away from the pantry door and pointed first to Tem and then to the pantry. He rose silently, went inside, and closed the door, leaving only his skateboard.

Once the orphan was in the closet, she asked, "How could Tony know any such thing? Data he found on the darknet?"

"He's really good at what he does. We call him the Pirate King for a reason."

That laughter again. "Tony? No, I am the King. The King of all the Pirate Kings. Who did he bother with this nonsense, besides you? He'll have clueless agents searching our linen drawers. Is that why you're here? To pick our bones ahead of your national security friends, those vultures?"

"He asked me to keep federal agents away because…" Here I was, protecting a guy from his mother. Who leaned on the closet door where she'd just stashed an orphan.

"Because why? He's sentimental?" Her hand floated up, fingering a pin on her sweater—that Lenin pin—though I bet this mother of dragons didn't make one unconscious move in her life.

"Because Tony thinks you were a Soviet spy."

"Oh, Good Lord in Heaven, no."

"A lot of what-ifs made him guess that." I couldn't argue that point with any strength. Tony *guessed.*

"There are many better what-ifs that he might consider." The accusation put her nose badly out of shape.

"I'm listening."

"What if in the early Nineties," she began slowly with that infuriating sly smile, "while white kids in dorms were rocking out to Madonna and the Gin Blossoms, a small horde of East Coast fraternity brothers came to Seattle, on their way to being rich software executives?"

"Well, that happened, didn't it? For a few hundred of them."

"What if one of them inserted a backdoor into crucial security technology?"

Now we were arguing where I have knowledge. "Most of those execs rushed to give the NSA and the FBI the secret backdoors to all their software. And hardware. More than a few of us have spent hundreds of thousands of hours seeking unknown backdoors."

"Ah, the NSA's mistress." The curve of a smile along her elegantly painted lips. Have I made it clear that Clarissa really didn't like me?

"So why are Doreen and Wendy dead?"

"My guess, Ms. Byron?"

"Will it prevent more people from dying?"

"I'm not sure." She touched that pin again, the only hesitant move she made. "Someone on the darknet is selling backdoor exploits to other countries. People who might know the secrets are being killed to keep them quiet forever."

"Are you and Tony writing a thriller movie together? He's searching for a rogue U.S. agent—the rogue that he insists has hacked your computer system."

She set her china cup and saucer in the tiny kitchen sink. "From how Tony harassed me last week, I believed he was working that possibility. Perhaps for one of his own extortion schemes?"

"He's better than that. Technically." I set my fragile cup and saucer aside. Tea is not my thing.

"Tony's illicit adventures always cause problems for his business partners and friends." A sly smile. Just like Tony's.

I did not mention my own notion, that I was the target of cybermobsters and that I'd drawn malevolent attention to her friends. Instead, I jumped back into what I came for. "Tony fears you were once a Soviet spy. Were those women under your control?"

She laughed. It might be what a hundred men longed to provoke for decades, but that deep, forbidding sound chilled me. "A busy international mogul like Tony shouldn't waste his time watching TV thrillers. Is he ratting on me to the FBI?"

"Besides malingering in the trauma unit, he's—" I took a breath. "He's a U.S. agent. He guessed *Soviet* when he couldn't find your name on the OPM list along with Wendy's and Doreen's. And because that's what he's thought for years."

She stared at me, boring holes in my soul. For the first time I noticed one blemish of age: the folds of her eyelids drooped in perpetual sadness. As if she'd gazed upon the world's well of sorrow and could never look away.

"Sad," she said, "that such a sweet boy grew up to think badly of me. It's exactly what they said back in those days, to expect the worst from the children of working mothers."

"Two women are dead." I persisted. "Tony got blown up in front of me. Whatever is going on, help me find out who else might be targets."

"Those women didn't accept the safety I offered them."

"Doreen and Wendy and Patricia chose to be in danger?"

The tiniest tremor at the corner of her right eye. Though perhaps I imagined that, because next she threw up her hands, surrendering.

"Fine. We need to get busy right now, Ms. Byron."

"First, let Tem out of the freaking closet. I can't concentrate when you act bat-shit crazy."

She angled her head, thinking, then stepped aside. She opened the door and, with an elegant flourish, waved me into the closet.

Which was empty.

Save for soup cans lining one wall. She touched something on the wall, and a hatch opened, revealing narrow metal stairs that led down into a light well.

She motioned for me to descend.

"I was a spy," she said. "For the FBI."

▪

Under Clarissa's apartment, a good half of Natalia's hardware shopping list was arrayed on metal racks, the kind from your local hardware megastore. The power and cooling load must be spectacular, though most everything looked brand-new, save a few pieces in a corner, displayed like a museum of old servers.

"Mostly headless," Clarissa said, as if she read my mind. "Solid-state drives run much cooler than those old monsters. And most of the crunching is in the cloud. Tem, what did we find last night?"

He didn't turn from the two screens he studied. "We're down to the seven you guessed when we started, minus two where Wendy never worked. So five."

"For eight years, I ran a contracting business." Clarissa addressed me, but leaned over Tem's shoulder, directing his attention to one area of the screen. "When value rose in the tech sector so fast, companies did what Microsoft did. They contracted out services that didn't contribute to patents or their code base."

Tem nudged her hand toward another area of the screen. She nodded, then turned her attention back to me.

"I provided executives with highly skilled assistants."

"Judge Yates was an attorney, not an executive assistant."

"Not then she wasn't. She was like the others in skill and intelligence, the kind who know your thoughts before you think them. Good degrees. Security checks. Bonded. Well-organized, well-groomed. For the very few execs who were unhappy with an assistant, I came and provided service myself until I sourced a suitable replacement."

"The women who received ransomware—they worked for you? Why are they dead?"

"Yes, Ms. Byron, to the first question. They reported to me." She pointed Tem's attention to another area of the computer monitor. "The second answer is still unknown. Tell us what you found, Tem."

"The four names we started with last night each worked at one time or another at these companies." He read a list of technology startups from long ago. "I built a matrix for who employed which assistant over specific time periods. These points show where any exec joined another company and asked for their assistant to come with them."

Before commenting, Clarissa asked for two more data points: who bought the original startups and which execs stayed on after a buyout. Tem showed where he'd gathered that data.

"I'm seeking the unhappy people." Clarissa still didn't look at me when she spoke. "Of course. What more should we be looking for, Ms. Byron? Since Tony thinks you can help."

"I'm meeting someone in fifteen minutes." I checked the time on my phone. "I'll be back this afternoon."

"We won't wait."

Tem began to read from one column: the list of technologies built, bought, and sold.

"Just those five companies," Clarissa pointed, then listened as Tem read a couple of dozen early Nineties innovations.

"Font rendering for screen and print."

"No," Clarissa said. "Not enough money."

"Read-write technologies for disk storage."

"Low value, but maybe."

Some early Plug and Play technology that required hardware, operating system, and firmware interaction rated a Yes.

A series of BIOS technologies, including Zeus, about which Daniel Llewellyn had chatted with me over drinks.

"What about Zeus?" I pointed to the crossed-out text, where the hand-drawn star beside it was also scratched out. "Did Patricia Yates work there?"

Tem studied the screen. "For only a month."

Clarissa considered it, not tossing my question to the wind the way she often did. "She didn't bring us anything from that assignment."

"Such as?"

"These women brought me every build from every code tree, at each place they worked. Patricia never picked up even one Zeus build."

"Industrial theft? You are effing kidding me." Startled, I lost track of my theory about mobsters coming for me.

"All my agents were well qualified and well trained," Clarissa said, snooty as an Afghan hound.

"The government used secretaries to steal code under development? From U.S. companies? Before 9/11 ever happened?"

"Executive assistants, not secretaries." Clarissa upbraided me like my eighth-grade English teacher. "Are you criticizing the technical capabilities of my workers? Or the strategy I was asked to execute?"

This whole time, I'd been trying to read data over her shoulder, past Tem's shoulder. The breakdown of the technologies was much more refined than what Tem read from the list.

"Executive assistants carry purses," Tem said. "Other people copied out the code trees."

"So government-sponsored industrial spying in the Nineties is getting your workers killed? This far into the future?"

"Yes, it appears so." Clarissa folded her arms again, thoughtful. "Surely it's bad actors within the government, trying to cover up something. It's so sad that Tony thought—"

"Are we finally coming to a meeting of minds?" But I was late for meeting up with Brad. "Keep looking for what technology it might be. I'll come back this afternoon to sniff who's watching you. May I bring my partner?"

Clarissa looked at Tem, who nodded.

Before heading for the stairs, I said, "If you tell trauma-care people who you are, Clarissa, they'll let you visit."

She seemed surprised. "Do they know who Tony is?"

"Not a clue. Unless Tony's people show up to identify him."

"He wouldn't like it if I messed that up for him, I'm sure."

▪

Scurrying through the rain, which once more fell with a vengeance, I took shelter at Espresso and Shoeshine. While waiting for my shot-in-the-dark, I used Tony's throwaway phone to check my voice messages, finding one from Zak.

> "There's a question only you can answer. If we send you a contract, can you sign an NDA and Standard Form 86?"

Using one of my burnerbot phone numbers, I sent a text message to Zak. My phone rang immediately. Zak's call forwarded to this handset.

"E-contract coming your way now, Sam."

Back into the rain, I headed for the office. Through the not-very-magic technology of e-signatures (tapped on a phone while I crouched under that cheap umbrella), within five minutes I had a contract (federal contractor pay—*fphtt!*). Zak called back.

"Make a Krypptikk project and send me the answer. What were the markers we found when we auditioned on that mystery code a couple of years ago? They took away the source, so I don't have access for research. It's bugging me in our current crisis. But I can't remember the markers."

"Give me a second. I'll send a Krypptikk invitation."

Face wet from gazing skyward while thinking about what we'd found back then, I ducked with the phone into the protection of my jacket as I tapped an answer for Zak.

> ***KRYPPTIKK JOB: #QUESTCODE_PRIVATE***
> Invited Members: sbyron; Zak Monroe
> *[ZakM accepted and entered project]*
> *SByron:*
> Ticket#1: Markers identified as follows:
> .
> .
> .

Those dots indicate that I'm not sharing private details.

Natalia would not be pleased with the low contract amount, but I'd be paid a second time for work I'd already done. Isn't that a professional win? Have to count it, because I'm not winning at anything else so far in this new business.

▪

At the office, Harley was ending a phone conversation. Outside the glass front door, a yellow Caution-Wet-Walkway sign shaded a calf's heart stabbed with an ornate Renaissance Faire dagger.

After hello, I said, "My Grandma Flo would hate to see a perfectly good beef heart go to waste."

"SPD was here to greet me this morning, so they have a report from me," Harley said. "And I talked with your detective friends about the mugging while they sniffed around."

"Thank you." Instead of arguing, I was appreciating more and more the presence of our receptionist. He handed me the receipt for what ended up in evidence bags as search-warrant takeaways: Tony's coat, its pockets empty; the check from the psycho-clown cookie jar. Both Tony and I were too ascetic to leave more clues.

Harley pointed to the caution tape across the street, left over from Tony's catastrophe. "That's logged as an attack on our business. You were on the job when the mugging happened. The laptop theft is company business, especially with missing customer assets. And that." He pointed to the calf heart. "It took the first SPD crew a few moments to get on the same page about what I think they need to investigate."

"Thank you again. Sincerely." I kicked my wet shoes into the office closet. At the back of the closet was a pair of Day-of-the-Dead–themed canvas low tops, left from move-in day. But also: socks. Though previously worn, the socks warmed my rain-wrinkled toes.

Harley said, "Did you see the cardboard sign? 'Friday is a good day to die'? Now the online death threats I reported to the FBI are linked up with these assault-and-threat cases."

"A successful morning, then. That was my night." I pointed to the police tape fluttering in the wet breeze and told the story—omitting Clarissa, still—and watched Harley's cop face settle in place.

"Malevolence." He meditated on the word. "Some creep opened the door to hell."

"Or at least Heck. If you talk with the investigators again before Natalia and I get back to the office, make sure they know every single thing you do about my mobster stalkers. Maybe..."

Natalia came in, bustling from daycare dropoff and having to park a couple of blocks away. Harley and I caught her up on our adventures.

"Blessed Freyja, what an evening you had! Nightclub, guests, hospital. So you didn't make much progress on that malware code?" She rested her hand on her chin, studying me.

"Tony's in Harborview." I redirected Natalia's attention to the most significant problem.

"Which he's been on the trajectory for since you met him." She shook a finger, as if I needed scolding. "I'm sorry he's hurt. But is this a surprise, given how he lives? Running down one unlit alley in the darknet, then turning the corner and running farther from the light."

"I'll give him your well wishes when I see him."

She was already scrolling through her morning messages and then typing task lists in Krypptikk.

> ***KRYPPTIKK JOB: CLIENT#1_MONROE***
> *NDragon:*
>
> > Ticket #3: Find ISP addresses on laptops from Client#1 and Client#202 and related GPS location.
> > Time Estimate: 0.5 days
> > Dependency: 1) Whether email is the malware delivery vector. 2) Lack of hardware for speedy research.
> > Start Time: TBD after morning field trip.
>
> CrossRef: Client#202_JONES

She pointed to the task list. "I'm gathering precise data to show how slowly our work progresses without Dogs of War hardware—"

"If things were different," I said, feeling a bit beaten and bitter, "they wouldn't be like they are."

"If only we could identify what things are like right now."

Harley asked, "What can I do?"

"Some research for me?" I'd had half a moment to consider next steps since talking with Zak. "Look in the security forums to find a government contact for reporting federal breaches. And then search for Anthony Hong Moon King, and anyone who uses a screen name that remotely resembles Honey Bear."

"What project should I use to track details?"

"The Debris_Byron one, I suppose."

Harley put on his reading glasses, switched the security TV to the news station, and then turned to his bank of monitors. On the news stream, the motley camo-clothed hordes continued to protest access and ownership in the Potholes Deadlock. The access I needed was to Evan Mulasky's attention. I imagined him assigned to hanging about in a black Suburban carryall, bored as hell.

Harley said, "By the way, you have a Friend request on your sock-puppet Facebook account." Listen to Harley, all up on in-crowd names for online disguises. "It's from a guy named Doug from Tukwila. He also DM'd you for a dinner date, to talk about the Sonics returning to Seattle."

Natalia gave me the side-eye. My kind-of, sort-of father-in-law was circumspect as hell. I answered both of them.

"It's Dan Llewellyn. Accept the Friend request, please. Harley, I appreciate all you're doing. I'll answer the dinner invitation."

"Friends?" Natalia's eyebrows were groomed to be inquisitive.

"Last night Dan played guitar with Jason Taylor and me. He's a good bass player. And a very persuasive person."

"He plays bass? Well, that makes all the difference for our forensics careers. Let's go meet more of his friends. Then we can talk."

Natalia and I grabbed our jackets and left to greet Brad. Time to go meet that ten-gallon douche nozzle, Luke Connor, and endure one more recruiting pitch for aDVers.

12

Fortress around Your Heart

BRAD ARRIVED IN A BMW crossover to pick up Natalia and me. Not the Maserati. Victor Pearl, that journalist, got to ride shotgun, so Natalia and I scooted into the backseat, which bore the impression of a child's safety seat. A multicolored early-learning baby toy had lodged itself between the front seat and the jockey box.

"Didn't know you had kids, Brad." I buckled in behind him.

"Doesn't everyone now?" He checked his mirrors, then leaned his arm over the seat, looking behind as he made a radical ninety-degree turn while backing onto the street.

"You have kids, Ms. Byron?" Victor asked.

"Yes, a sixth grader," I said, claiming Pippi as mine. And reiterated the appointment to myself to call her before bedtime. "She's away with her father right now."

"I have four," Natalia said, because she knows it always gets a rise out of people. "Two from my body, two of my wife's."

Brad didn't respond—he knew this from the recruiters' report, the same way Dan knew too much about me.

"How's your mother? I'm so sorry she's ill." Couldn't make myself ask: *Is she just ill, or did someone try to kill her?*

"Doctors think she'll be okay." Brad made a right turn to zoom down Twenty-third Avenue East.

"Do you need to be with her? We can make the trip to visit Luke on our own."

"No, it's fine. They won't let me sit with her until this afternoon." Brad's shoulders raised with tension. He was grinding his teeth. After a moment, he said, "I can use that as an excuse to get us out of there if Luke gasses on, which he does."

"It's her heart?" I prodded for more. "Patricia mentioned that it was affecting her health."

"That's why I insisted on the bio-monitor." Brad pounded the steering wheel. "Thank God."

I liked Brad better this way, tension leaking from his pores, pretending control, better than how I'd always known him: cool, always in command. Wished it didn't take pain and worry for him to be human.

"Did you talk with her yet?"

"No, she's sedated. They had to do a tracheostomy for an airway obstruction. For which they haven't yet diagnosed the cause." He accelerated sharply after the traffic light at Jackson. "Damn, I'm glad she's alive."

Brad drove like a bat out of Dante's hell, though there aren't bat-roads between Capitol Hill and Mercer Island, except for a short stretch on the I-90 bridge. He took the first exit for the island and headed south, jerking us along the winding road, speeding up and then coasting through curves. *BMW offers a drivers school,* I did not say. I bit my tongue to keep my thoughts to myself, then stopped so I wouldn't bite it off in the midst of jerking through another set of thirty-degree curves.

The rain picked up again, falling in sheets, the wipers barely able to keep up. Rivers of water escaped the ditches and ran across the road. We passed a late-model SUV—no, it was dark blue, not black. On Brad's instrument panel, the anti-lock braking display blinked repeatedly like a Christmas light.

What I most wanted to say: *Let me effing drive!*

Grasping the seatbelt with my left hand, knuckles knocking against the window, and clutching Natalia's hand like we're on the circular part of a Six Flags roller coaster, I pondered why I'd chosen to render my fate to others' choices.

For one thing, if we committed to aDVers, we'd have the hardware and staff to search through the problems like the ones we were currently wrestling. Except if there were more people at risk, tomorrow was Friday, which the ransomware mobsters—and my own stalkers—declared was the day to die. Therefore, why was I on this field trip? I should be in Clarissa's basement or my own Clean Room looking for—what?

After the last cryptic info dump from Clarissa, I needed to share insights with Natalia and Harley, to determine how to put pieces together. Hard to think clearly about Clarissa's mysteries while my heart thumped as Brad took a thirty-five-mile-an-hour blind hairpin turn by crossing totally into the other lane.

As diversion, I sent my bread-&-butter note to Dan.

Sam:
Thnks Fr th Mmrs. Dinner sounds nice. Where?

DougFromTukwila:
My boat? Any requests?

Sam:
I Wanna Be Sedated

DanFromTukwila:
Hard Days Night?

Sam:
Cherry Bomb

It was dawning on me that, one, Dan couldn't help but learn that someone got blown up outside my house, and then, two, if Natalia and I decided to go to work for aDVers, I'd have to eke a professional reputation out of this comic-book friendship that Dan and I seemed to be building. I was about to text back something sane, when he responded, and then went silent.

DanFromTukwila:
R – E – S – P – E – C – T

Wish I was in fact the genius Dan insisted I was.

Not feeling it.

In the way that one often does, I checked my phone messages to take my attention off Brad's driving, wishing I'd see something from Evan Mulasky.

> ***KRYPPTIKK JOB: #QUESTCODE_PRIVATE***
>
> *ZakM:*
>
> Send invoice.
>
> *SByron:*
>
> OK. Funny: Was just talking with Dan Llewelyn last night about our adventure.
>
> *ZakM:*
>
> Holy sh33t!! Spent all morning trying to get thru his people to speak to him.
>
> *SByron:*
>
> Want his private number?
>
> *ZakM:*
>
> You must be smokin' hot in your new gig.
> Setting the world on fire?
> Knocking 'em dead?

Why yes, yes I am. Unfortunately.

> *ZakM:*
>
> Gotta go.
> HOWEVER...I don't have permission to say much yet.
> But we found trails that lead to your White Knights.
> Be careful out there.

If I keep getting messages like this, how do I stop looking for black SUVs and post-Soviet bad guys? Obsessive back checking isn't helping to advance any of my research.

▪

On the far southwest end of the island, Brad pulled into a driveway that barely left room to get a car off the road, leaving the BMW's rear-end exposed to other drivers coming around a ninety-degree bend. Brad fiddled with the intercom, seeking admittance.

It seemed that the gate would be better placed farther off the road, but once we passed through, the reason for its placement became obvious. The twelve-foot laurel hedge that hid the house from the road also concealed a moat-like ditch and a ten-foot high metal fence with what seemed to be artsy razor wire along the top.

Only the first sign that we'd entered a medieval fortress.

The man who opened the door for us wore black, his collared shirt revealing pumped biceps, his impassive face marred by acne, his side-arm nestled against chiseled pecs.

If you met my cousins, you'd know I'm used to people who open-carry within the boundaries of their land. What I wasn't used to: this guard studied first Brad and then Victor intently, nodded, and let them pass. Natalia and me? We were condiments, ketchup passed along with the meat. The guard didn't look at us twice, just herded us toward the living quarters.

We passed two metal doors in the wide corridors, each with blinking electronics along both sides. Their massive metal frames interfered with any "open concept" that a future realtor might want to describe in selling this house. In fact, its outstanding sales feature: the interior was one giant panic room.

Though I never saw the kitchen, so what do I know?

Past the last door, the hall opened to a room as wide as the entire house. Floor-to-vaulted-ceiling windows opened to Lake Washington, where the sky still dropped a major portion of the Pacific Ocean, rain so thick that Seward Park across the lake was only an outline. In front of the windows, three large dogs—a Malamute, a Doberman, and a Ridgeback—claimed ownership of the large, cowhide-covered sofas. A finger snap from Luke kept them in place, so they watched us but we escaped being jumped on. The whole space reeked of fruity pipe smoke.

"Hello, y'all! How's it hanging?" Luke beamed at us from beside one window. He pumped Brad's hand, then Victor's. "Mr. Pearl. Haven't seen you about these parts since—"

"November, two years ago. We talked about your Second Amendment campaign."

"Ah, yes. Now you're writing me up again. What's the occasion?"

"The anniversary of the launch of Zeus. It's this Friday. A red-letter day."

"Nothin' rings people's bells like Golden Oldies, eh? Like playin' 'Born on the Fourth of July' when you want people thinking about glory and how great this country is."

Luke turned his attention to Natalia and me, while I pondered whether anyone paid attention to the lyrics when "Born on the Fourth of July" played.

"Hey, miz-z-z!" Luke hissed the consonants. "Got my ass in a crack with ol' Daniel last night. He called to remind me that there's girls who can run rings around me. And how I should ought to show respect."

"I'm from here," I said. "I know how real people talk. No offense was taken."

He grinned—one of those guys who got out of every ass-crack by offering the same grin as when he was five years old. "Daniel says you proved yourself with the big boys, better'n us. Better'n we ever done did, however famous it made us."

"I can't claim that," Natalia said. "Wouldn't dream of it."

"Nor I." I agreed, eyes wide. "Your Zeus project is more than legendary. It reached into most every life on the planet."

"Before 64-bit demanded universal firmware changes." Luke's voice scratched with resentment. Victor had a pad and pen, and seemed to be writing down what we said.

"Change happens. Natalia and I don't have a legacy like yours. We're just hackers."

Beside me, Natalia squirmed. If I were clairvoyant, I believe Natalia's subvocalization read: *WTF? This asshat?* How I wish I had one moment to tell her everything that happened since I ate a box-lunch sandwich with her the day before.

"I like that," Luke said as he came toward us, finally ready to shake hands with *the grrrls*. A sawed-off shotgun lay on the sofa behind him. "I better get to the business Dan bugged me to do, proving to you how he's got the best game in town."

He said *bidness*. His online curriculum vitae said Lakeside, the top Seattle private high school, and summa cum laude from Burlington, where he'd met Dan. My illicit, hide-out-in-the-Olympic-backwoods uncles don't say *bidness*. People from the Northwest only hear *bidness* on TV. I know the Northwest backwoods in my bones, whether it's the crappy commune or unemployed logger variety. More than a dozen of those guys might appear at a Byron family cousins reunion—if even one of them had an idea how to organize such an event beyond buying an extra twelve-pack of tall ones and three dozen weenies at Costco on the day before the Fourth of July.

So far, I had no clue why Luke performed this cracker act.

He turned his back on us womenfolk to talk jive with Victor, while Brad (who clearly didn't want to be there, whatever he claimed earlier) stared out the window, where that veil of rain still masked the landscape.

For thirty seconds Natalia sent questions with her eyes, with a twitch along the left side of her face, and with a WTF pursuing of her lips.

I twitched back: *Message received. Ready, player?*

Two-factor authentication for trust. No other message attached.

She blinked once, lifted a brow in assent.

Then Luke clapped his hands, I guess for attention.

"Shall we get down to it?"

"Actually, Mr. Connor," I began.

"Luke. It's got to be Luke. My old pappy is Mr. Connor. Even if you don't want me to call you Natasha and Samantha, you gots to call me Luke."

"Dan did a good job last night of convincing me, after you dropped by to say how-ya."

Again I felt Natalia squirming by me. But she said, "What we'd really like is to see what you're doing now. Lu-uke."

My friend Natalia is just the best.

▪

Brad bailed out of the conversation—he had to talk with Patricia's doctors—and retreated to a corner, away from the window, to bend his head over his phone, done with us. Then Victor looked at his phone, said he had to connect with his boss, bailed to the other end, tapping furiously on his phone.

Meanwhile, Natalia had put a nickel in Luke, and he talked and preened and wanted to teach us things.

"Dan says if I convince you to go to work for him, he'll lend me your genius."

"That's kind."

Luke chuckled. "Dan doesn't know what I got here. Maybe you geniuses will find things to learn from."

Natalia said, "We see that you prize security. There's always something to learn from people who are serious."

"You betcha. Of course, living here makes it the safest of places, because they like to protect each other."

"Who?"

"The Jews, of course. Surrounded by them here. Of course, that didn't work so well for them on 9/11."

Okay, this meeting just went south. All the way past the Equator to Antarctica.

"But that was an inside job," Natalia said, having learned better than me to get along by going along.

"Some didn't check their messages," Luke said. "But we get to today, when it's important to protect Israel since it's not time yet for the apocalypse. Those fundies praying for Armageddon are whack jobs, reading Revelation when they ought to be studying *Jane's Defense Weekly*. You know what I'm saying?"

"I do." Natalia agreed vigorously.

"It's who has the hardware, right? And the software to make it sit up and beg?"

We um'd and uh-huh'd. It took only a skoosh of feedback to keep his mouth going. But Natalia interrupted.

"Mr. Con—Luke. Would you show us your server-client configure-ation? I'm still setting up our business and would love to steal ideas."

More preening. And then the tour of the northern quarter of his living space, where a set of towers hummed, and banks of monitors were hung to avoid reflection from the massive windows. He named each element of the configuration—I mean more than giving details about boards and components: he effing had a name for each unit, like how you name a dog. All female names. *"Because that's who does the real work, eh, ladies?"* His entire server setup belonged in the Museum of History and Industry, down at South Lake Union. Not one of his pricey pieces of hardware had been updated for the last five years. To say it nicely, if quantum computing is the next big threat to security on the Internet, Luke Connor was not in the vanguard.

"Don't touch." He spoke sharply, but then slimed a smile for Natalia.

"Who consults for you?" Natalia asked, her hands plunged deep in her jeans' back pockets. Trying clairvoyance once more, I guessed that she didn't want his server crud to get on her hands, not that she had to keep from touching his antique hardware.

"Looking for customers for your little *bidness*?" That boy-wolf grin again. "My buddies set me up, after they got me thinking about what it's possible for someone like me to do."

"Ex NSA?" I asked brightly, however much I'd never want that label applied to me.

"What do they know? Oh!" He put his hand over his mouth, pretending he was a bad boy. "Not to insult what girls like you have to do these days to get a paycheck. You'll forgive me?"

"No offense." I shrugged. Didn't finish speaking my whole thought: *No offense could be greater than yours.*

Luke rubbed his palms, excited to share his secrets. "There's a group of us working together. Most are ex-Mossad. They came to me, got me thinking about what I know how to do in the world. Now that we got terrorists twintering their plans." Yes, he said *twintering.* "And especially when they be embedding their propaganda as hidden images in their video, well, then you're talking up my alley. And Tirkel and Osborne can kiss my lily-white ass."

Natalia, big-eyed, nodded. "So you get up and fight radical Islam every day. Truly?"

We'd been sent there to be recruited for aDVers. Instead, we find this—*person*—that some agent from who knows where had recruited as a useful idiot. Somebody has to get up every morning and rattphukk on the twintering, I guess.

"Are you safe?" Natalia drew close to Luke, clutching the sleeve of his shirt, glancing back and forth between Victor and Brad. She dropped her voice to a whisper. "Is all your protection to ward off kidnappers?"

"When you have a certain reputation, you got to take care." He effing patted her hand. "For what I'm doing, there's every reason to expect a full frontal."

"Oh my!"

Natalia never once in her life, before that moment, squeaked *oh my*. Very hard to compete. But I tried.

"Are you crunching your decrypt in a private cloud? Do you have a seven-gen datacenter in your basement? Quad cores in sets of twenty-eight? FPGAs for parallel computation?"

"You got it, sister." He nodded as if what I said made sense. Field-programmable gate arrays are real things, but I'd just recited a recipe for word salad. Unless Luke was jerking my chain, it made no sense that the massively brilliant Daniel Llewelyn might ever have spent three seconds with Luke, the total effing idiot.

"You're the math girl, right? Daniel said you got a kind of magic he wants. Says you always been a great team player. Me, I go it alone. I do what I know how to do, right up to my very limits. Then it's time to pass it on to my friends, who got datacenters for crunching bongo kinds of data. Make Google look like amateurs."

He damned well meant Israel, without ever saying the word. For the time Natalia spent drawing Luke out, I tried to make sense of it. I know several mathematicians and analysts who work there, all on the cutting edge of tomorrow. There's no way Luke Connor's intellect added jackapples in their world.

The black-shirted muscle man beckoned Luke from the iron-door passage, indicating with his thumb and little finger that a phone call was the issue.

"You girls want to excuse me? I won't be a moment. Woulda–shoulda–coulda be finding coffee for you."

When Luke passed through the iron door, Natalia sighed heartily. Then she started it, not me.

"'Space Cowboy.'"

"'My Heroes Have Always Been Cowboys.'"

"'Cowboys from Hell.'"

"'Mamas Don't Let Your Babies Grow Up to Be Cowboys.'"

"'Cows with Guns.'"

Before we totally cracked ourselves up, Victor scowled, then growled at us. "The problem with people like you is that you've never been anywhere truly dangerous. Never felt your heartbeat while wondering if a bullet might tear it open the next minute."

Okay, that came from off the wall. But Natalia smiled warmly. Didn't assert any history, like having been a child in Kosovo. Instead, she did what she does: asked questions. "Where did you serve? Somalia? Afghanistan?"

"Infantry? Airborne?" I asked. Yet I gave Victor an out. "But you're a journalist. I've heard they see the worst of the worst, with no weapon in hand."

Victor hesitated, his hooded eyes darting left and right. "Kosovo with the peace forces. Then Iraq as a reporter. Kosovo changed the way my eyes see the world."

"I've heard Kosovo was hard," Natalia said, still not sharing any personal history.

"Yeah. Not like what the poor fuckers found in the Nazi camps. But it changes you when you stare into a mass grave, even when it's too cold for the creepy crawlies or disintegration of bodies in the heat, like in Iraq."

"That must have been awful for you," she said.

Victor dipped his head as if she'd given a benediction and then responded to her smile as if she were flirting. "It was harder than you read about here in the news. But it's not right to share that kind of horror with girls like you."

"It's kind of you to spare us," she said. Me, I was ready to run screaming from the horror of Victor, the leavening atop the rotten grain of Luke's paranoid fantasies. And Brad? Too wrapped up with the cardiac doctors to even glance our way.

Between dog funk, pipe smoke, and guys gassing b.s., I needed to breathe. The nearest glass wall included a sliding door, so I stepped out onto the deck and into the grey day, sheltered from the worst of the rain by the generous overhang. The lake was delightfully choppy, and the cold air felt good. I stared through the veil of rain at the choppy lake waters for a minute before I glanced down.

Giant boulders piled beneath it, the deck hung out over the water's edge, another roll of fancy razor wire strung between water and rocks. The place had everything but gun turrets. I looked up, in case I hadn't spied them yet.

"Girl, you'd like to be catchin' your death out here." Luke appeared nearby, too near, and had his arm around my shoulder to lead me back inside. Black-shirt steroid man stood close to my other side.

"Help her in," Luke said. "This girl's special. And ol' Daniel has her back."

Black-shirt held the door. Inside, Luke pointed to a tray, offering us coffee from a French-press vessel.

What else did we learn on this visit? At the far end of non-allied libertarianism is a rich man, living on proceeds from a patent while asserting radical anti-tax truisms (which contribute to his well-being). You'll be happy to know that however much tyranny threatens liberty, under existing laws Luke expects to live to be one hundred and ten years old without any disruption of his personal pursuit of happiness.

Free. The way God meant us to be.

"And best of all for this house," Luke finished counting off the virtues of living at the far end of Mercer Island, "I can see who's within listening distance, depending on their hardware."

"It's like Krak de Chevalier," Natalia said.

Luke frowned, not understanding. "Crack?"

"The Crusader castle in Syria."

"Ah." The word *Syria* scatted his thoughts, like BBs on pavement. "Chickenshit kings in Europe gave up on the Holy Land, and now their Euro inheritors want to repeat history. Heroes push civilization ahead, and then the cowards stay home to harvest the gold and let the borders shrink. It's time to surge forward and drain blood."

"Seriously?" I should have bitten my tongue to draw blood, because I sent him into a tirade.

"Oh, I bet you girls are some of those who want to be scared about using the Big One. We don't even need to be going there, given the gains that people like us are making against the ragheads. They play crafty, but they just don't understand engineering like we do." He bumped me with his elbow. Good lord but I endured a lot of unasked touching that morning. "But look at that Krak castle in Syria. It's white ingenuity that built that, right? And we're building the best walls now."

Actually, it was Syrian slaves. And the Crusaders imported that engineering back into Europe, rather than the other direction. But Luke had more to say.

"Here." He held out a manila folder of news printouts. "There aren't many in my circle now that'd appreciate what this means. While I can't show you how I been helping my friends, here's a peek under the skirt at the outcomes. Israel isn't shy, like they are in this country, about saying how they're winning the fight."

See? He said it: he's helping Israel. At least he thinks so. Natalia passed his victory clippings to me one by one after she read them.

"Wow, this was you?"

He shuffled, aw-shucks style. "With a little help from my friends. Of course, I'm behind the curtain."

All of these cases were well publicized, at least in the security community. All included U.S. partnership. One of them was a project Natalia worked on when she was at—never mind, she can't put that on her resume. Two of them were projects Zak and I worked on. To my knowledge, none of them involved information sent to or received from a jerkoff cowboy hacker. Luke's whole cyber-sleuthing scene had less substance than a roadside daiquiri stand in hell. My skin crawled. A knot formed in my throat, keeping me from screaming.

Blessedly, Brad had to be on his way, so we said heartfelt faux goodbyes and left Victor there to finish his interview.

Walking to the car, Natalia's nose wiggled in the way it does when she tries to stop herself from laughing.

"What?" My whisper sounded more like a croak.

She held up her cellphone, which was prompting her to connect to an available wireless network. She punched a couple of buttons, then showed me the successful connection icon. Brad, meanwhile, started his car. Over its quiet purr, Natalia said, "Let's drive by later for giggles, to see what else is open on Mr. Paranoia's unsecured wireless network."

13

Why Can't We Be Friends?

SINCE VICTOR ELECTED TO STAY behind to finish his interview, it was just us three in the BMW on the long and winding road back to I-90 and Seattle. Natalia rode shotgun, and I sat behind her.

"Interesting." Natalia's voice lilted in a way that one might take any meaning from the word.

Brad glanced swiftly her way, then back at the road.

"It's a tribute to Dan's loyalty." He beat his thumb on the steering wheel, like you do when listening to music. We weren't listening to music. "That guy's been a freaking crank since long before I met him."

"You've known Luke a while?" Natalia's voice warmed to friendly interview mode.

I didn't join in, just listened while I checked my messages.

> ***KRYPPTIKK JOB: #QUESTCODE_PRIVATE***
>
> *ZakM:*
>
> Wow. I say your name, and Mr. Llewelyn is on the phone to work with us.
>
> *SByron:*
>
> Happy 4U. Do I get a bonus as facilitator?
>
> *ZakM:*
>
> Heh.

Ah, one thing went right this week. Then Brad's answer roused my attention. His voice sounded tight.

"Since I interned on Prometheus. My sophomore year."

That's what Patricia said, that Dan mentored Brad long ago, before we met at Princeton. Once Brad let out that first complaint about Luke Connor, he uncharacteristically began a quiet rant. For many people, being behind the steering wheel is like a truth serum.

"The day I walked in the door, I found the dev team bonded around hating Luke. We had to listen to that loser unload his b.s. day and night—mostly night, since he never showed up until four o'clock. Always bitching about what's unfair, how he's badly compensated, how the future of H-1B visas meant the demise of America as a world power."

"Met guys like that before." Natalia, the master of neutral statements that keep the conversation flowing.

"They had me run the builds. I swear, Luke never checked in significant lines of code. Didn't fix his bugs in a timely way."

"Let me guess," Natalia said. "He never worked on other people's code in his spare time. Never commented his own code, other than to stick his name beside a Contact-Me flag."

"You got it." Brad hit the turn signal with a vengeance and jammed on the gas as he merged onto the I-90 bridge. "And Luke always got away with being a snot, however much the team culture emphasized mutual respect."

"My sympathies," Natalia said. "Been there. Got the t-shirt."

It's the cliché we repeat because, in the tech sector, they do reward over-compensated developers with logo'd t-shirts.

"What did that groupie Victor have to say for himself?" Brad said; he wasn't actually asking. "How he ran psy-ops against computer-illiterate warmongers in Kosovo? About his undercover journalism in the darknet? About to sell a book, is he? I wonder who'd pay him to fluff Luke Connor's butt. Or who'd pay for an article on a jerk like Luke?"

"*Jane's Defense Weekly*," I said. "If you listen to Luke tell all about his adventures."

We then rode in silence to the Mount Baker tunnel.

When we passed through the darkness into daylight again, the rain had stopped. Brad said, "Luke expressed a grand sense of his code and how valuable it was. Nobody else saw it. Except Dan. Who took Luke with him whenever he changed teams. Talk about unearned privilege."

"It confirms my belief." Natalia gazed out the passenger window, not seemingly impassioned by Brad's complaints.

"That Luke got where he is on a big, fat sinecure?" Brad shifted down abruptly, exiting I-90.

"That there's a secret factory in Area 51 which creates Bad Programmer clones." She paused. "Why did Dan insist we talk to Luke Connor? This was the oddest but not the most enjoyable recruitment meeting I've ever been invited to."

Had to clear my throat to speak. "It wasn't meant to recruit us. It was a warning."

Brad's shoulders hunched up. A puzzled frown wrapped half way around his head. "What?"

"Dan wanted us to see what happens to people who believe they can go it alone."

It took Natalia half a second. Then she blurted, "Freyja's golden tears, deliver me."

We left Natalia on Fifteenth East near our office, while I asked to stay with Brad, since I wanted to get back to Harborview and he was on his way to Swedish hospital, both of which sit atop Pill Hill.

"Visiting a friend?" he asked while I climbed into the passenger seat beside him.

"Family." I reserved the right to keep one-half of my life out of the other half. But I endeavored to be more like Natalia, to keep the social conversation going. "I'm surprised to hear you castigate Luke." I weighed my words. "You've got that CEO thing down, never letting people know what you think."

"Do you hold that against me, Sam? Is that what gets in the way of seriously considering our offer?"

"Honestly, I appreciate that you've always known what you want. And made sure you got it. What do you want now, Brad?"

"Same as last we met. To be a superhero in the computer world. And I'm on the brink. Otherwise, I'd be just another project manager, skeezing through each day." He turned on a blinker, but didn't change lanes. "Though I suppose if I settled for that, it'd relieve the pressure."

"Could you do that? Settle for something less? I don't think you could. Which is a good thing."

We zoomed up Spring Street, which passes for a backroad up First Hill. Brad cleared his throat. "In grad school, all during that hack-a-thon, when you were telling everyone what to do, I kept seeing that Celtic tattoo in the web near your thumb, while I was trying to decide. Down the rabbit hole into algorithms I didn't understand? Or pursue a path where I could lead?"

"You chose a hard path. Which is good."

While Brad searched for parking on the First Hill side streets, he didn't seem to hear me, still arguing with a former me in the hack-a-thon lab. "You geniuses can't do for yourself what I do for you. I can put physical, legal, and managerial structures in place just like that." He snapped his fingers. "I make possible the greatest imaginable future for geniuses to do their work. People like you, not jerkoffs like Luke. I hope you're coming to aDVers."

"I can't decide by Friday, so I guess the answer is still No."

"You have to!" He slammed the steering wheel, startling me. "What do you need? Tell me. I'll do whatever it takes to make it happen."

"There's a set of important problem I'm researching. It takes all my time right now." For example: Tony getting blown up in front of me took all the mind space not consumed by solving his puzzle: who else was in danger?

"More important than the aDVers mission? We have to focus on human trials in the U.S. as soon as possible." He parked more aggressively than I do. But since he'd gotten increasingly tense the closer we came to the hospital, this obviously wasn't about me. Especially since, when he switched off the engine, he said, "I have a wife and kids. That I go home to at night. Do you geniuses go home to an algorithm?"

Just, wow.

For some people, their mother almost dying can be a crazy Wonderland truth serum.

"If it matters, Brad, please believe that I admire what you've achieved. And what you're trying to do at aDVers."

"Then you'll join us? We need the best. Without you, we're stalled. Can't you see that I've personally created the best possible world for your work?"

"Brad, my decision isn't based on our personal relationship."

"Personal relationships are what make the world run. That's my experience. I learned that from Dan Llewellyn."

Too tired, too stretched, I mistakenly said what I thought.

"Here's my experience, Brad. People praise what I do. Want me on their team. I'm flattered and dive into the work. Then I realize they want me for their own purposes, to contribute to their personal success. Natalia and I work together for mutual benefit, for shared goals. I'm not willing to give that up to work inside a corporate entity."

A corporate entity that wants me, so it can satisfy demands from the NSA. If I wanted to do that, I could go to Virginia, where at least I'd have someone to sleep with. And I'd see Pippi at dinner every night.

Brad dropped his passion and turned ice cold. "This is an opportunity to work on shared goals with Dan Llewelyn, as a mentor and a partner. Who in the world would pass that by?"

"Yeah? I get effing 'mentoring' when some guy is trying to keep me on his project, to meet his goals. No true understanding of collaboration. So I'm inclined to stick with my one partnership, my posse of two."

"That's sad, Sam. I worry that you'll end up an unused tool like Luke Connor. Or Victor what's-his-name. But the collaboration and real team work you want? We have it at aDVers."

"You should worry about your mother, Brad. Not me."

He folded in on himself, as if I'd kicked him in the gut. After a few seconds, he grabbed the steering wheel, pulling first and then beating on it. "She must have said goodbye to you, and then sat down and said hello to her own mortality."

Since I still had too many what-ifs and not enough facts, I couldn't share my fears with him. I rested my hand on his, where he clutched the steering wheel as if it might keep him from sliding into hell.

He sniffed. Then put the key fob in his pocket and opened the door. "I almost lost my mother—maybe I will soon—and I feel that I don't even know her."

"She told me how much she admires you." But she didn't tell me her secret. "Stay with her now, every hour you can."

Out on the street, he called after me. "You can't do your best work alone, Sam. Isn't that obvious?"

▪

It's a couple of blocks' hike from Swedish hospital over to Harborview and its world-class trauma unit. By the time I hit the elevator button, I'd become consumed by the insanity that Luke Connor represented. Not the tacky cowboy stuff, which you can find everywhere.

What did his "ex-Mossad" friends have Luke doing for them? Broadcasting propaganda via kiddie hacks? Tampering with the few remaining systems that had Zeus firmware, systems so ancient they run only in rural areas where there's electricity only on alternate Tuesdays?

Or did someone set up a scam, intending to extort him later, like a Nigerian Prince scheme, but posing as former Mossad? I couldn't figure who it was that Luke Connor served as a useful idiot, because I couldn't figure where "useful" might be possible.

Dan is rich, and Dan is loyal. Maybe Dan pays people to appear in camouflage and combat boots to discuss conspiracy theories with Luke, to keep Luke out of aDVers and other Real World business. The lack of rational sense drove me crazy, so I stood outside the elevator texting Dan Llewelyn.

> ↬Sam:
> Interesting field trip to visit Luke this morning.
> Thanks for the introduction. So many lessons learned.

> ↬Sam:
> Can I ask? Are the Mossad agents a present from you?

Actually, I didn't send that last message. No use making my new friend Dan think I'm a total lunatic.

Even with lack of sleep as an excuse, I wasted headspace on that Space Cowboy, even though no one was paying me to think about crazy rich guys. In fact, now that I'd finished Zak's mission, the only paying clients I had were Brad (who didn't, at this moment, need to hear my suspicions about Patricia's malware) and Tony.

While I waited for the elevator and glanced at my phone for an answer from Dan, a tap on the shoulder caused me to nearly lose my shit. I whirled, elbows out.

"Hey, be cool." It was Tem. Who seemed to be adept at ducking my elbows.

"Are you still stalking me?"

"Your receptionist said I'd find you here. You need to look at all the new crap on your social."

His printouts included several of the same messages and same Internet service provider address as the last research he shared.

"Friday is a good day to die."

"Great. Thanks. It's a good thing it's only Thursday. What else have you learned from all your hackery?"

"You'll have to ask Clarissa," he said, wandering off when the elevator finally arrived.

At the trauma-care nursing station, I asked the dude at the desk about Tony's status, repeating that I was his sister.

"Well, half-sister." I smiled, remembering to account for the missing Asian and African portion of my heritage.

"He's drifting in and out, but stable. We expect to move him to another floor later this afternoon."

"That's good news, right?" The hallways thrummed with a calm, quiet announcement over the speakers.

Bong-bong, Code Blue. Check your email.

The nurse blinked, listening to the message. "Yes. Do you want to see if the officer will let you in?"

He walked me through the corridors to a room at the end of the farthest hallway. The door was closed. The nurse knocked and pushed the door half open. "Ma'am, Mr. King's sister is here. Can she come in?"

Though I didn't hear an answer, the door was cast wider and I was inside with the sound of respirator, suction, and beeps that I hadn't heard since the day my grandmother didn't get to come home to die.

Clarissa sat on the guest chair, tidy and composed in a snow-white blouse and no-nonsense navy business suit, accessorized with a necklace: FBI credentials on a chain. No hellos.

"Your information proved useful last night." She watched Tony, not me. "The agency was able to fax positive identification to the SPD.

The damage isn't terrific. Only as bad as a kid who overspent at the reservation fireworks."

Tony's eyes move behind closed lids, his face like a badly sunburned beach boy. For the first time since we met, he looked vulnerable. Tied to the bed with tubes. Shallow breaths. But he was alive; if not one hundred percent awake, the animating soul of Tony was present.

"I'm happy to have helped."

"You didn't. I had to manufacture all of it. And I need to get him out of here." She turned her attention to me finally. "The security footage from my building shows a black SUV parked in the three-minute Wait Zone from the time you came inside until you left. The car then drove down the block and came back in the direction you walked."

"Please tell me you're kidding."

"You promised Tony you'd not get the FBI involved—"

"That wasn't the FBI or the NSA."

"Then what agency?"

"This whole thing isn't about Tony. Tem told you about me, didn't he? Those gangsters, the White Knights of the New Russian Revolution, are looking for me again."

"Oh, child. The world doesn't revolve around you."

"You're with the FBI, Clarissa. You can ask the locals—"

"I'm not with the FBI now. I'm with…it doesn't matter." She had her hand on Tony's arm, the one without a shunt, taking his pulse. He didn't respond to her touch any more than a sleeping person might.

"The year I worked in Hong Kong, Tony became disaffected with our way of life. Realistically, I couldn't take him along. That work was just about getting certain people out and other people in place. Wendy ending up there—well, there is such a thing as pure coincidence. Except, of course, I made the introductions that led to her marriage."

"Matchmaking spies?" I still did not understand how that woman's brain worked.

"She wasn't a spy. Merely a conduit. But yes. Doreen and her attorney. Patricia Yates and her civic-minded architect. You put people in appropriate circumstances and connections are made. If not on the first try, then eventually. Look at the raw material I started with: each an attractive, educated woman with unshakeable poise, the grace and wisdom of a woman who's reached a certain age, has a positive outlook, emotionally stable. An ambitious, wealthy man will fall in love."

"No one went into hiding after leaving your…team?"

"Patricia and Doreen stayed in town. Patricia kept her name. The others are scattered."

"Who? Where?"

"Doesn't matter. No others have contacted me. So if it's Argentina or the British Virgin Islands or Crete or Brussels, if they haven't called me, there's no trouble."

"Have you checked obituaries? Police reports for deaths?"

"Are you going to West Virginia to advise them on how to dig for coal?" Clarissa really didn't like challenges from me.

"So, you're absolutely positive no one else is at risk? What about the people who passed packages to your workers?"

"No one but me will ever know."

"And you passed packages to—"

"You surrendered your security clearance, Ms. Byron. You don't get to know."

Tony stirred, enough that her hand visibly moved where it rested on his arm. She studied him for a while and then began quizzing me instead of helping to find people in jeopardy. And I still had no realistic way to corroborate anything Clarissa said.

"What did Tony tell you, Ms. Byron? All of it, I mean. Not the thin broth you served this morning."

"He's chasing stolen crypto that a lot of people want. He's trying to identify the sellers and possible buyers."

"What stolen crypto?"

"He doesn't know. He thought maybe you might be selling it, and that's why Doreen and Wendy—"

"Tony, for God's sake." She waggled a finger at him, scolding. He opened his eyes, which startled me, but apparently not Clarissa. "Whoever's passing code, it has to be from inside. Is your organization so damned compartmentalized now that it can't look down and count its own toes?"

"Splain." Tony tried to talk through the tubes.

It's plain? Explain? There's pain?

Clarissa was still scolding him. "First, let's be clear. There's no spook in my system. Except you, whom we traced. There's only Tem and me. So when you can speak, you can apologize. A spook in my system! Do I insult *your* talents?"

"*Ssss.*"

Which didn't mean "no."

"And Russians? If you didn't lie to Ms. Byron, and you actually think that…well, I must be really good at what I do." She clapped her hands. "Let's get to work before anyone else shows up here."

She explained our morning conversation to Tony, whose eyes scanned rapidly behind his closed lids while she talked. He was awake, because he opened his eyes and took a deeper breath each time she paused in the middle of explaining her view of the Real World.

In the Nineties, Clarissa ran a placement service for executive assistants, only the best. Her employees? High-performing, medium-level office staff who'd begged for field work. They all understood their mission: to help identify foreign spies and saboteurs who might inflict harm in a new hot sector of the economy. The women were bonded, well-trained administrators who supported up-and-coming executives. Clarissa created and managed processes to harvest code under development, for purposes of national security.

"Not Soviets, Tony. And not malevolent in any way. But that life was too exciting for my workers to settle back into internal office routines afterwards. Most retired or married or otherwise left intelligence work after we closed the program."

"*Nary.*" Maybe Tony said, *"Sorry"*?

"Industrial espionage?" I asked; she didn't answer.

"The program stopped after Y2K pressures ended, even before 9/11 caused a massive strategy change in the tech sector. My crew got on with their lives. Until Monday when that malware spread, and some of my former team members sent me email, worried that it was about our old work."

Clarissa opened her attaché case, a slim and elegant black leather executive number that could never be mistaken for a cousin to my lost messenger bag. "To find an answer, our thesis is simple. Certain software that we captured remains mission-critical to the government. An internal bad actor—the one Tony chased—determined that my team and I know a secret about that software. The stolen OPM list allowed that bad actor to trace those women back to our work in Seattle."

"*Yesss.*" Better enunciation from Tony.

"Bad actor? Tony's rogue agent?"

Seeming to scold me now, or at least tutor me, Clarissa said, "Who else has the means to dig this deeply into the past? To find seemingly unrelated people so quickly? Make no mistake, Ms. Byron, that SUV that followed you? The threats? We're dealing with a rogue individual from a U.S. agency, if not a whole unit."

"Show Tony what you showed me this morning."

"Yes. We triangulated the projects we worked on with—" Clarissa paused, but only for dramatic emphasis, "—informed understanding of how deeply any project might have continued a life inside federal systems. We're down to two."

The list was the same one as from that morning, where she'd X'd off Prometheus and Zeus from consideration. Clarissa and Tem hadn't made much progress.

"No. The OPM list is a red herring." I'd reached that conclusion on the journey between Clarissa's hacker basement and the Hacker Comedy Theatre on Mercer Island. "Please listen. These women's sons called me, so I contacted Doreen and Patricia. The connection is that their sons both know me, not that they used to work for you."

"But the malware..." The beautiful thought lines in her forehead deepened, because she was pondering what I claimed, not because she hated my interruption.

"Likely thousands of people got that malware," I said. "Wendy and Doreen contacted you for help. But Zak and Brad contacted me. Doreen and Wendy were killed just so I'd be frightened into..."

Had to stop to clear my throat.

"'S'not right." Tony wiggled as best he could, shaking his head. Clarissa took away the oxygen cannula. "Timing's wrong for Wendy. She was already dead when I called Sam."

"Still—"

"No way the White Knights know that you and I have..." He had to get his breath.

"Shared information?" Clarissa prompted.

"A personal connection." He tilted his head, uncomfortably, to peer at Clarissa's list. "It's Prometheus. I thought I was looking for stolen crypto, but no other technology on the list is as crucial as Prometheus. You, Sam, are the coincidence."

"No, I'm the only person who knows the victims or their sons. They don't know each other. The White Knights—"

"Are in the darknet, trying to buy Prometheus." Tony seemed to relax a bit.

"But they don't know the feds once paid me to try to hack it." I was getting goosebumps. "Oh no. If they followed Zak or Brad because of Prometheus, then they found me by accident."

Tony wasn't relaxed. He jerked, disturbing his lines. The hardware at the other end of Tony's tubes complained about the disruption, beeping loudly. "Then the only person more valuable than you is Dan Llewelyn. Get me—"

Two critical-care nurses came through the door, neither gracious nor verbal in shuttling Clarissa and me to the hallway.

Clarissa leaned against the wall, arms folded. "Tony's wrong. The Prometheus project has no potential to put my workers in jeopardy. Dan Llewellyn ran the toughest possible security in those days. It has to be Tony's first guess, a rogue from inside the federal system."

"Then maybe that rogue agent found Doreen through Zak. He's working with Dan on the current generation of Prometheus. So, who else, Clarissa? Who else from your team worked on Prometheus or Zeus?"

"Patricia worked for the Zeus team, but never transferred any code. I worked as Dan's assistant for a month during Prometheus, when I couldn't place anyone else." Again, the slight deepening of the thinking lines across her forehead. "The only others alive from that project are Charlie Thomas, who's in Seattle. Dan Llewelyn. Luke Connor. But Luke Connor is—"

"A useful idiot. And Dan has strong personal protection. Leaving Charlie Thomas."

"Yes, but Charlie's practically off the grid. No phone. No Internet." She stirred, no longer leaning on the wall. "I'll have to go—"

"No, stay with Tony. I'll do it. Where?"

"Down on Eastlake." She was writing on the printout she'd shown Tony. "Here's Charlie's address and a note to introduce you. But with that malevolent SUV following you, please don't visit Charlie without protection."

"Who do I call? FBI? SPD?"

"No. Whoever attacked Tony listens at those posts. Take Tem along. He's waiting for me downstairs."

"Tem? He gets all Kung Fu Fighter with his skateboard?"

"Do you have friends who can be helpful?"

▪

Yes, I have friends. In the hall by the elevator, two paces past the "no cell phones" sign, I called Harley and asked him to pick me up at Harborview. Then I got impatient about elevators that stayed on the first floor interminably and ran down the stairs, trying to contact Zak.

Zak, who was battling intrusive hacks of a secret technology, was once more looking at that mythical gift from the gods, Prometheus.

Tony had probed in the underworld for dark-market sale of a stolen security technology. And now, from his crispy-critter critical-care bed, Tony declared that it had to be a Prometheus breach that had gotten two women killed.

On the surface, "digital watermarking technology" seemed a strange technology for the White Knights of the New Russian Revolution to be chasing through the darknet, much less killing people over. How?

The *creation* of the technology is from Dan's world. Tirkel, Osborne, and Rankin won the race to create the definitions that became public. Media businesses jumped on that form of digital watermarking for copy protection of movies and for monitoring broadcast theft.

Here we enter Tony's pirate world. The public watermarking technology is huge in the media world, where corporations want to protect their property. Consumers mostly consider it either an annoyance ("Why won't this DVD play on this device?") or a manifestation of corporate stupidity, because no one can prove the technology you might know as "DRM" serves a beneficial economic purpose. That is because hacking a consumer application of DRM is easy, and therefore it's not worth money on the dark market or elsewhere.

But if I claim that consumer DRM isn't particularly useful, then why would any government need its own watermarking technology? Such a technical solution for secrecy offers certainty that an image is genuine, whether from a battlefield or from espionage activities. Or if the watermark is robust, it could be used to absolutely prevent making copies. That has to be why, when Dan's Prometheus team came in one turn of the moon behind Tirkel et al., they won a single, unique customer. Prometheus had evolved to be the U.S. government's private, secure digital watermarking solution.

Therefore, the use of Prometheus technology—the *application*—is in Zak's world. The world I endeavor to avoid: national security, where it's paramount to know that broadcasts, video, and images are authentic. And, I assume, it's crucial for passing information that cannot be forged or tampered with.

Now the next part of the puzzle to consider is *distribution* of this private technology. Are we in the White Knights' world, as I maintain? The monetary value would be immense for anyone able to sell Prometheus technology to foreign actors, whether a government or a criminal enterprise. Suppose you could read or copy or transform images and visual content that the U.S. needs to keep absolutely secret?

If I could peer through the darkly tinted windows of the SUV that followed me, would I see eastern European cybermobsters? Or rogue agents of a U.S. security organization?

Whoever it is, they are pursuing people who touched Prometheus in any way, and they aren't merciful.

Tem loitered in the downstairs lobby, watching everyone who entered the building. We went to wait by the curb for Harley.

14

Garden of Serenity

NATALIA AGAIN CLAIMED SHOTGUN, SO Tem and I climbed in the back of the Jeep. Harley accepted my directions without a question, and we rode in silence for a few moments. Then Harley spoke.

"Sam, I'm going to ask a reasonable question in the midst of this chaos. Please tell the truth."

"What? I didn't do anything wrong." I reacted as if we were both back in the juvenile detention unit in the Limberlost sheriff's office. That part of me never got beyond age fourteen.

"Did you eat? And when will you get some sleep?"

Harley pointed to the paper sack in the passenger foot-well, which proved to contain a box lunch. While I was unwrapping a sandwich, Harley kept glancing in the rear-view mirror at Tem.

"Sam, you want to hand the other box to your friend? He looks a bit peaked. Now, tell me what we're doing."

"We're looking for a guy who might be in danger, like Judge Yates was. Or who has a clue about who's sending ransomware threats."

My explanation had to be enough. I still couldn't tell either Harley or Natalia that a rogue U.S. agent was involved—and even if I could, I still wasn't totally convinced. Tem was not ever going to say more.

Bouncing in Harley's no-suspension Jeep like Toad's Wild Ride, we careened down to Lakeview Avenue, past the forest of concrete pillars that hold up the I-5 freeway, and then we all slipped forward in our seats on the steep lane down to Fairview East. (You get a full lake view higher up, but only a fair view right alongside Lake Union. Our Seattle forefathers must have longed to be poets.)

Fairview Avenue is another Seattle-in-transition neighborhood. On the lake, new designer floating homes lined the last houseboat moorings the City Fathers will allow. Along the bluff above the lake, a new bank of apartments appeared each month, poured from the same 3D-printer mold as my new hyper-closet.

But where we traveled along the northern end of Fairview, a few dozen dwellings remained, now resembling a movie set: a huddle of cottages along the lakeside, the one-room dockworker shacks from the Twenties; to the east, close up against the bluff, stood old houses reclaimed in the Seventies, ferns still swinging from macramé hangers in the front windows, their tiny yards filled with ceramic pots and reclaimed ironwork displayed as art.

Harley eased off the gas. Natalia and I tried to identify house numbers, since the phone's GPS map couldn't report well amid the jammed-together cottages with dirt driveways winding off the roadway.

"Right there," Tem said from the backseat. "One on the right is a higher number, the other is lower. So it must be down that driveway."

Harley parked on the shoulder, which was a fancy name for compressed gravelly dirt scattered amid broken, weed-filled macadam. I shoved my shoulder against the passenger door, since that's the only way it opens, and stepped out into a long, tire-track puddle. Oh well, it's not as if wet feet are terminal.

"Maybe only Natalia and I knock?" I looked at my motley posse emerging from that rusted-out Jeep.

"Fine." Harley leaned against that Jeep, arms folded. Same posture as whenever he arrived to watch his deputy talk to miscreants. (The same way he would with whoever skated through Mrs. Waddington's barn, launched off the hay-loading dock, and scared hell out of her dogs. Though in the Pacific Northwest, some of us believe that an unused barn with a concrete floor should automatically be considered to be in a public trust and opened for its highest and best use. Oh geez, Harley was right, I was getting giddy. But not from lack of sleep. I admit to true fear.)

Tem settled beside Harley, arms also folded, but not leaning on anything and a head and a half shorter. Glancing back, I saw Harley talking, his head not turned to Tem. Then Tem spoke. An expert was about to extract more from Tem than I had managed.

Natalia and I tramped down the gravel drive to the two-room cottages huddled under the shelter of cedar trees, trees so large that they must have been planted just after the first settlers stripped the original forest. The cedar shingles of one tiny house hosted a Zen-like moss garden on the north side. The cabin we wanted was well-tended, though a year past when the white shiplap siding needed new paint. A single stone step led up to the front door, where a hand-carved sign hung from a sisal cord: In the Garden.

Down there under the cedars, cabins nestled hip to ass. There was no room and no sun for a garden.

"See the p-patch across the street?" Natalia nudged me.

Back up the gravel driveway.

Natalia waved to Harley and Tem, pointing to our next destination, a half-block south to one of Seattle's more magnificent p-patches. Tem glanced where we pointed, but kept talking to Harley, who'd settled into full listening mode.

The Fairview p-patch is among the best of Seattle's many glorious gardens. Roses hung on the rail fence, sunflowers tilted their heads, having offered most of their seeds to song sparrows and finches. It was early October, and we'd had a drenching rain, but the garden still offered bounty, though many gardeners had begun to put their plots to bed for the winter. A child's Eden of pumpkins still awaited harvesting; the red chard and Brussels sprouts would offer fresh greens into November.

But a weekday afternoon, after the downpour, the garden seemed deserted, save for one person in overalls and tall rubber boots who was methodically spreading winter compost over a planting bed, its walls created from stacked concrete slabs, as if this garden had been reclaimed from a destroyed civilization. A pile of withered corn stalks lay on a tarp in the pathway, ready for the communal compost heap.

"Hi," Natalia waved. "We're looking for a guy who lives around here. Charlie Thomas? Is there any chance you know him?"

The person with the rake proved to be a woman, about Brad's age, forty-something, with a striking sunburn, a chopped thatch of prematurely grey hair, breasts that jostled under her overall bib, and hands that spent lots of time in the garden.

"I'm Charlie. Who are you?"

"Friends of Clarissa Dalloway," I said. "She sent us."

A mischievous smile. "The real or the fictitious Clarissa?"

"Hard to tell the difference."

Charlie liked that answer. "Is Clarissa all right? She usually walks here, most afternoons."

"She's with her son. In the trauma ward at Harborview."

"Her son?" Charlie shook her head, an always-another-wonder gesture. "Never knew. What does she need? I'm happy to help."

"We came to warn you." I handed her the note from Clarissa. "You may be in danger. Because of your previous work with Clarissa."

Charlie looked at the note—"my friend Sam Byron"—and handed it back to me.

"Clarissa doesn't have friends." She resumed raking compost. "And Clarissa insisted there was no danger. That I was serving my country. How is it different a quarter century later?"

"We believe someone sold Prometheus secrets—perhaps a backdoor or a trap door. They've killed or tried to kill four people who might know. You're on the list of who might know about Prometheus."

"There is no such backdoor. Dan Llewelyn raised holy hell to make sure of it." Charlie stepped out of the bed, then pointed to a bench near the toolshed. "But yes, we should talk."

▪

Natalia had a message on her phone—childcare issues—and wandered back toward the Jeep to answer.

"I prefer to talk out here," Charlie said. She settled beside me on the bench, then brushed compost off her jeans. "This garden is more than a happy place for me. It's the key to serenity in my life."

"It is peaceful."

"And you have full view of whoever might be listening, even if it's from a boat on the lake."

"Uh." I hedged, hoping to offer a neutral answer. "Luke Connor expressed similar thoughts earlier today."

"But Luke Connor huffs paranoia like an addictive drug. I'm merely a realist."

"You agree there's a possibility that you're in danger?"

She pointed to a plot that held a tangle of vines. "Look at that. We had such a warm September, we're still picking tomatoes. You should take a basketful home."

Since I'd now gotten used to all these old-time coders playing Sphinx, taking their time to get to the topic at hand, I just waited. Charlie slipped a plastic bag from the pocket at the top of her overalls.

"A piece of shortbread?"

The cookie needed its wax paper wrapper. It nearly melted before I took a bite.

"One hundred percent organic," she said. "I trade what I grow with folks across the Cascades, so even the wheat and sugar are properly sourced. The butter is from the first wholly organic dairy in the Skagit Valley. The lavender is mine. From that patch right there. Oh, I should have warned you that it isn't vegan."

"Not a problem." And I shouldn't talk with my mouth full.

She didn't take a cookie. Instead, she stretched out beside me, crossing her rubber boots at the ankle, looking out over Lake Union while she talked.

"I do believe you about Clarissa," she said. "That's her handwriting, and she'd never send anyone she didn't trust."

"Is it true she has no friends?"

She pointed to where Tem was talking with Harley. "That boy. That's the only one I know about."

"Tell me about Prometheus. You worked on it?"

"Yes, what a pressure cooker. When that effort failed, we jumped right into the Zeus project. At the end of that death march, I spent a weekend by the ocean—though taking that much personal time was heresy on the Zeus team—and I decided that life shouldn't demand so much excess cortisol." She offered me a second cookie as soon as I wadded up the paper from the first one. "People who aren't in the industry don't understand. They tend to call us workaholics, but it's not that."

"It's because the problems to be solved are totally absorbing. I can't imagine leaving this life." I bit into the second cookie, feeling how true that was. My only quarrel was with the nature of the problems I had the opportunity to solve. And who paid me to solve them.

"Neither could I. Until it was too much. To stop, I chose a quiet and frugal path. Though I'm not poor. I'm like a rock-n-roll one-hit wonder, living on residuals."

"Tell me about Prometheus. Several of us are convinced that rogue agents are trafficking Prometheus secrets on the darknet. I believe that either sellers or purchasers are making life dangerous for your former coworkers."

Charlie said, "I once suspected that one of the developers coded a backdoor. When I brought my evidence to Dan, he asked me to do all I could to find it."

"The result?"

"You had to be on the team to know this, but I started by going line by line through Luke Connor's code."

"Brad Jones told me what a pill Luke can be to work with."

"Pill? Luke is twelve years old at heart." She laughed. "But what a kind person Brad is, to state it so nicely. When I knew him in those days, Brad was a flaming ball of ambition. He was quite upset about the implementation I found."

"You found a backdoor?"

"I found a crude Easter Egg, listing everyone's name, except Brad Jones's. That piqued Brad. But nothing matched Dan's fury. The only time I've seen him angry. He chastised Luke in front of the team, as if he wanted to drive the lesson home through public humiliation. Because an Easter Egg was known even back then to present an enormous security hole."

"He made Luke remove it?"

"Beyond that. Dan asked for more tests from me. I couldn't find proof, but I told him my coding skills weren't sophisticated enough. Dan himself picked up the details from my work and went through every line of code in the project. At the time, I deeply appreciated how Dan took me seriously and pursued the problem. Still do."

"So, no backdoor?"

"Nothing anyone with Dan's skills could find. When Dan sold Prometheus to the government, I was interviewed about what I knew about the code. I told the same story I'm telling you now, which they'd already heard from Dan. I believe they pursued another deep investigation, making sure the code held no surprises."

"And besides searching for Easter Eggs, you smuggled code for Clarissa?" A touchy area. I wasn't sure what words to use to discuss industrial espionage. Or theft. Also, I wanted another cookie, but wasn't going to ask.

Charlie said, "The FBI made its pitch over several interviews. You know how persuasive Clarissa can be. It took me thirty days to decide, but I finally agreed to pass Prometheus code to the government. Later, they bought the patent and took away all the code. I always believed they knew…"

"What?"

"The FBI knew that I told Dan about their pitch. I didn't agree to help until Dan convinced me that it was a decent idea, to cooperate with the government."

"And you knew it was the FBI because you got a U.S. paycheck?"

"No, because the interviews were downtown in the Federal Building. And no, I've never been employed by the government, only private companies. I was paid through a holding company in the West Indies. I declared it on my taxes and donated it to the Riot Grrrls Code on Fire Foundation."

The foundation that gave me a scholarship the first year I was at UW as a fast-track undergrad. I felt the conflicting circles of Reality versus Coincidence tightening around me.

Charlie seemed lost in thought. Then she laughed softly. "Dan laughs at the whole Easter Egg affair now. We were talking about it over Christmas dinner last year. He worked so hard to make sure Prometheus was clean, and then a year later the government paid him an immense sum to add a backdoor for them. So he'll be shackled to that code for the rest of his life, consulting on the care and feeding of

Prometheus secrets." She sobered, apparently drawing back from that personal memory. "To answer your question: the government version of Prometheus, yes, it has a backdoor. The original Prometheus code, no. At least within the bounds of Dan Llewellyn or any government security people to find it."

Discarding any notion of a third cookie, I kept my personal opinion off my face: that in the Nineties, there was slim-to-no chance that code reviews were as rigorous as any I'd be paid to do now.

Instead, I thanked Charlie for the background stories. "Now, I'm going to repeat the warning Clarissa sent me to deliver. It's extremely likely that your life is in danger. Just because you worked where you did. And because you knew Clarissa."

"My security system isn't as rustic as my house."

"The three women who were attacked had the best security imaginable. Yet two of them died this week."

Charlie sobered and seemed to draw within herself. She sat up on the bench, hands on her knees, prepared to move.

"What does Clarissa want me to do?"

"Go where no one might look for you. Tell no one where you are. Until Clarissa lets you know it's safe." I hesitated. "Though she says you don't use phones or computers."

"Not from my own home. I have an email address that I consult. But only from Internet cafes or the library."

"Then you are paranoid already?"

"Prepared. Not paranoid. I got advice at the rise of the Internet from Dan Llewelyn. And I took it to heart, to protect both my assets and my privacy."

"Fine. Let us help you get where you need to go."

"I'll just go to Dan for safety. It's a promise he always repeats, that if I need protection, he's always there."

We reached conciliation quickly enough, and I texted Dan.

> ✆2068888888:
> This is Sam Byron. I met Charlie Thomas, who's convincing me the value of joining your team.

While we waited for Dan's answer, Charlie and I traded small talk, about what it means to have a friend like Dan.

"'Friends like Dan' isn't a real concept is it? There's no comparison." I meant, being friends with someone that wildly rich.

"You mean who's honest and loyal to his friends?" Charlie took my words in an entirely different direction. "Who'll go beyond the bounds of reason to take care of his friends?"

"My experience is new. We've only just gotten to know each other outside of security research labs. We played music together last night." Was it just last night? Or half a lifetime and an explosion ago?

"Really? Dan must think a good deal of you. He plays only with people that he believes aren't…what's a good word?"

"Sucking up?"

"Close enough. When you have money," she tapped her nose, indicating herself, "you have to be diligent about keeping users out of your personal space."

I raised my hand in query, not understanding.

"Oh, too much Nineties jargon, eh?" she said. "Users and takers? Surely that concept about relationships remains in popular culture? People who associate for what they can use you for, not because there's true personal affinity."

"Ah, thank you. Yes, I understand the premise. I'm happy that Dan has tried to be friends." My phone buzzed with a text.

> DougFromTukwila:
> Charlie's my angel. Truth Goodness and Beauty.

> 2068888888:
> She needs help with a problem. Can I send her your way?

> DougFromTukwila:
> You Can Count on Me
> Tell Charlie I'm at my boat. See you at dinner?

"At his boat?" Charlie smiled reading the message I showed her. "It's just the other end of the street from here. I can walk."

"No, we'll call a cab and wait with you. Please don't come back until we let Dan know it's safe."

"But my things, my cat—"

"Dan has minions. Let him send someone to take care of it."

"And Luke Connor?" Charlie rose. "Have you warned him? Luke might be hard to convince."

I rose, too. "We're trying to find and take care of anyone who might need protection."

"What protection can you give Luke that he can't take care of himself? He's…a bit right of center."

"He's a bit right of sane."

With my handy throwaway phone from Tony, I called a cab company, repeating the address of the garden, not Charlie's house. As tedious as it can be to wait for a cab in Seattle, by the time Charlie had moved the pile of corn stalks to the compost heap, stashed all her tools, and locked the shed, the cab pulled up behind Harley's Jeep.

15

Colliding Circles

WHEN I RETURNED, NATALIA WAS tapping her phone noisily. Tem was still deep in true confessions with Harley.

"I was born here, but my mom and dad were undocumented. I don't know where they came from, or how. Clarissa knocked on my apartment door five days after my mom didn't come home. I was thirteen. Helped me get access to my parents' assets. Taught me to impersonate my mom online. But now I do my part to look after her."

Harley glanced my way. "Ready to go?'

"You bet," Natalia said. She tucked her phone into her bag.

"Wait a second." I'd made the decision: time to share everything with my team. So, out on the dirt-end of Fairview Avenue, I explained each piece carefully:

> Tony has been chasing a rogue agent who's selling Prometheus secrets on the darknet.
>
> His mother worked for the FBI to harvest industrial software code, including Prometheus.
>
> Zak was working with another team busy searching for who had obtained Prometheus secrets.

And then I repeated Charlie's story.

Silence reigned.

Tem spoke first. "So, at least two backdoors."

"Or," Natalia said, "Luke Connor and his fake Mossad agents are selling the original Prometheus—"

"—Extraction trapdoor," she and I said together.

And then we mutually stopped breathing for a heartbeat, considering: most likely, Prometheus wasn't being used merely to verify the authenticity of digital media like photos and video. Prometheus was the mythical gift, remember? It's most likely part of the watermarking solution for government databases, to detect tampering, trace leaks, maintain data integrity.

The kind of protection that was breached when the OPM database was hacked, when the list of spies was leaked to purchasers on the darknet.

"If you met this guy Luke," I said to Harley, "you'd see he's squirrelly enough to nest in trees and eat nuts."

Natalia described our morning with the hyper-paranoid cowboy. Then she urged us into Harley's Jeep. "Let's head back to Mercer Island. I want to listen some more before it's time to pick up my kids."

People climbed into the Jeep. For a few blocks, there was only the rattle and clatter of the Jeep over noisy concrete.

"What are we going to listen to?" Harley had the driver's seat, and once again Natalia took shotgun. I was in back with Tem, getting comfortable on the vinyl seat that half a dozen Owens family dogs had had their way with.

"His open wireless network." Natalia scrolled through the map on her phone. Finding Luke's address, she tilted the phone to show Harley the roads to choose. "I bet we find sideband messaging leaks."

"Is it legal?" Harley had already jerked the Jeep up the hill toward that abrupt I-5 entrance from Lakeview Drive.

"Absolutely," Natalia said. "I've testified with data taken in public that way. Completely acceptable evidence."

By the time we reached the I-90 merge lane south of downtown, we'd all agreed that Luke's backdoor in Prometheus must be what was being sought by my White Knight friends, by Tony and his team, and likely by several foreign actors. Tem and Natalia began to speculate:

> Luke's hackery chateau sent the ransomware, to silence anyone from the early development era.

Luke's "ex-Mossad" people murdered Doreen and Wendy.
And tried to set Tony on fire.

If anyone asked, and if I was free to say what I believe, then I'd have one message for the world.

SamsaraByron, World's Best Forensics Analyst:
Don't add backdoors in firmware or software for the government or anyone else.
You cannot guarantee someone won't open that door.

The World:
But what about the need to find terrorists?

SamsaraByron, World's Best Forensics Analyst:
Don't add backdoors. Others **will** open that door.
Do I need to say it three times?

"So, not your Russian boogeymen," Tem said.

"They could be involved with Luke. We still have to prove who sent the ransomware."

Once more Harley said, "This eavesdropping is legal?"

"Yes," Natalia said.

"And wise?"

While Natalia explained to Harley how she listened on open wireless networks, Tem chimed in about research he'd read and things he'd tried. Just a jolly batch of hackers rumbling down the interstate in a rusty red Jeep. For me: time to message Zak, even though we didn't have proof that Luke had sold his Prometheus backdoor.

KRYPPTIKK JOB: #QUESTCODE_PRIVATE

SByron:

Luke Connor from the original Prometheus project:
He knows about a backdoor that very likely migrated with the code the government purchased.
He talked about sharing secrets with foreign agents.
Still researching details.

ZakM:

Tell me where to look.

SByron:

Code likely went in with an Easter Egg that was removed. Check documentation in the Prometheus project history.

ZakM:

Can you give my customer enough for a warrant?

SByron:

He has a hokey hacker factory at his house.
I have two witnesses that he bragged about hacking in collaboration with former Mossad agents.
Is that enough?

ZakM:

Running it up our customer's chain.

SByron:

Attached Natalia's initial report on server signatures & ISP. Here's IRL street address.
Caution. Guy's armed to his oxygen-fixing gills.

.
.
.

▪

"No, I'm not kidding. Absolutely no trespassing."

Harley set the handbrake after stopping along the shoulder four car-lengths beyond Luke's fortress. He left the engine idling, though the Jeep was old enough that "idle" was a soft rumble. "Not one single action goes beyond the bounds of the law."

Natalia retrieved two laptops from her expensive bag and began fiddling with the software on one.

Tem said, "I can help."

"Okay. Sit back, Junior, and stay tuned to this station." She handed him the first laptop, which displayed a text-only window. From where I sat, it appeared to be sampling across network bandwidths, mostly reporting null. Natalia switched her attention to the other laptop.

"Cute." Natalia stared at the laptop she held. "Someone in the house uses Whacker. Even after last month's bad press."

Whacker: a new social network that people sent each other invitations to use, until a white-hat agency showed that Whacker security was leakier than your grandmother's rusted sieve. And a less kind hacker posted Whacker conversations between two political operatives colluding on a rattphukker smear campaign.

Tem hung over Natalia's seat, eager to see what she found, reading aloud for Harley's benefit and mine.

> "You paid us to deal with anyone sniffing for you."
>
> "I don't want to know details."
>
> "Do we have cover? Do you have preferred methods?"
>
> "Don't ask me how. Do what I contracted for."

Harley said, "If that's legal to capture—"

"Swear it is, on the graves of my children's six grandfathers." Natalia crossed her heart, balancing the laptop with her other hand.

Harley gripped the steering wheel, as if we were still on that jaunty ride, watching for potholes. "There's no identifying information. You don't know who's talking to who. What possible good will it do to steal that conversation?"

"It's not stealing." Natalia adjusted something in her software. "It's the same as listening to a conversation on the bus between two people sitting behind you."

"But it's worthless," Harley growled. "For law enforcement, it might as well be word salad."

"You be Grumpy, I'll be Sneezy." She punched his arm lightly, then scrambled to steady her laptop. "We'll leave when—"

"I've got it," Tem said. "Addresses both ways. Holy shit, Batman!"

Because I'd turned to see what Tem's laptop showed, I noticed movement out the Jeep's mud-smeared back window: Luke's black-shirted security-muscle guy was striding down the shoulder toward us.

Harley said, "Oh-oh. Hang on. Let's go."

But he wasn't looking in the rear-view mirror as he released the handbrake and accelerated. Out the front windshield, a convoy of black carryalls headed our way, as rapidly as the curving two-lane road allowed.

Harley kept the Jeep just under the posted speed. A quarter of a mile on, a pair of state patrol cars blocked both sides of the curving roadway, another pair of Mercer Island city police on the shoulder. They weren't letting anyone pass to the south. In our lane, they stopped each driver. Three cars on, it was our turn for Harley to explain that we were out looking at real estate opportunities. He flashed his law-enforcement ID when he produced his driver's license, which got us rapidly on our way, back to the city.

After days of trying to contact Evan Mulasky, I was surprised how little it took to make wheels turn. That simple hint to Zak, and here was action within an hour. Which was another reason why I sought to preserve the Great Wall of China between me and the NSA. A message from Zak bumped me out of my reverie.

KRYPPTIKK JOB: #QUESTCODE_PRIVATE

ZakM:

After talking with Mr. Llewelyn, we have enough technical details to solve our crisis.

SByron:

What was the problem?

ZakM:

Can't discuss. But customer liked your data. Seeking a warrant.

SByron:

We saw them on their way. Out on the island.

ZakM:

Wut? Wow. Did not know.

We rode in silence, not counting the Jeep's subtle early-Nineties roar and the traffic noise on the I-90 bridge. Inside the Mount Baker tunnel, Tem spoke.

"You said you wouldn't call the FBI. Then you did."

"No, I didn't." Not directly.

"Then what happened?"

"Beats me."

All that anxious bubbly excitement from eavesdropping? I settled back to a more familiar feeling: fear and loathing.

"It's the same ISP," Tem said.

"Internet service provider?" Harley was still learning his acronyms. "Same as what?"

"Same as Sam's White Knight death threats."

▪

At the office, Harley swept up garbage that had been tossed at our front door. Natalia went to her workstation, letting Tem follow her, as if he'd been elected chief acolyte. She transferred data from her two laptops and then began running tools. I listened to her explaining each step to Tem, not arguing when he had other suggestions. Whatever he'd been doing in Clarissa's basement, it wasn't kiddie hacking.

By the time she gave Tem a workstation to monitor output, I set to my own tasks. Natalia settled beside me, and we actually got some work done for a few minutes.

Yes, people who do the kind of work we do can sit beside each other, making progress, communicating continuously, yet work in companionable silence. Just the click of the keyboard if any of us types loudly.

KRYPPTIKK JOB: CLIENT#202_JONES

NDragon:

Ticket #2: Search Client#202 backups. Close ticket.
Results: Identified first backup where malware appears. System log shows a crash and reboot before install time. So I checked the previous backup, which contains the delivery package before it installed itself.

SByron:

Fantastic work!

NDragon:

Ticket #3: Set up a throwaway system to run the install while our tools capture all results. Starting now.

NDragon:

Without Dogs of War, these search-&-discovery loops will take until my kids graduate high school!

SByron:

Hope it can't detect our tools.

NDragon:

Ha! Bet we find source & phone-home details by tonight.

We paused to high-five, since it was our first headway on the ransomware mystery.

Harley was packing up his leather satchel, preparing to depart. "Come spend the night on the island."

I'd been messaging Zak (no response), Dan (offline, it seemed), Brad ("can't talk; sitting with my mother through some tests"), and my sister Eliot, just to exchange thoughts with someone who lived outside the lunacy of my world.

"Maybe I'll come out tomorrow." I'd decided to shower before meeting with Dan Llewelyn. "But you should take Tem. He can't go home since people were watching his house earlier."

"Really recommending the island, Sam." Harley made a move to complete an Owens family hug, but I had my phone up as a barrier. "Listen, we can snag a redeye flight to D.C. tomorrow. Monday's a holiday. Come along. Just to get away."

"You agree that my Russian mobsters are out and about? Or do you think I'm in the same danger as Doreen and Patricia?"

"It's just getting dang lonely around here without Pippi and Matt and Roz."

"There's no extra beds here." I called to Tem. "Go with Harley. He's got Wi-Fi, food, and a bed at his house."

Tem didn't look away from the monitor Natalia set him to watch. "I'll couch-surf with friends. It's fine."

"Ha!" Natalia jumped from her chair, darting a finger at her monitor. "Just look at—"

Sirens blared, deafening.

Four black armored vehicles appeared in the street, as if from nowhere. Officers crowded out of the doors away from our office, setting up a cordon. More SPD vehicles blocked the streets as far as could be seen from our office.

And an officer on a speaker-horn called out. "Everyone inside, do not leave. Shelter in place. Please lie down for your safety. "

"Dang." Tem stared out the window. "We're swatted."

"Maybe it's real." No one heard me over the repeated commands from the SWAT officer to shelter in place.

"Do exactly as you're told." Harley got on his knees, then lay on the floor, hands behind his head. "Don't speak except to answer questions."

"Freyja save us!" Natalia lay down. "Late fees at daycare again."

The lead SWAT officer stated his name over the speaker and then said, "I understand there's a situation here. We want to help."

Our office had glass doors and windows with full view from the street, so our saviors could see four people lying on the floor. Harley followed the instructions to indicate whether we were under duress—the commanding officer never said "hostage," but that's apparently what they'd expected to find. It took fifteen minutes to determine that our little team was neither a threat nor under threat. During that time, the tactical team cleared the entire building, all four floors. With the fire department and building manager to give them access.

Here's what I learned in that part of the day's thrills:

> Even if you only see their boots, a SWAT team scares the bejeezus out of you.
>
> Even if the team leader says, "We're here to help," you aren't feeling it when your nose is jammed on the floor.
>
> A dyed-and-polished concrete floor amplifies noise, especially when your ear is two inches from the concrete and most of the noise is from steel-reinforced boots.
>
> You can't make your brain work on the problem that absorbed you moments before. But you can obsessively compose a single text message to send as soon as you get to stand up.
>
> You'll wish you'd peed twenty minutes earlier for the entire fifteen minutes you spend on the floor.

"This is a mistake." Even with his face to the floor, Harley still sounded authoritative. "ID is in my rear pocket."

Once Harley was known, he answered all questions. We were allowed to stand, each with a personal officer checking our ID.

"I believe it's called swatting," Harley explained to the team leader. "I've been sending SPD the worst of this week's harassment. Including death threats. I'm not surprised, but..." They stepped into the building foyer, so I didn't hear the rest.

Tem also indicated his ID was in his pocket. "I'm just delivering sandwiches." He had the sack from Harley's Jeep in his hand. "My boss'll kill me if I don't get back."

His personal SWAT guy sent Tem outside to speak with yet another officer.

My SWAT officer—a woman—turned me around while she inspected my clothes. So I had to stare out our office window at a dozen guys in distressed hoodies who'd gathered across the street, all in Mr. Robot masks, all scraping shame-on-you signs with their fingers. My own fingers tingled. My arms were falling asleep, clasped behind my head that long.

"Ma'am?" Natalia asked as the female officer checked the pockets of her pants. "Is there any progress on tracing that anonymous tip? Because I think whoever it is might be standing across the street."

When officers stepped into the street, all the mini-Mr. Robots scattered, running up alleys and across nearby parking lots. Tem stood on an opposite curb, yelling. I assumed he called names or tags of kids he recognized. A uniformed officer crossed to speak with him, then began writing down whatever it was that Tem said. Which I'm inclined to think didn't include naming names.

Swell. We'll never make friends in this neighborhood. Our first two weeks cannot have left anyone on the block thinking we're the kind of neighbors you invite to the barbeque.

About the time the entire SWAT team agreed with Harley that there'd been a hoax, my favorite detectives appeared, Jeremiah looking more and more like a haggard Colombo, while Carlos seemed to have a stay-pressed suit and spine.

Natalia made a brief statement, and produced that daycare pickup excuse, which seems to work great, especially if there's one other parent in the mix to grant credence to the primacy of avoiding daycare late fees.

After all courtesies were exchanged, the SWAT team departed, leaving us with the detectives. On his way out the door, one of the

SWAT officers said to Jeremiah, "At least the SPD outcome beats bat-ass on Mercer Island." I believed that's precisely what he said *bat-ass*.

"What?" Far too impulsive, I caught Jeremiah's sleeve. "What happened on Mercer Island?"

"Alcohol and Firearms went to serve a warrant. But the guy blew himself up instead of answering the door."

ATF. Not bat-ass. Of course.

Jeremiah seemed matter-of-fact about that agency's business, until I said that I knew Luke Connor, that he'd been stalking me online, and that I had solid guesses about what drew a SWAT team to his house.

▪

As soon as the detectives and the SWAT team left, I switched the cable TV to the local station Harley used to monitor the Potholes Deadlock. Just after I turned up the volume, Tem slipped back into the office. Natalia followed not many steps behind him. At my inquiring glance, she shrugged.

"What? I just remembered it's not my turn for pickup."

Harley shushed everyone so we could hear the news.

> "...Bureau officers and local law enforcement serving a warrant were surprised by an explosion that shook southern Mercer Island this afternoon.
>
> "...Several dogs at the home were transported by animal control officers to a shelter.
>
> "...The police have not yet identified any persons involved in the incident. But our reporters have learned that the home belongs to software millionaire Luke Connor, well known in the Seattle area for his anti-tax and Second Amendment activism."

"Luke killed himself."

Beyond numb, I replayed my thoughts from the night in the trauma unit: this is all my fault. I'm the one who reported him, via Zak, to the over-ambitious national security apparatus.

Natalia denied that with a single shake of her head. "No, he's not the kind."

Having heard the story of our morning visit, Tem said, "I bet he had an accident when he tried to destroy his dorky datacenter."

Not convinced, I swallowed any it's-my-fault guilt, but it lay in my belly like a stone. A sharp-edged, volcanic basalt boulder. Because, it seemed, the White Knights stalking me sprang from Luke's network.

"We need to get back to work," I said. The place to find solace. "I'll get to what I can tonight. When we come in tomorrow—"

Natalia said, "I'm not coming in tomorrow."

"You have to come in!" Anyone might misinterpret my heart-felt plea as a whine. "We need to finish the ransomware research."

"It's a three-day weekend," she said. "Therefore, school and day-care are closed Monday. I drew the short straw, so it's me on at-home kid duty."

Harley kept on scrolling through #Debris_Byron filth on his computer. "School's closed Monday. Tomorrow's Friday."

"Exactly." Natalia packed up to leave. "Sam's thug friends insist Friday's a good day to die."

"If they didn't get blown up on Mercer Island," Tem added.

"Whichever way, I'm not coming to the office tomorrow. Nobody should come in, after what we learned today."

"We didn't learn everything." I endeavored to plead the importance of the social case. "We need to solve the ransomware story definitively."

"The triangulated point between the ransomware and its author is Luke Connor's ISP." Tem didn't look up from the monitor, which lit his face rather ghoulishly. No one had turned on the overhead lights since the swatting. "It's a mundane task to finish drawing that line."

Natalia nodded twice.

"We need to prove it," I insisted once again. "Other people might still be in danger. It sure wasn't Luke Connor who killed those women."

Natalia shakes her head only once when she's absolutely refusing. "I set notices for the tool output. We'll both receive a notice when the analysis is done. The results will be in the cloud, to study from any bunker where you choose to crouch."

"Are you safe at your house?" Harley said.

"We won't be home." She slung that beautiful bag over her shoulder. "Time for a Pacific Northwest weekend getaway."

My partners were taking the White Knights' threats so seriously that my rising anxiety dialed up to Eleven.

And yet.

"The White Knights don't want me dead." I was trying to stick to rational discourse and not hear last year's attack replay in my head. "They want me scared and vulnerable. They want me alive and working for them."

"Count me scared," Natalia said. "And refusing to be vulnerable."

"I'll walk you to your car. And you two," Harley stopped to shake a cautionary finger at Tem and me, "wait until I can take you somewhere safe."

When the door closed behind Harley, Tem said, "If they exist. The White Knights of the New Russian Revolution."

"Of course they exist. I saw them on Limberlost Island last year."

"Maybe Luke was pretending to be what he knew would scare you."

"Maybe they were in league together. And now all they're missing is a fool they used as a tool."

"Cowboys and outlaws?"

"Beats me. But your detective work with the ISP address doesn't convince me that it's over or that we're all safe."

"So go home with Harley."

Back to Limberlost Island, which was where these thugs had trapped me last time? Nope.

The safest place was my room upstairs, with double security codes, a long view to the street—and multiple notices that SPD already had about its occupant being under attack. While waiting for Harley to return so I could argue that point, I sent a message to Zak.

KRYPPTIKK JOB: #QUESTCODE_PRIVATE

SByron:

Congrats on the SWAT, I guess

ZakM:

It pissed off people here.

They still need a money trail.

SByron:

Your project might tie in with Doreen's malware.

Give me a name for SPD and FBI to contact.
Other people might be in danger.
Including you.

ZakM:

Wow. From your old mobster friends?

SByron:

Yeah. Hanging in there?

ZakM:

I'm handling life marginally well.
Wish you were here.

Then I wrote the text message I'd composed while my nose was pressed to the office floor during the swatting event.

Sam:
Please keep Charlie safe. You've heard about Luke? At least, we guess it's Luke.

DougFromTukwila:
I just heard. I'm shocked.

Sam:
I'm pissed

DougFromTukwila:
I'm sure law enforcement did best possible.
I didn't know Luke was that far into his fantasy world.

Sam:
Misfired last message. I'm pissed – I sent his ISP and street address to the FBI. But BATF got him first.

DougFromTukwila:
???

Sam:
Luke's ISP address is same as death threats sent to me.
And ask your NSA friends about Prometheus on the darknet.
Luke was selling it.

Tem argued aloud with a Deadlock protestor on TV who was declaring that every patriotic American should consider armed confrontation with our oppressive federal overlords for the sake of family and to ensure the freedom of future generations.

He cried, "Do the math, idiots," at the same moment that a message buzzed my phone.

DougFromTukwila:
Investigating. Upset. Upset 4 U. Charlie is safe.

Sam:
Upset? Yr upset?

I about squeezed my phone to death to keep from texting one more word back, not recognizing until that moment the depths of my rage. Not because the fourth richest man in Seattle had flakey friends. I'm sure they all have flakey friends. Rather, because I gave the FBI real-time, full access to my entire electronic life. And I assume they shared all that data with the NSA. I shared all my own research findings with the FBI and, through Zak, with the NSA.

Because, they said, they could protect me. As part of the effort to protect everyone in the Free World.

Except a sk8ter-boy in a basement and Natalia in high-heeled boots were more useful, armed only with faux-RadioWhack sideband pickups.

"Wannagettapizza?" Tem stuffed an energy bar into his mouth with one bite. Snatched from our kitchen food supply. He switched off the TV. "Before Harley sticks us in an atomic bomb shelter?"

DougFromTukwila:
Still joining us for dinner? Charlie's here.

16

In the Concrete Forest

"YOU GOT ME LOOKING OVER my shoulder, too." Harley was back in five minutes, just as I'd finished work in the Clean Room, setting tools to run on code from Doreen's and Wendy's computers.

"Paranoia strikes deep," I murmured, an instant reaction.

"So this is what it feels like to be you?" He chewed his lip. "Has it been this way since those Russian hoods came after you last year?"

"Until this week, mostly I didn't think about it."

"Truly? 'Cause that paranoia I felt out on the street got me to thinking. After that swatting, if we had to call the cavalry for help, like as not, 9–1–1 won't believe us."

"There's other protections against forces of evil." Tem rocked on his heels, hands jammed in his jeans.

"What?" Harley huffed. "Voodoo? Power of prayer?"

"There's running before you're chased." Tem, inscrutable, copped a Sphinx-like expression.

"Yeah?" Harley hadn't yet decided what to think of Tem. "Let me know how that works for you when you test it. Are you both ready to go?"

"What exactly is our goal?" Tem asked. "We shelter in place, living like refugees?"

"If I was you, I'd do like me." Harley assumed a Viking stance. "Eat a decent meal. Get some sleep. Get up in the morning and make a plan. And I still recommend my house out on Limberlost. If you're not doing that, we need to trade phone numbers, so we're all in touch."

We shared numbers. Tem still insisted on couch surfing, and I had a dinner date with Dan. It did occur to me to change clothes before dinner, but my jeans seemed to have survived the day, and I was too exhausted to have a single fuck left to give. I found a button-up cardigan in the office closet and tugged a plaid hoodie over it.

While Harley waited patiently, he tuned the security TV to cable news again. In that day's episode of the Potholes Deadlock, muzzle-loader duck hunters shouted at camo-clad militia, and I'd swear I saw Evan Mulasky in the line of FBI observers.

After locking up the office and heading out the door, we agreed that Tem could fetch a laptop and check his own tools and reports from Clarissa's basement. Then Harley would drop Tem with friends and chauffeur me to my dinner with Dan.

Harley said, "When you see him, take up Mr. Llewelyn's offer of personal security. Tomorrow's Friday." I agreed at that point, not in an arguing mood. From the back seat of the Jeep, I sent Natalia a text, asking the existential question.

Sam:
What should I say to Dan? Do we accept his entire offer?

NataliaDragon:
My partner says yes. She finds this week of dead and bombed clients a tad depressing.

Sam:
You?

NataliaDragon:
I'm about there, teetering on the edge of Yes.

Sam:
Tony paid us $100K. Can we run a few months on that?

By that time, I didn't expect the second payment from Tony for two reasons. I hadn't solve the problem he hired me for, except now we knew Clarissa wasn't a Russian spy. But also, Tony might no longer own his investigation. No contract, no one to bill.

> NataliaDragon:
> Launching Byron&Dragon was a half-baked emotional reaction. Not typical for you or me to jump like that.

> Sam:
> Maybe.

> NataliaDragon:
> Should have at least thrown the rune stones, consulted the all-seeing Odin.

At the Galahad Apartments, Harley stayed in the Jeep while I followed Tem, because I wanted to see the results of the analysis Clarissa had been running. And once more, I felt awe at what Tem and Clarissa had built in the basement.

At one workstation, Tem called up a log and studied it.

I said, "Can you put it in the cloud somewhere, for both of us? Harley isn't going to like waiting for long."

He acted instead of answering, texting me a link to access it. "That's your account. Can you memorize the password?"

"Yeah. Let's go."

While he bagged a laptop, I fingered the hardware. I needed to satisfy my curiosity. "Why in all that's holy did Clarissa grift that *New York Times*?"

"She says it's important to keep fit."

After I acknowledged the message Tem sent, I had another one to answer.

> 1(206)#######:
> Those guys after you now. I will protect you.

> Sam:
> Nicky, go screw yourself with a barbed stake.

Leaving the Galahad building, Tem had his usual board and backpack. I carried a second skateboard for him, that janky homemade skateboat for traveling on city streets when the tide is rising. Out on the sidewalk, I slapped the board down to try it while Tem advised me not to hurt myself.

Left foot over front truck bolts, right foot over back bolts. (I've already confessed that I'm a plain old regular rider.)

Rocked toe to heel to feel the board, finding the stiff motion you'd expect from a homemade board and hearing the low-class sound of loose bearings.

Leaned forward, then back with weight on my heels.

Felt good. I should skate over to Dan's yacht, make sure he knows he's hiring the girl who scraped more skin off her knees fifteen years ago than any other skater in the VFW parking lot on Limberlost Island. Toes forward, I kicked off, softly bouncing the board up over the first sidewalk hump.

"Hey! This deck needs new grip tape!" I called to Tem.

Surprisingly, Tem (as little as I knew him) didn't have this homemade wonder in perfect order. But then, maybe he hadn't yet gotten to that chore, since the rainy season just now crept up on us after a long summer and a warm, comfortable autumn.

A black SUV crept up the street, pausing by where Harley idled in the Jeep.

"This way!" Tem hissed. "Through the gate!"

Grabbing that board, I followed, leaping a hedge and running across a good citizen's backyard.

▪

People under stress swear. Known scientific fact. More stress, more blasphemy.

Following Tem, I squished and splattered through alleys, yards, and mucky city-park greenways. Skating when it was possible, running when it wasn't. Across the crown of the hill and into the pricier neighborhoods. I didn't start swearing until we ran down that steep four-story open-air stairway from Tenth Avenue East to Lakeview.

In times past, I didn't used to swear while running. Didn't ever look down, never expected to slip. Old at thirty? I swore at every element of the environment, even at Tem, since the slippery dude seemed to glide even while running, as if he had no sinews or joints. Yet after the first flight, I found that same physical rhythm.

The great thing about that endless concrete staircase? No one older or bigger can gain on you, whether you're running up or down.

And I'm still fit enough that I can swear out loud without becoming winded.

We ran down the stairs. We ran like you run in your dreams, where you might suddenly be aloft, flying instead of running. Blackberry brambles couldn't grab us. Nattered concrete couldn't trip us. Moss parted and allowed firm footing. If our feet ever touched the ground.

The last ten steps above the street were more blackberry-infested than the rest, because these vines had the possibility of reaching sunlight, and competed to grab space in the open well, though most berries had been stripped by stair-climbers, leaving only the sun-shrunken nibs farther up the vines, where the yellow jackets still hoped for a taste of sugar. The longest of the trailing vine, like a monster in the movies, snagged Tem's sleeve. When he jerked free, the vine recoiled, slashing my face and snaring my hair, so that I had to peel the thorny coil away with bare hands, scratching my knuckles and smearing more blood on my face.

We hit the sidewalk on the east side of Lakeview Avenue, where water trickled across, another lost forest creek, leaving a trail of slime and mud. Tem held out his arm, stopping me from running into the street without regard to traffic.

Harley came past in the Jeep, but didn't recognize us in time to stop before the Jeep traveled up the narrow northern side street.

That black SUV—had to be the same one—trailed after the Jeep. Tem and I dashed across Fairview, forcing a south-bound Prius to jam its brakes, forcing the Rav4 behind it to screech its brakes and then lean on the horn. Tem and I splashed recklessly through the massive puddle at the bus stop, and then sprinted down under the I-5 roadbed.

"Which way?" Team shouted.

"Down!"

"They'll just find us on Eastlake."

"Too many options!"

We'd hit the first fork—the place on the dirt-bike trail where years before Tony must have realized he'd already lost the race. A fearless freak's paradise: a dense forest of concrete pillars planted regularly, with trails that became ramps, man-made cliffs of crushed rock engaged in wire, stairs with rails for the faint of heart.

Above, tucked into the cavern where I-5 launches itself across the concrete forest, homeless shelter-seekers huddled. Roused when we ran into their territory, they called out to us.

> "If it's cops, they're on your ass!"
>
> "At eight o'clock your time!"

My heart beat twice while deciding which direction. I glanced back.

What do you expect the stalkers in your nightmares to look like? I expected—in my dreams, on the street, in my bed late at night—a carload of eastern European mobsters. Fat heads, dressed in black, swarming from their SUVs. Just like last time, just like the fake-Russian mobsters outside my house on Limberlost last year.

Peeking back, while running over rough ground, what did I see chasing me? What I didn't expect: the other end of the culture, hacker wannabes with issues.

Victor Pearl.

Slender Man from Espresso and Shoeshine.

Steroid Man from Luke's personal guard.

All of them bulky, not as agile as Tem or me.

One of them—Steroid Man—had a gun pointed at me, while Victor Pearl reached inside his jacket.

Our homeless lookout squad shouted out directions.

> "Go right!"
>
> "Straight now!"
>
> "Hey, gun man! Your mama sucks cock!"
>
> "Blackberries at one o'clock."

"Give it up, assholes!" Tem shouted.

Though breathless, I joined in. "The NSA has everything we know. No use killing us."

Victor shouted, "We can do it for pleasure. You dumb—"

Never mind. Like I said, people swear under stress.

A gunshot rang out.

Adrenalin hit me like an ungrounded current.

Shouts and screams from the people in the freeway-cave jangled my fear even more.

> "Hey, man. No guns!"
>
> "Our kids play here, asshole!"
>
> "Not cool!"
>
> "Runners, behind you at seven o'clock."

The homeless, roused from their own safe perch, scrambled down onto the pathways, screaming invectives at our pursuers. One remained up above, shouting directions from their aerie.

> "Behind you at seven o'clock."

Tem and I took off skating. One foot in front of the other.

Pushed, pushed again. Back foot across the deck, my front toe pointed toward escape and freedom. I leaned forward for a toe-side turn, my heart pumping harder each time I kicked forward. I forced myself to breathe evenly, comforted by the sensation of the board's truck bolts under foot.

Our pursuers couldn't run in silence. Their boots pounded on concrete. Huff of breath, louder than the freeway roar. Then we couldn't hear them over the noise of the angry, pursuing hoard who cursed unwanted intruders in their concrete forest.

Tem and I, we skate for freedom.

We skate for glory.

We skate to get from point A to point B.

We skate. And we know the way in this forest.

Feet pounded behind us.

We reached the first man-made plateau, where it appears that the cliff must drop off thirty feet or more.

"I'm going over!" Tem shouted.

That cliff: it's where Tony once lost track of me amid the massive concrete pillars. And I performed that move again.

I skated off the cliff.

Into concrete pillars as thick and densely planted as the trees that once grew here.

Back foot on board tail, shoulders in opposite direction of upcoming turn, pressure on the tail, I moved into the turn that came up soon after the landing. The front of the board lifted off the ground as I swung my shoulders and followed the momentum. The board rotated to make the turn. The familiar feel of concrete beneath me, where I'm master of my fate. Yes, fearless.

A gunshot.

Okay, still afraid. Adrenaline again shot through, my fingers tingly with needles.

Tem fell back, alternately skating and running behind me, then he darted ahead and branched to the right when I had no choice but to shoot ahead. Thirty yards later, he repeated, darting to the left this time.

He was drawing attention away from me. Balanced in his goofy way on his front foot, weight forward, he dragged his back foot, braking instead of taking another of the caged-rock terracing walls. Me, I shot over this perceptual cliff and came down once again on an unseen paved walkway.

Flying. Flying across the hillside, the motion calmed me, where the mechanics of flying on that janky board replaced fear.

▪

You can't see it from the concrete footpath, but the drop is only ten feet to another path hidden below. You have to be accelerating to make it. You have to know the immediate ninety degree turn in the path and be prepared for it. You have to be able to jump the next ten-foot cliff immediately, and then duck under the brambles.

It's October. The pillars are freshly painted, graffiti-free for the moment. The Himalayan blackberries continue their effort to capture all ground stolen from the indigenous people since those East Coast settlers first leveled the old-growth forest down to pure mud. Tem and

I alternated running amid the patches of trails left by urban-dwelling hunter-gatherers, and the trails the skaters and dirt-bike crews had hewed under the freeway.

"Split up!" he called, once again thirty feet in front of me in the concrete forest.

Another gun shot.

The local ledge-dwellers screamed their anger, and it echoed like the waking of the undead, louder than the persistent pounding of rush-hour traffic overhead.

Push, push, accelerate, then back foot across truck bolts. Blood roaring. No thought. Only motion.

Tem and I split up, both of us moving parallel under the freeway, Tem winding through the lower paths, me finding my way among the pillars and maze of paths directly under the massive traffic-laden roadway above.

The vibration up my legs when I hit concrete, the *sluff sluff* echo and slowed movement when I hit packed earth. The *crunch* of gravel and *snap* of twigs, barely heard under the constant freeway roar. Each change in sound beguiling me, urging me to look back; each alteration in the feel of the earth below me, a Richter scale amplification of fear. I didn't have time or space for fear.

Twenty yards after I lost track of Tem, I began winding down the hill, wondering why I ever felt safe to ride here alone in daylight, much less this close to dusk. The pounding of my heart let up as I eased toward the city streets and finally emerged from the concrete forest into open air. The freeway noise proved even louder on the side streets than under the actual roadway. Crouched behind a dusty Volvo crossover parked on the narrow side street, I checked back for my pursuers. Over freeway and the blood pounding in my ears, all that could be heard was that pack of the undead homeless, screaming for vengeance.

"Fucking calling the cops, you asshole!"

"Watch out! There's kids here, mo'fo!"

Winding amid the narrow side streets and alleys, skirting past the tiny fenced backyards, still skating, I dodged the pedestrians creeping home from a hard day's work. Got yelled at for skating recklessly where cars can't see skaters. Then I hit Eastlake Avenue and the four-lane open-air exposure of a major arterial.

Steps away, Slender Man held Tem, using one hand to wrench up both of Tem's arms behind his back, while the other held a pistol at Tem's neck. I stomped on the board's tail. It flipped up. Slender Man looked back at the sound of my janky wheels, but I'd caught the board and swung, bashing his head before he could make a decision.

Tem kicked him in the nuts. Twice.

Midway through Tem's second kick, an SPD car arrived. Harley stopped his Jeep in a yellow-striped no-parking space on the other side of Eastlake. His brakes squealed.

We need to check those brakes come the weekend.

▪

The people who lived under the freeway did a better job of mauling Victor than Tem and I managed on Slender Man. But then, that led to a larger, complicated argument about who was in the wrong once the third and fourth set of SPD cars arrived.

Which makes me happy to have my neighbor Harley as the official Byron&Dragon receptionist and driver. Not that I didn't stop Slender Man all on my own.

It's just that I'm out of practice. It's been years since I last explained to law enforcement what I was doing out skating on public roads in bad light. Plus, Harley has a better vocabulary for straightening out chaos while red-and-blue lights are flashing.

Meanwhile, Steroid Man had disappeared, which I felt deserved more attention than anyone in a uniform seemed inclined to give. However, Harley had memorized the case numbers he'd been discussing with the SPD over the past couple of days, which got more attention than anything else.

By the time detectives Jeremiah and Carlos arrived, most of our helpers from under the freeway had disappeared, leaving only three of the most vociferous, insisting that they'd been attacked, shot at. Two officers recorded those men's observations of the deadly jeopardy that Victor and Slender Man had brought to the neighborhood.

Gradually, the common story became known through these key forces: Harley, for calm and clear-headed statements; the three homeless heroes, for consistent and concise descriptions of the marauders who attacked us; Jeremiah and Carlos, for adding that I'd been harassed for days and needed police protection.

Tem?

Melted into the gathering dusk, became a shadow when the clouds thickened and threatened rain again. Gone as soon as the nearest officer misdirected his attention.

From that point, Harley and I just followed along as asked. For the first time that day, I didn't have to look over my shoulder. SPD had its own methods, and people had assignments to haul Victor and Slender Man away, to finish taking statements from anyone who'd gathered on the sidewalk, to walk through the forest under the freeway, to do what they could to find Steroid Man—the SUV's license number Harley provided when he first called 9–1–1 to report the chase.

When the rain began to fall, fat drops fast and hard, Harley and I sat in the unmarked car with the two detectives, collaborating to make sense of the afternoon's excitements. In the front seat, Harley cradled Tem's janky skateboard.

Jeremiah offered alcohol wipes. I washed my face and hands.

"Just blackberry thorns?" He sounded kind.

It stung as bad as you'd guess it might, and required several swipes before the cloth came away clean. Couldn't do anything about my shirt or the dark splotches on my faded black jeans. My rich-lady's leather jacket needed to find another life. After Jeremiah deposited my alcohol wipes in a bio-hazard bag, I asked to use my phone to text Dan about being late for dinner.

DougFromTukwila:
I can send my car, if that helps.

Sam:
Thanks – no, just backed up behind projects

DougFromTukwila:
That math and moral dilemma thing?

"The other witnesses say that you know how to run when someone's chasing you." Jeremiah made the universal running symbol with his two fingers.

"We skate to be free."

"Let's see where we are." Carlos, in the driver's seat, began ticking items on his fingers. "A murder on Tuesday—did we tell you the medical examiner confirmed that? An explosion sends a mysterious man to the trauma ward. A series of death threats, which you insist are from Russian mobsters. Juvenile vandalisms. A false swatting—but we agreed that's part of the juvenile vandalism, right?"

"Yeah, correct."

Harley spoke up. "A mugging and property theft."

Carlos held up five fingers. "More?"

Harley cleared his throat. "We were on Mercer Island just before the real SWAT began over there. Sam visited that house earlier today."

"The Internet service provider he used," time for me to speak, "is the same as the source of those White Knight death threats."

You could read both Jeremiah's and Carlos's thoughts like an LED traffic billboard:

Ph—ough—kk.

Still coughing freeway-forest dust, I said, "The event on Mercer Island is likely the most important thing today. But I can't say any more without…"

"Your best friends at the FBI?" Carlos began punching messages in his cellphone.

"You can't say even a tiny bit more?" Jeremiah prompted. "By the way, you look like hell. Not your usual charming self."

"Do you want me to speculate?"

"Please," all three men said at once.

"My best guess," which had simmered from the moment I glanced back to see who was chasing me, "is that Luke Connor, who blew himself up on Mercer Island, was selling U.S. cryptology secrets."

"Who to?" Jeremiah asked.

"From what he said this morning, Luke believed it was Israel. The three guys chasing me work for Luke. And I suspect they attacked

Doreen Monroe and Judge Yates, because those women knew Luke possessed that technology."

"Judge Yates?" Jeremiah frowned, though in the dimming light it was increasingly difficult to read his expression. "I testified in her court several times."

"Me, too. But only once."

"It's inconceivable that she'd be part of any conspiracy."

"Those women," I said, "got caught in a massive paranoid sweep of anyone who might know anything."

"How did you get involved?"

Brushing past that question, I continued with my surmise. "Luke Connor was so inept, he probably didn't mean to kill himself, only destroy his computers."

"Which had the evidence that might prove every one of your guesses," Jeremiah said.

"Yes. Like, how they found those women? Who they sold secrets to? Everyone that might be involved?"

Carlos asked the million-dollar question, that I suppose I'll get asked until I'm old and grey. "Do you work for the NSA? Are you helping chase terrorists?"

"No. I was hired to remove computer malware. Which I believe was sent to find connections between several women."

Carlos glanced at his phone. "Okay, Mr. Owens. Sheriff. You probably want to go home. Sam has friends downtown who want a conversation, too."

Harley opened the door, but before he stepped out into the rain, he pointed a finger at Detective Jeremiah. "You and those friends need to make sure Sam sleeps somewhere safe tonight."

Me, I was texting Dan a request for a raincheck, and then reading the response.

DougFromTukwila:
Breakfast with Egg Man? Milky Cereal?
My chef does a mean Omelette From Outer Space

So Dan wasn't, it seemed, emotionally devastated by the loss of his old friend Luke Connor. Remind me not to be so poorly thought of by old friends as Luke when I get to the end of my days. A motion from the car's front seat caught my eye.

Jeremiah held out an evidence bag, more than large enough for that phone. "Should we look at that?"

I considered. All I'd lose was the opportunity for Nicky to harass me up until I bought a new phone.

"Let me make a quick call."

After I left an email message to assure Pippi that no one was chasing me, so she could sleep without bad dreams, I passed the phone over to Jeremiah.

Once more, I surrendered my phone without a warrant, because I'm a good citizen with few secrets. And once more, they took away a PIN-protected, encrypted phone but didn't ask for PIN or keys. Do you suppose there's a mountain of uncracked phones in evidence lockers? Do they wipe those phones and donate them to shelters? Is there a cavern under a mountain in Nevada that holds seized encrypted phones, like spent uranium?

17

Personality Crisis

▪
▪
▪

WE ONCE MORE GOT COZY IN an East Precinct interview room. Two junior federal agents joined us. Agent Mulasky Skype'd in from his motel room north of the Potholes Reservoir.

"Our officers picked up the third individual," Jeremiah said. "He crashed his vehicle while fleeing. They're patching him up at Harborview right now."

"All notes and background files have been shared," Carlos began. "The FBI has the code under question. We defer to federal expertise on that."

"Can you summarize again for me, Ms. Byron?" Evan asked. He sounded as tired as I felt. Yet he had the luxury of calling in from his bed in a Motel 8. Likely his coffee was no better than the thin brew we sipped from paper cups. Jeremiah offered me a granola bar, which took a lot of saliva to swallow. "I can't make the connection between your mobster bad guys and that fellow on Mercer Island."

"Yeah, I'm still trying." I'd been working to make connections since the early hours in the trauma ward. My summary in two parts—in which I said "crypto" because explaining Prometheus watermarking technology wouldn't help in this discussion:

> My fraudster White Knights have been seeking to buy stolen security technology on the darknet. Federal agencies are seeking potential sellers and buyers.

> Luke Connor appeared to be selling that stolen technology internationally.
>
> Someone used the stolen OPM list to find and hack anyone who had access to the original technology. Those women were threatened and then killed because their names were on the list.
>
> The White Knights and Luke Connor were connected, possibly partners.

"I once did research on that particular security technology." I drew the threads as close together as I understood them. "That's why I'm being pursued."

"How did you uncover the association between those women and the OPM list?"

"Tony King told me. He was about to show me details, but was attacked. Another FBI agent—"

"No." One of the junior agents stirred when I mentioned Tony. "We don't know this individual, outside of research files into his online activities, going back a decade. Several attempts to obtain a warrant for him were quashed because of lack of evidence."

"I'll be back in town tomorrow afternoon," Evan said. "I'll interview him then."

"He's gone," that junior agent said. "The hospital released him to an FBI agent. We haven't found out who yet."

Lots of noisy silence.

It wasn't time to explain my doings with yet another agent they couldn't identify. No, best not to say anything about Clarissa, like I originally promised Tony.

"Let's research that come the morning. Now, about the explosion on Mercer Island?" Evan prompted. "I have a brief from Alcohol and Tobacco. The warrant that ATF tried to serve came from confidential informants who report illegal possession of explosives."

"Do you think Alcohol and Tobacco will want to talk with me?" I asked. "I was at that house earlier in the day. The owner was armed to the teeth. And paranoid."

Evan sighed the sigh of a man who's been on his feet for days, talking to and listening to overwrought people who read an astigmatic version of the Constitution.

I wanted to be reassuring. "That's how the explosion relates to those dead women. I believe Luke Connor was selling those security secrets on the darknet, because he worked on that software years ago. Two of the guys chasing me tonight were at Luke's house. And I saw a couple of them on Capitol Hill just after Mrs. Monroe died. But I don't have hard data for you yet."

"Yet?" That single word from Evan escaped as an exhausted whisper.

"My partner and I are analyzing the malware that three women received. We hope to trace the source. Earlier today, we picked up network details outside Luke Connor's house. Perhaps we'll be able to triangulate data by tomorrow."

"Outside? Not when you were visiting?"

"That's the irony. Luke's setup wasn't secure, but he was selling national security information. At least, I believe so." I remembered Harley's warnings. "Our receptionist made sure we weren't breaking any laws, capturing unsecure broadcasts from that house."

Jeremiah finally spoke. "She means Sheriff Owens from Limberlost County. He works in her office. He's been helpful with elements of our investigation. Especially for the harassment and death threats."

We must have gone over what I knew three times as a whole, plus various pieces made for a fourth pass. What data did Byron&Dragon have? What threats did we receive? Who was at Luke's house when he explained that ass-cracker paranoid stuff about Mossad agents?

"And your best guess, Ms. Byron? Without data?" Evan yawned, on camera.

"The guys chasing me work for the White Knights. Luke was involved with the White Knights. That security technology is worth millions—billions—to the right buyer."

"These aren't good directions for investigation," Evan said.

"Thanks. That's what I've told my receptionist all week."

"We haven't made progress finding your White Knights in the past year. Traces, like smoke in a mirror, but nothing there when we focus."

"Maybe those three in custody will have answers." I had high hopes, still, of being free of whoever was chasing me and killing innocent retired executive assistants.

"Right now, those three belong to SPD. We'll just be sitting in." Evan laughed, rueful. "Meanwhile, gentlemen. I hate to ask, since we're in your house, but could you excuse us to speak with Sam for just a moment?"

With the SPD detectives gone from the room, Evan said, "You have some notion of a rogue agent. Yet the only name you can give us is Anthony Moon."

Glancing between the two junior agents in the room, I decided quickly, and then tried to sound as nice as possible.

"Evan, this has to be only between you and me."

After his guys departed, Evan first dug deeper into national security questions. What was the nature of work I did with Zak for the NSA? What did Tony say about his security work and his rogue agent suspicions? How did I decide that Luke's homemade conspiracy ravings were related to sale of government security secrets?

I said, "However random the data seems, I believed Tony's claim—that whenever he talked to anyone inside the FBI about details he learned, it resulted in dead agents."

In the end, Evan and I had a list of questions no one could answer, similar to the list I'd been working on for two days:

> Who sent those women that malware?
>
> Who were the agents Luke claimed to be working with?
>
> Was there ever an FBI project to capture software code?
>
> Does an agent codenamed Honey Bear run honeypots?

"But the key question," I insisted, "is whether stolen government security software on the darknet has led to murder."

I'm sure Evan was as unexcited as I was about the prospect of spending another day struggling with those unanswerable questions. However, I promised to be ready at eight the next morning when an agent would come to my office to receive copies of all malware and research logs in my possession. I guess we were ignoring that I'd already posted most of this to a cloud share for them. Finally, SPD guys offered me a ride, with the promise that their Capitol Hill patrols would check my neighborhood throughout the night.

On the way home, longing for bed, I begged my escorts to stop at the all-night gas station on Twelfth Avenue so I could buy a phone, having no intention of sleeping alone with no phone. Plus I needed at least yogurt, a box of crackers, and an apple, since I'd missed the chef-prepared dinner on Dan's boat. The officers were gracious about waiting, but the cashier dude didn't seem grateful that a patrol car idled outside.

In the back seat of the car, I set the phone's PIN and installed an encryption application, and then went online to my account and redirected my calls and texts to this new number. My escorts idled again near my apartment. One of them walked me inside and rode upstairs with me before saying good night. "Don't let the bedbugs bite," he called from the waiting elevator.

Inside my post-modern monk's cell, I charged my phone, and then reset all the building security codes, triple-checking everything. Because I still had unanswered questions about who was out there.

Unfortunately, while I was setting the security alarm, I caught a glimpse of myself in the brush-your-hair-before-you-leave mirror inside my apartment door. A Kabuki actor caught in a rainstorm. Those blackberry thorn scratches needed more alcohol. And I deserved acetaminophen, at the very least.

▪

The time flashed on my phone, indicating that it was too late to return calls to Pippi or Matt. She'd left a voice-mail message, pleading for bedtime girls' talk. Several texts from Matt begging for the same (not the girl-talk part). I set an alarm to call early in the morning, so I'd catch them before school and work.

Natalia left me a text, asking about the dinner with Dan that never happened. I sent back the news that the meeting wouldn't occur until the next day. And I still hadn't decided what to say to Dan. But since I was going to spend the next few days working with the FBI—without compensation—I felt the needle tipping toward Dan and Sanity, versus Independence and Chaos, as our first week's projects proved to be.

Then I read Natalia's project updates.

> ***KRYPPTIKK JOB: CLIENT#202_JONES***
>
> *NDragon:*
>
> Ticket#3: Task complete, closing ticket.
>
> *NDragon:*
>
> Full report on byron&dragon server in this folder.
> Package delivers grabbag of well-known malware.
> Only significant code is new shieldware.
> It shuts down the laptop's anti-virus and then unpacks the payload.
> Lots of Ourobouros - code hatches & eats itself recursively.
> 1 package harvests email addresses & sends to server.
> Another sends computer's GPS location to same server.
> Ransomware is only a skeleton. Just mounts billboard. Doesn't send response or freeze files. Final package uninstalls everything, deletes packages.
> Leaves billboard app + that common signature you found.
>
> *NDragon:*
>
> Found server address that the harvesting package sends to. But the site displays an FBI seizure notice.
> So transferred whole research package c/o Evan at FBI.
> Hope Evan tells us what they know someday.
>
> *NDragon:*
>
> Xref: New ticket in Client#1_Monroe to run same research. We can forward results to Evan's office when it finishes.

FBI seizure notice for a web domain? Usually that means legal seizure and asset forfeiture. Which should mean the FBI was already working on the same puzzle we were. So I expected we'd soon hear again from Evan or someone from his team.

Unless it was a fake notice that appeared at the site, intended to cause an ill-informed web visitor to pause and read while bots embedded malware on the visitor's computer. No, Natalia would detect that. So: real seizure notice.

I'd gotten halfway to the shower, to be followed by bed, when the video-doorbell rang. Someone down on the street wanted me. Under the closed-circuit camera at the door, a very wet Brad Jones hunched over like an injured man.

"Sam? Can I come up? I need to talk."

What-the-everlasting-eff.

While he rode the elevator, I crawled hastily back into jeans. Half-shredded Vans and no socks. Grabbed a sweater with ragtag sleeves that smelled like Matt because it was his sweater. The mirror by the door insulted me, but I decided to never again comb my hair for anyone. Ever.

After hellos, I gave Brad a towel and told him to hang his coat in the shower to drip itself dry.

If anyone in the Western hemisphere needed a drink, it was Brad, so I poured two shots of Mischief whisky, jelly jar for Brad and my Grandma Flo's fake-crystal sherry glass for me.

He spoke from the bathroom, while he rubbed his head dry. "My shoes are wet too."

"No worries. Won't hurt my floor."

He accepted the offered drink and sat in my one chair. Since the only other sitting place was the bed, I half-stood, half-leaned against the ledge that pretends to be a kitchen counter.

"How's your mother? Better, I hope?"

"Mmm." He shook his head, but so tense his neck scarcely turned. Pale and drawn. "Not good." A sip of his drink. Another pause before he spoke. "She had another cardiac episode. She's in intensive care again. They kicked me out."

"I'm truly sorry to hear it. We only met once outside of court, but I deeply admire her."

"Outside of court." He repeated and then pondered what I said. "I forget you do that. An expert witness. Other people know you in a different way."

"Was she better during the day? Did you have a chance to speak with her?" I was feeling bad for him, given all the distress he revealed. And I wanted Judge Yates well again and able to say whether she'd been attacked. But my day had involved too much fear and exertion. He needed to talk about whatever he'd come for and then go away and let me sleep.

"Through much of the day, they wouldn't give me a prognosis. So I spent the afternoon in misery, until they let me sit with her. Then she roused. All the vitals improved. But now…"

"I'm so sorry." I try not to say that all the time, but there are moments when nothing else will serve. "What can I do for you, Brad? Have you eaten? Do you want me to call for a ride?"

As if the words didn't want to escape his throat, he spoke in low, ominous tones. "She said someone tried to kill her." He grasped that jelly-jar glass as if he had to hold on to something. Grasped it so hard, the glass shook, the whisky sloshed. "Then she went into stress. And they threw me out."

"Geezus, Brad." Best response I could manage, given that I wasn't surprised like he was. Her words fit with everything that had happened, and I'd guessed as much since I first heard the EMTs were with her.

"Now she's worse. They say it's hours until I can see her." Wound up tight, his jaw muscles knotted, Brad choked out the words.

"Are you going back tonight, to wait?" I was trying to understand why he was in my room. He could have simply called me.

"They have my cell number. I'll go back when they call."

"Have you talked with SPD?" Jeremiah and Carlos needed to hear this confirmation of suspicions.

"Can't go to the police…I mean, I guess I will. But they won't take it seriously. Or even believe me."

The SPD guys already had me as their favorite crazy lady. They'd have no problem with Brad. "Why are you asking me?"

"Because when I said, 'Who?' like an idiot, she said, 'Ask Sam.' And then she pointed at me. Took all her strength to lift her hand. And she kept saying, "You. You. You." That's when she went into cardiac arrest again."

"I'm so sorry." What else could I offer him?

"Why? That's why I came here. Why 'ask Sam'? Why point at me? What did you tell her? What did you say about me?"

"Nothing. We talked about—"

"What, Sam?" Grimacing as if in agony, he clutched my sweater sleeve, stretching it, pulling me toward him.

"We talked about events in her past, events that might have led to that ransomware on her computer."

"Ransomware? Not just a virus?"

Wiggling out of his grasp, I said, "She was going to call a friend for information. Or for permission to speak."

"Like attorney-client privilege?"

"From old friends, I think. She knew I've been trying to find others with that same malware who might be in jeopardy."

"Who? Who in the world would want to kill my mother?" He reached out toward me again, but I dodged. "Was it someone she defended or prosecuted? When she was a judge?"

To a reasonable extent, I felt sorry for him. And worried about the overwrought passion he'd brought into my room. He needed someone to console him, to help him calm down, yet I couldn't pull up buckets of pity. Too tired, mostly.

"Can't say more. I'll give you SPD people to contact. They will be interested in what she said, since—"

"Goddamn it, Sam." He banged the jelly jar on my table. "We're talking about my mother. You know something. Tell me what's going on. What do you know?"

My new phone buzzed, causing it to jitter a couple of inches across the table. Just an ordinary text.

> T-E-M:
> victor works for same agency that does adverse security – easy to find if U search – interesting

I read the message. Then read it once again. Still readjusting my neural pathways, I glanced up. Brad stared down at the table, the tension in his hand still rattling that glass against the table top. Of course, Brad can read upside down.

"Victor?" he said, as if puzzled. "Victor Who's-It? What did he do?"

The street-level video-doorbell rang again. It was Jeremiah.

"Ms. Byron, are you home for the night?"

The security display showed a bird's eye view of the street, where Jeremiah held his hand up toward the camera, making the universal running sign with two fingers.

"Sam?" Brad had hold of my sweater sleeve again, both hands this time. "What do you know? You look—"

Tossing my sherry glass at Brad's head, I ripped for the door, slammed my palm on the emergency panel in the hall, setting off the fire alarm, and then I hit the panic bar full force, bursting the fire door against the concrete wall.

And I ran—jumped—a full flight before looking back. By then, a trio of SWAT guys passed me, one falling back to make sure I was okay. Probably not anyone I'd met earlier that day. Likely, all those guys from the afternoon's faux-swatting were sleeping peacefully.

Which it seems I'd never be allowed to do again.

And the neighbors in this building? They're going to kill me if no one else kills me first.

▪

"Wish you guys wouldn't make a habit of this."

This time, even Carlos laughed.

And this time, I didn't have to sit in a cold conference room. The interview was in the warmth and comfort of my own home, small as it is. I ate my dinner, an apple and cup of yogurt, while trying to remember the last full meal I'd eaten (with Tony). I opened my little bag of crackers and lined them up on a plate as I talked with the detectives, who had endured about as little sleep as I had. And they had to sit on the bed, because the room had no other way to accommodate three people.

Chilled, I pulled my sweater closer around my neck—my blanket from Pippi now gone—but then smelled Matt again, even though I'd sweated in fear while wearing his sweater. Left me feeling so lonely.

Jeremiah led the explanation. "One of the three chasing you asked for his attorney, who worked for the personal security agency. Neither was prepared for the charges we presented."

"Attempted homicide?" Me. They wanted to kill me.

"Actual murder. And conspiracy," Jeremiah said. "One of his friends left physical evidence at Mrs. Monroe's house. Then the guy wouldn't listen to his attorney, couldn't shut up. He insisted they were just doing their job, that the exec they'd been hired to protect ordered them to scare people."

"Like me?"

"I don't have details. But he spilled that his partner killed Mrs. Monroe and Judge Yates. As a freelance extra."

Carlos—who managed to look sharp, even after this day—said, "The guy insisted three times that his supervisor said, 'Just take care of it. It's what I pay you for.'"

And I'd been in that fishbowl conference room while Dan tried to persuade us to help aDVers save the world, when Brad opened the door while telling a crew of security guys: *Just take care of it.*

And what Brad had said to me: *I'll do whatever it takes.*

"His attorney convinced the guy to quit talking," Carlos said. "Our interviewers are still talking with the other one."

"There's three guys." Although exhausted, I could still keep track of up to three numbers. "You said you caught the other one. When I first saw him, he was security at Luke Connor's compound."

Jeremiah said, "That's who our guy claims was the self-appointed assassin. Unfortunately, guy number three didn't make it out of the emergency room at Harborview. His friends can now lay all blame on him."

Carlos said that SPD first guessed that orders came from the aDVers leader, Brad Jones.

"When we couldn't find Mr. Jones, we triangulated his phone to your address."

"It's still hard to believe Brad was responsible for all this." Not that several other people in my life didn't turn out to be someone else. "But his mother says she was attacked. How could Brad—"

"Maybe that one person went beyond his assignment," Jeremiah said. "But we can't interview him to ask why he was at Mrs. Monroe's house. Based on our chatty guy, we have a warrant to look at Judge Yates's house tomorrow."

"And here we are." Carlos closed his notebook.

"Thank you. Kind of destroys my original idea about the White Knights of the New Russian Revolution." I felt disappointed in myself, for the paranoid ideation. And yet: I was no longer being chased!

"Our chatty guy said their cowboy supervisor got the idea about the White Knights from an online search," Jeremiah said. "Tomorrow the FBI gets a turn with him. We hope—"

"Wait. Cowboy supervisor? That's Luke Connor." Oh no. Poor Brad. Screwed over by Luke one final time. "Brad Jones is a straight-arrow executive. No one would ever think to call him a cowboy."

Carlos frowned, that bony ridge above his eyes tight with concern. "What do you mean?"

"Because of that word, cowboy. They must work for Luke, not Brad. Ask them again."

Busy messaging through his phone, Carlos became even more grim.

"We hope this is all closed soon. And that you get to sleep."

That's what we wished each other when we said goodbye.

I found the tossed sherry glass, rinsed it, and restored it to the shelf, wondering if Brad was finding jail as cold and boring as I did that time when law enforcement made a mistake about me.

Me, I had to check the security codes and settings for my doors again, and then once more made sure the alarm was set so I woke in time to call Pippi and Matt.

18

Death or Glory

THE SLEEPING PART OF THE night would have gone better if I hadn't kept waking up worried about Brad, wondering if they'd sorted him back into the good-guy pile.

I got up at dawn's crack to call Pippi. Matt was already gone. That call would have felt better, since she declared a successful night's sleep—after talking with Matt and telling the truth—if I hadn't used my half of the conversation to keep telling lies, reassuring her that I've been in no danger.

"Don't worry about me, sweet one."

Just after I called Pippi, Zak sent a plain old ordinary email: he'd passed his Krypptikk access for our Client#1 project to his supervisor; he wasn't to speak with me about the project any more.

But hey: SPD had identified the person who killed his stepmother. However, I wasn't allowed to talk to him about that yet.

My usual baby-footprint barista was tending the customers at Espresso and Shoeshine, though too busy to say more than a perfunctory hello. At least, finally, she remembered my drink without my prompt. Drinking my shot-in-the-dark, standing at the bar, I pondered what Natalia and I should do, given that either events or law enforcement had silenced or jailed or disappeared all the clients who had hired me to help their mothers.

While I sipped coffee, I fielded early-morning texts from Natalia: what had I decided about aDVers?

Too much to communicate in text, and I wasn't about to call and discuss it while she was feeding her kids and driving off to their Pacific Northwest weekend getaway.

I internalized the other element of Natalia's messages: If we don't go to work for aDVers, then Byron&Dragon needs to find serious work. Even if I managed to free Tony's check from the SPD. I sketched a list:

1. Ask Evan for investigative work.

And secretly wish I could work on what we'd started with the ransomware and any possible connection to Luke Connor.

2. Ask Z-Crypto for work related to Prometheus.

No. I inked a heavy line through that idea. Not ever begging Z-Crypto for squat.

3. Ask Brad to reconsider contracting versus employment at aDVers.

Unless Brad was still being interrogated and arraigned for who knows what. And our last conversation hadn't ended well.

Tem manifested beside me in the espresso store. Disappeared. Then reappeared in a moment with his drink, apparently liking a great deal of milk with his caffeine. He showed me his phone. A message dated from last night.

> ✆1(509)########:
> Bye! I'm off with a friend who's a nervous flier. Reminds me of traveling by merchant ship. Tight quarters sailing all around SE Asia. But such lovely men to travel with. Lock the house till you hear from me.

"When I answered," Tem said, "I got a rude no-such-number bounce-back from the carrier."

"So she's gone." Which I'd assumed when "someone" with FBI credentials absconded with Tony.

"Probably crossed the Canadian border by the time you put Charlie Thomas in that cab. Unless Clarissa chose Mexico. It's getting cold in Canada."

"C'mon, Tem. Read the message. If she went to Canada, it was only to catch a flight to Asia."

Ultimately, I recruited Tem to help prepare files for the FBI.

"Wish we had your files, too."

Tem scowled. "Not giving our data or methods away. Unless Clarissa says so."

"We have gaping holes to fill. If anyone is ever to understand what happened." It wasn't until I could say it aloud to someone who'd know what bugged me about the last night's developments. "We have no clues that lead to Tony's rogue agent. And no Tony to help us probe."

Once I started, I proceeded to full core dump.

"Look, it's clear Brad Jones isn't involved in any of this. He's living his life's dream. He's got kids and a wife. Why risk all that with Luke? He despised Luke. And Victor."

"And why try to kill his own mother?" Tem asked the $100K question. Except my $100K was in an SPD evidence file. Unless they forwarded it to the FBI with every other scrap of my life.

"He didn't. He wouldn't. "

"If you say so."

"I've known Brad a long time. If something was up with him, I'd see it."

"Like you did with Tony?" Tem stuffed a couple of envelops with the memory drives we'd prepared.

"No, it'd be something twisted. A hint that foreshadows acts of terrible passion." I continued. Tem's calm wasn't contagious. "The only deep passion Brad ever revealed was over his mother's health. And about Luke being a jerk."

"So not Brad. Just Luke?"

"Except Luke wasn't capable of the kind of hackery required to find Clarissa's workers. Or to find Tony, like someone inside an agency might. Sure, Luke could hire muscle, but he needed brains. And who'd trust Luke as a partner? He blabbed like an idiot to Natalia and me."

"Unless he was gaslighting you."

"No. Charlie said Luke was always an idiot. Or at least an officially certified assbiter."

"If that Luke guy didn't do the hacking himself, he was rich as hell. He paid for it. And that Victor guy did psy-ops as a mercenary. I found his book about it online. So…"

"What?"

"I'm still down with Luke and gaslighting, Sam. Doesn't take a genius to execute."

"Or else Luke hired the White Knights as his hackers. Dwellers of the darknet."

"Paranoia strikes deep." Tem wrote labels for those envelops with a fine-point Sharpie.

"It's not paranoia when people really are chasing you."

We finished labeling and boxing up memory drives. Tem asked, "Want to come over and dig into what Clarissa and I gathered?"

"Didn't she say to leave the house locked?"

"Yeah. But I moved all the hardware last night." He grabbed his skateboard and backpack. "Except for two museum boxes that contain old email and tax records for the apartment."

Tem, of course, disappeared into the ozone before the trio of federal agents arrived, thirty minutes early. I expected the same agents from the previous night's conversation, and was ready to do an audit with them, comparing the inventory list against the labeled contents.

The smallest and oldest of the three introduced himself as Special Agent Ian Travis. He presented his FBI credentials and showed me a warrant from U.S. District Court. The other two agents were silent and but wore FBI jackets.

"Should I call my attorney?"

"If you like." Special Agent Travis seemed unspeakably bored. "But you aren't accused of a crime."

As long as you respect the warrant, he said, only with his attitude speaking. Someone forgot to tell him that I'm a cooperating partner.

I pointed the way to the Clean Room and asked if they wanted coffee before we started.

"No, ma'am. Thank you."

I glanced at my phone to read and answer a text.

↩MattOwens:
This is Pippi. I have a surprise. (Don't tell Matt I'm teasing you.)

↪Sam:
Matt can see his messages, goofy girl. I love you.

And I'd lost any appetite I ever had for surprises.

The FBI guy motioned for me to sit in one of the chairs. He stood beside me while the other two agents proceeded to remove every hard disk from every computer in the room and in the general office. "And your cloud-based servers, ma'am?"

Then he stood and watched while I deleted everything related from the cloud. That fourteen-year-old delinquent sk8ter-grrrl who lives inside me? Complete no-show for the entire time that Ian-with-the-badge breathed noisily beside me and watched me capture before-and-after directories onto the storage media he provided. The "after" resembled Natalia's dumb report: empty.

When I was signing *their* inventory list, the agent said, "In cases where the owner isn't accused of participating in a crime, we typically return the hardware within this time window."

He pointed to a statement at the top of the inventory sheet that showed a time space over which Natalia and I might as well take an extended vacation, since it'd be a spring before we were back in business.

This time, however, I got to keep my crappy mini-mart cell phone. Jeremiah, my SPD friend, called while the FBI carryall was driving away. The hellos and chatting aren't interesting. First, Brad Jones was free, identified as a non-participant. The White Knights, per Victor's and Slender Man's stories, were invented by Luke Connor to harass me, to divert me from getting in Luke's business. The main part of the barebones story that Jeremiah shared:

"Our cases moved to U.S. District Court. We aren't working on any felony cases at the moment. We'll assign an officer to track any future harassment of you or your business. But the FBI assures us that your involvement in this event is over."

▪

Obviously, the rogue agent Tony had been pursuing might be Ian, the by-the-rules agent who stood beside me while every cybertrace of the last week's work was boxed up and hauled away. Then again, perhaps Ian was only doing his job. Still not sure which is creepiest.

I locked up the office and grabbed more coffee before going to meet with Dan for our delayed breakfast.

Tem reappeared two blocks further down Capitol Hill.

"The FBI got it all?"

"Each bit and byte." Ha ha. The espresso tasted especially bitter.

"Will they find proof in those files?" Tem seemed more anxious and emotional than I'd seen before.

"What do you mean, proof?"

"That a U.S. agent is selling a crucial security asset? Without the data you gathered, how do we prove anything?"

"The reality?" I poured the rest of the bitter brew into a leaf-filled gutter. "We don't. We have nothing."

"Your business is shot?"

"No, we can still push the Byron&Dragon business ahead. We'll figure that out. I mean, we can't point to any crime."

"But when they see what's in your files—"

"They don't want our data to analyze." It felt a bit strange telling Tem, of all people, not to be optimistic. "They just don't want us to have those files. Whoever 'they' are."

He slapped down his skateboard, scooting beside me as I walked, both of us down the middle of a north Seattle back street. "We can reconstruct some of it. You have access to Mrs. Yates's backups."

"Everything we really need to know got blown up yesterday, or it's stored on the web server that has an FBI seizure notice. We have no details about foreign interests. Nothing about any Prometheus back-door. No way to find Tony. Or even prove Tony is real."

In fact, I can't prove to anyone, even myself, that there's any such a thing as the evolved secret version of Prometheus.

"If you're going to see that guy Dan," Tem kicked his board up, caught it, tucked it under his arm, "I'll come along. It was his security guys who attacked us."

"No, they were Luke Connor's guys."

"If I don't come, what are you doing to be safe?"

"Living in my own skin. Nothing is threatening me. The guys SPD arrested invented the White Knights. To divert my attention."

Tem had apparently been infected by Harley's concern and nagged me, so while he watched, I texted Harley to say where I was going and when I'd call him next. I texted Matt, who didn't answer. I texted my SPD friends, and then even Evan.

Sam
SAM BYRON IS GOING TO BREAKFAST.
JUST SO YOU KNOW.

"See you." I started to walk down the hill.

"Wait." Tem caught up beside me, his phone out, punching buttons. "Take a cab. A real one that has to call on the radio to say where they pick passengers up and drop them off."

"Seriously?"

"Like, I just met Harley yesterday. I don't want him going all Viking berserker on my ass if I let you do stupid stuff."

While waiting for the cab, Tem and I debated at length whether I do stupid stuff. I maintain not—except for texting while walking in unsafe places.

"You're walking off down the street," I called after Tem. "All alone. How is that only stupid when I do it?"

By the time the cab took me to Lake Union to rendezvous with Dan and Charlie, another storm was fixing to blow, but it remained dry. I got out of the cab when we reached Fairview Avenue. No black SUV cruised by to scare me, and no one demanded my attention. It was only a couple of blocks' walk, but it gave me enough time to excavate the bold postpunk Samsara who's ready to lunch with the super-rich.

After the week's trauma, I still wanted to be in charge of my own future, even if my research business had been carried off in FBI evidence boxes. I remained inclined to say no to the aDVers offer, as irrational as that sounds. For one, I'd have to report to Brad Jones, who I'd hit in the head with a sherry glass the night before.

Second, my chief interest in keeping this breakfast date: I wanted to hear from Dan how he felt about his "friend" Luke betraying his country and murdering people.

Too soon, I reached the pier where Dan's sailboat was docked, and so had to deal with another reason I can't be rich: I don't like boats. Can barely tolerate planes. If I'm playing music and the band is on poorly built risers, I think about loss of footing instead of key changes. The long dock swayed before I even stepped on it. The guy at the gate was the second-floor doorman at that fake speakeasy. Now dressed for weather, with only a narrow overhang to shelter him, he recognized me, greeted me with a warm smile.

"Ms. Byron, good to see you again. Mr. Llewelyn is expecting you. It's the vessel at the end of the dock."

I'd thanked him and started down the dock when he called after me. "It was a pleasure hearing you two play together the other night. I know Mr. Llewelyn appreciated it, too."

Waving again, I trod the wooden dock, my belly drifting to one side, my knees to the other, as a boat's wake washed up. A pair of men in white passed by, the kitchen crew; they also greeted me warmly and then left the dock for the parking lot.

On Lake Union, patches of glassy water shattered and scattered, then darkened and boiled where the wakes of two boats crossed. The sky shifted from the morning tumble of benign cumulous to a malignant mass of thunderheads, the Expressionist skies of dystopia, the chaos of the deep erupting as the lake quivered, shedding blues and greys to reveal a churning, angry green flecked with a froth of anxious, wind-tortured waves.

But then, maybe it was an ordinary Seattle squall seen through the outrage I felt about Agent Ian and whoever used the FBI to destroy my research.

Dan hailed me from the final boat slip, where he sat with Charlie Thomas in the stern of his ship, both of them bundled up in pea coats and watch caps. Instead of the fiberglass monster I'd expected, the boat was a historic vessel, formerly a harbor fishing boat, now deeply restored, with gleaming mahogany trim and fresh, white shiplap. Nostalgia incarnate. If you don't mind the floor moving when you step aboard.

We were dining al fresco. Charlie and Dan sat under a canvas awning, though I didn't believe the rigging could resist the impending storm. Two empty director's chairs waited alongside an antique wooden table. White linen tablecloth, crystal goblets, tulip glasses for mimosas, which Charlie offered as I sat down.

"Not for me, thanks. I have to work later." And I don't like to drink when the table's moving.

"The sailors have their spinnakers out." Dan pointed to the half-dozen sailboats whose spinnakers bellied in the morning wind, the orange, yellow, and rainbow sails vibrant under grey skies. "How long do you think they'll last?"

"I'm not a weatherman," I said.

"But you know which way the wind blows." He grinned, but that expression faltered and dimmed. Charlie watched him, didn't crack a smile.

"Raindrops will indeed fall on their heads."

"When the rain comes…" Dan trailed off, not finishing the rest of the lyric, if that's what he intended.

Food had already been served, but Charlie hadn't touched hers, and I can't remember what was on my plate. I seized the nearby French-press carafe and poured a dark, thick steam into a white china mug. Then clutched the mug. To warm my fingers, if nothing else.

Dan had set aside his breakfast when he stood to greet me. Seated again, he laid his knife and fork across the plate. He tipped his tea cup to check the contents, his hand shaking, perhaps with the motion of the boat. "It was delightful yesterday, working with your friend Zak Monroe. He's brilliant."

"Yes. Our work together was always a joy."

"Does that memory make you long for team work again?"

Zing. Here we go. "I have a team, Dan. At Byron&Dragon."

The stupid boat rocked. I grabbed my mug. Hot coffee spilled over my hand. Brad climbed aboard and slumped in the director's chair next to me. Then he righted himself, took a deep breath, and adopted the posture and air of a CEO. Never looked at me once, though I was ten inches away.

Holding a grudge, I guess. But the mistake wasn't mine.

"Ah, Brad! You finished in time to join us." Dan lifted his mimosa glass to greet him. "The attorneys did their job?"

"Yes, but mostly thanks to Victor. He made it clear I wasn't involved. That he worked only for Luke. Then the FBI turned up, and they sent me on my away."

He had a ruby-red, egg-shaped bump on his forehead. He took the napkin from his place setting, spooned ice out of a water glass, and clutched it to his head. Though I felt bad about that, I felt worse for having feared him.

"I'm sorry, Brad. The police said—"

"It's fine." Brad's voice was hoarse. He made a motion as if pushing away my hand, except I hadn't reached out. "They explained the misunderstanding."

"Is your mother—"

"She's stable. Thank you for asking." Didn't feel as if he was in fact appreciative, but then, I did smash him in the head with a glass.

Dan offered Brad a mimosa; and Brad seemed to need it at least as badly as he'd needed the Mischief the night before, but he declined and instead reached for the French press and poured a cup of coffee.

In his best, master-control CEO voice, Brad asked, "What the ever-loving fuck was Luke up to?"

At least I knew that answer, mostly. I just had no proof. "He was selling U.S. security assets to foreign entities. Israel, at least. Maybe not as mastermind, but…"

You'd think I'd hit Brad on the head again. "Luke? What did he have to sell?"

"Prometheus code. And a backdoor into it." I had no reason to keep that a secret, especially since Brad worked on the team in those days. But I was watching Dan, who seemed more intent on stirring his tea than the crisis around Prometheus. "It's been for sale on the darknet since—"

"Prometheus on the darknet?" Brad, astonished, clutched his middle, like a man punched in the gut.

"Oh no!" Charlie murmured. The first words she spoke. "Brad shouldn't know."

A ripple of understanding washed over Brad, like the waves rocking the boat. He forced himself to be calm like a man wrestling a demon. Dan huddled in his pea coat, no sign of emotion.

"The FBI will rip us apart." Brad pressed one hand hard on his left eye, like you do when a migraine starts. The wind picked up, and the sky grew darker. "Luke Connor has doomed aDVers."

"No," Dan said. He waved a hand, like a magician making a bird disappear. "It ended with Luke. They have no reason to look further. They'll just insist on the best possible security solutions from aDVers. So we need Sam more than ever."

Brad wasn't looking at me. "So we still need to convince her? And then I spend a year cleaning up after Luke Connor?"

"No." The long O of Dan's whispery voice made me shiver. "With Charlie's help last night, we fended off any ill effects."

My insides burned from more than anger over being gaslit by Luke and Victor. I'd been so blind it was immoral, even if the outcomes weren't the result from my own stupidity.

"Innocent women died. Alone. Afraid." I could catch fire from my burning insides. Explode like a human grenade. "How did you patch that up?"

The wind amplified the sailboats' wake, so that waves cascaded over the dock. The sailboats skidded and dipped, rose and shuddered again across the surface of the lake, breaking the bleak reflection of ambient light.

"When I was a child…" Dan began in the tone he used when he'd explained times past at the faux-speakeasy. "I believed all became known when we die. That God granted all knowledge when you went to heaven. Don't…believe it now. But don't you wish it could be true?"

"Never thought about it," Brad said, his voice seeming to echo from the depths of an existential funk. "Raised agnostic."

"I'm curious," I said. "I'm compulsive about logic."

Dan said, "A month ago, when Z-Crypto was contracted to determine whether packages on the darknet contained Prometheus secrets, Luke asked his security guys to double-check possible connections. He begged to do it himself, since he hadn't been allowed leadership before."

"Luke!" Brad exploded. "Luke should—he shouldn't have been allowed to lead his own dogs."

"How did Luke know about the Z-Crypto contract?"

Dan didn't answer.

That's the moment when I truly understood. Brad, still sounding gut-punched, exhaled a guttural moan.

"What did you tell Luke to do?" I stared out over the water, knowing I sat across from the author of all the corruption Tony had been chasing. Was I in greater danger than ever before? No: Dan and his friend Charlie had "fixed" everything—including the removal of any proof I held. I had one remaining question. "And how anyone could trust Luke Connor with anything of value?"

"What I said—" Dan stopped, as if trying to remember.

Brad had his head in his hands. "Let me guess. You said, 'Deal with it. That's what I pay you for.'"

"It's like…" Dan faltered again. "Who was that king who cried, 'Will no one rid me of this troublesome priest?' I allowed too much authority. With Luke in the middle, I should have checked closely. Believe me, I didn't ask for anyone to die. Especially not those women."

"Or Luke Connor?" I said. "It's convenient that he's not available to answer for any of this."

"Luke did that himself," Charlie said, breaking out of her silent-witness performance, but then she folded her hands and settled back again in her director's chair.

"And attacking Sam Byron?" Brad beat a tattoo on the table top with his thumb, drumming the same heart-pounding anger I felt. "I answered questions for most of the night about attacks on Sam."

"No!" Dan, shouting, banged his glass while setting it down. "I put Sam and Zak Monroe on the watch list. But only because they'd peeked at Prometheus once. Not for…"

So: I wasn't a genius. Merely in the wrong place. "That's why you wanted me at aDVers? To keep me from intruding?"

"No, I wanted you for what you are. Truly." Dan sipped his mimosa, as if it consoled him.

"How did Sam end up on Luke's kill list, then?" Brad poured more coffee. I tried to imitate his stern, calm demeanor.

"Luke's people had chased Tony Moon for weeks, trying to divert his attention. Though they didn't know who it was until Tony appeared in Hong Kong and then at Sam's office."

Damn if I was going to fall into that abyss again, thinking everything bad that happened was because of me. Though it did appear, at that moment, that Tony had successfully protected Clarissa by not visiting her personally.

I asked, "Who sent the feds after Luke yesterday?" Charlie shifted in her chair, but otherwise, the two of them acted as if they didn't hear my question.

Dan said, "When I came home from playing music Wednesday night, Luke insisted Sam was an NSA agent, working with Tony to find who was selling Prometheus. I asked for all work to halt. All trails erased. Luke swore he'd handle it."

The boat rocked again from other sailors' wake. Wind chilled my bare ears. The lake was not a wine-dark sea, but the angry waters had been stirred by a primitive god calling damnation down on a world of betrayers and dupes.

"Why do any of this?" I pretended that I was as astute as Dan claimed. "Why sell dangerous secrets? For money? You can fund a company the size of aDVers."

"We need untraceable funding for our human trials."

Brad half rose, profoundly agitated. "Those governments sponsored our tests as humanitarian collaborations."

Dan waved him down, a weak brush of his hand against the wind. "You are a true innocent, Brad. We put it all in place before you joined aDVers. If anyone asks—they won't, I promise—you know nothing about the bribery required to enable human drug experiments." Dan shakily sipped from his tulip glass.

"At least that's true." Brad fumed.

"We built whole hospitals just to have the small wards and clinics we needed. We paid entire extended families to participate in tests, gave them housing. We paid for hardware, wet work, education, the salary and housing of nursing staffs. I'm not rich enough to buy whole countries and cities. This way, other friendlies helped support our testing program."

"You damaged national security for the sake of your human drug trials?" My voice sounded mild, though the witch raging inside longed to scream.

"Oh no, never." Dan folded his arms, rocked himself as if wracked with despair. "I've always held a fail-safe block to Luke's backdoor code. Luke only sold to friendly nations, but I always remained ready to stop any misuse. Yesterday, I sent that block to your friend Zak. Backdoors are closing today on all major assets. Likely the NSA team stayed up through the night to test and field the solution."

"What now?" Brad asked. "You'll have to explain all this, at least to the FBI—"

"No. Don't upset their efforts to find other purchasers. Besides sending the fix to Z-Crypto, I sent details to my partners at the top. They know how to proceed. And I promise you, they don't want a word of this in public. All they'll share with the FBI will be about Luke as mastermind."

"Luke as a mastermind." Brad sniffed. "Masterminded his way into destroying aDVers."

"His debacle won't affect your work. We must succeed. You must succeed." Dan grasped his glass with both hands. The glass rattled against the tabletop. One more failure of insight from Sam Byron. I'd observed his breathlessness. His tremors. I can count, but never add.

"Ah, you see, Sam? We didn't advance…our research…in time to help me. Even though I was the first human subject. My case is too far along, so all it bought me was one more year. Gave me…" He took a long moment to catch his breath. "One more chance to make a new friend. To help Brad to achieve…"

"Help me?" Brad exploded, knocking over his coffee cup so that a dark stain ran across the tablecloth.

"Yes. A new opportunity. A wide open field." Dan seemed to fold up inside his pea coat, becoming smaller by the moment.

"Am I the new friend?" I jammed my napkin on the table to keep Brad's coffee from running into my lap.

"Yes." His smile wavered, lips parchment white. "I consider the dawn of that friendship a final blessing. A mercy."

The tulip glass fell from his hands. He leaned to the side, his hands grasping the rail. He stood, stumbled. And then vomited over the side. Charlie rushed to him. But he pushed her away.

I was not feeling any mercy.

"Was it you or Luke who hired the White Knights? To run darknet payments? To hack for Luke? Did they murder those women for you?"

Dan frowned. "There is no such thing as White Knights. They aren't more than—"

He stumbled. Charlie again reached for him.

"No!" she cried. "Do it another way!"

He shoved her, but she was immovable. Instead, he leaned away from her.

"It's done."

He pitched over the side. The boat rocked with a wave, knocked against the moorings.

"God!" Brad ripped off his jacket, kicked off his shoes, perched on the rail.

Charlie pulled him back. "That's his plan. Stop!"

Brad shrugged her off and jumped. I grabbed a grappling pole, hoping to help. First thing: using the pole to keep the damned boat away from the dock, so it didn't smash into it while Brad and Dan were under water. I jumped back to the dock for better footing, a greater chance to offer help.

Brad surfaced twice, gulped air, and sank again. At last he came up, towing Dan by his coat. He grasped the pole I held, then grabbed one of the boat's bumpers to stay afloat while we wrestled Dan onto the dock.

From there I started old-style CPR and mouth-to-mouth. What you're supposed to do for drowning. Blow. Check for chest rise. No sign. Finger to feel for carotid pulse. Not there. I knelt over him and started chest compression. Counted to thirty. By then, Brad was out of the water. He blew air while I pressed, then he begged to take over the compressions. While he again counted to thirty, I searched for a defib-rillator—and failed.

I shouted down the dock to the security guy, begging for a defibrillator. The security guy had disappeared. My throat raw from shouting, I went back to spell Brad, the way he'd spelled me.

A voice several slips down yelled, "I'm calling 9–1–1!"

When I looked, it seemed to be Nicky. When I looked again, no one was there.

That's when I noticed Charlie, who stood in the boat's tiny galley, calmly washing dishes.

The EMTs appeared, with a defibrillator. And better training than mine. Brad and I stepped back, Brad's drenched clothes soon soaking mine, because we ended up clasping each other, like a brother and sister frightened by what the adults had done, Brad crying, the ugly kind, like when a parent dies.

Here's me on Friday morning—*a good day to die*—calmly answering EMT questions about what happened. Mr. Llewellyn seemed unsteady, complained of difficulty with a chronic neural condition. He slipped. Fell into the water. Brad hauled him out. Enough CPR to break his ribs. No defibrillator.

We sat in the director's chairs wrapped in wool blankets that Charlie brought from the cabin, waiting for law enforcement, me fighting nausea with the sway of the anchored boat. The rain refused to fall, yet the wind churned white froth on the dark lake, shifted colors of grey in the near-black skies, and whipped the lakeside trees and autumn-dead perennials with a passion, a synesthesia of torment.

Charlie sat beside Brad, taking Dan's chair. Tears straggled down one cheek. "A classical tragedy. Did you read Shakespeare in school? A stag pulled down by wolves. Courageous, beautiful in his dignity. Defenseless against fate." She looked up. "I'm not heartless. We sat up the night together, Dan explaining while he repaired everything after the mistakes Luke and his people made."

"Repair." Brad repeated the word. He was shaking, his teeth chattering. The EMTs had checked him for shock, but that's what it looked like to me. I added my blanket around him and grabbed a pea coat from the galley.

"He planned it this way," Charlie said. "Now we have to let him go."

To be clear, Dan had swallowed something while we talked, before he went over the side. We weren't meant to fish him from the lake. And I knew I needed to say so when SPD arrived. Not just out of anger that someone chose to escape responsibility for perpetrating horrors.

Except: when law enforcement did arrive, the SPD officers came with Special Agent Ian Travis and asked to take our statements. But asked damn few questions.

▪

What Tony asked me: *Didn't you complain that it's not good for society to have a rich man running his own social agenda?*

I hadn't thought that through sufficiently.

No White Knights of the New Russian Revolution.

Merely the lingering stench of gaslight.

▪

Brad offered Charlie and me a ride, but I wasn't excited about going back to an office devoid of hard disks or huddling under a blanket in the upstairs closet where I lived. Besides, I didn't want either of them in my physical space at that moment.

Instead, I took the South Lake Union trolley to downtown and got a replacement phone at the fancy cellphone store. My messages included only one of interest: an invitation to a jam session with Jason Taylor. Real musicians only. I caught the Number 26 bus and then walked down to his rehearsal space, though I'm not free to disclose where that is. The least challenging secret of the past week.

The whole journey, I kept circling back to Tuesday's questions: Am I a stooge for federal crimes against humanity, or am I helping law enforcement tackle dangerous criminal activity?

I'm not good at abstractions. I have to anchor ideas in real action.

So I'm silent about Clarissa. And Tony. If the security state used Tony and Clarissa as agents, someone knows. If that someone believes either of those two has gone rogue, it's their business. Not mine.

I called Pippi and Matt again, but the instant voice-mail meant his phone was turned off.

19

It Gets So Dark after Sunset

IN JASON'S MASSIVE STUDIO, WE took turns, but basically, I spent the entire afternoon on rhythm guitar. Loud. Shredding.

High volume.

Chords.

Scales.

Beat.

Key changes.

Closer to pure mathematics than anything I'd done all week. And no moral dilemmas.

A good afternoon: breaks to eat (catered, but vegan); standing out on the porch to watch it pour rain and talk music; phones turned off, so we were only on Planet Music. One front-porch discussion and a decision: I took on a project for Jason Taylor, to meet the challenge of stopping hacks to his website.

Next stop in my career: suggesting strong passwords to protect spreadsheets.

Karl (our mutual attorney) sat in, master of hand rhythm instruments. At one break, I mumbled an *any news?* query. He shook his head. And then nodded. "We're countersuing for the neighbor's beachfront, since your aunt's ownership predates everyone in the neighborhood. But your brother Pete—he couldn't reach you yesterday."

"What? He's in jail? Held for ransom?"

"He wants to lease your aunt's house for his film crew. He has backers and deadlines for a documentary on racial justice in Limberlost Island history."

"That'll make him popular in the neighborhood." And solve a fistful of my problems for a while. "Is Pete going to live there?"

"That's the idea—that the whole crew lives there."

"Including all the videographers who've been living at my house in Leschi?" The house I'd rented to Pete when I started living with Matt.

Agreeing to that was a no-brainer. With rental income to cover Aunt Lucky's living expense, I could stop worrying for a while. And I could move back into my own house, if Pete was no longer mooching off me. At the final break that afternoon, I agreed to Pete's proposal and then showed Karl how we use Krypptikk, since he was curious.

KRYPPTIKK JOB: CLIENT#3_TAYLOR_WEB

Invited members: byron&dragon; Jason Taylor; Karl Schwann

SByron:

Ticket #1: Define and implement security protocols and processes for Jason Taylor Band website.

Ticket #2: Create site manager documentation.

[Karl accepted and entered project]

[NDragon accepted and entered project]

NDragon:

Where's the contract and billing rate?

Timeline?

SByron:

You're supposed to be on vacation.

NDragon:

Thank Freyja, you're alive! Friday's almost over.

It didn't seem right to ruin Natalia's weekend with news about our hardware. And Jason's dinky task was all the work we had, though he promised to tell his friends about Byron&Dragon.

What a calming, stress-free afternoon it had been. The only hitch: I hadn't been playing guitar enough lately, so by late afternoon, my fingers were ready to bleed.

On the way back to Capitol Hill (with a lot of walking, since the bus connections between Fremont and the Hill suck), I got my first text on my new handset.

> ✆1(509)########:
> Weather is warm & muggy, the women are beautiful.
> Mother is traveling with a former dojoig paramour.
> She believes in a future for my technothriller fantasy work.
> Me, I'm sorting sickpay & workplace safety with my supervisor.
> Meanwhile, made it through 5 of Bowie's top 100 books.

> ↳Sam:
> Call when you're free. I'm apparently easy to find.

Tony. A burnerbot phone number. But on the positive side: he's okay; seems Clarissa is, too. Though I had to go to the Internetz to figure out about the paramour: DOJ Inspector General.

So, not pirates; not grifters, either of them. Or so Tony says. And perhaps my attorney can get the FBI to pay that hospital bill.

▪

In the office, Harley and Tem sat at what's become the receptionist's workstation, eating pizza and watching a news update on the Potholes Deadlock. Between stuffing his mouth with pizza, Tem read Twitter updates off his phone from journalists and participants, live from the occupation. He talked through the slab of pizza he'd stuffed in his mouth.

"Wannnsum?"

"Thanks, I—"

On the other side of the office, Natalia's workstation was switched on, with three monitors filled with social media pages. Harley had his systems up with several searches in progress, but none of it looked like #Debris_Byron work.

"How are you working? The FBI took—"

Tem swallowed before he could talk. "Harley helped me haul my equipment over. We got most of the Clean Room set up. Your software tools are still installing."

Peeking into the Clean Room, I found, if not Dogs of War, then at least Dogs of Border Skirmishes.

Tem took another bite and started talking again. "Natalia can swear in four languages. Didn't like hearing about the FBI and your hardware. Made me sign a W-4 form and an employment agreement before she'd share passwords to the cloud." Stuffed another slice in his gob.

The office water-closet door slammed open. Zak emerged, still zipping, then surprised to find the space no longer an all-male zone.

We're not lovers, never were, but Zak's embrace was as comforting as four hours of extraordinarily loud music.

After happy-to-see-you, et cetera, I asked what conference he'd come here for, how much free time he'd have.

He grabbed a pizza slice. "I quit. I finally saw the ethical compromises that drove you away. I came here, hoping to work as a contractor until I find a job."

"Seattle?"

"Yeah." He wasn't much better than Tem with the hand-to-mouth eating business. "I'd forgotten that it's impossible to find good pizza in Seattle."

Without looking away from the news broadcast (the FBI had banks of super-bright lights shining on protesters, who huddled under tarps against the night-time chill), Harley said, "Hope you learned your lesson, young lady."

"What lesson?" This week, it's been like the repeating bad dream where I signed up for too many credit-hours and it's too late to drop any classes. Can't tell what lessons I'm learning.

"That you need a strong team. It's no good going out and trying to do it all by yourself. Like I always told my deputies."

While they all made guy-type plans—Tem to stay with Zak at what was now his house on North Capitol Hill, Harley headed home to Limberlost Island, all three agreeing to see each other Monday morning, since a small business doesn't close for Columbus Day.

"Seattle doesn't have Columbus Day," Tem said. "It's Indigenous Peoples Day."

"What'd ya celebrate with? Salmon and kinnikinnick?" Zak laughed at his own dumb joke.

"I don't celebrate Hallmark holidays," Tem said. "But I'm skating in West Seattle tomorrow, if you want to come."

"Delridge?" Zak asked.

"Yes. And, actually, you mean pemmican. Kinnikinnick is a smoking mixture."

They were headed out the door while I was reading a Krypptikk project message.

KRYPPTIKK JOB: CLIENT#202_JONES

BJones:

Sending aDVers contract with a 6-month retainer.
Secure access for Byron&Dragon to use all facilities.
Is this correct figure?

...

NDragon:

Archiving Client#202 project.
Billing final project hours.

SByron:

Thank you for the offer, but Byron&Dragon declines.
We are overbooked for the coming year.

If this was a movie instead of happening in the Real World, I'd be waking up with blackout amnesia, accused of killing my lover. Or perhaps once again losing the son I didn't know I had. Or I'd find out that I'm married and my seven children have missed me so much.

Oh, so very much not funny. And thinking that made me miss Matt and Pippi so much, a pain ran through my middle and wouldn't let go.

Instead, it seemed to be that Byron&Dragon had new hardware and twice as many employees and contractors. And still, no significant clients or prospects. Though the day's postal mail had an offer from my insurance company to settle for ninety percent of what I'd been hoping to get back from last year's debacles. Tempted to accept, I scanned and sent the offer to Karl for his advice. I needed a shower and a night in bed before committing to anything.

Harley promised to lock up (after consuming more pizza and more fanboy watching of the FBI operation at the Potholes Reservoir). While I waited for the slowest elevator in the world, I read a text—from Matt!

🖑MattOwens:
Monday is Columbus Day, long to see you.

🖑Sam:
Seattle doesn't have Columbus day.

"But it is a holiday." Matt's voice purred in my ear.

Better than a comfort hug from Zak.

Better than air after being suffocated.

When I surfaced from Matt's embrace, I had only the single most obvious question.

"Where's Pippi?"

"She and Roz are meeting Harley at the ferry. They're going to the island tonight. Pippi's idea is that I want to be with you for the night."

"Smart girl."

"Also, I want to have that conversation you've been avoiding, about doing whatever you want." He touched my left earlobe in that gentle way he knows will drive me over the edge. "Because this is all I want."

▪

Friday night about killed me. I'm so old that by the time the clock displayed two a.m., the best part of the night was a hand with guitar callouses, large but just the right size, resting on my inner thigh. It'd be too hot, if it were summer. But it was October, and we were listening to the falling rain.

"Those guys out at the Potholes Reservoir—"

"Law enforcement or protestors?" I asked.

"They're protesting about federal grazing fees and irrigation allotments, right?"

"No. They're protesting the arrest of one of their friends for possessing armor-piercing Teflon bullets and a large store of C4 explosives." I'd picked that much up from Harley's obsession.

"Huh." He was quiet for a minute, his breath warm in my hair. "A bunch of them have families. And they're off camping in the wilderness, likely to get arrested."

"Instead of using the courts and the legislature." Listen to me, all up on the side of the law, as if I trusted it.

"And they've got federal and state and county law enforcement out there."

"All wet as a drowning duck right now." As my Grandma Flo always says.

"I made a mistake." Warm hand gone from my thigh, Matt held me close. "Taking Pippi to Virginia was a bad idea. Even with Roz there, she's missing her friends. And you. And Harley. And everyday life. Roz is homesick. Pippi's homesick. And I'm gone from dawn until her bedtime or later."

"It's only six months."

"Yeah. That word 'only' works for me. Except in the night when I miss you. But do you remember how long half a year lasted when you were eleven?"

"Distinctly." It was the year after my brother Pete and I left my father's hippie commune and began living next door to Matt and the huggy Owens family.

"So when I said I wanted you to be free—"

Oh no. One more stupid mistake I made, as bad as texting while walking. "Does Pippi want to come home? Because if she does, I'm right here."

"I want you to be free, so—"

"Being with Pippi, what Pippi needs—that has nothing to do with freedom."

▪

Saturday morning, after the second time, but before we got to the third time, the video-doorbell rang from street level. We weren't supposed to meet Pippi until mid-afternoon.

"I swear to Natalia's pagan gods, I'm moving back to my own house, with or without Pippi. And digging a moat. I want life to get back to normal." I got up from my narrow bed carefully, having to scoot past Matt. I switched on the street-cam, hoping it wasn't yet another visit from the SPD.

No, I wish it were SPD.

Instead, it was Huck, my Deadhead father, long grey hair tied back in a Willie Nelson braid, pukka-shell necklace at his throat. Neil Young's lost fringed leather jacket. Returned from Hell-n-Gone.

"Missy, can you come down here and straighten this out? Me and your uncle Bob—"

"Where the heck have you been?"

"Traveling. We followed Dr. Dog and Buddy Guy for the summer. But that's done. We brought your car back."

"Thanks. Leave the key under the floor mat."

"No can do, Missy. That dipshit guy Nicky is out in the street yelling that we're car thieves. Bob got a hold of his collar when the dang twerp tried to run. And now all these kids out on the curb are telling the parking meter lady that the FBI is coming with guns."

"What exactly," I tried to be patient, "am I supposed to do about it?"

"Whatever you can. And hope for the best. It's like I always taught you, sometimes doing karma only makes it worse."

"Just go, Huck. Those kids are harmless. And the FBI will likely come soon for Nicky."

Matt snuggled up behind me, still warm from bed, and whispered in my ear. "The FBI already came. Twice."

"Boy, howdy." From what the security camera revealed, Huck glanced back out to the street. "Your uncle Bob and me, we had our hearts set on buying you breakfast. To thank you and all."

Matt tickled my ear. "You're thinner than you were this summer. And I'm hungry. Come on. Say yes."

He stepped away and pulled on his jeans.

"Besides, it's just what you asked for, Sam. Life is back to normal."

■ ■ ■

Sam's Cheat-sheet

acquired

When one corporation is bought by another, where the terms involve stock, cash, and other financial incentives. It's not quite the same transaction as when you "acquire" a Tiger Milk bar by exchanging cash for physical goods.

adware

Software that displays advertising to generate revenue. The business goal is, roughly, to capture clicks as a way to measure eyeballs (the number of people who viewed the ad), and to auction the value of those clicks to advertisers. Adware is a prime economic driver of the Internet. Sometimes adware is also malware. See malware below.

backdoor

Special code created and embedded in software that allows anyone who possesses the backdoor "secret" to bypass any security or authentication features of the software.

Big Data

A large amount of stored data that can be analyzed for insight. For example, all the searches on a major web presence such as Google or Facebook are stored and then analyzed using a variety of tools and methods to understand trends, human behavior, or any other wild guesses that might lead to insight.

biometric identifier

Your fingerprint or palm print. Your iris and retina. Your DNA. The geometric points of your face used for facial recognition. The gait of your walk. Your voice. The unique timing with which you type on a keyboard. You possess all kinds of unique secrets.

block

To prevent explicit attempts at communication. For example, your email program gives you the ability to block selected senders so that you never see their email.

bounty hunting

Some software and networking companies pay a "bounty" to security researchers who report "vulnerabilities." The goal for bounty programs is to increase "citizen" involvement in the effort to reduce cyber threats.

burnerbot

In this context, it's a web application that creates alternative phone numbers for texting, messaging, or calls. The burner number offers privacy to whoever has created the number, because callers cannot determine the identity of the individual or company linked to the burner number.

darknet, dark-web

In general, an overlay network on top of the Internet that requires specific software for access and typically uses a non-standard communication port. Often "darknet" refers to a private network, like Tor, that supports file sharing and other hidden services. The breadth of use of the darknet spans from privacy and whistleblowing purposes to illicit porn, drug, and computer crimes.

digital watermarking

Think "DRM" on your DVDs. It's an undetectable addition to digital media—pictures, video, databases—for purposes of copy protection or authentication, or to detect whether the data has been tampered with.

doxxed

A revenge tactic advanced in the 1990s: searching the Internet for data, images, and documents ("docs") about an individual, and then publishing related personal details on the Internet to expose the individual. Doxxing is a standard tactic for online harassment.

encryption

The conversion of data so that only authorized users can read it. A common public-key encryption application for encrypting messages is PGP—Pretty Good Privacy.

executable cell biology

Computer models that describe biological phenomena, typically to gain insights about molecular mechanisms.

forensics analyst

Generally, a professional who follows scientific methodology in support of criminal and legal investigations. In my world, the focus is a cyber security professional who investigates hacking, cyber fraud, industrial and political espionage, or terrorist communications.

geek

A term I use to describe myself, which I gave myself permission to use without reference to any standards that might be used to judge whether I qualify.

machine learning

A field in computer science that combines computational learning theory and pattern recognition, resulting in software that "learns" from data by making iterative passes to identify patterns without being programmed to perform a specific analysis.

malware

Any malicious software that's built to disrupt a computer system or hack sensitive data or networks. It includes any varieties of viruses, rootkits, Trojan horses, ransomware, and spyware.

NDA (nondisclosure agreement)

A confidentiality agreement between two parties that restricts the ability to share information exchanged between the two parties. In the software industry, it's common that employment agreements include a signed agreement not to disseminate any of the company's confidential information.

non-compete agreements

In the software industry, employment agreements commonly contain a provision that, upon termination of employment, the worker will not exploit confidential information belonging to the former employer. Allowed clauses and enforcement varies from state to state in the U.S., and California is now the most progressive, having outlawed all but a small number of cases.

ransomware

A type of malware that restricts access to a computer, usually stipulating that you must pay a ransom to remove the malware. The technologies involved include a Trojan virus, encryption, and an untraceable payment system.

recovered

In this story, the repaired, unlocked, and restored files and data on a computer that has been infected with malware.

Slender Man

A fictional paranormal fright figure created by Eric Knudsen in an Internet forum that subsequently went viral, resulting in considerable fan art, stories, and video.

startup

In the computer industry, an entrepreneurial venture where a company is formed to advance a combination of new technology, business processes, and markets that results in a fast-growth business model. Typically, as soon as the business model is proven, the startup is acquired by a larger corporation, and that acquisition rewards the startup's investors.

steganography

The ancient technique of hiding a message within something else—an image, video, a document. "Paul is dead."

Tor

Free software for anonymous communication, directing Internet traffic through a volunteer worldwide network, for the specific purpose of protecting the privacy of users in confidential conversations.

trapdoor

The complex mathematical function in encryption that serves to "unlock" the encryption, like the key that opens a padlock.

Trojan virus

A kind of malware the disguises itself as legitimate software, seemingly harmless but with underlying malicious purpose.

virus signature

The unique pattern of a virus's code. Anti-virus software keeps a database of the "signatures" that describe specific patterns.

About the Author

ANNIE PEARSON lives and writes in Seattle. In addition to the *Rain City* series, she also writes the *Accidental Heretics* adventure series (as E.A. Stewart).

The *Rain City* series focuses on life in contemporary Seattle, among people whose work drives their hearts' desires, often in conflict with other love affairs.

Annie Pearson posts about writing and eclectic project planning at www.anniepearson.com.

Acknowledgments

I am grateful to my deep readers, Susan Urban, Martin Fossum, and Jacyn Stewart. I am deeply indebted to Waverly Fitzgerald for the Mondays and Thursdays spent writing together through the winter—and for being an inspiring and insightful teacher. Many thanks, as always, to my editor, Elizabeth Bjorkman.

From Jugum Press

RAIN CITY SERIES by Annie Pearson

When odd things happen to quirky people under grey skies

The Grrrl of Limberlost

A murder in a Seattle coffee house. A murder on a decaying boat dock on Puget Sound. Samsara Byron, the security expert, insists this has nothing to do with her. She's heroically fending off an attack on the world's cyber infrastructure—if she could only get a cell signal.

Artemis in the Desert

Eliot Arden, a Seattle artisan, and Sean Frederick Wentworth, the steampunk manga artist, undertake the same motorcycle journey they traveled ten years before. But this time, dreams and desires might just heat up like red slickrock in the sun. Or is that fire sparked by a 900cc bike sliding sideways down a backcountry highway?

Nine Volt Heart

He said, "I love you." She said, "You don't even know the real me." He said, "Great title for a song. Key of G? Can we try close harmony?" Jason, the singer-songwriter, and Susi, a music teacher, meet by accident in Seattle. Secrets, songs, and stalkers quickly entwine their lives in unpredictable ways.

ACCIDENTAL HERETICS SERIES by E.A. Stewart

Lost in the Languedoc Crusade

Bone-mend and Salt (Book 1)

Fight or beg for mercy when enemies turn an unjust war against you? Three ruined crusaders battle conspiracy and disaster while trapped in the new war against the Cathar heresy. Swords and grit must defend against deceit.

Trebuchets in the Garden (Book 2)

How do you prepare for the dawn of the Inquisition? Three embattled crusaders seek justice and respite amidst terror, siege, and conspiracy—as zealots prepare to ignite the next heretics' pyre.

www.jugumpress.net

www.ingramcontent.com/pod-product-compliance
Lightning Source LLC
Chambersburg PA
CBHW070658180626
46817CB00006B/2429

* 9 7 8 1 9 3 9 4 2 3 4 1 2 *